Miracle of The Rose

WORKS BY JEAN GENET

Published by Grove Weidenfeld

The Balcony
The Blacks
Funeral Rites
The Maids *and* Deathwatch
Miracle of the Rose
Our Lady of the Flowers
Querelle
The Screens
The Thief's Journal

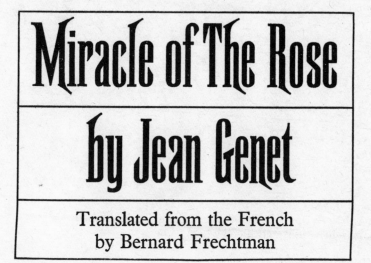

Miracle of The Rose
by Jean Genet

Translated from the French
by Bernard Frechtman

GROVE WEIDENFELD
NEW YORK

Published by Grove Weidenfeld
A division of Grove Press, Inc.
841 Broadway
New York, NY 10003-4793

Originally published in *Œuvres Complètes* by Librarie
Gallimard, Paris, France, under the title *Miracle de la
Rose*, copyright © 1951 by Librarie Gallimard.

Library of Congress Catalog Card Number 66-58157
ISBN 0-8021-3088-7

Manufactured in the United States of America

Printed on acid-free paper

First Grove Press Edition 1966
New Evergreen Edition 1988

10   9   8   7   6   5   4   3   2

Miracle of The Rose

OF ALL the state prisons of France, Fontevrault is the most disquieting. It was Fontevrault that gave me the strongest impression of anguish and affliction, and I know that convicts who have been in other prisons have, at the mere mention of its name, felt an emotion, a pang, comparable to mine. I shall not try to define the essence of its power over us: whether this power be due to its past, its abbesses of royal blood, its aspect, its walls, its ivy, to the transient presence of convicts bound for the penal colony at Cayenne, to its prisoners, who are more vicious than those elsewhere, to its name—none of this matters. But to all these reasons was added, for me, another: that it was, during my stay at the Mettray Reformatory Colony, the sanctuary to which our childhood dreams aspired. I felt that its walls preserved—the custodial preserving the bread—the very shape of the future. While the boy I was at fifteen twined in his hammock around a friend (if the rigours of life make us seek out a friendly presence, I think it is the rigours of prison that drive us toward each other in bursts of love without which we could not live; unhappiness is the enchanted potion), he knew that his final form dwelt behind them and that the convict with his thirty-year sentence was the fulfilment of himself, the last transformation, which death would make permanent. And Fontevrault still gleams (though with a very soft, a faded brilliance) with the lights emitted in its darkest heart, the dungeon, by Harcamone, who was sentenced to death.

When I left Santé Prison for Fontevrault, I already knew that Harcamone was there, awaiting execution. Upon my arrival I was therefore gripped by the mystery of one of my fellow-inmates at Mettray who had been able to pursue the adventure of all of us to its most tenuous peak: the death on the scaffold which is our glory. Harcamone had "succeeded." And as this success was not of an earthly order, like fortune or honours, his achievement filled me with amazement and admiration (even the simplest achievement is miraculous), but also inspired the fear that overwhelms the witness of a magical operation. Harcamone's crimes might have meant nothing to me had I not known him at close range, but my love of beauty (which desired so ardently that my life be crowned with a violent, in fact bloody death) and my aspiration to a saintliness of muted brilliance (which kept it from being heroic by men's standards) made me secretly choose decapitation, which has the virtue of being reproved, of reproving the death that it gives and of illuminating its beneficiary with a glory more sombre and gentle than the shimmering, silvery velvet of great funerals; and Harcamone's crimes and death revealed to me—as if taking it apart—the mechanism of that glory which had at last been attained. Such glory is not human. We have never heard of any executed criminal whose execution alone haloed him as the saints of the Church and the glories of the age are haloed, but yet we know that the purest of those who were given that death felt, within themselves and on their severed head, the placing of the amazing private crown which was studded with jewels wrested from the darkness of the heart. Each of them knew that the moment his head fell into the basket of sawdust and was taken out (by the ears) by an assistant whose role seems to me strange indeed, his heart would be garnered by fingers gloved with modesty and be carried off in a youngster's bosom that was adorned like a spring festival. I thus aspired to heavenly glory, and Harcamone had attained it before me, quietly, as the result of murdering a little girl and, fifteen years later, a Fontevrault guard.

I arrived at the prison with my hands and feet chained. I had been prepared by a very long and rough trip in the armoured police-train. There was a hole in the seat, and when my gripes got too violent because of the jolting, I had only to unbutton. It was cold. I rode through a countryside numbed with winter. I imagined the hard fields, the hoar-frost, the impure daylight. My arrest had taken place in mid-summer, and my most haunting memory of Paris is of a city completely empty, abandoned by the population which was fleeing from the invasion, a kind of Pompeii, without policemen at the crossings, a city such as the burglar dares dream of when he is tired of inventing ruses.

Four travelling-guards were playing cards in the corridor of the train. Orléans . . . Blois . . . Tours . . . Saumur. The car was detached and switched to another track, and we were at Fontevrault. There were thirty of us, because the police-car had only thirty cells. Half of the convoy was composed of men of about thirty. The rest ranged from eighteen to sixty.

While the passengers looked on, we were attached in pairs, and with our hands and feet chained we got into the Black Marias that were waiting for us at the station. I had time to note the sadness of the crop-headed young men who watched the girls go by. My chain-mate and I entered one of the narrow cells, a vertical coffin. I noticed that the Black Maria was divested of its charm, that air of haughty misfortune which, the first few times I had taken it, had made it a vehicle of exile, a conveyance fraught with grandeur, slowly fleeing, as it carried me off, between the ranks of a people bowed with respect. It is no longer a vehicle of royal misfortune. I have had a clear vision of it, of a thing which, beyond happiness or unhappiness, is splendid.

It was there, upon entering the prison-wagon, that I felt I had become a true, disenchanted visionary.

The wagons drove to the prison. I cannot tell how it looked from the outside—I can tell this about few prisons, since those which I know, I know only from the inside. The cells of the wagon were closed, but from a jolt of the vehicle as it mounted a paved slope I gathered that we had gone through a gate and that I was in the domain of Harcamone. I know that the prison is at the bottom of a valley, of an infernal gorge from which a miraculous fountain gushes, but nothing stops us from thinking that it is at the top of a high mountain; here, in this place, everything leads me to think that it is at the top of a rock, of which the ramparts are a continuation. Although this altitude may be ideal, it is all the more real, for the isolation it grants is indestructible. Neither the walls nor the silence has anything to do with it. We shall see this in the case of Mettray Reformatory, which is as far-flung as the prison is high.

Night had fallen. We arrived amidst a mass of darkness. We got out. Eight guards, lined up like footmen, were waiting for us on the lighted steps. At the top of a flight of two stairs the wall of darkness was breached by a huge, brightly illuminated arched door. It was a holiday, Christmas perhaps. I had barely time to catch a glimpse of the yard, the black walls of which were covered with mournful ivy. We passed an iron gate. Behind it was a small inner yard lit up by four electric lamps: the bulb and shade, in the form of an Anamite hat, are the official lamp of all French prisons. At the end of this yard, where, even in the darkness, we sensed an unwonted architecture, we passed another iron gate, then went down a few steps lit by lamps of the same kind and suddenly we were in a delightful square garden adorned with shrubbery and a fountain around which ran a cloister with delicate little columns. After mounting a stairway sculpted in the wall, we found ourselves in a white corridor and then proceeded to the record office, where we remained a long time in a state of disorder before our chains were taken off.

"You there, you going to put out your wrists?"

I extended my wrist, and the chain pulled up the hand, sad as a captured animal, of the fellow to whom it was attached. The guard fumbled at the lock of the handcuffs; when he found it and inserted the key, I heard the slight click of the delicate trap that was freeing me. And that deliverance to enter captivity was to us a first affliction. The heat was stifling, but no one thought it would be so hot in the dormitories. The door of the office opened into a corridor that was lit up with cruel precision. The door was unlocked. A convict on the maintenance staff, probably a sweeper, pushed it slightly, put his smiling face in, and whispered:

"Say, boys, if any of you have butts, better let me have 'em, because . . ."

He broke off and disappeared. Probably a guard was coming. Someone shut the door from the outside.

I listened to hear whether the voice would cry out, but I heard nothing. Nobody was being tortured. I looked at one of the fellows who were with me. We smiled. We had both recognized the whisper which would be for a long time the only tone in which we could speak. We sensed all around us, behind the walls, a stealthy, silent but zealous activity. Why in the dead of night? In winter, darkness came on quickly, and it was only five in the afternoon.

Some moments later, likewise muffled, but remote, a voice, which sounded to me like that of the inmate, cried out:

"Regards to your fanny from my dick!"

The guards in the office heard it too but didn't bat an eyelash. Thus, as soon as I arrived I realized that no convict's voice would be clear. It is either a murmur low enough for the guards not to hear, or else a cry muffled by a thickness of walls and anguish.

As soon as each of us gave his name, age, occupation, and distinguishing marks and signed with the print of his forefinger, he was taken by a guard to the wardrobe. It was my turn:

"Name?"

"Genet."

"Plantagenet?"

"I said Genet."

"What if I feel like saying Plantagenet? Do you mind?"

". . ."

"Christian name?"

"Jean."

"Age?"

"Thirty."

"Occupation?"

"No occupation."

The guard gave me a dirty look. Perhaps he despised me for not knowing that the Plantagenets were buried in Fontevrault, that their coat of arms—leopards and the Maltese Cross—is still on the stained-glass windows of the chapel.

I had barely time to wave a stealthy good-bye to a youngster who had been in the convoy and whom I had singled out. It is less than fifty days since I left him, but though I would like to adorn my grief with the memory of him, to linger over his face, he flees me. In the Black Maria that took us from the station to the prison, he managed to get into the same narrow cell (the guards made us enter in pairs) as a tough-looking pimp. In order to be chained to the pimp, he had resorted to a trick that made me jealous of both of them and that still bothers and, owing to a deep mystery, attracts me, tearing a veil so that I have a luminous insight. And ever since, when time hangs heavy, I mull over this memory in my prison, but I cannot get to the heart of it. I can imagine what they did and said, what plans they made for the future, I can fabricate a very long life for their love. But I weary quickly. Developing this brief incident—the child's manoeuvre and his entering the little cell—adds nothing to my knowledge of it, in fact destroys the charm of the lightning manoeuvre. In like manner, when Harcamone hurried past me, the beauty of his face lit me up, but when I observed it at great length, in detail, the face faded. Certain acts dazzle us and light up blurred surfaces if our eyes are keen enough to see them in a flash, for the beauty of a living thing can be grasped only fleetingly. To pursue it during its changes leads us inevitably to the moment when it ceases, for it cannot last a lifetime. And to analyze it, that is, to pursue it in time with the sight and the imagination, is to view it in its decline, for after the thrilling moment in which it reveals itself it diminishes in intensity. I have lost that child's face.

I picked up my bundle: two shirts, two handkerchiefs, a half-loaf of bread, a song-book. And, with an already plodding gait, not saying a word to them, I left my travelling companions, crashers, pimps, hoodlums, thieves sentenced to three years, five years, ten years, and lifers, and went to join other crashers, other lifers. I walked in front of the guard through very clean, white hallways which were brightly lit and smelled of fresh paint. I passed two trusties who were carrying on a stretcher the eight monumental registers containing the names of the eleven hundred and fifty prisoners. They were followed by a young guard and a clerk. The two prisoners walked in silence, their arms straining beneath the weight of the giant volumes which could have been reduced to a small notebook. In shuffling along on their selvaged slippers, they bore the full weight imparted by so much sadness and thus seemed to be thudding the floor, lumberingly, with rubber boots. The two guards observed the same silence and walked with equally solemn steps. I almost saluted, not the jailers, but the books which contained the so illustrious name of Harcamone.

"Hey, you going to salute?"

This was said by the turnkey who was escorting me, and he added:

"Unless you already feel like getting the works."

Prisoners are required to salute the guards. As I neared them I ventured, with difficulty, the ridiculous salute which is so incompatible with our flabby, gliding gait on heelless slippers. We passed other guards, who didn't even look at us. The prison lived like a cathedral at midnight of Christmas eve. We were carrying on the tradition of the monks who went about their business at night, in silence. We belonged to the Middle Ages. A door was open at the left. I entered the wardrobe. When I took off my clothes, I felt that the brown homespun prison outfit was a robe of innocence which I was

putting on in order to live near, in fact under the very roof of
the murderer. Trembling like a thief, I lived for days on end in
a state of wonder which none of the lowliest daily pre-occupa-
tions was able to destroy: neither the crappers nor the stew
nor the work nor the confusion of the senses.

After assigning me to a dormitory, Number 5, they assigned
me to the workshop where camouflage nets were being made
for the German army which was then occupying France. I had
made up my mind to keep out of the intrigues of the big shots,
of the guys who pay for larceny, who pay for murder, but in
the wardrobe I was given a pair of trousers that had belonged
to a bruiser—or an inmate who must have acted like one. He
had made two slits in it for false pockets, which were forbidden. They were waist-high and cut on the bias, like those of
sailors. When I walked, or was inactive, that was where, in
spite of myself, I put my hands. My gait became what I hadn't
wanted it to be, that of a big shot. The outfit included a brown
homespun jacket without collar or pockets (though a convict
had pierced the linng and thus made a kind of inner pocket).
It had button-holes, but all the buttons were missing. The
jacket was very threadbare, but less than the trousers, which
had been mended with nine patches, all more or less worn with
age. There were thus nine different shades of brown. The two
false pockets had been cut diagonally at stomach-level with, I
imagine, a paring-knife from the shoemaking shop. The
trousers were supposed to be held up by the buttons alone,
without belt or braces, but the buttons were all missing,
which made the outfit look as sad as a wrecked house. In the
shop, two hours after my arrival, I made myself a raffia belt in
the form of a rope, and, as it was confiscated every evening by
a guard, I would make another the following day. There are
inmates who make a new one every single morning, that is,
say, for ten years, three thousand times. The trousers were too
short for me. They reached only to my calves, so that my long
underpants and pale white legs were visible. The underpants
were white and the letters A.P., which stand for *administration*

pénitentiaire, were stamped on them in thick ink. The undershirt was made of homespun, also brown, and had a small pocket on the right side. The coarse linen shirt was collarless. The sleeves had no cuffs. Nor buttons either. There were rust spots on the shirt which I feared were shit-stains. It was stamped A.P. We changed shirts every two weeks. The slippers were made of brown homespun. They would get stiff with sweat. The flat forage cap was made of brown homespun. The handkerchief had blue and white stripes.

I add the fact that Rasseneur, whom I had met in another prison, recognized me and, without consulting me, got me into a mob. Apart from him, I recognized no one from Santé or the other prisons. Harcamone was the only one who had been with me at Mettray, but he remained invisible in the death-cell.

I shall try to tell what Harcamone meant to me, and thereby what Divers meant to me, and above all Bulkaen, whom I still love and who finally indicates my fate to me. Bulkaen is the finger of God; Harcamone is God, since he is in heaven (I am speaking of the heaven I create for myself and to which I am devoted body and soul). Their love, my love for them persists within me, where it acts and stirs my depths, and though what I felt for Harcamone may be mystic, it is none the less violent. I shall try to tell as well as I can what it is about these handsome thugs that charms me, the element which is both light and darkness. I shall do what I can, but all I can say is that "they are a dark brightness or a dazzling darkness." This is nothing compared to how I feel about it, a feeling which the most worthy novelists express when they write: "The black light . . . the blazing shade . . . ," trying to achieve in a short poem the living, apparent synthesis of Evil and the Beautiful. Through Harcamone, Divers and Bulkaen I shall again relive Mettray, which was my childhood. I shall revive the abolished reformatory, the children's hell that has been destroyed.

Can it be that the world was unaware of, did not even suspect, the existence of three hundred children who were organized in a rhythm of love and hate in the fairest spot of

fairest Touraine? There, among the flowers (those garden
flowers and those which I offer to dead soldiers, anxiously, lest
they not suffice, have been, ever since, my infernal props)
among the flowers and rare varieties of trees, the Colony led
its secret life, worrying the peasants for fifteen miles around,
for they feared that a sixteen-year-old colonist might escape
and set fire to their farms. Furthermore, as every peasant was
given a fifty-franc reward for each runaway child he brought
back, the Mettray countryside was the scene, night and day, of
an actual child-hunt, complete with pitchforks, shotguns and
dogs. If a colonist went out at night, he strewed terror through
the fields. Rio, whom I cannot think of without being moved
by his maidenly sweetness, was about eighteen when he tried to
run away. He dared set fire to a barn so that the panic-stricken
peasants would get up and run to the fire in their nightshirts
without taking time to lock the door. He entered unseen and
stole a jacket and pair of trousers in order to get rid of the
white canvas breeches and blue twill smock that were the
uniform of the Colony and that would have singled him out.
The house blazed away magnificently. Children, so it was
reported, were burned to a crisp, cows perished, but the bold,
remorseless child got as far as Orléans. It is a known fact that
young countrywomen always leave a jacket and pair of trousers
on the clothes-line in the hope and fear that a runaway will
steal them, move the line, which rings a bell, and so be caught.
Traps laid by women's hands surrounded the Colony with an
invisible, undetectable danger which threw pairs of frightened
kids into a wild panic. The mere memory of this causes me,
within my affliction, a greater affliction, fills me with frightful
gloom at the thought that this childhood world is dead. Only
one phrase can express my sadness, the one that is always
written at the end of a prince's visit to the scenes of his former
loves or the scenes of his glory: ". . . and he wept . . ."

Fontevrault, like Mettray, could be rendered by a long list
of the couples which were formed by names:

Botchako and Bulkaen

Sillar and Venture
Rocky and Bulkaen
Deloffre and Toscano
Mouline and Monot
Lou Daybreak and Jo
Bulkaen and I
Divers and I
Rocky and I.

I lived for a week in the bewilderment of arrival, familiarizing myself with the prison discipline and regimen. A simple regimen, a life that would be easy if it were not lived by us. We got up at six. A guard opened the door. We went to the stone-flagged corridor to get our clothes which we had left there before going to bed. We then got dressed. Five minutes in the washroom. We drank a bowl of soup in the refectory and then left for the shop. Work until noon. Then back to the refectory until one-thirty. Again to the shop. At six o'clock, mess. At seven, to the dormitory. I have just set down, exactly, the daily schedule at Mettray. On Sunday we would stay in the shops, inactive, sometimes reading the list of names of the abbesses, appointed by royal decree, who had reigned over Fontevrault. To go to the refectory at noon, we had to cross yards that were infinitely sad, sad because of the abandonment that already dooms to death the admirable Renaissance façades. Black faggots are heaped in a corner, near the abbey chapel. Dirty water flows into gutters. The grace of some architectural jewel is sometimes wounded. I got involved in the complications of love affairs, but the daily preoccupations with work, meals, exchanges, the occasional devices whereby a convict craftily carries on a private life behind his official, visible life, and, in addition, a rapid acquaintanceship with the inmates, did not prevent me from bearing, almost painfully, the weight of Harcamone's presence. One day, at meal time, I couldn't refrain from whispering to Rasseneur:

"Where is he?"

And he, in a breath:

"In Number 7. Special cell."

"You think he'll get it?"

"Sure thing."

A kid at my left who guessed we were talking about that death put his hand to his mouth and muttered:

"It's great to die gloriously!"

I knew he was there, and I was full of hope and fear, when I had the privilege of witnessing one of his appearances. It happened during a recreation period. We were lined up near the death-cell, waiting our turn to be shaved by a convict (we were shaved once a week). One of the superintendents had opened Harcamone's door. He was accompanied by a guard who was casually entwining his gestures with a thick chain, as thick as those by which the chairs are attached to the walls. The superintendent entered. Though we were facing the wall, we could not help looking, despite the fact that we weren't allowed to. We were like children whose heads are bowed during evening service and who look up when the priest opens the tabernacle. It was the first time I had seen Harcamone since leaving Mettray. He was standing, with the full beauty of his body, in the middle of the cell. He was wearing his beret, not drooping over his ear as at Mettray but set almost on his eyes and bent, forming a peak, like the vizor of the caps of old-time hooligans. I received such a shock that I can't tell whether it was caused by the change in his beauty or by the fact that I was suddenly confronted with the exceptional creature whose story was familiar only to the well guarded chamber of my eyeballs, and I found myself in the situation of the witch who has long been summoning the prodigy, lives in expectation of it, recognizes the signs that announce it and suddenly sees it standing before her and—what is even more disturbing—sees it as she had announced it. It is the proof of her power, of her grace, for the flesh is also the most obvious means of certainty. Harcamone "appeared unto me." He knew it was recreation time, for he put out his wrists, which the guard attached with the short chain. Harcamone dropped his arms, and the chain hung in front of him, below his belt. He walked out of the cell. As sunflowers turn to the sun, our faces turned and our bodies pivoted without our even realizing that our immobility had been disturbed, and when he moved toward us, with short steps, like the women of 1910 in hobble-skirts, or the way he himself danced the Java, we felt a temptation to kneel or at least to put our hands over our eyes, out of decency. He had no belt. He had no socks. From his head—or from mine—came the roar of an airplane engine. I felt in all my veins that the miracle was under way. But the fervour of our admiration and the burden of saintliness which weighed on the chain that gripped his wrists—his hair had had time to grow and the curls had matted over his forehead with the cunning cruelty of the twists of the crown of thorns —caused the chain to be transformed before our unastonished eyes into a garland of white flowers. The transformation began at the left wrist, which it encircled with a bracelet of flowers, and continued along the chain, from link to link, to the right wrist. Harcamone kept walking, heedless of the prodigy. The guards saw nothing abnormal. I was holding the pair of scissors with which, once a month, we were allowed, each in turn, to cut our fingernails and toenails. I was therefore barefooted. I made the same movement that religious fanatics make to seize the hem of a cloak and kiss it. I took two steps, with my body bent forward and the scissors in my hand, and cut off the loveliest rose, which was hanging by a supple stem near his left wrist. The head of the rose fell on my bare foot and rolled on the pavestones among the dirty curls of cut hair. I picked it up and raised my enraptured face, just in time to see the horror stamped on that of Harcamone, whose nervousness had been unable to resist that sure prefiguration of his death. He almost fainted. For a very brief instant, I found myself on one knee before my idol, who was trembling with horror, or shame, or love, staring at me as if he had recognized me, or merely as if Harcamone had recognized Genet, and as if I were the cause of his frightful emotion, for we had each made exactly the gestures that might be so interpreted. He was deathly pale, and those who witnessed the scene from a distance might have thought that this murderer was as delicate as a Duke of Guise or a Knight of Lorraine, of whom history tells us that they fainted, overwhelmed by the smell and sight of a rose. But he pulled himself together. His face—over which a slight smile passed—grew calm again. He continued walking, with the limping gait of which I shall speak later, though it was attenuated by the fetters on his ankles, but the chain that bound his hands no longer suggested a garland and was now only a steel chain. He disappeared from my sight, whisked away by the shadow and the bend of the corridor. I put the rose into the false pocket that was cut in my jacket.

This, then, is the tone I shall adopt in speaking of Mettray, Harcamone and the prison. Nothing will prevent me, neither close attention nor the desire to be exact, from writing words that sing. And though the evocation of Bulkaen may bring me back to a more naked view of events, I know that, as soon as it ceases, my song, in reaction against this nakedness, will be more exalted. But let there be no talk of improbability or of my having derived this phrase from an arrangement of words. The scene was within me, I was present, and only by writing about it am I able to express my worship of the murderer less awkwardly. The very day following this prodigy I forgot all about it in my infatuation with Bulkaen.

Blond, close-cropped hair, eyes that were perhaps green but certainly grim-looking, a thin, lithe body—the expression that best renders it is: "grace in leaf and love at rest"—an air of being twenty years old: that's Bulkaen. I had been at Fontevrault a week. I was going down for the medical examination when, at a turn of the stairway, I saw him. He was dressing or undressing. He must have been swopping his homespun jacket for a newer one. I had time enough to see, spread across his golden chest and wide as a coat of arms, the huge wings of a blue eagle. The tattoo wasn't dry, and the scabs made it stand out in such relief that I thought it had been carved with a

chisel. I was seized with a kind of holy terror. When the
youngster stood up straight, his face was smiling. It was
gleaming with stars. He was saying to the crony with whom he
was making the swop, ". . . and besides, I've been given a
ten-year injunction."[1] He threw his jacket over his shoulders
and kept it there. I was holding a few cigarette butts in my
hand, which was on a level with his eyes because of our
positions on the stairs—I was on the way down. He looked at
them and said, "Someone's got cigarettes." I said "I have"
and kept going, feeling a little ashamed of smoking Gauloises.
The cigarette is the prisoner's gentle companion. He thinks of
it more than of his absent wife. His charming friendship with it
is largely due to the elegance of its shape and the gestures it
requires of his fingers and body. It was boorish of me not to
offer Bulkaen one of my white maidens. That was our first
meeting. I was too struck by the brilliance of his beauty to
dare say another word. I spoke of him to no one, but I carried
off in my eyes the memory of a dazzling face and body. I
prayed for him to love me. I prayed for him to be the kind of
person who could love me. I already knew he would lead me to
death. I know now that this death will be beautiful. I mean
that he was worthy of my dying for him and because of him.
But may he lead me to it quickly. In any case, sooner or later
it will be because of him. I shall die worn out or shattered.
Even if, at the end of this book, Bulkaen proves to be contemptible because of his stupidity or vanity or some other ugly
quality, the reader must not be surprised if, though aware of
these qualities (since I reveal them), I persist in changing my
life by following the star to which he points (I am using his
terms, despite myself. When he sent me notes later on, he
would write: "I've got my star . . .", for his role of demon
requires that he show me this new direction, He brings a
message which he himself does not quite understand but which

[1] In the original, *interdiction de séjour*: a punishment, which does not
exist in English and American law, whereby a criminal is banished from
an area for a given time.—Translator's note.

he implements in part. Fatality will first utilize my love of him. But when my love—and Bulkaen—disappear, what will be left?

I have the nerve to think that Bulkaen lived only so that I could write my book. He therefore had to die, after a life I can imagine only as bold and arrogant, slapping every paleface he came across. His death will be violent and mine will follow close on his. I feel that I'm wound up and heading for an end which will blow us to bits.

The very next day, in the yard, during recreation, Rasseneur introduced us to each other, at a moment when several fellows were plaguing a homely, unlikable old queer. They were pushing him around, bullying him, making fun of him. The most spiteful of all, possessed of a cruelty that seemed completely unwarranted, was Botchako, who had the reputation of being the most formidable crasher in Fontevrault, a brutal individual who usually said nothing to the jerks and even less to the queers, whom he seemed unaware of, and I wondered why he had suddenly let loose on this one. It was as if he were all at once giving vent to insults that had been accumulating a long time. His irregular but firm teeth seemed to be curling his lips. His face was freckled. One imagined he was red-headed. He hadn't the shade of a beard. He wasn't jeering with a smile, as were the others; he was nasty and insulting. He wasn't playing but seemed to be taking revenge. Rage set him ablaze. He was regarded as the biggest fucker in the jug. Ugliness is beauty at rest. When he spoke, his voice was hoarse and hollow. It also had some acid scratches which were like cracks, like fissures, and, considering the beauty of his voice when he sang, I examined his speaking voice more attentively. I made the following discovery: the irritating hoarseness, forced by the singing, was transformed into a very sweet, velvety strain, and the fissures became the clearest notes. It was somewhat as if, in unwinding a ball of wool at rest, these notes had been refined. A physicist can easily explain this phenomenon. As for me, I remain disturbed in the presence of the person who revealed to me that beauty is the projection of ugliness and that by "developing" certain monstrosities we obtain the purest ornaments. Under the spell of his words, I expected to see him strike the jerk, who dared not make a movement, not even of fear. He instinctively assumed the sudden, shifty, prudent immobility of a frightened animal. Had Botchako made a single move to strike, he might have killed him, for he would not have been able to check his fury. It was known in the prison that he never stopped fighting until he was completely exhausted. The features of his pug-nosed face manifested the power of a solid, stocky, unflinching body. His face was like a boxer's, tough and firm, hardened by repeated blows, beaten like wrought-iron. There was nothing soft or drooping about its flesh. The skin clung to dry muscle and bone. His forehead was too narrow to contain enough reason to stop his anger once it got going. His eyes were deep set and the epidermis of his chest, which was visible though the opening of the shirt and homespun jacket, was white and healthy-looking and absolutely hairless.

Above the yard, on a kind of raised cat-walk, Randon made his rounds without stopping. From time to time he would look down into the yard where we were standing about. He was the meanest of the guards. In order that he not notice the cruelty of the scene—he would have had the guilty ones punished for the sake of virtue—the big shots and the jerk himself made their attitudes and gestures look inoffensive, even friendly, while their mouths were spewing insults, though in a muffled voice that veiled their malevolence. The queer was smiling with the utmost humility, as much to put off the guard as to try to mollify Botchako and his cronies.

"You bitch, you swallow it by the mouthful!"

With a single twist, unique in the world, Botchako hitched up his pants.

"I'd shoot it up your hole, you punk!"

Bulkaen was leaning against the wall with his elbow, in such a way that his head was under his arm, which looked as if it

were a crown. This crown-arm was bare, for his jacket was, as
always, simply thrown over his shoulders, and that enormous
coil of muscle, his baron's coronet on the light head of a child
of the North, was the visible sign of the ten years of banish-
ment that weighed on his delicate pate. He wore his beret the
way Harcamone did. At the same time, I saw his neck, the skin
of which was shadowy with grime; from his round shirt-collar
emerged a wing-tip of the blue eagle. His right ankle was
crossed over the left, the way Mercury is always depicted, and
the heavy homespun trousers, as worn by him, had infinite
grace. His smiling lips were parted. From his mouth came a
breath which could only be perfumed. His left hand was poised
on his hipbone as on the handle of a dagger. I haven't invented
this posture. That's how he stood. I add that he had a slender
figure, broad shoulders and a voice strong with the assurance
that came from the awareness of his invincible beauty. He was
watching the scene. Botchako was still spitting insults and
getting more and more nasty.

Lou Daybreak, the most isolated of us because of his name,
made a vague gesture. Lou's name was a vapour that
enveloped his entire person, and when you pierced the softness
and approached him, when you passed through his name, you
scraped against the thorns, against the sharp, cunning
branches with which he bristled. He was blond, and his eyebrows looked like spikes of rye stuck to his stylized brow. He
was a pimp, and we didn't like him. He hung out with other
pimps, whom we called "Julots" or "Those Gentlemen" . . .
and they often got into brawls with our mobs.

We thought that this gesture—his hand dropping on
Botchako's shoulder—was an attempt to make peace, but he
said, with a smile:

"Go on, marry him! You're in love with him. Anyone can
see it!"

"Me? Marry a queer?"

Botchako's face expressed exaggerated disgust. There was
no reason for Lou to talk as he did, for though the pimps and

the crashers, who formed distinct groups, did speak to each other about trivial matters having to do with work and life in common, they never took the liberty of going too far. I was waiting for Botchako to go for Lou, but he turned away and spat. Lou smiled. There was a movement of hostility in the group of crashers. I looked at Bulkaen. He was smiling and shifting his gaze back and forth from Botchako to the jerk. Amused perhaps. But I dared not think I was in the presence of two guys (Bulkaen and the queer) who were basically identical. I was watching Bulkaen to see his reaction to the queer's gestures. I tried to detect a correspondence between their gesticulations. There was nothing mannered about Bulkaen. His excessive vivacity made him seem somewhat brutal. Was he carrying within him an abashed and quivering fag who resembled the pathetic jerk that everyone despised?

Would he love me? My spirit was already flying off in quest of my happiness. Would some unexpected happening, some blunder, alike and equally miraculous, link us by love as he was linked with Rocky? He related the great event to me later on. I translate his language: Rocky and he had met at Clair-vaux Prison. They were released the same day and decided to work together. Three days later, their first burglary made them rich: a wad of banknotes. "Sixty thousand francs," said Bulkaen. They left the rifled apartment and went out into the street and the night, floating with elation. They dared not count and split the booty in the lighted street. They entered the garden of the Square d'Anvers, which was deserted. Rocky took out the bills. He counted them and gave thirty to Bulkaen. The joy of being free and rich gave them wings. Their souls tried to leave their cumbrous bodies, to drag them heavenward. It was real joy. They smiled with glee at their success. They rose to the occasion, as if to congratulate each other, not upon their skill but their luck, as one congratulates a friend who has come into money, and this happy impulse made them embrace. Their joy was so great that there is no knowing its essence. Its origin was the successful job, but a small fact

(the embrace, the accolade) intervened amidst the joyous
tumult, and despite themselves it was this new fact that they
considered the source of the happiness which they named love.
Bulkaen and Rocky kissed. They could not break away from
each other, for happiness never produces a movement of withdrawal. The happier they were, the more deeply they entered
each other. They were rich and free—they were happy. They
were in each other's arms at the moment of deepest happiness:
they loved each other. And as this merging was energized by
the mute fear of being caught, and also because their mutual
solitude made them seek a friend as a shelter in which to hide,
they married.

Bulkaen's gaze turned away from the scene that pained me
and it settled on Rasseneur, the friend who had introduced
us—but his head had to make a quarter-turn and his gaze met
mine on its way to Rasseneur. I thought for a moment that he
had recognized me as the fellow of the day before. My face
remained impassive, indifferent, and his, now that I recall it,
was, I think, somewhat arch. He started a conversation. When
the ten-minute recreation period was over, I shook hands with
him without wanting to seem as if I were bothering to look at
him, and I made a point of this calculated indifference by
pretending to be overjoyed to see a friend who was going by,
but I carried Bulkaen off in the depths of my heart. I went
back to my cell, and the abandoned habit of my abandoned
childhood took hold of me: the rest of the day and all night
long I built an imaginary life of which Bulkaen was the centre,
and I always gave that life, which was begun over and over
and was transformed a dozen times, a violent end: murder,
hanging or beheading.

We saw each other again. At each of our meetings he
appeared before me in a bloody glory of which he was
unaware. I was drawn to him by the force of love, which was
opposed by the force of supernatural but brawny creatures
who kept me from going to him by fettering my wrists, waist
and ankles with chains that would have kept a cruiser anchored

on a stormy night. He was always smiling. Thus, it was through him that the habits of my childhood took hold of me again.

My childhood was dead and with it died the poetic powers that had dwelt in me. I no longer hoped that prison would remain the fabulous world it had long been. One day, I suddenly realized from certain signs that it was losing its charms, which meant perhaps that I was being transformed, that my eyes were opening to the usual view of the world. I saw prison as any ordinary roughneck sees it. It is a dungeon where I rage at being locked up, but today, in the hole, instead of reading "Tattooed Jean" on the wall of the cell, I read, because of a malformation of the letters carved in the plaster, "Tortured Jean." (It's because of Harcamone that I've been in the hole for a month, and not because of Bulkaen.) I walked by the murderer's cell too often, and one day I was caught. Here are a few details: The carpentry shop and the shops where camouflage nets and iron beds are made are in a court in the north part of the former abbey. They are one-storey buildings. The dormitories are on the first and second floors of the left wing, which is supported by the wall of the former chapter-house. The infirmary is on the ground floor. In order to get there, I had to go by way of the sixth or seventh division, where the death-cells were located, and I always went by way of the seventh. Harcamone's cell was at the right. A guard, who sat on a stool, would look inside and talk to him or read a newspaper or eat a cold meal. I would look straight ahead and keep going.

It must seem odd that I walked through the prison all by myself. The reason is that I had arranged things, first with Rocky, who was an attendant in the infirmary, and then, when he left prison, with his successor. While at work, I would pretend that something was wrong with me, and the attendant would send for me to be treated. The guard in the shop would merely ring up his colleague and let him know I was coming.

The exact vision that made a man of me, that is, a creature

living solely on earth, corresponded with the fact that my femininity, or the ambiguity and haziness of my male desires, seemed to have ended. If my sense of wonder, the joy that suspended me from branches of pure air, sprang chiefly from my identifying myself with the handsome thugs who haunted the prison, as soon as I achieved total virility—or, to be more exact, as soon as I became a male—the thugs lost their glamour. And though my meeting Bulkaen revives dormant charms, I shall preserve the benefit of that march toward maleness, for Bulkaen's beauty is, above all, delicate. I no longer yearned to resemble the hoodlums. I felt I had achieved self-fulfillment. Perhaps I feel it less today, after the adventures I am describing, but I felt strong, not dependent, free, unbound. Glamorous models ceased to present themselves. I strode jauntily in my strength, with a weightiness, a sureness, a forthright look which are themselves proofs of force. The hoodlums no longer appealed to me. They were my equals. Does this mean that attraction is possible only when one is not entirely oneself? During those years of softness when my personality took all sorts of forms, any male could squeeze my sides with his walls, could contain me. My moral substance (and physical substance, which is its visible form, what with my white skin, weak bones, slack muscles, my slow gestures and their uncertainty) was without sharpness, without contour. I longed at the time—and often went so far as to imagine my body twisting about the firm, vigorous body of a male—to be embraced by the calm, splendid stature of a man of stone with sharp angles. And I was not completely at ease unless I could completely take his place, take on his qualities, his virtues. When I imagined I was he, making his gestures, uttering his words: when I *was* he. People thought I was seeing double, whereas I was seeing the double of things. I wanted to be myself, and I was myself when I became a crasher. All burglars will understand the dignity that arrayed me when I held my jimmy, my "pen." From its weight, material, and shape, and from its function too, emanated an authority that made me a man. I had always needed that steel penis in order to free myself completely from my faggotry, from my humble attitudes, and to attain the clear simplicity of manliness. I am no longer surprised at the arrogant ways of youngsters who have used the pen, even if only once. You may shrug your shoulders and mutter that they're scum. Nothing will prevent them from retaining the jimmy's virtue, which gives, in every circumstance, a sometimes astounding hardness to their youthful softness. Those who have used it are marked men. Bulkaen had known the jimmy, I could tell at once. These kids are crashers, therefore men, as much by virtue of the kind of nobility conferred upon them by the jimmy as of the risks, sometimes very great, which they have taken. Not that any particular courage is needed—I would say, rather, an unconcern, which is more exact. They are noble. A crasher cannot have low sentiments (I intend, starting here, to generalize. You will read later on about the baseness of hoodlums.), since he leads a dangerous life with his body, for only the crasher's body is in danger, he does not worry about his soul. You are concerned for your honour, your reputation, you devise ways and means of saving them. But the crasher takes risks in the practice of his trade. His ruses are the ruses of a warrior and not of a sharper. It is noteworthy that during the war of 1940 real burglars did not try to live by what became common among bourgeois and workers, by what was then called the "black market." They knew nothing about business. When the prisons were filled with honest people who had been driven from the woods by hunger, they lost their fine, lordly bearing, but the crashers remained a haughty aristocracy. The great evil of this war has been its dissolving the hardness of our prisons. The war has locked up so many innocent people that the prisons are merely places of lamentation. Nothing is more repugnant than an innocent man in prison. He has done nothing to deserve jail (these are his own words). Destiny has made an error.

I did not get my first jimmy from a yegg, I bought it in a

hardware store. It was short and solid, and, from the time of
my first robbery, I held it as dear as a warrior his weapons,
with a mysterious veneration, as when the warrior is a savage
and his weapon a rifle. The two wedges, which lay next to the
jimmy in a corner of my room—the corner quickly became
magnetic, hypnotic—lightened it and gave it that air of a
winged prick by which I was haunted. I slept beside it, for the
warrior sleeps armed.

For my first burglary I chose a few houses in Auteil and
looked up the names of the tenants in the phone book.[1] I had
decided to operate as luck would have it. I would break in if
nobody was home. I casually passed the concierge's window in
the first apartment house. In my trousers, against my thigh,
were my jimmy and wedges. I started on the fifth floor so as to
run less risk of being disturbed. I rang once. No one answered.
I rang twice. Finally I set up a peal that lasted two minutes so
as to be sure the apartment was empty.

If I were writing a novel, there might be a point in
describing the gestures I made, but the aim of this book is only
to relate the experience of freeing myself from a state of
painful torpor, from a low, shameful life taken up with prostitution and begging and under the sway of the glamour and
charm of the criminal world. I freed myself by and for a
prouder attitude.

I had trained myself by breaking open doors in safe places,
my own door and those of my friends. I therefore carried out
the present operation in quick time, perhaps three minutes.
Time enough to force the bottom of the door with my foot,
insert a wedge, force the top with the jimmy and insert the
second wedge between the door and the jamb, move up the
first wedge, move down the second, wedge the jimmy near the
lock, and push . . . When the lock cracked, the noise it made
seemed to me to resound through the building. I pushed the
door and went in. The noise of the lock as it gives way, the

---

[1] There is a Paris directory arranged by street and house number.—
Translator's note.

silence that follows and the solitude that always besets me will govern my criminal entrances. These are rites, the more important as they are inevitable and are not mere adornments of an action whose essence is still mysterious to me. I entered. I was the young sovereign who takes possession of a new realm where all is new to him but where there surely lurks the danger of attacks and conspiracies, a danger hidden along the road he takes, behind every rock, every tree, under the rugs, in the flowers that are tossed and the gifts offered by a people invisible by virtue of their number. The entrance was large. It heralded the most sumptuous home I had ever seen. I was surprised that there were no servants. I opened a door and found myself in the big drawing-room. The objects were waiting for me. They were laid out for the robbery, and my passion for plunder and booty was inflamed. To speak properly of my emotion I would have to employ the same words I used in describing my wonderment in the presence of that new treasure, my love for Bulkaen, and in describing my fear in the presence of the possible treasure, his love for me. I would have to allude to the trembling hopes of the virgin, of the village fiancée who waits to be chosen, and then to add that this light moment is threatened by the black, pitiless, single eye of a revolver. For two days I remained in the presence of Bulkaen's image, with the fearful shyness of one who carries his first bouquet in its lace-paper collar. Would he say yes? Would he say no? I implored the spiders that had woven such precious circumstances. Let their thread not snap!

I opened a glass cabinet and carried off all the ivories and jades. Perhaps I was the first crasher ever to leave without bothering about cash, and it was not until my third job that I felt the sense of power and freedom that comes from discovering a sheaf of bills that you stuff into your pockets. I closed the door behind me and went downstairs. I was saved from bondage and low inclinations, for I had just performed an act of physical boldness. I already held my head high as I walked down the stairs. I felt in my trousers, against my thigh, the icy jimmy. I amiably wished that a tenant would appear so that I could use the strength that was hardening me. My right hand closed on the jimmy:

"If a woman comes along, I'll lay her out with my pendulum."

When I got to the street, I walked boldly. But I was always accompanied by an agonizing thought: the fear that honest people may be thieves who have chosen a cleverer and safer way of stealing. This fear disturbed my peace of mind in my solitude. I dismissed the idea by means of shrewd devices, which I shall describe.

I was now a man, a he-man. The broad-shouldered kids and pimps, the children of sorrow with bitter mouths and frightening eyes, were of no further use to me. I was alone. Everything was absent from the prisons, even solitude. Thus, my interest in adventure novels wanes in so far as I can no longer seriously imagine myself being the hero or being in his situation. I stopped plunging into those complications in which the slightest feat, criminal or otherwise, could be copied, be carried over into life, be utilized personally and lead me to wealth and glory. Thus, it was now extremely difficult for me to re-immerse myself in my dream-stories, stories fabricated by the disheartening play of solitude, but I found—and still find, despite my new plunge—more wellbeing in the true memories of my former life. Since my childhood is dead, in speaking of it I shall be speaking of something dead, but I shall do so in order to speak of the world of death, of the Kingdom of Darkness or Transparency. Someone has carved on the wall: "Just as I'm guarded by a prison-door, so my heart guards your memory . . ." I shall not let my childhood escape.

Thus, my heaven had emptied. The time to become who I am had perhaps arrived. And I shall be what I do not foresee, since I do not desire it, but I will not be a sailor or explorer or gangster or dancer or boxer, for their most glorious representatives no longer have a hold on me. I stopped wanting, and I shall never again want, to go through the canyons of Chile, for

I have stopped admiring the clever and sturdy Rifle King who
scaled their rocks in the illustrated pages of my childhood. The
excitement was over. As for things, I began to know them by
their practical qualities. The objects here in jail have been
worn out by my eyes and are now sickly pale. They no longer
mean prison to me, since the prison is inside me, composed of
the cells of my tissues. It was not until long after my return
here that my hands and eyes, which were only too familiar
with the practical qualities of objects, finally stopped recognizing these qualities and discovered others which have another
meaning. Everything was without mystery for me, but that
bareness was not without beauty because I establish the difference between my former and present view of things, and
this displacement intrigues me. Here is a very simple image: I
felt I was emerging from a cave peopled with marvellous
creatures, which one only senses (angels, for example, with
speckled faces), and entering a luminous space where everything is only what it is, without overtones, without aura. What
it is: useful. This world, which is new to me, is dreary,
without hope, without excitement. Now that the prison is
stripped of its sacred ornaments, I see it naked, and its nakedness is cruel. The inmates are merely sorry creatures with
teeth rotted by scurvy; they are bent with illness and are
always spitting and sputtering and coughing. They go from
dormitory to shop in big, heavy, resounding sabots. They
shuffle along on canvas slippers which are eaten away and stiff
with filth that the dust has compounded with sweat. They
stink. They are cowardly in the presence of the guards, who
are as cowardly as they. They are now only scurrilous carica-
tures of the handsome criminals I saw in them when I was
twenty. I only wish I could expose sufficiently the blemishes
and ugliness of what they have become so as to take revenge
for the harm they did me and the boredom I felt when confronted with their unparalleled stupidity.

And it grieved me to discover this new aspect of the world
and of prison at a time when I was beginning to realize that

prison was indeed the closed area, the confined, measured universe in which I ought to live permanently. It is the universe for which I am meant. It is meant for me. It is the one in which I must live (for I have the organs one needs to live in it), to which I am always being brought back by the fatality that showed me the curve of my destiny in the letters carved on the wall: "M.A.V."[1] And I have this feeling (so disheartening that after my mentioning it to Rasseneur he exclaimed: "Oh! Jean!" in a tone of such poignant sadness that I felt an instant expression of his friendship), I have this feeling during the medical check-up or during recreation when I meet friends, new and old, those to whom I am "Jeannot with the Pretty Ties", those I knew at the Mouse-trap, in the corridors of Santé and Fresnes Prisons, even outside. It is so natural for them to make up the population of prison and I discover I have such close ties with them (professional relations, relations of friendship or hatred) that, since I feel so much a part of this world, it horrifies me to know that I am excluded from the other, yours, just when I was attaining the qualities by means of which one can live in it. I am therefore dead. I am a dead man who sees his skeleton in a mirror, or a dream character who knows that he lives only in the darkest region of a being whose face he will not know when the dreamer is awake. I now act and think only in terms of prison. My activity is limited by its framework. I am only a punished man. To the usual hardships of prison has been added hunger, and not a child's hunger—for our hunger at Mettray was the gluttony natural to children who are never sated, even by abundance. Hunger here is a man's hunger. It bites the bodies (and gnaws the minds) of the least sensitive brutes. Behind the walls, the war, which is mysterious to us, has shrunk our loaf of bread, our food allowance, and the big shots have been hit in the rightful object of their pride, their muscles. Hunger has transformed the prison into a Great North where wolves howl at night. We live at the confines of the Arctic polar circle.

[1] M.A.V., *mort aux vaches,* death to the cops.—Translator's note.

Our skinny bodies fight among themselves, and each, within itself, against hunger. This hunger, which at first helped to disenchant the jail, has now become so great that it is a tragic element which finally crowns the prison with a savage, baroque motif, with a ringing song that is wilder than the others and may dizzy me and make me fall into the hands of the powers summoned by Bulkaen. Despite this affliction—for though I take a man's stand, I realize that I am leaving a larval world of prodigious richness and violence—I want to try to relive my moments at Mettray. The atmosphere of the prison quickly impelled me to go back—in going back to Mettray—to my habits of the past, and I do not live a single moment on earth without at the same time living it in my secret domain, which is probably similar to the one inhabited by the men who are being punished, who walk round and round with their heads bent and their eyes looking straight ahead. And the fury with which I once turned on Charlot has not yet emptied me of the hatred I vowed him, despite my air of indifference, when, in the shop, because I reacted vaguely, or perhaps not at all, to one of his jokes, he shook me by the shoulder and said, "You in a fog or something?" I instantly felt the hatred we can bear a person who violates our dearest secrets, those of our vices.

At times, each of us is the theatre of a drama which is occasioned by several elements: his real loves, a fight, his jealousy, a projected escape, which merge with dream adventures more brutal than real ones, and the men who are then wracked by the drama suddenly thrash about, but in silence. They make stiff gestures. They are brusque, taut, set. They hit out as if fighting an invisible soldier. Suddenly they relapse into their torpor; their very physiognomy sinks to the bottom of a swamp of dreams. Though the warden may say we are sluggish, the more subtle guards know that we are deep in these gardens and they no more disturb the submerged convict gratuitously than a Chinese disturbs an opium-smoker. Charlot was not an absolute tough. He therefore could not permit himself to screw me. And though he could later knock hell out of anyone who needled him, there hung over him the infamy of having made with his own hands, when he was broke, a black satin dress so that his girl could cruise for trade. I hated him for that blemish and for his shrewdness. In fact, my nerves couldn't stand the provocations, however slight, of a jerk or weakling. I would let my fists fly at the merest trifle. But there would have been no need to let fly at a tough, and it was not only because of fear, but because the toughs never even annoyed me. There issues from those I call "toughs" a potency that still dominates, and that soothes me. At Mettray I beat the daylights out of a little jerk who ran his hands over the window-panes with a squeaking sound. A few days later, Divers did the very same thing and thus tugged at all my nerves, which wound about him and climbed lovingly over his body. If my memories of the Colony are awakened by Bulkaen in particular, by his presence, by his effect on me, the danger will be doubled, for my love of him already threatened to deliver me to the former powers of the Prison. And because in addition to this danger is that of the language I shall use in talking of Mettray and Fontevrault. For I tear my words from the depths of my being, from a region to which irony has no access, and these words, which are charged with all the buried desires I carry within me and which express them on paper as I write, will re-create the loathsome and cherished world from which I tried to free myself. Furthermore, as the insight I acquired into commonplace things enables me to indulge in the play and subtleties of the heart, my heart is caught in a veil again, incapable of fighting back when the lover practises his wiles. Charms master and throttle me. But I am glad to have given the loveliest names, the most beautiful titles (archangel, child-sun, my Spanish evening) to so many youngsters that I have nothing left with which to magnify Bulkaen. Perhaps, if words do not meddle too much, I shall be able to see him as he is, a pale, lively hoodlum, unless the fact of remaining solitary, alone with himself, unnamable and unnamed, charges him with an even more dangerous power.

The green faces of the plague-stricken, the world of lepers, the nocturnal sound of rattles, a voice against the wind, a tomb-like atmosphere, a knocking on the ceiling, do not repel, do not horrify so much as do the few details which make an outcast of the prisoner, the deported convict or the inmate of a reformatory. But within the prison, at its very heart, are solitary confinement and the disciplinary cell from which one emerges purified.

The origin—the roots—of the great social movements cannot possibly lie in goodness, nor can they be accounted for by reasons which are openly avowable. Religions, the Frankish and French royalty, the freemasonries, the Holy Empire, the Church, national-socialism, under which people still die by the axe and whose executioner must be a muscular fellow, have branched out across the globe, and the branches could have been nourished only in the depths. A man must dream a long time in order to act with grandeur, and dreaming is nursed in darkness. Some men take pleasure in fantasies whose basic contents are not celestial delights. These are less radiant joys, the essence of which is Evil. For these reveries are drownings and concealments, and we can conceal ourselves only in evil or, to be more exact, in sin. And what we see of just and honourable institutions at the surface of the earth is only the projection, necessarily transfigured, of these solitary, secret gratifications. Prisons are places where such reveries take shape. Prisons and their inmates have too real an existence not to have a profound effect on people who remain free. For them, prisons are a pole, and, in prison, the dungeon. I shall therefore tell why I tried to have Bulkaen—for whom my love was so recent—sent to the hole.

But first, here is why I was sent to the punishment cell, where I began to write this account.

Just as when you walk at someone's side, his elbow and shoulder, despite your trying to walk straight, shift you to the right or left and may make you bump against walls, so a force shifted me, despite myself, in the direction of Harcamone's

cell. The result was that I often found myself in his vicinity
and thus rather far from my dormitory and workshop. I would
leave with a definite goal, though on the sly, either to bring
some bread to a crony, or to get a cigarette in another shop, or
for some other practical reason, and most of the time the goal
was quite far from the seventh division, where the death-cells
are located, but the same force always made me go out of my
way, or go too far, and I also noticed that as I approached the
secret goal, which was hidden behind the mask of a reasonable
decision, my pace grew slower, my gait more supple and
lighter. More and more I would hesitate to go farther. I was
both pushed forward and held back. Finally I would so lose
control of my nerves that if a guard came along I would be
unable to dash out of sight, and if he questioned me, I had no
explanation to account for my presence in the seventh division.
So that the guards imagined God knows what whenever they
found me there alone, and one of them, Brulard, once nabbed
me.

"What are you doing here?"

"You can see for yourself. I'm going by."

"You're going by? Where are you going? . . . And besides,
I don't like your tone. Take your hands out of your belt."

I was on a horse.

Even when I am very calm, I feel as if I were being swept
by a storm. This may be due to my mind's stumbling over
every unevenness of surface becuse of its rapid pace, or to my
desires, which are violent because they are almost always
repressed, and when I live my inner scenes, I have the exhilar-
ation that comes from always living them on horseback, on a
rearing and galloping steed. I am a horseman. It is since I have
known Bulkaen that I live on horseback, and I enter the lives
of others on horseback as a Spanish grandee enters the
Cathedral of Seville. My thighs grip the flanks. I spur my
mount, my hands tighten on the reins.

Not that it happens quite that way, I mean not that I really
know I'm on horseback, but rather I make the gestures and

have the spirit of a man on horseback: my hand tightens, I toss back my head, my voice is arrogant. The sensation of riding a noble, whinnying animal overflowed into my daily life and gave me what is called a cavalier look and what I considered a victorious tone and bearing.

The guard reported me, and I was brought up before the warden, in the prison court. He hardly looked at me. He read the charge, put a pair of dark glasses over his pince-nez and pronounced sentence:

"Twenty days in the hole."

A guard took me there, without letting go of my wrist, which he had held all through the hearing.

When a man in prison does all he can to make trouble for his friends who have remained free and is responsible for their being caught, he is called malicious, whereas the fact is that in such a case the malice is composed of love, for he lures his friends to prison in order to sanctify it by their presence. I tried to have Bulkaen punished, to have him sent to the disciplinary cell, not in order to be near him, but because it was essential that we both be doubly outcast at the same time, for people can love each other only on the same moral level. It was thus one of the usual mechanisms of love that made me a rat.

Bulkaen was never sent to the disciplinary cell. He died —shot—without getting there.

I am going to talk once again about this twenty-year-old crasher with whom the whole prison was in love. Mettray, where he had spent his youth, elated both of us, united and merged us in the vapours of our memory of monstrously exquisite hours. In our relations with each other we had fallen back, though not deliberately, into the ways and habits of the reformatory; we used the colonists' gestures, and even their language; and around us, at Fontevrault, there was already a group of big shots who had been at Mettray, whether friends of ours or not, but fellows we had known well, who were united by the same likes and dislikes. Everything was a game to him, even the most serious matters. He once whispered to me on the stairs:

"We used to plan escapes. For the slightest reason, with another little guy, Régis . . . We'd feel like eating apples, and off we'd go! Or it was the grape season, so we'd go for grapes. Sometimes it was to screw, sometimes for no reason at all. And sometimes we'd plan real ones, escapes, escapes for good. We'd manage so they didn't work out. All in all, we had a great time."

The prison regulations state that any convict who commits an offence or a crime must serve his penalty in the institution where he committed it. When I arrived at Fontevrault, Harcamone had been in irons for ten days. He was dying, and that death was more beautiful than his life. The death-throes of certain monuments are even more meaningful than their period of glory. They blaze before going out. He was in irons. I remind you that repressive measures are practised within the prisons: the simplest is loss of canteen privileges, then dry bread, solitary confinement, and, in the state prisons, the disciplinary cell. The Cell is a kind of big shed, the floor of which has a high polish—I don't know whether it's polished by brushes and floor-wax or by the canvas slippers of generations of punished men who walk in a circle and are so spaced as to occupy the entire perimeter of the hall without anyone's being first or last, and who walk in circles the way punished colonists at Mettray walked round and round the yard (with one difference, though a disturbing one: the drill had got complicated. Here, we walk at a more rapid pace than at Mettray, and we have to keep within boundary lines that go around the hall, making our circuitous march resemble a childish and difficult game), to such a degree that at Fontevrault it seemed to me I had grown up without stopping in my round. The walls of the Mettray yard have fallen about me; those of the prison have sprung up, walls on which I read, here and there, words of love carved by convicts and phrases written by Bulkaen, the most singular of appeals, which I recognize by the abrupt pencil-strokes, as if each word were a matter of solemn decision. Ten years have gone by and a ceiling has covered the sky of Touraine. In short, without my realizing it, the setting was transformed as I aged and circled. It also seems to me that every step taken by a convict is only the step, complicated and continued for as long as ten or fifteen years, which was taken by a Mettray colonist. What I mean is that Mettray, though now destroyed, carries on, continues in time, and it seems to me too that the roots of Fontevrault are to be found in the vegetable world of our children's hell.

At regular intervals, two yards from and parallel to the walls, is a series of masoned blocks with rounded tops, like the bitts of boats and wharves, on which the punished men sit for five minutes every hour. A husky assistant, one of the punished prisoners, supervises the drill. In a corner, behind a little wire cage, a guard reads his newspaper. At the centre of the circle is the can into which the men shit, a recipient three feet high in the form of a truncated cone. It has two ears, one on each side, on which you place your feet after sitting down, and a very low back-rest, like that of an Arab saddle, so that when you drop a load you have the majesty of a barbaric king on a metal throne. When you have to go, you raise your hand, without saying anything; the assistant makes a sign, and you leave the line, unbuttoning your trousers, which stay up without a belt. You sit on the top of the cone with your feet on the ears and your balls hanging. The others continue their silent round, perhaps without noticing you. They hear your shit drop into the urine, which splashes your bare behind. You piss and get off. The odour rises up. When I entered the room, what struck me most was the silence of the thirty inmates and, immediately, the solitary, imperial can, centre of the moving circle.

If the assistant had been at rest while supervising the drill, I would not have recognized his face, but sitting on the throne, with his brow wrinkled by the effort, he looked as if he were worried, as if he were straining with a difficult thought, and he recaptured the mean look of his youth—gathering his features—when his eyebrows, contracted by anger or bad temper, almost came together and I recognized Divers. Perhaps if I had been less in love with Bulkaen it would have pained me, even after fifteen years, to meet, in such a posture, the person I had loved so ardently at Mettray. Though perhaps not, for nobility was so apparent in his slightest movements that it was difficult, if not impossible, for him to seem humiliated. He got up without wiping himself. The odour—his odour—rose up, vast and serene, in the middle of the room, and, after buttoning himself, he resumed the rigid immobility of command.

"One . . . two! One . . . two! "

It is still the same guttural voice, a big shot's voice, that issues from a throat encumbered with oysters which he can still spit violently in the face of a jerk. It is the same cry and voice he had at Mettray. From my cell, I still hear him yelling. The pace of the marching will remain a hundred twenty steps a minute.

I arrived in the morning from a punishment cell in order to enjoy by means of words the memory of Bulkaen, who had remained above, in order to caress him by caressing the words which are meant to recall him to himself by recalling him to me, I had begun the writing of this book on the white sheets with which I was supposed to make paper bags. My eyes were startled by the light of day and smarting from the night's dream, a dream in which someone opened a door for Harcamone. I was in the dream, behind the door, and I motioned to Harcamone to cross the threshhold, but he hesitated, and his hesitation surprised me. Awakened by the guard during this episode in order to go from the hole to the big cell, I was still under the influence—which was painful, I don't know why—of the dream when, at about eight o'clock, I went to take my place in the circle.

After punishment in the disciplinary cell there is the severer one of being put in irons. This can be imposed only by the Minister of the Interior, at the warden's request. It consists of the following: The ankles are held by a ring which is attached to a very heavy chain; the ring is snapped shut by a guard. The wrists are bound by a lighter, slightly longer chain. This is the stiffest punishment of all. It precedes the death penalty and is, in fact, its forerunner, since, from the day sentence is pronounced until the day of execution, the feet of men condemned to death are in irons day and night, and their wrists and feet are chained at night and whenever they leave the cell.

Before speaking more fully about Bulkaen and Divers, who were the pretext for my book, I want to introduce Harcamone, who, when all is said and done, remains its sublime and final cause. I felt, as he did, the shock and dismal sound of the formula "preliminary hearing to confirm the mandatory sentence of life imprisonment."[1] When a man is convicted of theft for the fourth time, with mandatory penalties, that is, more than three months in prison, he is sentenced to "transportation." Now that the penal colony has been abolished, he will have to spend the rest of his life in prison. Harcamone was sentenced to "transportation." And I am going to speak of his death sentence. I shall explain later the miracle whereby I witnessed, at certain times, his entire inner, secret and spectacular life, but here and now I offer my thanks for this to the God we serve, who rewards us by the attentions that God reserves for his saints. It is saintliness too that I am returning to seek in the unfolding of this adventure. I really must go in quest of a God who is mine, for as I looked at pictures of the penal colony my heart suddenly clouded with nostalgia for a land which I knew elsewhere than in Guiana, elsewhere than on maps and in books, and which I discovered within myself. And the picture showing the execution of a convict in Cayenne made me say: "He stole my death." I still remember my tone of voice: it was tragic, that is, the exclamation was directed to the friends I was with—I wanted them to believe me—but the tone was also slightly muted because I was voicing a deep sigh,

---

[1] Life imprisonment, *rélégation perpétuelle. Rélégation,* confinement in a place of detention, formerly included transportation of habitual offenders to a penal colony.—Translator's note.

a sigh which came from afar, which showed that my regret came from afar.

To speak of saintliness again in connection with transportation will set your teeth on edge, for they are not used to an acid diet. Yet the life I lead requires the giving up of earthly things that the Church, and all churches, require of their saints. Then saintliness opens, in fact forces a door which looks out on the marvellous. And it is also recognized by the following: that it leads to Heaven by way of sin.

Those who are sentenced to death for life—the "transportees"—know that the only means of escaping horror is friendship. By abandoning themselves to it, they forget the world, *your* world. They raise friendship to so high a plane that it is purified and remains alone, isolated from the creatures who fathered it, and friendship—on this ideal level, in the pure state, as it must be if the lifer is not to be carried away by despair, as one is said to be carried off (with all the consequent horror) by galloping consumption—friendship becomes the individual and very subtle sentiment of love which every predestined man discovers (in his own hiding-places) for his inner glory. Living in so restricted a universe, they thus had the boldness to live in it as passionately as they lived in your world of freedom, and as a result of being contained in a narrower frame their lives became so intense, so hard, that anyone—journalists, wardens, inspectors—who so much as glanced at them was blinded by their brilliance. There the most potent pimps hew out—that's exactly the word—a dazzling celebrity, and when one feels, behind the wall that is more fragile than the past and equally impassable, the proximity of your world (paradise lost) after witnessing the scene which is as frighteningly fabulous as God's wrathful threatening of the punished couple, the audacity to live (and to live with all one's might) within that world whose only outlet is death has the beauty of the great maledictions, for it is worthy of what was done in the course of all the ages by the Mankind that had been expelled from Heaven. And this, in effect, is saintliness, which is to live according to Heaven, in spite of God.

It is by Harcamone that I am taken there, that I am transported beyond the appearances I had attained at the molting-time of which I have spoken. My faith in Harcamone, my devotion to him and my profound respect for his achievement strengthened my bold will to penetrate the mysteries by performing the rites of the crime myself, and it must have been my abhorrence of the infinite that accorded me this faith and trust. If we are free—available—and without faith, our aspirations escape from us, as light does from the sun, and, like light, can flee to infinity, for the physical or metaphysical sky is not a ceiling. The sky of religions is a ceiling. It ends the world. It is a ceiling and screen, since, in escaping from my heart, the aspirations are not lost; they are revealed against the sky, and I, thinking myself lost, find myself in them or in the images of them projected on the ceiling. Abhorring the infinite, religions imprison us in a universe as limited as the universe of prison —but as unlimited, for our hope in it lights up perspectives just as sudden, reveals gardens just as fresh, characters just as monstrous, deserts, fountains; and our more ardent love, drawing greater richness from the heart, projects them on the thick walls; and this heart is sometimes explored so minutely that a secret chamber is breached and allows a ray to slip through, to alight on the door of a cell and to show God. Harcamone's crimes—the earlier murder of the girl and, closer to us, the murder of the jailer—will appear to be foolish acts. Certain slips of the tongue in the course of a phrase give us sudden insight into ourselves by substituting one word for another, and the unwelcome word is a means whereby poetry escapes and perfumes the phrase. These words are a danger to the practical understanding of discourse. In like manner, certain acts. Faults sometimes—they are deeds—produce poetry. Though beautiful, these deeds are none the less a danger. It would be difficult for me—and impolite—to present a report here on Harcamone's mental faculties. I am a poet confronted with his crimes, and there is only one thing I can say: that those crimes gave off such a fragrance of roses that he will be scented with them, as will his memory and the memory of his stay here, until our waning days.

And so, when he killed the guard, Harcamone was taken to a special cell, where he remained until the hearing in the Criminal Court, and it was not until late afternoon, after the death sentence, that he was placed, for the forty-five days of the appeal period, in the death-cell. It was from that cell, where I see him as a kind of Dalai Lama, invisible, potent and present, that he emitted throughout the prison those waves of mingled joy and sadness. He was an actor whose shoulders bore the burden of such a masterpiece that one could hear the creaking. Fibres tore. My ecstasy was shot through with a slight trembling, with a kind of wave-frequency that was my alternate and simultaneous fear and admiration.

Every day he had a one-hour recreation period in a special yard. He was in chains. The yard was not very far from the punishment cell where I am writing. And what I often took for the sound of my pen against the inkwell was the very faint, indeed one might say, as of any mournful sound, the very delicate sound of the condemned man's chains. An attentive or predisposed or pious ear was required to perceive it. The sound was intermittent, for I sensed that Harcamone dared not walk too much lest he make known his presence in the yard. He would take a step in the wintry sun and then stop. He hid his hands in the sleeves of his homespun jacket.

There is no need to invent stories of which he is the hero. His own suffices, and, what is quite exceptional in prison, his truth is more becoming than any lie. For convicts lie. Prisons are full of lying mouths. Everyone relates fake adventures in which he plays the role of hero, but these stories never continue in splendour to the very end. The hero sometimes gives himself away, for he needs sincerity when he talks to himself, and we know that when the imagination is vivid it may cause the inmate to lose sight of the dangers of his real life. It masks the reality of his situation, and I don't know whether he is afraid of falling into the depths of the imagination until he himself becomes an imaginary being or whether he fears a collision with the real. But when he feels imagination overcoming him, invading him, he reviews the real risks he runs, and, to reassure himself, he states them aloud. Bulkaen used to lie, that is, of the thousand adventures he invented, which composed a light and fantastic lacework skeleton and organism for him, loose ends stuck out of his mouth and eyes. Bulkaen did not lie to advantage. He was not calculating, and, when he tried to be, he made errors in calculation.

Though my love for Divers and my adoration of Harcamone still excite me, Bulkaen, despite the levity I discovered in him, was the thing of the moment. He was he who is. I did not imagine him, I saw him. I touched him, and, thanks to him, I could live on earth, with my body, with my muscles. Shortly after seeing him with the queer, I met him on the stairs. The stairway, which goes from the floors on which the workshops and refectories are installed, to the ground floor, where the offices, prison court, medical room and visitors' room are located, is the main meeting-place. It is cut into the stone of the wall and unwinds in shadow. That was where I almost always saw Bulkaen. It was the lovers' trysting-place, particularly ours, and it still vibrates with the sound of the kisses exchanged there. Bulkaen ran down the stairs two at a time. His shirt was dirty, bloodstained, open in the back as the result of a stab. At the bend, he stopped short. He turned around. Had he seen me or sensed my presence? He was shirtless; his torso was naked beneath the jacket. It was another inmate—a new one—who had passed me, had, in silent flight on his slippers, passed Bulkaen, had, in the twinkling of an eye, come between the kid and me and, in so brief a time, had once again sparked the thrill of seeing Bulkaen in the theatrical conclusion that I wished for him. He turned around and smiled.

I pretended, for two reasons, not to recognize him. Firstly, so that he did not regard my eagerness as a sign of my

love—which would have put me in an awkward position in
relation to him. Though the fact is, I was wasting my time, for
he admitted to me later that he had read everything in my eyes
the first time we met. "I could tell right away. I could see you
got a kick out of being next to me." Secondly, because I had
seen him until then in the company of big shots, particularly
pimps who couldn't admit me to their clan since I was a
newcomer, and I didn't want to look as if I were playing up to
them by associating too openly with one of them whom I had
no right to treat otherwise than I did them. Furthermore, I
had a feeling that the crashers were at odds with the pimps.
. . . It was he who came up to me and put out his hand.

"Hello, Jean!"

I still don't know how he knew my name.

"Hello," I answered casually, in a tone of indifference and
in a very low voice—but I stopped:

"Well?"

His lips remained slightly parted after whispering that word.
There was no telling what his question was about, and his
body was hardly at rest for his whole body was questioning.
"Well" meant "How goes?" or "What else is new?" or
"What's up, kid?" or all of them together. I didn't answer.

"Say, you look healthy! I don't know how the hell you
manage, but you always seem rarin' to go!"

I shrugged slightly. A prisoner who did not know us stopped
on our stair on his way down. Bulkaen looked him in the eyes
in such a way that he dared not say a word to us; he dashed
off. Bulkaen's gaze delighted me with its hardness. I could tell
what my fate would be if ever such a gaze transfixed me, and
what followed frightened me more, for in order to alight on me
his eyes grew milder until they were only a moonbeam
quivering with leaves, and his mouth smiled. The walls
crumbled, time turned to dust, Bulkaen and I remained
standing on a column which kept raising us higher. I don't
think I even had a hard-on. The prisoners continued on their
way down in silence, one by one, invisible to our solitary

encounter. There was a great rustling of leaves, and Bulkaen screamed at me:

"How the hell do you manage? You probably eat your head off!"

I still didn't answer. He continued his whispering, very low, without ceasing to smile, for we realized that behind the bend of the stairway the guards were counting the prisoners on their way down to recreation. Behind the walls, the commissary, the offices. We had to speak very low. Also behind, the Warden, the countryside, the free people, the towns, the world, the seas, the stars, everything was close to us though we were far away. They were on the watch, they could take us by surprise. His smile tried to put them off the track; Bulkaen muttered quickly:

"You've always got cigarettes. . . ."

At last he was telling me what obsessed him. He showed what was on his mind. . . .

"It gets me down not having cigarettes. I'm not fit for the ash can. No butts, not a thing, not a thing. . . ."

As his smile reached these last words, it gradually faded. He had to talk quickly and quietly, we were in a hurry, almost the whole division had gone down. A guard might have come up and found us there. Under that double pressure, Bulkaen's voice and what it was saying seemed to be reeling off a drama, a crime story.

"I'll croak if it goes on. . . ."

My attitude didn't encourage him. I still kept my mouth shut. At times I couldn't understand his whispers. I cocked my ear, I listened carefully. Behind the walls I could sense the presence of our past life, of our days in prison, our sorrowful childhood. He said:

"You don't have a butt on you, do you, Jean?"

Without letting my face show any feeling, though I was annoyed, I simply put my hand into my jacket pocket and took out a fistful of butts, which I handed him. He seemed not to believe they were all for him, but his face was beaming. And I went down, still not saying a word, with a casual shrug. I was already downstairs, outside, when he finally arrived. We were locked up in the same little yard. He came straight to me and thanked me, then immediately, to justify his chiseling, informed me that he had been in prison from the age of twelve. And he specified: "From twelve to eighteen I was in a reformatory. . . ."

I asked: "Where?"

"At Mettray."

I remained calm enough to ask:

"What family? Joan of Arc?"

He answered "that's right" and we reminisced about Mettray. He accompanied each of his important but rare remarks with a broad, open, flat movement of his left hand, which seemed to come down suddenly on the five strings of a guitar. A male gesture whereby the guitarist mutes the vibrations of the strings, but it is a calm gesture of possession, and one that produces silence. I gave way to my passionate nature. The love I had been damming up for several days broke through its reserve and flowed out in the form of great pleasure in finding a Mettray colonist in my division. The word pleasure isn't quite right. Neither is joy, nor the other synonyms, nor satisfaction, nor even felicity or delight. It was an extraordinary state since it was the fulfillment of what I had been desiring (though with a vague desire that remained obscure to me until the day of my encounter) for twenty years: to find in someone other than myself the memory of Mettray, as much perhaps in order to relive Mettray as to continue it in my adult life by loving in accordance with the ways of the past. But added to that state of happiness was the fear that a slight wind, a slight shock, might undo the result of that encounter. So often had I seen the fondest dreams turn to dust that I never dared dream of Bulkaen, of a young, hale, handsome boy with a faithful heart and stern gaze, and who would love me. A youngster who would love robbery enough to cherish thieves, contemptuous enough of women to love a hoodlum, and also honest enough to remember that Mettray was a paradise. And suddenly, at the same time as the Colony showed me that despite my talent and training as a dreamer I had never ventured the fairest of dreams (I did approach it at times!), prison life was confronting me with the living fulfilment of that dream.

Bulkaen came from the depths of Mettray, sent forth by her, born God knows how, bred in the faraway, dangerous world of tall ferns, learnèd in evil. He brought me the most secret perfumes of the Colony, where we found our own odours.

But when I work on the fabric of our love, I shall know that an invisible hand is at the same time undoing the stitches. In my cell, I wove; the hand of destiny destroyed. Rocky destroyed. Although at the time of those first two meetings I did not know that he had loved, I did know that he had been loved. I sensed it. It did not take me long to learn of Rocky's existence in his life. When, for the first time, I wanted to ask a guy in his shop whether Bulkaen had gone downstairs, I tried to describe him, since I didn't know his name. The guy replied:

"Oh, you mean the little crasher who pukes on dough! Rocky's girl. Or, if you prefer, Bulkaen. . . ."

Rocky's "girl." . . . The crasher who pukes on dough! The convict thus informed me of one of Bulkaen's most amazing peculiarities: whenever he discovered cash while doing a job, a kind of nausea made him vomit on the bills. The whole prison knew it, and no one ever dreamed of joking about it. It was as strange as Harcamone's limp or Botchako's epileptic fits, as Caesar's baldness, as the Viscount of Turenne's fear, and this strangeness aggravated his beauty. Hersir destroyed. As did Divers' presence. I invented the most curious designs for our love, but I sensed beneath the loom the fatal hand that unknotted the kinks. Bulkaen would never belong to me, and I could not weave firmly on the mere basis of a single meeting, even of a whole night of love. The following is the usage of the expression "It was too good to be true." I had the feeling that no sooner had life brought us together than it would separate

us, to my shame and sorrow. And life was so cruel as to make
Bulkaen disappear just as I was putting out my arms to his
apparition. But for the time being I enjoyed tremblingly the
precarious happiness that was granted me.

So I could see him whenever I liked, could go up to him,
shake his hand, give him what I had. I had the most avowable
of pretexts for approaching him: my fellowship with a former
colonist and my fidelity to Mettray. That same evening he
called out to me from his row:

"Hey, Jean!"

I imagined him smiling in the darkness. When he smiled, we
all felt our knees give way.

I was lying down. I hadn't the force to spring up and rush
to the door, and I yelled back:

"Yes, what do you want?"

"Nothing. How goes?"

"All right. And you?"

"All right."

A tough voice broke sharply through the silence:

"Don't worry, he's imagining your little mug and beating his
meat."

Bulkaen seemed not to have heard this comment.

He said to me: "Good night, Jean." When he finished, his
voice was prolonged by a kind of chant. It was a cry from
another window:

"Boys, this is Roland talking! They let me have it! Hard
labour for life. So long, boys! I'm pushing off tomorrow for
Melun! So long!"

The silence closed again over the last word. All the beauty
of the evening and of Bulkaen's cry will be contained in that
child's noble farewell to his life. Though the windows are shut,
the waves he whips up will transmit his peaceful sadness to the
depths of our sleep. It is the commentary on Bulkaen's cry of
greeting. . . . "So long, boys, I'm pushing off tomorrow. . . ."
The simplest—the reader knows what I mean by simple—the
simplest of us is praying. It is an orison, the state that makes

you forgive, since it leaves you powerless when confronted
with the greatest crimes, that is, men's judgements, for that is
why it was granted us that evening to hear the very voice of
afflicted love. I then had to take a piss. Suddenly I was flooded
with the complete memory of so full a day, and I had to hold
my prick with both hands for it was too heavy. Bulkaen!
Bulkaen! The name enchanted me, though I still didn't know
his given name. Will he love me? I remembered his mean look
and his ever so gentle look, and his shifting from one to the
other when he looked at me was so frightening that, in order to
escape the fear, my body found nothing better to do than sink
into sleep.

Harcamone was given a life sentence after his fourth theft.
I cannot tell exactly how the idea of death occurred to him.
I can only invent it. But I know him so well that I am likely to
be right. I myself knew the tremendous despair of a life
sentence, and it was even worse that morning, for I had the
feeling that I was being damned forever.

I have just read the amorous scribbles on the wall of the
punishment cell. Almost all of them are addressed to women,
and, for the first time, I now understand them, I understand
those who carved them, for I would like to proclaim my love
for Bulkaen on all the walls, and if I read them, or if someone
reads them aloud, I hear the wall telling me of my love for
him. The stones speak to me. And it was amidst hearts and
flowers that the inscription "M.A.V." suddenly brought me
back to my cell at Petite Roquette, where, at the age of fifteen,
I saw those mysterious initials. I had long since—from the
time I learned their exact meaning—ceased to be affected by
the sinister glamour of the carved letters: "M.A.V.",
"B.A.A.D.M.", "V.L.F." When I read them, I merely read
"Mort aux vaches" (death to the cops), *"Bonjour aux amis du
malheur"* (greetings to friends in need), and now, all at once,
a shock, a sudden loss of memory, makes me feel uneasy at the
sight of "M.A.V." I now see these letters only as a strange
object, an inscription on an ancient temple. I feel the same

sense of mystery as in the past, and, when I become conscious
of it, I have the added feeling of being replunged into unhappiness, into the grief that was the substance of my childhood,
and this feeling is even more painful than what I felt in the
disciplinary cell when I took my place in a marching circle that
seemed eternal, for I realize that it is within myself that
nothing has changed, that my misfortune does not obey
external laws but that it is within me, a permanent fixture,
immobile and faithful to its function. So I feel that a new era
of misfortunes is opening in the very heart of the happiness
caused by my love for Bulkaen, a love which is enhanced by
his death. But this feeling of sorrow, along with the discovery
of the signs that accompany it, was aroused perhaps by my
amorous passion, which had the external form of my passions
at Mettray. This ardour was involved in the same childish and
tragic complications. I was thus going to live in the unhappy
mode of my childhood. I am caught in the mechanism of a
cycle. It is a period of misfortune—and not misfortunes—
which is opening when another is about to end, and there is
nothing to prove that it will not be succeeded by a third—and
so on throughout eternity.

When a man has been condemned to spend the rest of his
days in jail, death is at the heart of prison life, and prison is
the worst misfortune that can befall natures which are still
enraptured with the taste of freedom—I have said prison and
not solitude. At first, Harcamone wanted to escape. Like the
rest of us, he wanted, as soon as he arrived, to make a calendar
which would be valid for his entire confinement, but not
knowing the date of his death, he thus did not know the date of
his release. I too made a calendar, at first a ten-page notebook,
with two pages for each year, in which every day would be
marked. To go through it, I had to turn the pages, and that
takes time. In order to get an overall view of their twenty years
of detention, the hardened criminals detach all the pages and
paste them on the wall. I did the same. With a single glance I
can scan my penalty, can possess it. Over those twenty years

they indulge in the most frightfully complicated mathematics. They multiply, divide, juggle the number of months, days, weeks, hours, minutes. They want to arrange those twenty years in every possible way, and it seems as if the twenty years were going to be extracted from the numbers in purer form. Their calculations will end only on the eve of their release, with the result that the twenty years will appear to have been necessary in order to know the combinations contained in twenty years, and the aim and justification of the imprisonment will be these calculations which, placed flat against the wall, look as if they were being slowly swallowed up in the darkness of the future and the past and, at the same time, seem to be shining with so unbearable a present brightness that this brightness is its own negation.

Harcamone was unable to have a calendar. His dead life followed its course to infinity. He wanted to flee. He quickly considered all possible means, including escape. In order to escape, what was required, in addition to help from the outside, which Harcamone had never been able to arrange for, because he was as dull in free life as he was dazzling in prison (allow me to say a word about this brilliance. I would like to compare hardened convicts to actors—and even to the characters they impersonate—who, in order to reach the highest pitch, require the freedom provided by the stage and by its fabulous lighting, or the situation, which is outside the physical world, of Racine's princes. This brilliance comes from the expression of their pure feelings. They have time to be tragic and the necessary "income of a thousand francs"), what was required was a show of boldness, a constant will to take cunning precautions, which the sparkle that I have mentioned made difficult, impossible. A man with a powerful personality is incapable of cunning or guile or of putting on an act.

Harcamone therefore came round to death as the only way of shortening his captivity. He first thought of it in perhaps a literary way, that is, by talking about it, by hearing other inmates say to him, "It's better to croak," and his lofty nature,

which was hostile to sordidness, took over the idea and ennobled it in the only effective way, by making it familiar, by
making it an absolute necessity, whereby it escaped moral
control. He conversed with this idea of death in a tone of
intimacy, a tone that was practical and never romantic. But as
facing his death was a grave act, he did it with gravity, and
when he spoke of it, he did so without grandiloquence, though
one could nevertheless detect ceremonious attitudes in his
voice.

As for ways of taking his own life, the revolver and poison
had to be discarded. He could have thrown himself from the
top of one of the upper galleries. . . . One day he went to the
railing and climbed over. Squatting for a moment at the edge
of the void, he moved back a little, dazzled by the horror of it.
With his arms slightly behind him, he beat the air a while and,
for a brief moment, he was like an eagle flying from its rock.
Finally, mastering his dizziness, he turned away, sickened no
doubt by the sight of his shattered limbs on the ground. He
did not see Rasseneur, who reported the scene to me.
Rasseneur was alone with him on the gallery, but he had
stepped back, hugging the wall so as to leave Harcamone with
the impression of his solitude.

Harcamone chose to commit what was for him a rather
trivial act, one which, through the working of a fatal
mechanism stronger than his will, would cause his death. He
murdered, in an almost calm moment, the guard, a man
insolent with mildness and beauty, who had bullied him least
during his two years at Fontevrault. We know that Harcamone
died nobly during the four months following this murder. He
had to erect his destiny, as one erects a tower, had to give this
destiny tremendous importance, towering importance, unique
and solitary, and had to build it of all his minutes. It seems to
you impossible that I dare ascribe to a petty thief the act of
building his life minute by minute, witnessing its construction,
which is also a progressive destruction. Only a rigorously
trained mind seems to you capable of that. But Harcamone

was a former colonist of Mettray who had built his life there minute by minute, one might almost say stone by stone, as had all the others, in order to bring to completion the fortress most insensitive to men's blows. He approached Rose-wood (I learned all about the murder immediately), who suspected nothing, least of all that anyone might kill him, and least of all cut his throat, even if the cutthroat were Harcamone. Perhaps he could not admit the possibility of a jailor's becoming a victim, that is, a hero who was already idealized since he was dead and reduced to the state of a pretext for one of those brief poems which are the crime items in newspapers. I have no way of knowing how Harcamone happened to be present when the guard passed by, but he was said to have rushed up behind and grabbed him by the shoulder, as if he had wanted to kiss him from behind. I've done the same thing to my friends more than once in order to plant a kiss on their childish necks. (In his right hand he held a paring-knife which he had stolen from the shoemaking shop.) He struck a blow. Rose-wood fled. Harcamone ran after him, caught up with him, grabbed him again by the shoulder and this time cut his carotid. The blood spurted on his right hand, which he had not withdrawn in time. He was in a sweat. Though he tried hard to be calm, he must have suffered extremely at being borne all at once to the climax of his destiny and carried back to the time when he murdered the little girl, though he had the luck to perform his later murder with gestures other than those with which he had committed the earlier one, thus safeguarding himself from too great a misfortune. Since he avoided repetition, he was less aware of sinking into misfortune, for all too often people overlook the suffering of the murderer who always kills in the same way (Weidmann and his bullet in the back of the neck, etc.), since it is most painful to invent a new and difficult gesture.

He wanted to wipe his wet face, but his hand smeared it with blood. The scene was witnessed by some inmates whom I didn't know. They allowed the murder to be carried out and they overpowered Harcamone only when they were quite certain that Rose-wood was dead. Finally, Harcamone thought of doing something very difficult, more difficult than the murder: he fainted.

Hewn out of the rock, embellished by a thousand cruelties, constructed with boys who erect their lives stone by stone, the Mettray Colony nevertheless sparkles in the mists of an almost continuous autumn which bathe that existence, and autumn likewise bathes ours, in which everything has the tints of dead leaves. We ourselves, in our prison homespun, are dead leaves, and it is with a certain sadness that one moves about in our presence. We fall silent. A slight melancholy—slight not because it is infrequent but because it weighs little—hovers about us. Our weather is grey, even when the sun is shining, but the autumn within us is artificial, and terrible, because it is constant, because it is not a transition, the end of a beautiful day, but a finished state, monstrously immobilized in the mist of the walls, the homespun, the odours, the stealthy voices, the indirect looks. Mettray sparkled through the same sadness. I cannot find the words that would present it to you lifted from the ground, borne by clouds, like the fortified cities in old paintings, suspended between heaven and earth and beginning an eternal assumption. Mettray swarmed with children, children with charming faces and bodies and souls. I lived in that cruel little world: at the top of a slope, a pair of colonists, outlined against the sky; a thigh swelling out a pair of canvas trousers; the toughs and their open flies from which there escaped, in whiffs that turned your stomach, the scent of tea-roses and wisteria fading into evening; a simple child kneeling on the ground as if he were about to take aim, in order to watch a girl go by between the trees; another youngster who means to talk about his beret but thinks of his cap and says "my fez, my hood, my toupee"; Harcamone as a child, swathed in princely poverty; the bugle opening in his sleep the gates of dawn; the playless yards (even in winter, the snow isn't used for fights); but also the dark machinations, the

walls of the mess-hall painted with tar up to the level of a
child's head (what infernal mind, what gentle-mannered
director, conceived the idea of painting them, and of delicately
painting in black the inner walls of the cells in the quarter?
And who was it who thought of painting half-white and
half-black the walls of the cells of Petite Roquette, where
almost all of us had been before coming to Mettray?); in the
quarter, a mournful Corsican song reverberating from cell to
cell; a pair of torn trousers revealing a knee of piercing beauty
. . . and lastly, among the flowers in the Big Square, the
vestiges of the schooner where the sadness of being here,
locked up, makes me seek refuge at night. In the past, it was
rigged and masted, with sails and wind, amidst the roses, and
colonists (all of whom joined the navy when they left Mettray)
used to learn there, under the orders of an ex-sailor, how to
handle a boat. For a few hours a day, they were transformed
into cabin-boys. And throughout the Colony one still hears the
words topman, watch, first mate, frigate (this word designates
a chicken, a queer); for a long time, the language and habits
retained the imprint of this practice, and anyone on a quick
visit to the colony might have thought it had been born, like
Amphitrite, of the sea. This language in itself, and what
remained of the customs, created a fantastic origin for us, since
it was a very old language and not the one which had been
invented by generations of colonists. The children had an
extraordinary power of creating words as well. Not extravagant words, but in order to designate things, words which
children repeat to each other, thus inventing an entire
language. The colonists' words, invented for a practical purpose, had an exact meaning; "a gear" was an excuse. They
would say, "Not a bad gear." "To fox" meant to grumble.
The others escape me. I shall mention them later, but I wish to
state that these words were not argot. It was Mettray that
invented and used them, for they are not to be found in the
vocabularies of any of the other reformatories or of the state
prisons or of the penal colony. By mingling with other words

whose authentic nobility goes back to time immemorial, these
relatively new ones isolated us from the world even more. We
were a land that had been spared by a very ancient cataclysm,
a kind of Atlantis which preserved a language that had been
taught by the gods themselves, for I use the word "gods" to
mean the glamorous, formless powers, such as the world of
sailors, the world of prisons, the world of Adventure, by which
our entire life was ordered, from which our life drew even its
sustenance, its life. Even the word "guy," which is a naval
term, upsets me. Thinking about the idea would relieve me,
but merely touching upon it makes me feel uneasy at the
thought that Guy comes from so far away. My chest. . . .

Indeed it seems that when tragedians, while performing,
reach the heights of tragedy, their chests swell because of the
rapidity of their breathing. The rhythm of their life is
quickened. Their speech seems to be rushing headlong even
when it slows up, even when they wail softly, and the
spectator, who is a victim of this art, feels similar movements
within himself, and, when he does not feel them spontaneously,
he thinks he will enjoy the tragedy more if he provokes them.
He parts his lips, he breathes rapidly, he gets excited . . . and
so, when I think, by way of Guy, of Bulkaen's gentler
moments, of his actual death, of his deaths as imagined in the
secrecy of my nights, of his states of despair, of his falls, hence
of his culminant beauty—since I have said it was elicited by
the wretched disorder of his face—though I lie motionless in
bed, my chest swells, I breathe more quickly, my lips are
parted, my bust feels as if it were straining toward the tragedy
which the boy experienced, the rhythm of my circulation
quickens, I live faster. I mean that all this seems to me to *be*,
but I actually think that I haven't moved and that it is rather
the representation of myself, one of my images which *I see*,
confronted with the image of Bulkaen in his loftiest attitude.

Thus, Bulkaen had taken increasing possession of me. He
had surged into me, for I had let slip the avowal of a love
which he had long been aware of, perhaps as much from the

song in my eyes as from my gifts to him. He seemed so independent of the world around us that he appeared to me unaware not only of the strangeness of Harcamone's situation but of his presence here, his existence in our midst. He seemed to be unaffected by this influence, and perhaps no one but me—and, for other reasons, Divers—was affected by it. Botchako, whom I sometimes saw when I passed the overheated tailor shop, where he worked stripped to the waist like a Chinese executioner, was much more glamorous. The reason is that blood purifies, that it raises the one who sheds it to unwonted heights. By virtue of his murders Harcamone had attained a kind of purity. The authority of the big shots is lewd. They are men who can still get a hard-on, whose muscles are of flesh. The member and the flesh of murderers are of light. I mentioned him to Bulkaen:

"You've never seen Harcamone?"

"No."—He looked indifferent, and he added, without seeming to attach any importance to the question:

"Have you?"

The light flared. He suddenly seemed its purest essence.

At four in the afternoon, when darkness set in, the lights went on and the prison seemed engaged in an activity whose purposes were extra-terrestrial. The flick of a switch sufficed: before, the semi-darkness in which human beings were things, in which things were dumb and blind; after, the light in which things and people were their own intelligence anticipating the question and resolving it before it was raised.

The look of the stairway changed. It was a well rather than a stairway. There were exactly fourteen steps from floor to floor (there were three storeys). The white stone stairs were worn away in the middle, and so the guards, whose hobnailed shoes tended to slip, had to go down very slowly, grazing the wall, which, to be more exact, was a partition. It was painted ochre and adorned with scribbles, hearts, phalli, arrows, etc., which were quickly engraved by a feckless rather than ardent fingernail and quickly effaced by a trusty at the order of a turnkey. At elbow- and shoulder-level, the ochre was rubbed off. At the bottom, it flaked off. In the middle of each landing was an electric bulb.

In the light, I replied:

"Me? Yes. We were pals at Mettray."

That was false, and the light made my voice ring false. We had never been friends at Mettray. Harcamone, who already possessed the kind of glory he was to develop to its apotheosis, maintained a silence that seemed disdainful. The truth, I believe, is that he could neither think nor talk, but who cares about the reasons for an attitude that composes a poem? Bulkaen hitched up his pants with one hand and put the other on his hip:

"No kidding? Is he from Mettray too?"

"That's right."

Then he left without showing further curiosity. And I suffered the shame of feeling for the first time that I was turning away from my chosen divinity. It was the following day that Bulkaen sent me his first note. Almost all his letters began as follows: "Young tramp." If he had surmised that I was sensitive to the charm of the expression, he had surmised rightly, but in order to have realized it, he would have had to detect on my face or in my gestures certain signs or mannerisms that showed my contentment. But he hadn't, since he was never present when I read his letters and I would never have been foolish enough to tell him. The first time I had occasion to talk to him, I remembered that he was in for a jewel robbery and, not knowing his name yet, I called out: "Hey.... Hey... Jewel! Hey, Jewel!" He turned around, his face lit up. "Excuse me," I said, "I don't know your name. . . ." But he said very fast and in a low voice: "You're right, call me Jewel, that's all right." And then, almost immediately, so that I wouldn't suspect the pleasure it gave him to be called Jewel, he added: "Like that we'll be able to talk and the guards won't know who it is."

I learned that his name was Bulkaen a little later when I

heard a guard rebuke him for walking too slowly, and it was on the back of a photo that I saw his given name "Robert." Anyone but me would have been surprised that at first he told people to call him "Pierrot" and later "Jewel." I was neither surprised nor annoyed. Hoodlums like to change names or distort their real ones until they are unrecognizable. Louis has now become Loulou, but ten years ago it was transformed to P'tit Louis (Li'l Louis), which in turn became "Tioui."

I have already spoken of the virtue of the name. A Maori custom requires that two tribal chiefs who esteem and honour each other exchange names. It was perhaps a similar phenomenon that made Bulkaen swop Robert for Pierrot[1] —but who was Pierre? Was it Hersir, about whom he spoke to me in spite of himself? Or, since it is customary for hoodlums to be called only by a familiar form of their name, had he chosen Pierrot because there was no suitable nickname for Robert? But again, why precisely Pierrot?

His naive joy was hale and hearty, because of his youth, but even though I felt it when he called me "young tramp," I had to refrain from displaying the same joy. Therefore, he himself must have felt the slight thrill produced by these words when they are uttered affectionately: "young tramp," comparable, for me, to the caress of a broad hand on the back of a boy's neck.

We were still at the bend of the stairway, in the shadow.

I shall never sing sufficiently the pleated stairway, and its shadow. The fellows used to meet there. The toughs—those whom the judges call hardened offenders—the "black-ties" (because all or almost all of them have appeared in Criminal Court and wore, for the hearing, the little black bow-tie sold at the canteen, for the assizes are a more formal ceremony than the hearings in police court) find shelter there for a few seconds from the guards who hound them (and from the jerks who might squeal on them—though informing is more to be feared from a tough than from a jerk), and they concoct

[1] Pierrot is the familiar form of Pierre.—Translator's note.

escapes. As for their past life and the set-backs that have marked it, they choose to talk about such things in bed, from cell to cell, from chicken-coop to chicken-coop (the dormitory is a huge room with two facing rows of narrow cells—each of which has only one bed—separated by a brick partition but covered with a wire netting and closed by a grating. They are called the chicken-coops). The first evening, after the rounds had been made, I heard a strange invocation; it was phrased by an amazingly elegant voice: "Oh my solid, oh my fierce, oh my burning one! Oh my Bees, watch over us!"

A chorus of grave and fervent voices, which were moved to the depths of the soul that dwells in the voice, responded:

"Amen."

The lone voice that had sung out was that of Botchako the bandit. His invocation had been addressed to his jimmy, to the pry and wedges, and all the crashers in the dormitory had responded. No doubt the invocation was a parody, which it aimed to be, for amidst the cluster of voices a few other yeggs heightened the buffoonery (one of them even said: "bring your dough," and another added: "bring your fanny"), but in spite of itself the buffoonery remained *profoundly* grave. And my whole being, both body and soul, turned to my jimmy, which lay motionless though vibrant in my room in Paris. It still seems to me that those vibrations made that corner of my room a bit hazy, blurred, as if they had spread a kind of golden mist which was the halo of the jimmy—officers' sceptres and batons are pictured that way in conventional imagery. It vibrates like my indignant and wrathful prick.

Bulkaen asked me whether I had received his note.

"No, I didn't get anything."

He seemed annoyed, for he had given it to a trusty who was to have passed it on to me. I asked him what it said.

"Do you need something?"

"No no," he said.

"No? Then what was it about?"

"Oh, nothing."—He looked embarrassed. I understood his

embarrassment, which was perhaps feigned so that I would
insist or question him further, or so that I would guess without
asking questions. But I insisted. We both felt a deep shyness in
the other's presence, a shyness hidden behind rough gestures,
but it was the very essence of the moment since it was what
remains in my memory when my gestures have been scraped
away. I insisted:

"Then why'd you write if you don't need anything? I don't
get it."

"I sort of wrote about my friendship for you . . ."—I had a
feeling that my love had been discovered. I saw I was in
danger. Bulkaen was kidding me. I was being made a fool of.
This attitude, which, along with meanness, is the core of my
nature, permits me to say a word about that meanness. When I
was poor, I was mean because I was envious of the wealth of
others, and that unkindly feeling destroyed me, consumed me.
I wanted to become rich in order to be kind, so as to feel the
gentleness, the restfulness that kindness accords (rich and
kind, not in order to give, but so that my nature, being kind,
would be pacified). I stole in order to be kind.

I made a final effort to lock myself in behind a door that
might have revealed my heart's secret and enabled Bulkaen to
enter me as he would a conquered country, mounted, in boots
and spurs, holding a whip, with an insult on his lips, for a
youngster is never gentle with a man who worships him. I
therefore replied roughly:

"Your friendship? Who the hell wants your friendship!"

He was suddenly abashed, and his gaze lost its hard fixity,
its razor-like sharpness. He said, painfully, word by word, he
wavered: "Thank you, Jean, you're nice. . . ." I was
immediately ashamed of what I took for my toughness but
what was simply meanness, revenge on a kid who had just "got
the better of me." As a result of entering the prison at night,
when the lights were on, I shall retain, throughout the present
narrative, a kind of inwardness and the surprise of living a
monstrous Christmas eve—during the day too. Bulkean would

be the Redeemer, the gracious and living, even familiar
Redeemer. I was anxious lest everything stop and collapse. I
wanted to atone for my dull-witted remark, and I said, laying a
hand on his shoulder (that was my first friendly gesture, I
touched Bulkaen for the first time):

"Pierrot my boy, you're imagining things. If I'm nice to
you, it's because we were both at Mettray. I've got to be nice
because of Mettray. You can have all the pals you like, you can
be friends with them . . ."—but what I was about to utter was
too painful to me—since it would also be painful to write it—it
touched too much on my love, endangered it by allowing
Bulkaen to be unaware of it and to love whomever he
liked—and suddenly I felt within me one of the far too many
lacerations that lay my soul bare. I said:

"If I've got a crush on you, forget about it."

He took both my hands and said:

"No, Jean, I won't forget about it. It's important to me."

"It's not."—I was trembling. The mass might end, the
organs might stop playing. But a choir of young voices went on
with its canticles. He said:

"It is, Jean. You'll get to know me."

These words filled me with hope. We were pals, and I even
asked him to send me another note. I was capitulating. It was
then that we began to exchange the love letters in which we
spoke of ourselves, of plans for robberies, of prodigious jobs
and, above all, of Mettray. He signed his first letter "Illegible," as a matter of caution, and I began my reply with "Dear
Illegible." Pierre Bulkaen will remain for me the indecipherable. It was always on the stairs, where he waited for me,
that we handed each other the slips of paper. Though we were
not the only couple who carried on that way, we were probably
the most painfully agitated. Fontevrault was thus full of those
furtive exchanges which swelled the prison as if with repressed
sighs. At Fontevrault, the amorous nuns and sisters of God
came to life again in the form of pimps and crashers. There are
things one could say about destinies, but note the strangeness

of that of monastries and abbeys) which prisoners call the bee[1]): jails and preferably state prisons! Fontevrault, Clairvaux, Poissy! . . . It was God's will that these places shelter communities of only one sex. After the monks (they too in homespun) had chiselled the stone, the convicts modelled the air with their contortions, gestures, calls, their cries and modulations, their sea-cow vociferation, the silent movements of their mouths; they torture the air and sculpt the pain. The monasteries all belonged to a Lord—or Sire—who possessed true wealth, namely men and their souls, and the men gave him the best of themselves. They carved wood, painted leaded glass windows and cut stone. Never would a lord have dared collect rood-lofts or stalls or any polychrome wooden statue in a room of his castle. Today, Fontevrault is ravaged of its jewels of stone and wood. People without nobility, incapable of winning souls, have bought them for their apartments. But another and more splendid debauch fills the prison. It is the dance in the darkness of two thousand convicts who shout, sing, sizzle, suffer, die, froth, spit, dream and love each other. And amongst them Divers. I had read his name on the list of men who were in the disciplinary cell. And so here he was again, he who for so long (his absence itself was indiscreet) obsessed the little Mettray colonist. I recognized him on the can, as I have said, and I spontaneously associated his presence with Harcamone's death sentence. However, I never said a word to Divers about the murderer. Not a single one, for by the time I could speak to him freely I had already been informed that there was a painful relationship between them. No one knew the details, but the whole prison felt uneasy about it. And this silence was observed everywhere. It was so absolute that it was disturbing, for a particularly important event was taking place in the prison, an event of which everyone spoke and thought about but of which Divers and I said nothing, though it was perhaps the thing that drew us closer together. This silence

[1] *Abbaye* (abbey) and *abeille* (bee) are pronounced almost alike.—Translator's note.

was comparable to that of well-bred people when they suddenly smell the odour of a silent fart in a drawing-room.

When Divers returned to Mettray, he was introduced to me with great pomp, in the presence of the crowd, with all the display befitting the occasion, with the ceremonial that fate cannot resist when it wants to deal one of its great blows. When I was taken to the Mettray Reformatory, I was fifteen years and seventeen days old and I had come from Petite Roquette. At present, the kids who are at Fontevrault come from Lily Street (which is what we call the corridors of the ninth and twelfth divisions of Santé Prison, where the cells of the minors are located). In the mess-hall, a few moments after my arrival—I was in a state of nervous tension that evening (or perhaps I did it to prove I was very daring)—I threw a plate of soup in the face of the head of the family (I shall say a few words about the division of the Colony into "families"). I was no doubt admired for this gesture by the big shots who were stronger than I, but I was already distinguishing myself by a merely moral courage, knowing full well that I would not be beaten for such a gesture but would be punished according to law, whereas I was so afraid of being hit that I would not have dared to fight with another colonist. Besides, the bewilderment of being a newcomer in a world of boys who you feel are hostile is paralyzing. Bulkaen himself admitted this to me. He was given a thrashing the day of his arrival, and it was not until a month later that he dared fight back. He said to me:

"I suddenly realized I could fight. You can imagine what a lift it gave me. I was gay as a lark. I was alive again! All I had to do was get started in order to know I had the stuff."

It was the impossibility of killing my opponent, or at least of mutilating him hatefully enough, that kept me from fighting in the beginning; to fight in order to hurt him seemed to me ridiculous. I would not have minded humiliating him, but if I had lorded it over him, he would have felt no shame, for the victor was haloed with little glory. Only the act of fighting was noble. It was not a matter of knowing how to die but rather how to fight, which is finer. Nowadays, the soldier knows only how to die, and the bumptious individual retains the manly bearing of the fighter, all the hodgepodge of his trappings. I had to impress Bulkaen by something other than this moral courage, which he would not have understood. I sensed as much from the tone of his letters. The first of them was surprisingly amiable. He wrote about Mettray, about Old Guépin, and I learned that he had almost always worked in the fields. Here is the second, which I managed to preserve:

"Dear Jean,

Thanks for your note. I enjoyed it. But excuse me for not being able to write letters like yours. I'm not educated enough for that, because that wasn't the kind of thing I could learn at Mettray with Old Guépin. You know what I mean since you were there too, so excuse me, but believe me when I say I really like you, and if it's possible I'd like to go off with a fellow like you, someone who likes to go bumming and who's got big ideas real big ones. . . .

I want you to believe me when I say I probably see things the same way you do. Age has nothing to do with it, but I don't like kids. I'm twenty-two, but I've seen enough since the age of twelve to know what life's about. . . . I've sold all I had in order to eat and smoke because at my age it's hard to live on what they feed you here. . . .

Don't ever think I'll laugh at you, I'm not like that, I'm frank and when I've got something to say I don't care who hears it, and besides I've suffered too much myself to joke about your friendship which I'm sure is sincere."

A few words which he wanted to emphasize were put into brackets or set off by quotation marks. My first impulse was to point out to him that it was ridiculous to put slang words and expressions between quotation marks, for that prevents them from entering the language. But I decided not to. When I received his letters, his parentheses made me shudder. At first, it was a shudder of slight shame, disagreeable. Later (and now, when I reread them) the shudder was the same, but I know, by some indefinable, imperceptible change, that it is a shudder of love—it is both poignant and delightful, perhaps because of the memory of the word shame that accompanied it in the beginning. Those parentheses and quotation marks are the flaw on the hip, the beauty-mark on the thigh whereby my friend showed that he was himself, irreplaceable, and that he was wounded.

Another flaw was the word "kiss" with which the note ended. It was scrawled rather than written. The letters were muddled and made it almost indecipherable. I could see the horse that rears when a shadow falls.

He also said a few words about his robberies, his work outside, and how he loved it, and he displayed great artfulness in letting me know he was hungry. We are all hungry because of the war, about which we receive news which is so remote that it seems like ancient history; the rations have been cut in half, and everyone engages in an amazingly ruthless traffic. The war? The open countryside—the open countryside beneath a pink September evening. People are whispering, bats are flitting by. Far away, *at the borders*, soldiers grouse and see the dream flit by. But I was gleaming, and gleaming visibly. Being used to prisons, I knew how to get a double food ration; I bought bread and cigarettes from a few turnkeys, whom I paid in stamps. Bulkaen, without knowing how I did it, saw on my body the reflection of my wealth. Without asking me, he hoped for some bread. When he begged me for cigarette butts on the stairs, he had already opened his homespun jacket, revealing his naked torso, and, running his hands over his sides, had shown me how thin he was, but I was so struck at the time by the fact that the tattoo, which I had taken for an eagle tooled in the round, was the head of a whore whose hair spread right and left like two wings, that I wasn't aware of my annoyance. I was therefore disappointed again when I realized the ill-concealed meaning of his letter. I made a great effort to overcome my annoyance, of which I was conscious this time, by telling myself that hunger was general, that the toughest, sternest pimps were tortured by it, and that I had the privilege of witnessing one of the prison's most painful experiences, since the usual tone was raised to a pitch of tragic paroxysm by a physical suffering which added a grotesque element. I told myself too that friendship need not be absent from a relationship in which self-interest also had its place, and, instead of being brutal with him, I realized that Pierrot was young and that his very youth, and it alone in him, demanded bread. The next morning I gave him a roll, along with a friendly note. I wanted to hand it to him with a smile. I felt it would have been delicate not to speak, to make my offering lightly. I tried hard to be gracefully casual, but I was weighed down by all that love and I remained solemn. Love made me ascribe infinite importance to every gesture, even those to which I would rather not have done so. I pulled a long face in spite of myself and made a solemn gesture.

A little later he wanted my beret:

"I'm hot for that beret of yours," he said. And I exchanged it for his. The next day, it was my trousers.

"I'm itchy for your pants," he said. with a leer which I couldn't resist. And on the stairs we quickly took off our trousers and exchanged them. The men going by showed no surprise at seeing us bare-legged in the shadow. In seeming thus to scorn adornments, in casting off my own, I was moving toward the state of tramphood which lies almost wholly in appearances. I had just committed a new blunder. The exchange of notes became a habit. I slipped him one every day as he passed me his. He wrote admiringly about brawls and brawlers. And that was after the eagle's metamorphosis into a woman made me fear he was more virile than was apparent from his face. I had to avoid acts of moral courage that might have made me lose sight of physical courage. I return to Divers.

At Mettray, after the soup incident, I was given two weeks on dry bread (four days on a starvation diet and one day with a bowl of soup and a piece of bread), but the gravest comment

was that of the heads of families and other colonists who told
me, after my throwing the bowl, that I resembled Divers.
Physically, it seems. The Colony was still full of that gala
event, his stay among us. And when I wanted to know who
Divers was, everyone agreed that he was a tough customer, a
thug, an eighteen-year-old big shot, and immediately, without
knowing any more about him, I cherished him. The fact that
his name was Divers endowed him with an earthly and nocturnal dream quality sufficient to enchant me. For one isn't
called Georges Divers, or Jules or Joseph Divers, and that
nominal singleness set him on a throne as if glory had recognized him when he was still in the children's hell. The name
was almost a nickname, royal, brief, haughty, a convention.
And so he galloped in and took possession of the world, that is,
of me. And he dwelt within me. Henceforth, I enjoyed him as
if I were pregnant with him. Carletti told me, one day when we
were alone in a cell, that he had once had an experience that
was like a counterpart of mine. One morning, in prison (upon
awakening, his conscious personality was still entangled with
night), he slipped into the blue trousers, which were too big
for him, of a hefty sailor who was in his cell and whose clothes
(which are left outside the door for the night) had been mixed
up with his by a turnkey whose blunder had been planned by
the gods.

"I was his kid," he said.

And I, having only the name Divers as a visible, prehensible
asperity for grasping the invisible, shall contort it so as to
make it enter mine, mingling the letters of both. Prison, particularly a state prison, is a place which makes things both
heavier and lighter. Everything that pertains to it, people and
things alike, has the weight of lead and the sickening lightness
of cork. Everything is ponderous because everything seems to
sink, with very slow movements, into an opaque element. One
has "fallen," because too heavy. The horror of being cut off
from the living precipitates us—the word calls for precipice
(note the number of words relating to prison that evoke fall-

ing, "fall" itself, etc.). A single word that a convict utters transforms and deforms him before our very eyes. When I saw Divers again in the big cell, he was going up to a big strapping fellow to whom he said:

"Cut the strong-arm stuff." To which the yegg replied, nonchalantly:

"My arms are 6/35's." That was enough to transform the bruiser then and there into a dispenser of justice and to make Divers a promised victim. When he was mentioned to me, upon my arrival at Mettray, he was in prison at Orléans. He had once escaped, but the police caught him in Beaugency. It was rare for a colonist to be able to go farther in the direction of Paris. Then suddenly one day he returned to the Colony, and after a rather brief stay in the quarter, he was let out and was assigned to Family B, mine. That evening I could smell on his breath the pungent odour of the butts he had picked up among the laurels, an odour as heartbreaking as it was the first time I ever smelled it. I was ten years old. Walking on the sidewalk, with my head upturned, I bumped into a passerby, a young man. He was coming towards me, holding between his fingers, chest-high, hence on a level with my mouth, a lighted cigarette, and my mouth stuck to it when I stumbled against his legs. That man was the heart of a star. The creases formed by the trousers when one is seated converged at his fly and remained sharp, like the rays of a shadowy sun. When I raised my eyes, I saw the young hoodlum's brutal, irritated look. I had extinguished his cigarette between my teeth. I cannot tell which pain supplanted the other, the burn on my lips or in my heart. It was not until five or ten minutes later that I began to notice the smell of the cigarette and that, on licking my lips, my tongue encountered a few grains of ash and tobacco. I recognized that smell on the warm breath that Divers blew at me. I knew how hard it was even for members of "families" to get tobacco, let alone the colonists who were being punished in the quarter. Rare were the big shots to whom this luxury was accorded. Of what sovereign race was Divers? I belonged to him from the very first day, but in order to celebrate our marriage I had to wait until Villeroy, my boss at the time, left for Toulon to join the navy. The ceremony took place on a clear, freezing, sparkling night. The door of the chapel was slightly opened from within. A youngster put out his shaved head, looked into the yard and inspected the moonlight, and less than a minute later the procession emerged. Description of the procession: twelve pairs of doves or colonists between the ages of fifteen and eighteen. All handsome, even the homeliest. Their skulls were shaven. They were twenty-four beardless Caesars. At the head of it ran the groom, Divers, and I, the bride. I wore on my head neither a veil nor flowers, nor a crown, but around me, in the cold air, floated all the ideal attributes of weddings. We had just been married secretly in the presence of the assembled Family B, except, of course, the jerks, or bums. The colonist who usually acted as chaplain had stolen the key of the chapel, and we had entered it around midnight to perform the mock marriage. The rites were parodied, but true prayers were murmured from the depths of the heart. And that night was the loveliest of my life. Silently, because they were barefooted in plain cloth slippers and because they were too cold and too afraid to talk, the members of the procession made their way to the stairway of Family B, an outer wooden stairway which led to the dormitory. The faster we went and the lighter grew the moment, the faster our hearts beat and the more our veins swelled with hydrogen. Over-excitement generates magic. At night, we were light-footed. During the day, we moved in a torpor due to the fact that our acts were performed reluctantly. The days were the Colony's. They belonged to that indefiniteness of dreams which produces suns, dawns, dew, breezes, a flower, things which are indifferent because they are ornaments of the other world, and through them we felt the existence of your world and its remoteness. Time was multiplied there by time.

A few creakings of the wood barely indicated to the indifferent night that something unusual was going on. In the dormitory, the couples coiled round themselves in their hammocks, warmed themselves, made and unmade love. I thus knew the great happiness of being solemnly though secretly, bound until death, until what we called death, to the handsomest colonist of Mettray Reformatory. That happiness was a kind of light vapour which raised me slightly above the floor, which softened what was hard: angles, nails, stones, the looks and fists of the colonists. It was, if a colour can be ascribed to it, pale grey, and like the exhalation, scented with envy, of all the colonists who recognized I had the right to be who I was. It was composed of the knowledge I had of my power over Divers, of his power over me. It was composed of our love. Though there was never any question of "love" at Mettray. The sentiment one felt was not named, and all that was known there was the brutal expression of physical desire.

Mention of the word love between Bulkaen and me aged us. It made me realize that we were no longer at Mettray and that we were no longer playing. But at Mettray we obviously had more gusto, for the fact of not naming our feelings, out of shyness and ignorance, made it possible for us to be dominated by them. We submitted to them entirely. But when we knew their names, it was easy for us to speak of feelings that we could think we were experiencing when we had named them. It was Bulkaen who first uttered the word love. I had never talked to him about anything but friendship (it should be noted that when I let slip my confession on the stairs I did so in a form that hardly committed me):

"If I've got a crush . . . ," for I was not yet sure of the attitude he would adopt. I remained on guard because of the tattoo. Moreover, if he accepted me as his friend, whom was he dropping? Or who had dropped him? What was Rocky's place in the hierarchy of the toughs, Rocky, whom he had known at Clairvaux and for whom he fought? And, above all, who was Hersir and how had he loved him? It was not until later that he informed me that Hersir had been, some time before himself, Rocky's boy.

"Did you love him?"

"No. It was he who loved me."

"Rocky who loved the other one?"

"That's right."

"Then what the hell does it matter? Why are you always talking to me about that Hersir of yours?"

He gestured with his elbow, then with his shoulder. He said, with his usual scowl:

"Oh, it's nothing, it's nothing."

The first time I tried to kiss him, the expression on his face, which was very close to mine, became so hostile that I realized there was a wall between us which would never be broken down. My forehead knocked against his withdrawal and he himself collided, as I could see, with his aversion for me, which was perhaps his physical aversion for men. It's true that I imagine him, in all likelihood, with a girl at his arm, and I'm sure that, at first, he was a chicken only because of his good looks (and later, in addition, because of his enthusiasm for strength, his loyalty to friendship, his goodheartedness). So he drew back a bit. He still looked hostile. I said:

"Let me kiss you."

"No Jean, not here. . . . I assure you, outside, you'll see."—He was explaining his refusal by the fear of being seen by a guard (we were still on the stairs), but he knew very well that there was little chance of that. He started to leave and, perhaps to console me for staying so short a time, he said:

"Jean, you'll see, I'll have a surprise for you in a week." He said this with his usual graciousness, the graciousness that emanated from each of his gestures, from his scowls, from his words, even when he wasn't thinking of you. Another remarkable thing was that his graciousness seemed to spring from his toughness, or rather to have the same origin. It was sparkling.

I acted as if I weren't too disappointed and I didn't want to be so cruel as to tell him what he was at Fontevrault, what role he played among the big shots, or what he had been at Clairvaux, as I happened to learn from another convict (from

Rasseneur himself):

"He was taken for what he was, but you can't say he wasn't respected."

I forced a smile, as if Bulkaen's refusal were unimportant, and shrugged slightly at the surprise he promised me, but though my smile meant to be simple and casual, it could not remain so for long. I was too upset and hurt. I could feel tragedy welling up within me, for I felt I was rushing to my doom, and when I said:

"You little rat, you're stringing me along . . . ," I was already half-way up the altitude to which resentment was carrying me. Perhaps my words were sharp, my tone of voice—which I wanted to be bantering—shaken with emotion, quivering. He mistook the meaning of my words—unless, because of that shaken voice, he really discerned the true meaning which I wanted to conceal from myself—he said:

"You can stop giving me bread and cigarettes if you think I'm your pal just in order to get something out of you. I won't take anything more."

"Come off it, Pierrot. You can always pull the friendship line on me. You'll have your bread."

"No no, I don't want it, keep it."

I snickered:

"You know very well that won't stop me. You can play me for a sucker as much as you like, I'll always give you what you need. And it's not because I've got a crush, it's because I've got to. It's out of loyalty to Mettray."

I was about to resume the slightly literary tone that would alienate me from him, that would cut the too immediate contact, for he would be unable to follow me. But, on the contrary, what I actually did was to quarrel with him in a sordid way, to reproach him for what I gave him. I didn't want to be strung along. My haughtiness, my magnanimity—which were feigned—were exasperating him. I added:

"Your good looks, which I can't help seeing, are payment enough."

I have since realized that this remark clearly expressed the passion I was trying to conceal. At the expression "good looks" he made a gesture of annoyance, a rough gesture, which showed how he felt about me, a gesture which told me to go to hell. He said:

"So what . . . so what . . . my good looks, my good looks, what about it? That's all you talk about! "—His voice was hostile, lewd and hollow, as always, and muted out of cautiousness. I was about to reply; a guard was coming up the stairs. We parted hastily, without a word, without looking at each other. The situation seemed to me more ominous because it had been cut short. I felt my abandonment, my loneliness, when the dialogue between us no longer maintained me ten feet above the ground. If he had been simply a queer, I would have immediately known what act to put on: I would have "played it tough," but Pierrot was a smart crasher, a kid who was perhaps sore at heart—and cowardly, as males are. Had I been brutal, he would have perhaps responded likewise, whereas he could still be caught in the trap of unexpected gentleness. His meanness, his trickiness, his violent reversals, his straightforwardness, those where his sharp angles. They were his brilliance. They fascinated. They hooked my love. As Bulkaen could not be without his meanness, could not be that demon without it, I had to bless it.

I remained upset for a long time, less because of his apparent indifference to what I gave him and still less because of the rejected kiss, which was proof of his lukewarm attitude toward me, than because of my discovering a hard, granitelike element which was often visible to me and which made his face a landscape of white rocks beneath a sky devoured by an African sun. Sharp edges can kill. Bulkaen, without realizing it (or realizing it), was heading for death and was leading me to it too. And in abandoning myself to his order, I moved a little further away from Harcamone's. The feeling—in the course of a conversation with Pierrot—of having begun to undergo rather than to decide—continued in what might be called a normal way. I belonged, it seems, to Pierrot.

Tonight, as I sit and write, the air is sparkling. The most sorrowful female head, with the softest blonde hair I have ever seen, the saddest woman in the world, is nodding slightly. The Prison is in her brain, under the brain-pan, like an abscess. It causes what she calls her "vapours." Let the Prison emerge from her forehead, or ear, or mouth, and the woman will be cured, and the prison itself will breathe a purer air. We see the frost on the windows, and that splendour is a mockery since it is all we are allowed to admire, without being able to indulge in the cosy joys that usually accompany it. We have no Christmas, no chandeliers in our living-rooms, no tea, no bearskins. Thinking so much about Bulkaen has worn me to a frazzle. When I lie down, I feel tired all over, especially in the arms, near the shoulders, and the following expression flits across my mind: "my arms are weary of hugging you and of not being able to hug you." In short, I am so obsessed by desire that all words and each of their syllables evoke love. "To push back the aggressor" suggests "to push back shit," aggravated by an idea of grease[1]. . . . I suffer at never having possessed Bulkaen. And death now prevents all hope. He refused on the stairs, but I invent him more docile. His eyes, his eyelids are trembling. His whole face is giving way. Does he consent? But what prohibition weighs upon him? While a stern will thrusts aside the images which are not of him, my mind strains eagerly toward a vision of the most enticing details of his body. I am obliged to invent the amorous postures he would assume. This requires great courage, for I know that he is dead and that this evening I am violating a corpse (it is probably a "rape followed by violation without deflowering", as the Judge sometimes says of a little girl who has been tumbled, but the fact remains that death terrifies and imposes its morality, and that the image of Bulkaen which I conjure up has its real double in the realm of the infernal

[1] The sound of the word *"graisse"* (grease) is contained in the word *agresseur* (aggressor).—Translator's note.

gods). I would need all my virility—which is mainly a mental attitude rather than physical courage and appearance. But just as I am about to enter him in thought, my member softens, my body grows limp, my mind drifts. . . . I live in so closed a universe, the atmosphere of which is thick, a universe seen through my memories of prisons, through my dreams of galleys and through the presence of convicts: murderers, burglars, gangsters, that I do not communicate with the usual world, or, when I do perceive it, what I see of it is distorted by the thickness of the wadding in which I move with difficulty. Each object in your world has a meaning different for me from the one it has for you. I refer everything to my system, in which things have an infernal signification, and even when I read a novel, the facts, without being distorted, lose the meaning which has been given them by the author and which they have for you, and take on another so as to enter smoothly the other worldly universe in which I live.

The air is sparkling. My pane is frosted over, and it is indeed a joy to see the frost. From the dormitory we never see a nocturnal sky. The windows are forbidden us, since at night we occupy small cells in a big room which are laid out in two facing rows. And sometimes we commit an offence so as to be sent to the hole where at night we can see through the skylight, which is often unmasked, a patch of starry sky and, even more rarely, a piece of moon. The air is sparkling. Mettray suddenly takes the place—not of the prison in which I live—but of myself, and I embark, as formerly deep in my hammock, on the remains of the half-destroyed unmasted ship among the flowers of the Big Square at Mettray. My longing for flight and love disguises her as a mutinous galley that has escaped from a penal colony. She is the "Offensive." I have roamed the South Seas on her through the branches, leaves, flowers and birds of Touraine. At my order, the galley cleared out double-quick. She sailed beneath a sky of lilacs, each cluster of which was heavier and more charged with anguish than the word "blood" at the top of a page. The crew, now composed of all the moguls from here, who were formerly big shots at Mettray, bestirred itself slowly, with pain and difficulty. Perhaps it wanted to be roused, for it was oppressed by the princely authority of the captain who kept watch at the post which is called, on galleys, the Tabernacle. The captain's past will remain mysterious to you, as it is to me. What crimes brought him to the naval colony and what faith enabled him to stir up the galley? I ascribe everything to his good looks, to his blond curls, his cruel eyes, his teeth, his bare throat, his exposed chest, to the most precious part of him. But all I have just said exists through words, whether flat or luminous. Will it be said that I'm singing? I am. I sing Mettray, our prisons and my hoodlums, to whom I secretly give the pretty name "petty tyrants." Your song has no object. You sing the void. Words may conjure up for you the pirate I want to speak of. To me he remains invisible. The face of him who commanded the galley of my childhood is forever lost to me, and in order to speak accurately to you about him I have a right to use as a model a handsome German soldier—I even desire him—who shot a bullet into the charming neck of a fifteen-year-old kid and who returned to his barracks no less clean, no less pure, heroized even more by that useless murder. He remains pale in his funereal uniform, and is so proud when he sees his bust emerge from his tank that I thought I was seeing the captain at his post. He will serve as model for my description of that figurehead whose face and body have worn away, but if I start using this subterfuge to revive my galley, am I quite sure that all of Mettray will not be described according to models quite different from the reality and chosen, as chance would have it, from among my lovers? But what does it matter! If I restore such a limbo bit by bit, it is because I carried it scattered within me. It is because the colony is contained in my loves or else my only loves are those that can revive it.

The sailors, the pirates of the galley, had the same bearing as the captain, though without that crown of darkness. We were sailing on a fair sea and would not have been surprised to

see the waters open with the thrill of carrying such a burden
and swallow it up. The ship swarmed with muscular torsoes,
brutal thighs, heads of hair, necks from which polished oak
tendons projected as they turned; also, one could tell that
behind the daring trousers were the loveliest tools in the Royal
Navy, and I was reminded of them in prison by the equally
heavy member of Divers, which was darker and yet more
radiant than ever, so that I wonder whether its brilliance was
not due to the proximity of Harcamone, who daily moved
toward death. I never knew anything definite about Divers'
relations with Harcamone. Though the whole prison was
darkened with a kind of sadness when it associated those two
names, nobody could tell the reason why. We felt there was a
link between them, and we suspected it was criminal since it
remained secret. The oldtimers were at one in remembering
that Harcamone, continuing to live in his world (of higher
lineage than ours), used to humiliate the trusties. Not that he
refused to obey, but by his subdued gestures—for his gesticu-
lation was very sober—he assumed in their presence, without
meaning to, insolently authoritative poses which made him
dominate the turnkeys and inmates. Divers was aware of his
authority (at Mettray, the head of the family once ordered a
newcomer, a sickly boy, to read the family's greetings to the
director on New Year's Day, and it was on this occasion that
Divers uttered the famous saying: "It's not fair!"). No doubt
he was thinking of the power that should have been his because
of his beauty, because of its superiority to all other virtues.
Being jealous, he may have wanted to appropriate Harcamone's artful gestures of command and, in order to make them
more effective with his flock, to eliminate the true lord, to
provoke the fight that ended in the death of the guard. You,
the reader, now know that we were wrong.

I had become particularly friendly with the pilot. (Note how
I speak of that galley on which, though I could have been the
master, I accorded myself only the lowliest post, that of
cabin-boy, and sought the friendship of my mates. You'll say

that I wanted to be a cabin-boy so as to enjoy the love of the whole crew, but you ask why I didn't choose, by inventing some other story, of kidnapping or of boarding a boat, to be a fair captive.) Perhaps I had vowed the pilot this friendship because of the melancholy, of the loneliness too, which never left him and so made me think he was gentler, more tender, more affectionate than the other sailors. For all the buccaneers were brutes, which I wanted them to be. I continued on ship the life I had led at Mettray, but with even more cruelty, with such cruelty that I could thereby project my real life and perceive its "double," which too often was invisible. I was the only cabin-boy on board. In the evening, with my calves abraded and my hands sore from coiling the stiff ropes (precisely those which we use in our shops at Fontevrault to make the camouflage nets that will be the enormous tulle which veils the phalli of the Nazi cannons when they spit), I would go and squat beside the pilot (if the captain did not allow me to stretch out on my bed). I stayed on until it was rather late. The *Subtle* plunged ahead into a fog of stars. I pointed with my toe to the Big Dipper, then, bumping my forehead into sails, stumbling over capstans and anchors, I went back to my hammock. In the Mettray dormitory my hammock was near the window. Beneath the moon and stars I could see the chapel, the Big Square and the little cottages of the ten families. Five of them form one side of the square, the other five form the side opposite, the chapel stands on a third, and, facing it, the lane of chestnut trees runs down to the road that leads to Tours.

My head is spinning, I'm pitching with dizziness. I have just written the words "chestnut trees." The yard of the Colony was planted with them. They bloomed in the spring. The flowers covered the ground and we walked on them, we fell on them, they fell on us, on our caps, on our shoulders. Those April flowers were bridal, and chestnut blossoms have just bloomed in my eyes. And all the memories that crowd on me are obscurely chosen, in such a way that my stay at Mettray

seems to have been only a long mating broken by bloody
turmoils in which I saw colonists whack each other and
become a mass of bleeding flesh, red or pale, and hot, with a
savage fury, ancient and Greek, to which Bulkaen, more than
any other, owed his beauty. Indeed, his fury was constant. And
though his youth seemed to me too young, too weak and fresh,
I bear in mind that the old crashers, who are strong and
clever, were once young and that in order to have become what
they are they had to be as tough as he when they were his age.
He lived in a state of unrest. He was the arrow that keeps
vibrating and will not come to a stop before the end of its
course, which will be the death of someone, and his own.
Though I never knew anything definite about his skill as a
crasher, I can sense it from his suppleness and trickiness
—though the kind of cleverness necessary on the outside is
different from what works here. He was no doubt the furtive
crasher who casts a rapid look about and whose gesture was of
the same nature. He had a casual gait, but if he came upon a
corridor or bare wall, a quick and sudden leap thrust him to
the right or left and concealed him. Those brusque movements
which flared up in his supple casualness destroyed it; they
were streaks of lightning that clung to his elbows, to his
broken bust, his knees, his heels. As for me, I'm a crasher of a
different kind. None of my movements is more rapid than
another. I do all things without sudden haste. My gait is
slower and calmer, more reposed and staid, more certain. But,
like me, Pierrot loved robbery. The crasher's joy is a physical
joy. The whole body is involved. Pierrot must have hated
racketeering, though he naively admired the great racketeers,
just as he admired books and their authors, without loving
them. When he was burgling, he thrilled from top to toe. "He
lubricated."

He burst into a silent laugh.

"Cut it out, Jean. You slay me."

"What. . . ."

"But even all alone . . . (his voice is a murmur, he barely

speaks, I have to listen carefully, to draw closer. Night is coming on. The stairway is dark).

". . . Jean, I did most of my jobs *solo*, because with someone else, you understand. . . ."

I understand and I note his gesture of disappointment!

"I did them *solo*! "

The child was teaching me that the true stuff of Parisian slang is gentle sorrow. I said to him, as I did every time I left him:

"Got anything to smoke?"

He did not answer my question but smiled faintly and whispered, holding out his hand:

"Come on, give with the butt! Cough up! Clear the horizon!"—Then he made an ironic military salute and ran off.

The very day after the mysterious nuptials which I have described, I left the Colony forever without having been able to spend a single night with Divers, my first encounter with whom I have not yet related. One May evening, amidst the fatigue of a holiday in honour of Saint Joan of Arc, with the oriflammes drooping beneath the weight of a ceremony that was at last over and the sky already changing colour like a lady's make-up at the end of a ball, when nothing more was expected, he appeared.

The first directors of the Colony must have realized what a magnificent garden the yard became when it was decked with the national colours, because for a long time any holiday was seized as a pretext for pinning flags on the trees and walls, in the rose-bushes and wisteria. Red cotton and cheese-cloth inflamed the chestnut trees; the bright greens of the early branches were shot through with red, blue and especially white, for the Colony did not forget that its founders were nobles and that its benefactors, whose names are still inscribed on the walls of the chapel, were: His Majesty the King, Her Majesty the Queen, Their Royal Highnesses the Princes of France, The Royal Court of Rouen, The Royal Court of

Nancy, The Royal Court of Agen, all the royal courts of
France, the Countess de La Rochejaquelein, the Count de La
Fayette, the Prince de Polignac, in fact a list of five or six
hundred lilied names, written out in full and accompanied by
titles, as can still be seen on the most beautiful tombstone in
the little cemetery, between the poor mound of Taillé (eleven
years old) and that of Roche (twenty years old): "Marie
Mathilde Julie Herminie de Saint Crico, Viscountess Droyen
de Lhuys, Lady of the Orders of Maria Luisa of Spain, Theresa
of Bavaria and Isabella of Portugal." Interspersed among the
tricolored flags were white and pale blue oriflammes with gold
fleurs de lis. They were generally arranged in clusters of three,
the one in the middle being blue and white. On Joan of Arc
Day, this fabric instilled a light joy into the newness of spring
and the fresh greenery, it purified the air. On the trees in the
Big Yard, the souls of a race of handsome young cocksmen,
seemingly indifferent to an apotheosis among the branches,
fierce-eyed lads with violent bodies and hostile loves, spurting
abominable insults between their white teeth, were moistened
with a gentle dew. But on Assumption Day, however, those
same cloths became, in the sun and dust and amidst dead
flowers, a kind of demented bunting. They presided with
haughty weariness over some royal ceremony of which we witnessed only the preparations or, if you like, the settings, for
the personages were too sublime—and their dramas too grave—
to be seen by us.

It was in the middle of this kind of huge, unused altar that
new colonists sometimes made their first appearance. Around
five in the afternoon (for that was also when boys who had
been punished and who were to be reprieved were let out), I
immediately noticed a colonist nobler than the others. He had
both hands in his pockets, thus raising the front of his blue
smock, itself rather short, and revealing to the dumbfounded
afternoon a fly lacking a button, which must have popped off
under the heavy shock of a fag's stare, the kind of kid about
whom one says:

"You've got eyes that make fly-buttons pop!"

I noticed this and also the dirt around the opening of the fly. Then I was struck by the toughness of his expression. I remember too his . . . and I cannot, even mentally, without a frightful pain in my chest, conclude the word . . . smile. I shall burst into tears if I utter in their entirety the words which betoken a single one of his charms, for I realize that in mentioning them I would be depicting Pierrot. But he had what Pierrot doesn't have: his cheekbones, his chin, all the prominent parts of his face, were, perhaps because of the compact blood vessels, darker than the rest. He seemed to be wearing a black tulle veil, or only the shadow of that veil. This is the first article of mourning that will adorn Divers. And the face was human, but, to be accurate, I am obliged to say that it was continued in movements that made it cease to be so and that changed it into a griffon, and even into a plant. It remained in my mind like the faces of angels engraved on glass and painted on stained-glass windows, faces that end, with the hair or neck, in the form of an acanthus leaf. Anyhow, Divers had that crack, which was intended by the architect, as was the pathetic breach in the Coliseum which causes eternal lightning to flash over its mass. I later discovered the meaning of the crack, which was a second sign of mourning, and of the even more theatrical one that furrows Bulkaen, that furrows all the big shots, from Botchako to Charlot—Charlot to whom my hatred clung and still clings, whom I felt within me, certain that some day a pretext would be found for that hatred to discharge violently.

We entered the mess-hall. A little yegg said to me:

"Did you see her? One of them is back!"

"Who? Who's back?"

"A doe."

You now understand the meaning of the expression "to doe."[1] A person who runs away, a person who escapes, is a doe. Quite naturally, and without anyone's daring to make a

[1] *Se bicher* (to clear out); *biche* (a doe).—Translator's note.

gesture or say a word, Divers sat down at the first table, that
of the big shots. As the tables were set out like those of pupils
in a classroom, with four colonists, on one side only, facing the
desk of the head of the family, I beheld the back of that
prodigy who deigned to eat and even to show delicate dislikes
after coming out of the hole. Indeed, he pushed a few bits of
undercooked vegetables to the edge of his iron plate, whereas
all the others ate everything. When we went out into the yard
for afternoon recreation, which lasts only a few minutes, he
joined the group of Toughs who—an extremely rare thing
—shook hands with him. It was not customary at Mettray for
colonists to shake hands openly. I think that this is to be
regarded as a secret agreement on their part to reject whatever
recalls civilian life and might make them miss it. It should also
be regarded as a certain reluctance felt by a "tough" who wants
to become a "man" and is therefore averse to any show of
friendship. And perhaps the colonists were somewhat ashamed
to perform among themselves a gesture which was habitual
among the guards but from which the guards excluded them.
As soon as he drew near the group, the released colonist saw
all hands reach out to him. He was breaking customs by his
mere presence, though he himself was still attached to them,
for he was somewhat abashed at the sight of the open hands,
hardly realizing that they were held out for him. We shall have
occasion to note that the colonists who come out of the
"punishment quarter" at Mettray, or out of the "disciplinary
cell" here, spontaneously assume the self-satisfied, arrogant
attitude of a tough, just as, during the war, any French soldier
assumed the pretentious air of a man who had died on the field
of honour. I was watching the new colonist from the top of the
stairs at the entrance of the mess-hall; I was standing with my
back against the doorframe, but that slightly leaning posture,
and that support, and that pedestal, made me look too important. I walked a few steps away, with my head bowed. I dared
not ask who he was, lest I seem silly—for though I was not a
big shot, nevertheless the fact of my being the elder brother's

chicken gave me a kind of status as a well-protected grande dame, and in order to maintain my prestige in the eyes of the jerks it was important that I not seem ignorant of what all the big shots knew (toughs and big shots are the two terms that designated, as they do here, the masters, the chiefs). The bugle blew taps. To get to the dormitory, which was on the first floor, we lined up in double file at the bottom of the outside stairway, of which I have spoken, and marched up the stairs. The newcomer stepped into line beside me. As he approached, he wet his lips; I thought he was going to speak, but he said nothing. The gesture was only a tic. I was not yet aware that he resembled me, for I did not know my face. We went up the wooden stairs. I did not have the audacity, in his presence, to put my hands into my pockets (fear of seeming too much like a big shot and too much his equal). I let them hang. That was humbler. He stumbled against the iron edge of a stair and I said to him, trembling slightly, "Watch out. The elder brother'll get after you, especially since you've just got out of the hole." He turned his head to me and answered with a smile: "To do that he'd have to have a little more hair on his chest." Then he added: "Is he your big shot? Tell him to go pad his knees." I didn't answer, but I lowered my head, and I would like the cause to have been an obscure sense of shame at having a big shot other than this insolent tough. He also uttered between his teeth the words "*Maldonne*" and "*la Caille,*"[1] expressions not used in the families, and he seemed to me to have returned from far away, from a dangerous adventure, for those words, coming from him, were like the black velvet sea-weed that a diver brings up around his ankles. One feels he was involved in games or struggles that partake of amorous play and the fancy-dress ball. He was, in effect, a residue of the underworld. The quarter thus had a life even more secret than ours, a life to which the rest of the Colony

---

[1] *Maldonne,* literally misdeal, conveys the idea of "barking up the wrong tree"; *la Caille* might be rendered as: "that creep".—Translator's note.

seemed impervious. It appeared to me less vicious because more turbid. The hardness and limpidity of Bulkaen's expression were due perhaps to sheer stupidity, to shallowness! Intelligence has vacillations that stir the depths of the eyes, that veil them. This veil passes for mildness, which perhaps it is. Mildness, a hesitation?

A hammock next to mine was free and was assigned to the newcomer by the head of the family himself. That same evening, I gave him a stunning present. During drill in the dormitory (the rite of going to bed), all noise except the rhythmic clicking of our heels on the floor was forbidden. The elder brother in charge of the drill was at the other end of the dormitory, near the head of the family. In taking from its slot the spar from which the hammocks hung, Divers knocked it against the wall. The head of the family growled:

"You there, can't you watch what you're doing?"

"Who did that?" yelled the elder brother.

For some seconds the silence in the dormitory grew more intense. I did not look at Divers.

"He won't own up, no danger of that!"

Then I turned slightly and raised my hand.

"Well, which of the two?"

I looked at Divers in amazement. He too had raised his arm, though reluctantly, and was already lowering it.

"It's me," I said.

"You should have said so. K.P. for you tomorrow."

Divers had a quizzical smile at the corner of his mouth and the gleam of a conqueror in his eyes.

For a brief moment the same gesture had made us accomplices in a slight imposture, and now I stood there alone, stupidly, with my hands emptied of their offering. After drill, when we were in bed, we chatted for a moment. He courted me slightly while Villeroy, the elder brother of the family and my personal big shot, was reporting to the head of the family, in the latter's room, on the day's events (perhaps he was playing stool-pigeon). I hardly answered, for I was afraid of revealing

my preoccupation: "Tell me about the quarter where Divers
still is." I was waiting for the captive male to talk about
himself, and first about the quarter, which was still mysterious
to me. I dared not look at him, but I could imagine his little
head raised above the hammock. I said in a whisper:

"Were you there long?"

"There where?" he said sternly. I got flustered.

"Where? In the quarter . . . where you were . . ."

I awaited his answer anxiously, amidst a silence that was
beginning to rustle softly.

"In the quarter? For a month."

A month. I dared not tell him that I had been at the Colony
more than a month and had never seen him there before. I was
afraid of annoying him and of his remaining silent. There was
whispering around us. Life was starting. Taps had blown.
Despite myself, I said simply:

"But . . ."

"Well, I'm back. With the nippers, you know, handcuffs.
They put 'em on me, the rats! But it didn't get me down. You
can be sure of that. I purposely let the chain hang in front of
me, like a fancy bracelet. People were squinting at me, you can
imagine, since Beaugency."

If, twenty years from now, while walking along the beach I
met a stroller wearing a big coat and if I spoke to him about
Germany and Hitler, he would look at me without answering,
and suddenly, seized with panic, I would pull up the flaps of
the coat and see a swastika on his lapel. I would stammer:
"So you're Hitler?" Thus did Divers appear to me, as great,
as evident, as pure as divine injustice. In short, I was confronted at the same time with the disturbing mystery of Divers
and of the quarter. It was little guys like him that I heard
marching in the yard the day of my arrival, when I was taken
to the council room to see the director. He was sitting at the
table with the green cover, beneath the crucifix. I could hear
the clacking of the little but heavy sabots that were moved by
the little feet of colonists. The director made a sign and the

guard pushed the window. The director scowled with annoyance. His jowls quivered, and the guard shut the window
completely. We could still hear the sound of the little sabots. I
could see the director's face growing angrier and angrier and
his grey jowls moving more and more and faster and faster. I
felt no desire to smile because I wasn't really sure that he
hadn't sent for me to punish me already.

"You are here . . ."

His voice tried to cover the sound of the sabots.

". . . You will not be unhappy. The other boys . . . The
Mettray Colony is not a penitentiary, it's a big family."

He spoke more and more loudly, and I suddenly felt myself
blushing for him. I took upon myself his shame and suffering,
I felt the same uneasiness as when I heard attempts to jam a
radio broadcast (German at the beginning of the war, English
at the end), those desperate efforts to destroy a dangerous
message, to prevent its being received, though it gets through
anyway and succeeds in sending out its call.

During our stay at Mettray, Divers did not use all his ways
and means of surprising me. The very afternoon when I saw
him again, fifteen years later, on top of the can in the disciplinary cell, one of the guys whispered to me as I was about to
return to my coop:

" Riton-la-Noïe' is asking for you."—"La Noïe" means
night.—I answered likewise in a whisper:

"Riton-la-Noïe? Never heard of him."

"He's the trusty. There he is, behind you."—I turned
around. It was Divers. He was leaning against the wall and
looking at me. His right hand was hanging at his thigh, back-
side out, the very position in which he used to take hold of his
prick.

Hiding from the guards, we made a few invisible movements
of approach. I went straight over to him, unhesitatingly, as a
friend, as a pal. Despite that gesture and posture which were
all too reminiscent of the big shot of the old days, my love for
Bulkaen did not allow anything but friendship. No doubt,

when I saw him again (Bulkaen was still alive, above my head, working in the shop, sleeping in the dormitory), there was no element of tenderness in my friendship, though a slight tenderness did seem to well up or to disappear far off in the depths of me.

Thus, Mettray blossomed curiously in the heavy shadow of Fontevrault. The Colony was ten or fifteen miles from the prison and its race of vicious bruisers. It had a dangerous glamour for us, a glamour of cabinets in which poison is stored, of powder-magazines, of embassy ante-chambers. Bulkaen disregarded my allusions to the Colony and talked about the future. In reply to a letter in which I told him about my passion for distant journeys, for going places, he spoke of plans for fleeing, for escaping, for a free life, in which I was involved. Then he went on to talk about women and confided to me that after making love he felt like bashing their heads in with the bidet, but all these passages in the letter were silenced by the one that revealed his misery: ". . . When the job was over, my pals would go see the girls and I'd go off my myself, all alone." How could he who was so charming write such a thing? Could it really and truly be, and was it possible that no one realized how miserable the child was? In another letter he added: "You know, Jean, I wasn't a jerk. Lots of bigtimers were proud to be seen with me." He was not unaware of the glamour he possessed. He had had the experience of Mettray.

We lived beneath the stern gaze of the Prison, like a village at the foot of a feudal castle inhabited by steel-clad knights, and we wanted to be worthy of them. In order to resemble them, we observed the orders that reached us secretly from the castle. Through whom? I cannot help saying that everything was in league with the children that we were: the flowers spoke, the swallows and even the guards were, willingly or not, our accomplices. Like Mettray, the Prison was guarded by a race of old jailers to whom beastliness was natural. To them we were dregs. They openly hated the inmates, but cherished

them in secret. In addition, they were—they are—the jealous
guardians of loathsome ways and customs. Their comings and
goings wove the limits of an inhuman domain, or rather the
meshes of a trap in which abjection was caught. Some of them
live for a quarter of a century, and often more, amidst hoodlums whom at the same time they contain. Every new convict
was immediately not merely pushed around by brutal gestures,
but, even worse, was drowned in the mockery and snarling
words that ordered all the vile measures, from the shearing of
the hair to the wearing of the hood, and one feels that the
guards are on intimate terms with the hoodlums, not because
there is intimacy between them in the usual sense of the word
but because there wells up from the hoodlums the horror in
which the guards are caught, in which they melt. A family air
merges them, as it merges masters and old servants, who are
the seamy side of the masters, their opposite and, in a way,
their unwholesome exhalations. The disease with which they
were inoculated was kept alive not only by the regulations, but
even more by the habits of the inmates and their personalities,
by the finical punctuality of the guards, who were sick with the
sickness of the big shots, and also by the stagnating immobility, or, if you like, the running around in circles in that
tightly closed domain.

We obeyed the men of the castle, and we were even bolder
than they. Even if, by virtue of some strong predisposition, a
boy had not loved the Prison, he would have been carried
away, would have been carried toward it, by the wave of love
that rose up to it from the Colony. At every moment a colonist
would have shown him what made it lovable. Before long he
would have realized that it was the perfect expression of his
truth. Legend, which embellishes everything, embellished the
Prison and its big shots and all that pertained to them, even,
and above all, their crimes. A word was sufficient, if uttered by
a Tough of the Family, in such a tone ...

Though we were moved by tragic spirits, the tragedy was
stricken with an extraordinary malady of love. Our heroism

was stained with acts of baseness, acts of fascinating cowardice. It was not uncommon for the fiercest toughs to play up to the guards with the repulsive purpose of getting special consideration. Informers are often found among the toughs. They are so sure of their power that they know a betrayal will not affect them, but the other little guys cannot for a single moment slacken in their will to be "regular." The slightest lapse would be fatal to them. They cling to loyalty as do others to virility. At noon, on a heavy, broad-rumped, hairy-legged nag that was still wearing its brass and leather harness, Harcamone, riding side-saddle with his legs dangling at the left, crossed the Big Square on his way back from cartage or work in the fields. He had had the audacity to hook at the edge of his tilted cap, near his ear and almost covering his left eye with a trembling mauve leucoma, two huge bunches of lilac. He must have been quite sure of his integrity. In the Colony, he alone could coyly adorn himself with flowers. He was a true male. The apparent rectitude of Bulkaen was due perhaps to his profound weakness. I know that he never compromised with the adversary. He often told me how he hated squealers, but I never saw his hatred so clearly as the time he spoke to me about "fairies," about the "little queers" of Pigalle and Blanche. We were on the stairs. Resuming in a low voice the conversation we had begun during the medical examination, he said:

"Don't go to those joints, Jean. The guys who go there aren't for you. They're the kind who sell, and they're all squealers."

He was wrong about queers being informers, but he wanted to show me how he hated stool-pigeons and also that he didn't want to be confused with fags. If those words are still so clear in my memory, it is because they were followed by others that were even more disturbing. He said to me:

"We'll beat it, Jean! As soon as we get the hell out of here, we'll head for Spain."

He freely let his dreams escape. He sat down on the stairs

and remained there with his head in his hand and his eyes closed.

"Jean, listen, imagine us in Cannes, on a pedal boat, in the water . . . it's sunny there . . . We'll be happy."

In the sentences that followed, he uttered the word happiness a number of times. He also said: "Down there we'll be as quiet as mice." I resisted the desire to take his shaven head in my warm hands and, as I was on a lower step, to rest it on my knees, which was on the step above. I felt the same grief I had often felt at Mettray when confronted with my helplessness. There was nothing I could do for him but caress him, and I had the impression that my caresses even aggravated his sadness, as in the past my caresse had saddened Villeroy when he had the blues. He said, in wonderment, with only the barest hint of anxiety: "Do you think the guys in our cell know that we . . . ?"

Villeroy was at Mettray because he had killed his father, a pork butcher. Villeroy was my man. As elder brother of Family B (each family, all of whose members occupied one of the ten cottages on the Big Square, which was covered with lawn and planted with chestnut trees, was called Family A, B, C, D, E, F, G, H, J, or L. Each of the cottages housed about thirty children who were ordered about by a colonist huskier and more vicious than the others. He was picked by the head of the family and was called the "elder brother." The elder brother was supervised by the head of the family, who was usually some retired civil servant, a non-commissioned officer, an ex-trooper), he had in his service a kid who was something like his squire, or page, or female attendant, or lady, and who worked in the tailor shop.

Mettray, now as I write, has been emptied of its fierce and charming demons. And for whom does Fontevrault have a bone? Our heaven has been depopulated. If we climb to our transoms, our eager eyes no longer have the luck to think they see the belfry around which the colonists must be playing in the Touraine countryside. And as our life is without external

hope, it turns its desires inward. I cannot believe that the
Prison is not a mystic community, for the death cell, in which
a light burns night and day, is the chapel to which we direct
our silent prayers. It is true that the more hard-boiled of the
hoodlums pretend to deny Harcamone's grandeur, for the
purity attained by blood—one speaks of the baptism of
blood—offends them, but I have noticed more than once in the
course of conversation a sign which showed that those least
prone to respect felt a certain reluctance to use harsh words
when talking about the murderer. In fact, one day, during the
medical check-up, Lou Daybreak, Botchako, Bulkaen and
others were standing in front of the infirmary and talking
about the death of Rose-wood and the act of killing. Each of
them expressed his opinion of Harcamone's worth. I had, so I
thought, completely freed myself from his hold But I didn't
talk about him. However, the discussion was cut short by a
single word from Bulkaen:

"He's what I call a man! "

He said it quietly, though with a slightly comic intonation.
Immediately the former power swooped down on me. Flowing
from my love of Bulkaen, waves of submission to Harcamone
broke over my head. I made a slight movement, as if I were
going to bend, or stoop. No one challenged the boy's remark.
We felt that only the youngest and handsomest of us could
decide whether Harcamone was a man.It was for him to offer
the palm-branch—the palm of Stephen the deacon—for that
palm, which was within us, was awarded by what was most
youthful in us. Bulkaen was the visible form of the quality that
made us pay deference to Harcamone's act.

"He's what I call a man," he said. And, after a silence, he
added:

"And him, at least, he shovels it up. He gets all the grub
and wine he wants."

Then he stood there, a little foolishly, with his legs too far
apart, like a young colt or a little calf. Indeed, Harcamone
received a double and even triple ration of bread and soup. He

was being fattened in his cell, like the ancient kings of the Isle of Nemi who were elected for a year and them immolated. And Pierrot, whose belly was devoured by hunger when he thought of Harcamone, must have been struck mainly by the latter's air of prosperity. Harcamone was stout. He was being bred. To the heart-breaking sweetness of being out of the world before death, was added, in Pierrot's mind, the pleasantness of the mild torpor that lulls a sated body to sleep.

Divers' presence here replunges me, as much as and more than does Bulkaen's, into my old life. Instinctively, in my cell, which, like the pearl, thus becomes orient, I turn to the east, toward the hole. The climate of prisons, the kind of lethargy that sends one to hell and makes our life as sordid as that of monsters, has something in common with sleep. I mean that when you are discharged, when you pass the gate, the memories that suddenly come back are those of the moments preceding the arrest. You "link up" with those moments as you do with the morning when you awake from an agonizing dream. And in the course of detention you sometimes cling to the movements, to the events which were getting under way when you lost footing, events which were like semi-awakenings that at times explode on the surface of a heavy sleep. You flounder a little, feebly, and you sink. You go back to sleep. Death does its work, once again it closes its door over you. I shuddered at the thought of Bulkaen's going to the hole. What if he stayed there, would he forget me? Would he not forget me? To whom did he talk about me? And if he does talk, what does he say? Who am I to his cronies? Now that I had found Divers, who, in spite of me, wanted to rake up the memory of our love at Mettray, I was afraid of Pierrot's turning up. Not that I had much to fear if Divers were indiscreet. I feared rather that his charms, which were still potent, might act on the youngster. And I feared too the ordeal of the crap can. I knew I could see him there without my love's suffering thereby, but I was not sure that I had the physical assurance, the bodily authority, to sit down on it myself in his presence without endangering my prestige. In wanting to go to the hole so as to be more deeply buried in abjection—I had the impression of descending when I went there, for my love of Bulkaen made me seek the most nauseating situations for us, perhaps so that we would both be more isolated there from the rest of the world, just as I lovingly imagined him plunging beneath my covers, releasing his worst odours, making me do likewise so that we would mingle in what was most private about us—in wanting to go to the hole I hoped to lure Pierrot there. But Pierrot remained upstairs, in spite of me, and perhaps, I also hope, in spite of himself. But I soon felt willing to rot there so that he might sprout, so that his new branches might deck the sky with flowers. And it was Divers, forgotten for a moment, whom I found there, and my love for Pierrot was going to be complicated by the memory of my past loves.

Like Harcamone, Divers had grown up. He was a man of thirty, with broad shoulders but an amazingly supple body, and he was elegant, despite the heavy dark-brown homespun clothes. He glided rather than walked. His legs were long and so sure-footed that I would have liked him to bestride me often so that I could be the furrow that the gaitered soldier and hunter bestride in the field. He has remained a crasher and has never banded with the pimps, for the pimps' bands differ from those of the crashers.

In the eyes of the pimps, the crashers are suckers, poor jerks who are in for trouble. Success with women gives the pimps a victorious, disdainful and also distant manner which they retain here, and which is envied by the crashers, who have remained kids. Divers is a sad kid. Now that Bulkaen has been shot and Harcamone beheaded, all that remains for me is to yield, not so much to a present love as to the memory of my love for Divers.

In the early days of our relations, Bulkaen had blurred my image of Harcamone. When Divers and I met again, he was no more than a friend. Now that Bulkaen was dead, my love for Harcamone, which had been damaged by the memory of

Bulkaen, emerged from the dungeon in which Bulkaen had
locked it. Finally, with Harcamone dead and myself softened
by many sorrows, and lonely too, my body slackened a little
when I saw Divers again. My gestures, without realizing it at
first, grew gentler. I leaned toward him like a woman. I loved
him with my usual violence. One makes love at first for the fun
of it, as a friend, in order to "come." Then passion follows,
with its vices, with its cults. I eventually drew the bewildered
Divers into that disorder; he was lost in the shadow that I
brought (it is woman's lot to cast shadow). In the disciplinary
cell he still suffers from the disease that embellishes him:
syphilis. I know nothing about this malady, except that it
colours the big shots' flesh with a greenish hue. It was impossible for me to learn from whom he had picked it up. He must
have had little experience of civilian life for fifteen years. He
told me he had spent a total of about eight years in jail, almost
three of them at Fontevrault State Prison, where he was
always a trusty.

I loathe and worship the trusties. They are bullies chosen by
the warden or the chief guard. Wherever I have been under the
supervision of a trusty, the one who held the sceptre was the
very one I would have chosen, not because of his physical
strength or brutality, but out of a secret preference, as one
chooses a favourite. He was almost always the handsomest. It
is said that when wild horses choose a king they select the most
harmonious of the pack. Wardens and chief guards select their
trusties in like manner—what a face they'd make if they were
told this!—and in like manner did the head of the family
choose his "elder brother" at Mettray. In Family B, the rules
of honour (the particular honour held in honour there, a
primitive honour in accordance with Greek tragedy, in which
murder is the most moral way of resolving a conflict), the
rules of honour were strictly observed, the elder brother being
loved as greatly as he was feared, and I have seen colonists
bite and claw each other before the impassive eyes of the
guards, fighting for reasons of precedence, for a rank denied

their elder brother. I have seen blood flow at Mettray from children's torsoes. I have seen youngsters die, killed. The guards did not dare make a move. Something like fumes of blood envelop the murderer and carry him off. Thus lifted, raised, with body erect, he reaches the bench of the accused, facing a Special Court clad in scarlet, which is the blood that has been shed, the blood in person, demanding vengeance and getting it. It is perhaps this gift of producing a miracle by a mere stab that astonishes the mob, alarms it, rouses it and makes it jealous of such glory. The murderer makes blood speak. He argues with it, tries to compound with the miracle. The murderer creates the Criminal Court and its machinery. In view of this, one thinks of the birth of Chrysaor and Pegasus, who sprang from the blood of Medusa.

Because guards don't make a move when a deadly battle rages, you think they're brutes and you're right. I like to think they were petrified by a wrathful spectacle, the grandeur of which was beyond them. What was their petty existence compared to the radiant life of the children? For the colonists were all noble, even the jerks, since they were of the sacred race, if not of the sacred caste. The Colony was surrounded by cottages that housed the families of the guards, large peasant families, ridiculously indigent compared to the luxurious colonists who were rich in possessing only their youth and grace, and their gestures too, which fashioned jewels in the air, and also their power over a people who tortured them without realizing that torture magnifies the person whom one thereby worships rabidly. The guards are vile brutes, necessary to the beauty of my sunken life. The death that keeps vigil within me would indeed be less sumptuous without them and the fiendish children. My childhood life was cruel and bloody, and the cruelty that flourished brutally at Mettray, among the children, was inspired by the coarser kind that adorned the men of Fontevrault.

To the glory of the trusty:

"Looking out on the drill of which he is in charge, he keeps watch from a secret dwelling-place, an inner cabin, something like the binnacle where the captain of the galley stands.

"While the punished convicts walk round and round, he sings to himself: I'm a buccaneer, what care I for glory!

"His eyes have the gold streaks of the narcissus, the narcissus engraved on the buttons of the uniform of the African Battalion. What are they doing there?

"When he drains off the last drops after pissing, he becomes a giant tree, a northern fir stirred by the wind.

"His knees gently take shape in my hand like certain huge snowballs. His knees! Hector's marvellous, astounding invocation: 'by your life, by your parents, by your knees . . .' By your knees! (What a scowl of contempt on Divers' face when he said to me, about Villeroy: "He can go pad his knees!")

"When the men who are being punished see him marching in front of them, they slyly say of his round and not very mobile buttocks: 'They gabble.'

"And then, that last stroke, that finishing stroke, his neck."

But I have written out this poem with less fervour as a result of knowing Bulkaen, to whom I bore as much tenderness as love, and from whom I hoped as much. Rid of Divers for a moment by virtue of this poem, lying in my little cell where I am locked up for the night, I can imagine myself sleeping with Pierrot in a big bed, and toward morning I sidle up to him. I again venture, as yesterday, a caress. I wake him. In the drowsiness of morning he stretches his arms and legs, presses his sprawling body against mine, which is now gathered together, He puts an arm around my chest, lifts his head and gently, deeply, places his mouth on mine. And after crediting him with such a tender gesture, I cannot believe that he could have remained unfeeling toward me, for if I have imagined that gesture it is because something about Pierrot suggested the image, something about him told me he was capable of it (perhaps a tic, a movement, a pout, something or other which I no longer recall but which is so alive within me that I continue it until this morning's kiss). Suddenly I think it is the icy hardness of his gaze that has made me believe in his tenderness, perhaps because of the idea that the iciness of his eyes would not resist my warmth. And when I think of the boy's abandoning me, my hand tightens around my pen, my arm invents a poignant gesture. If he knew how I suffer, he would leave death and come to me, for his cruelty was kind.

The "quarter" at Mettray corresponded to our disciplinary cell. When I arrived at the Colony one mild September evening, my first shock was caused when I was on the road, amidst the fields and vines, by a bugle-call which sounded just as the sun was setting. It rang out in a forest of which I saw only the gilded summit. I was coming from La Roquette Prison and was chained to the guard who accompanied me. I had not got over the horror I had felt, when I was arrested, of suddenly being a character in a film who is involved in a drama of which the agonizing outcome is unknown since it may reach just the point at which the reel is cut or burned, and so make me disappear in the darkness or the fire, dead before my death.

We walked up the road. The trees were getting denser, Nature was growing more mysterious, and I should like to speak of her the way islands occupied by pirates and savage tribes are sometimes spoken of in adventure stories. The traveller arrives in a land where the vegetation keeps watch over precious captives. There are cedars, catalpas, yews, wisteria, and all the trees common to the grounds of Renaissance castles, and that was the civilized setting required for Bulkaen's vigour. At the top of the hill, my guard and I passed a nun who was chatting with a powerful-looking young man in fawn-coloured boots. He was another guard. But the nun —Sister Holy Sneaker?—was old and ugly, and the second guard we saw was also ugly. He had a thick, black, handle-bar moustache and was wearing a pair of baggy, grey canvas breeches tucked into leggings, the lower edges of which curled up over the insteps with the same curve as the moustache and whose calves had the contour of the gaiters one sees in the illustrated hunting-catalogues of 1910. I thus gathered that the handsomest hoodlums in France would be hounded by the most ridiculous and vicious human species (save for some rare and highly disturbing exceptions, guards who were handsomer than delinquents and of such lordly bearing that we licked their boots). Finally I came to a square, like a village square, with a chapel and cottages. I felt we were at Mettray, and I was astounded and terrified to realize that we had got there without having to pass walls, fences, barbed wire and drawbridges. I arrived then on a mild September evening. A splendid autumn was opening the gate to the eternal grey season in which I am trapped, but the autumn for which I long is that season of wet forests, rotting moss and dead russet leaves. It is a rich, full-bodied autumn, recognizable by a thousand signs, even when you remain indoors, in a city, and such autumns, with their richness and sweetness, are denied us. We know only the bleak, impossible greyness within us, and this greyness, which is even bleaker when shot through with a ray of sunlight, is the faces of the guards and the dismal severity of the objects. But it is so sweet—for then I can thumb my nose at the world of guards and judges, even at your world—when in its mists I see again the gleam of Harcamone's radiant image. Merely by the remark he had made about him, Bulkaen had caused me to turn again to the idol from whom his love had turned me away. The murderer seemed to me more dazzling, which proves the delicacy of my feeling for Bulkaen. This love did not lure me to a nether region but, on the contrary, uplifted me and brightened my surroundings. I am using the very language with which mystics of all religions speak of their gods and mysteries. They arrive, as is said, in sun and lightning. It was thus that the condemned man appeared to my inner gaze, the vision being governed by my love for Bulkaen.

When I arrived at Mettray, I was first taken to the quarter, where I was stripped of all the clothes that belonged to my past life. Shortly thereafter I was alone in a cell, a poor little fellow wrapped in a blanket, squatting in a corner and reading

the following inscription which had been carved on a floorboard with a knife: "Pietro, the master of the vampires, that's
me!" Through the walls I could hear outside the pounding of
the heavy sabots that were moved by forty or sixty bare,
chafed little feet. Journalists and writers have spoken of the
punishment drill reserved for the boldest of the colonists. The
fury of the love which the colonists bore each other, the love
which bore them, which threw them into each other's arms,
was perhaps heightened by the despair of being deprived of all
other tenderness, of family affection. Hardness could shine
between their eyelids and lips, but they could not escape the
fact that they were forlorn children. As the provincial courts
also sentenced youngsters to the Colony, there was a general
convergence at Mettray of the young scum of France. La
Roquette is now a women's prison. It was formerly a convent.
While waiting to appear in juvenile court, we were kept there,
one by one, in narrow cells, which we would leave for a
one-hour recreation period every day. In the division yard we
would walk about in a circle, as in the quarter at Mettray, as
in the hole here, without speaking. We were supervised by a
guard, like those here, who all have their particular idiosyn-
crasy: Brulard rubs against the wall like a mangy horse;
Roly-Poly always curls his moustache when he talks; the
Panther speaks very gently, but once a day, with the voice of a
village cantor, he lets out with "Send . . . the Council Room."
When the inmates went back to their cells, each youngster
remained in the circle until the preceding one was locked up,
and, despite the precautions that were taken, we were able to
choose bosom friends. Love-letters, strung to threads, ran
from window to window and, with the help of a trusty, from
door to door. We all knew each other. When he arrived at
Mettray, the newcomer would inform us that "So-and-so is
coming up in two months." We would wait for him. Though at
La Roquette we would all go to mass because the chaplain
would innocently read to us, from the altar, letters from
former inmates, my companions, who had left for Mettray,

Eysses or Belle Ile, and through him we knew the whereabouts of Bébert the Legionnaire, Black Jim, Laurent, Martinelle, Bako, Dédé from Javel, little tramps, some of whom had a girl on the streets. They were petty pimps, but a short spell in the Colony transformed them and turned them into crashers. They quickly lost their languid manner. The cute little tramps had to become "toughs," and tough they remained.

It is only later that life tempers the colonists' rigidity, and the crashers they have become no longer have the rigorous intransigence of childhood. They have a graciousness of which we were incapable. This very morning Lou Daybreak asked a crasher—one of the most highly esteemed members of the gang—Velvet:

"You wouldn't have a hunk of bread, would you?" (I note the embarrassment in the pimp's voice and gesture; his extremely dignified attitude is ruffled by the humiliation involved in any request. The pimp wanted to be neither cold nor humble, and his voice cracked slightly.)

Velvet looked in his bag and took out a piece.

"Here, take what you need."

"What do you want for it?"

"Oh, nothing at all. Keep it."—And he walked away with a smile.

But the shills, the seasoned pimps, know that business is business, and among themselves everything is paid for. They are really men, capable of being businessmen.

Mettray made us tough-minded but generous.

Here too we wait for our friends, but we knew them in civilian life and, before that, at Mettray, at Aniane, at Eysse, at Saint Maurice . . . Thus, Harcamone had known Divers at Mettray and had run into him again in Montmartre, where they worked together in several robberies. And here, at last, is the explanation of the suspected relationship between Divers and Harcamone. Harcamone already had three convictions for theft. He was liable to life imprisonment when he was ratted on by Divers and convicted a fourth time. The judge gave him a life sentence. It was thus because of Divers that Harcamone was waiting to have his head cut off. When I learned this, I was surprised to realize that I felt no disgust for Divers. I wanted to share his secret so as to feel I was his accomplice and to rejoice with him at being the cause of one of the greatest misfortunes in history. I experienced a joy which was of a very rare quality because it put an end to a long-standing, cloudy anxiety. I was happy with Divers. I am still happy, with a grim happiness, a happiness charged with carbonic gas. Infuriated at not having been able to possess Bulkaen, I turn in despair to my former loves and let them lead me to the most illicit regions. For if Pierrot kisses me, I can believe in his love. Again on the stairway, and at the same turning, which had ended by being ours, he gave me a quick peck on the mouth and started to run off, but I had time to grab him by the waist, bend back his head and, drunk with love, kiss him. It was the sixth day of our friendship. It's this kiss that I often recall at night.

In order to afford myself pleasure in the loneliness of my nights, I would still occasionally imagine myself as having a very handsome young face and body so as to enjoy more easily the caresses of the captain of the galley. At times I would also invent other situations for myself, I would have, in thought, other adventures, forgetting to discard that youthful face and body, with the result that I once got involved in a story in which I sold myself to a very rich old man. But I still had that very handsome face, and I was amazed to learn that my good-looks were a kind of armour which protected my purity. I then understood why the handsomest adolescents give themselves without apparent disgust to the vilest old men. Nothing can defile them, their beauty guards them. If the most repulsive of monsters had wanted me at that moment, I would have given in to him. It then occurred to me that, thanks to his protective beauty, Bulkaen would venture to give himself to me.

Instead of pressing my mouth firmly against his, I imparted

to my lips a very slight trembling, so that they did not stick to his, they did not adhere. Our kisses did not melt into one. The slight trembling which made my mouth open on his and withdraw at each quiver (for the kiss was of a nervous, spas-modic kind) was caused perhaps by my desire not to lose all consciousness and sink into befuddlement but to remain pre-sent, careful to savour the pleasure. Indeed, a continuous contact of our mouths and an increasingly "fierce" pressure would have winded me, but that movement of the lips, which trembled as in a passionate murmur, kept heightening the consciousness of my pleasure. That shudder, as it were, also enhanced my happiness, for it made our trembling kiss seem to take wing, to be idealized. Pierrot let me hug him tightly, but at a faint sound of foosteps he broke away so sharply that I realized he had been on the alert all the time and that he had not been roused during the embrace, for on hearing the sound he would have had slight difficulty, despite his quick reflexes, in shaking off the excitement, and I who was stuck to him, would have detected that slight twinge, that unsticking of a subtle glue. He escaped from my arms so nimbly that I realized he had never nestled in them. That sign, which I now recall, along with others, obliged me to seek refuge in my old loves. For three months in which I helped Divers bear the ignominy of Harcamone's death, I lived a sunless life with him, a life spent by our minds, which were strained to the point of song, in the airless and lightless cell of a condemned man. Divers lived in the joy of having dared strike flush in the face a beauty more beautiful than he. I shared his joy and sorrow. And if I felt any indignation about his act, it was at night, when I thought of Pierrot. Thus, we lived gravely, at each other's side, with the certainty that Harcamone was dying slowly in the solitude of a cell. I also dreamed of committing a murder with Divers and laying the blame on some big shot of matchless moral rigour and physical beauty who would be sentenced instead of us. This desire freed me from a torment, a very slight one, which I felt when I thought about Divers, a torment that had deep roots in me or in the past. It seems to me that this wilful dream destroyed a clumsy and evil gesture. Perhaps I wanted to redeem Divers by taking his crime (was it this one?) upon myself. I was giving away my soul and grief, which were those of a lover.

In addition to the ten families, the Colony had another which lived apart, to the right of the chapel, near the cemetery. It was called "the Joan of Arc Family." I went there once, accompanied by a guard, to get some brooms for the mess-hall. When we left the barnyard, which was to the right of the chapel, we entered a lane lined with two hedges of hawthorne, roses, jasmine and no doubt other gorgeous flowers. We passed some youngsters who were on their way to the Colony. My excitement rose as we approached the family, which we called "the Joan of Arc." It had its own flag (blue and white) and was composed only of chickens, chickens of the big shots of the other families. I continued on my way among the same flowers, among the same faces, but I sensed, from a kind of uneasiness which came over me, that something was happening. The scents and colours of the flowers were unchanged, yet it seemed to me that they were becoming more essentially themselves. I mean that they were beginning to exist for me with their own existence, with less and less the help of a support: the flowers. Beauty too was detaching itself from faces. Each child who passed tried to hold it back, but it ran away. Finally, it remained alone. The faces and flowers had disappeared. I kept walking, far ahead of the guard, carrying my two brooms, and I contracted my buttocks as when one is frightened at night. However, I forced myself to make as few gestures as possible through which the Hell into which I was descending—a strange hell where even the very particular scent of Hell appeared in the bewildering guise of a rose-bush laden with sulphur roses—through which, as I was saying, the Hell could have wormed a finger and, seized by my whole mechanism, could finally have invaded me. I did not regain my peace of mind until I got back: less fearful beauty calmed me.

Because Pierrot started at Mettray in the Joan of Arc Family I have no way of telling which of the two, Pierrot or "the" Joan of Arc, benefited from the light shed by the other. Just as a cottage is changed into a palace and the servant-girl into a fairy in the illustrations of old magazines, so my cell is transformed by a stroke, of which I still see the wand that is about to disappear, into a stately chamber lit up by a hundred torches, and my straw mattress, continuing this transformation, has become a bed adorned with curtains that are attached by garlands of true pearls. Everything wavers beneath the rubies and emeralds; everything is made of gold, silk, mother of pearl; and in my arms I hold an unclothed knight, who is not Bulkaen.

I received another note from Bulkaen in exchange for mine. It was written in the careful handwriting which he used for penning the petition for reprieve in which, owing to his ignorance, he got entangled in barbarous sentences and pointed words and, before writing, in movements of the hand that were like sweeps of the leg in dancing, movements in which the clumsiness of his imagination tried to hide behind the agility and elegance of the hand. He asked me to write a few lines of verse about a subject which he gave me: "Jean, would you write a poem for me about two friends who loved each other a lot in prison? One of them goes away. The one who's left behind writes to him to say that he'll always love him and that he's waiting to join him, even in the penal colony, where they'll be happy." And he added: "Believe me, lots of men think that way in prison."

Those lines between my fingers! Ever since then, I can't help seeing Bulkaen in the penal colony where he should have been (for though I was robbed of my death, his death stole his destiny; it was Bulkaen whom I envisioned amidst the ferns when I wrote *The Condemned Man*). Pierrot did not even want to go to the penal colony—and to join Rocky—he wanted to hymn his desire. When I learned that Rocky was being sent to Saint Martin de Ré, I realized, on seeing Pierrot return from the sixth division, that he had just said good-bye to his former lover. He didn't see me, but I saw the look on his face; it was that of des Grieux when he saw Manon in the convoy of girls on the way to Havre de Grâce.

It was difficult at Mettray to go from one family to the other. Discipline was so tight that I am still amazed that the authorities found reliable men to apply it seriously. Viewed at close range, this seriousness was tragic. The director, the assistant director and the guards were, by dint of inhumanity, false directors, false assistant directors, false guards, children of a kind who had grown old in childhood and its mysteries. They were writing my story. They were my characters. They understood nothing about Mettray. They were idiots. If it is true that only intelligent people are capable of understanding evil—and hence the only ones capable of committing it—the guards never understood us. Each family lived in ignorance of the other families. And contact with the Joan of Arc family was even more strictly forbidden since it was composed, not of the youngest (let us marvel again at what aroused the indignation of an Albert Londres or an Alexis Danan: the members of each family were grouped not by age but by height) but of the smallest boys, all or almost all of whom were the chickens of the big shots of the other families, whom they met in the workshops, where classification by family did not apply.

It will be rather difficult for me to portray the characters in this book. The children all resemble each other. Fortunately, each of them was heralded by more or less strange particularities, just as each toreador is preceded in the bull-ring by his music, archers and ribbons. The portrait of Pierrot is more likely than the others to merge with those of all the colonists. He is indeed vulgar, but with a vulgarity that is haughty, hard, maintained by constant labour. His vulgarity is erect.

Is it possible that young men with such pure faces, faces so unmarked by vice and suffering, make love like everyone else? The angels proceed otherwise when they wish to enjoy the voluptuousness of possession: the lover is metamorphosed into

the beloved. At present, I need only evoke my childhood loves
to redescend to the depths of time, in its darkest dwellings, in a
lonely region, where I find only the Colony, formidable and
alone. She draws me to her with all her sinewy limbs, with the
gesture of sailors who pull a rope out of the water, placing one
hand in front of the other while the rope piles up on deck, and
I regress, with the Divers of old at my side, to a nauseating
childhood which is magnified by horror and which I would
never have wanted to leave. From the disciplinary cell, where I
spent two weeks, I arranged with an infirmary assistant to slip
me some phenobarbital in exchange for a few butts. This
century is certainly the century of poison, an age in which
Hitler is a Renaissance princess, in which he is, for us, a mute,
profound Catherine de Medici, and my fondness for poisons,
the appeal they have for me, sometimes makes me merge with
one or the other of these personages. Then the phenobarbital
led me to the infirmary in lordly state, pale and deathly-
looking. I was hoping, since the infirmary was near the disciplinary cell, to communicate with Divers, who I knew was
the trusty there, but the doctors gave me an emetic and after
analysing my vomit discovered the phenobarbital, and I was
sentenced to a month in the disciplinary cell for having
smuggled a dangerous drug into the prison. In that way, I
joined Divers more rapidly. When I entered the cell, he didn't
recognize me. I lowered my head at the sight of the crapper on
which he was sitting in state. When he got off, he ordered me
in a nasty tone—for he was nasty at first: "Get over there,
make it snappy," and he pointed to a place among the men
who were being punished. Then he looked at my face and saw
it, and he smiled, with the kind of sad, evil smirk we all have
when we recognize each other in prison. The smile meant:
"You too, you were bound to come. You couldn't live
anywhere else." I must mention that I felt slightly ashamed
when I told Bulkaen that I too had been at Mettray. I had not
been able to escape the usual fate—I turned my eyes away,
ashamed at not having been able to avoid the common lot, but

already strong and victorious, for the adventure that won me
three years in prison would be very beautiful. When I saw that
he had recognized me, I wanted to talk to him, but the guard
was watching us. It was only toward evening that we exhanged
a few words, and not until three days later, when we had re-
established our former intimacy, that I explained why I was in
the hole. He finally believed in my love for him. After fifteen
years of waiting, of seeking—for since his departure from
Mettray, my entire life, as I now realize, had been only a long
quest for him—I had risked death to see him again. And the
reward was worth so great a peril. Two beds away from me is
his same little face, contracted by some mysterious drama that
is unfolding, is being performed, if you prefer, on a secret
screen; his perfect set of imperfect teeth, his mean, shifty look,
his wilful, never satisfied forehead and, under the stiff white
shirt, the body that neither blows nor fasting could wither, as
noble and imperious as revealed to me on the rare occasions
when we went bathing in the summer, with its heavy torso, its
chest like the tool called a maul, at the end of a flexible
handle: his waist; his chest, which I still dare compare to a
top-heavy rose on a stem that always bends. I told him that I
now felt only a very true, very warm friendship for him, a
loyal fellowship. But such a feeling would not have made me
brave death and conquer it.

At Mettray, we offered prayer exactly eight times a day.
The procedure in the dormitory was as follows: when all the
members of the family were upstairs, the head of the family
locked the door and the session began. The colonists were all
lined up along the two wide sides of the dormitory, each boy in
his place, with his back to the wall. The elder brother called
out: "Silence," and the children stood still. "Take off your
sabots." They removed their sabots and placed them in a very
straight line, two yards in front of them. "Kneel!" cried the
elder brother. The colonists knelt in front of the sabots, which
were empty but steaming. "Pray." A youngster said the
evening prayer, and everyone made the responses: ". . .

Amen," but transforming this "Amen" into "come on." "On your feet!" They stood up. "Right about face," and they turned a half circle. "Three steps forward, march!" They took the three steps forward and their noses were against the wall. "Remove the rods." They lifted the big shafts which were hooked to the wall, and when the order was given, put the ends of them into notches cut in the vertical beams which had been put there for that purpose. And at each movement they thumped their heels on the floor to mark time. Then they undressed and continued the drill in their shirts. They "spread the hammocks," they "made their beds," "folded their clothes," and their shirt-tails flew in the wind, mischievously lifted up by the neighbours who wanted to see the little ass that gave them a hard-on. I loved those complicated bed-time rites. As we were always afraid of bungling one of the movements and being kicked with the clog that the elder brother had not yet taken off, we performed them with a gravity shot through with sceptical smiles which were quickly effaced. This fear was sacred since, in the omnipotence of his beauty and ferocity, the elder brother was a god to us. We went to bed after putting on the zinc underpants of which the big shots spoke, and we dreamed.

At Mettray I dreamed less of theft and burglary than of prostitution. Having a lover who knew how to burgle would probably have delighted me. There is no doubt that I would have loved him, but as a courtesan. Later on, I would be a beggar rather than a thief, and when I had to work out a plan for escaping from Brest Prison and getting Pilorge out of jail in Rennes, the first thing I thought of, since I had to destroy iron bars, was acid rather than a file and a metal saw. I chose guile, crafty slowness in the manly manner. And it was not till much later, after all those stages, that I decided to be a thief, to live at first by simple stealing, stealing from show-cases, and finally by burglary, This happened slowly. I went to theft as to a liberation, to the light. I freed myself from prostitution and begging, the abjectness of which becomes increasingly apparent the more I am drawn by the glory of theft. I am living my youth at the age of thirty, but my youth is old.

It is quite possible that in his own eyes Bulkaen was only a constellation—or, if you like, the crystalization of the jewels he had stolen. But the force he possessed was only the force of my love. His granite-like hardness was the rigidity that resulted from the tightening of all his fibres in the presence of my love—and particularly of my desire.—The more I weakened, the more he hardened, seemingly for me alone and by contrast. He stiffened with all my love, and the jewels set in his bulk made of him a sceptre, a hand of justice. There was no likelihood of his softening in my presence. He was comparable, in this respect, to the Colony, whose sparkling hardness was due to the fact that no colonist ever cried. The Colony never softened. It had a sense of decorum. Heroes and certain captains have adorned themselves with their victories by tacking to their names those of places they have forced and conquered. Thus, we get Devout of Auerstaedt, Scipio Africanus . . . Crashers adorn themselves with their loot, their booty. Bulkaen sparkled with his rocks. One day, I called out to him, on the q.t. as always:

"Pierrot?"

He turned his head. His eyes were hard, his eyebrows drawn. Between his teeth, so as not to be heard by any big shots, he said to me in a venomous whisper:

"I told you to call me Jewel! You understand, it's on account of the guards. They all know my name's Pierrot."

I shrugged.

"All right. I don't give a damn, only it sounds like a whore . . ."

"What d'you mean 'whore'?"

The expression on his face grew mean, as when I wanted to kiss him.

"You mean Kid Jewel sounds all right to you?"

"You're nuts. It's not on account of that. It's on account . . ."

"Of your jobs, the jewels, sure, I know."

I added in an ironic tone: "All right, I'll give you all the jewels you want." He told me to speak lower. I thought: "With my suffering. I'd feel I was praying."

In his mind he heard himself being called Bijoux (Jewels) with the courtly x. But when saying the word, no one knew whether or not there was this x[1]. One might have called him Bijou, meaning Kid Bijou. He himself did not mind—to a certain extent, he wished—that the origin of the nickname be known, but he wanted to seem to have had it for a long time so as not to seem responsible for it. He wanted to be rightfully noble.

At the beginning of this book, I spoke of a kind of disenchantment with prison. It came about gradually as I began to examine delinquents and criminals purely from the standpoint of practical reason. From this point of view, all criminal acts may seem foolish, for the gain is trivial compared to the penalty incurred if you fail, to the risk you run, and prison seemed to me—which it also is—a pack of poor devils. But if I go further, if my lights illuminate the interior of the big shots. I understand them better, I feel exactly as I used to feel about them and their work. My understanding was complete when Bulkaen once said to me: "When I do a job, when I break into a house, I get a hard-on, I lubricate." The reader will therefore not object to my presenting Bulkaen as a liberator.

It would pain me to have to say that men are my brothers. The word sickens me because it attaches me to men by an umbilical cord. It thrusts me back into the womb. The word binds us through the mother. It belongs to the earth. I loathe the brotherhood that establishes bodily contacts, but I mean "my brothers" when I think of the colonists. I must have loved my Colony for its influence to halo me even now. I mean—and as far back as I can remember—that it is a *precise stretch of time,* but that it irradiates, that this *present past* diffuses a dark vapour, composed chiefly, I think, of our suffering, which

[1] The x of *bijoux* is not pronounced.—Translator's note.

is my halo and to which I turn, in whose downiness I often forget the present.

My childhood rises to my teeth. That particular world of reformatories has, in my memory, the properties of the world of prisons, theatres and dreams: anxieties, falls, fevers, apparitions, inexplicable noises, singing, suspected presences. But I am brash enough to be of the opinion that prisons and children's homes do not depart sufficiently from the unusual. Their walls are too thin and not impervious enough. Mettray alone profited from a prodigious achievement: there were no walls, but only laurels and flower borders; yet nobody, to my knowledge, succeeded in escaping from the Colony itself, for the facility of doing so seemed to us very weird, protected by watchful spirits. We were victims of a foliage which was seemingly harmless but which, in response to the least daring of our gestures, might become electrified, raised to such a tension that we would have been electrocuted to the very soul. We all thought that in that sumptuous flora dwelt the perils of sleep, and its immobilities, which were laden with all the potentialities in the world. Watching over us, the better to spy upon us, was a demoniacal power specially directed against children. Once, during a recreation period, I tried to destroy the charm. I stood at the very edge of the narrowest limits of the Colony, near the trimmed laurels and a tall dark yew. There were flowers at my feet and grass so delicate, so familiar, that I suddenly thought I sensed a sympathetic relationship between it and me, and I felt self-confident. I made the movement of removing my feet and my sabots, which were too heavy for running. I wanted to flee. I was already on my way. The colonists behind me were shouting their usual insults. I could imagine their illicit doings, their equivocal murmurs . . . I had a terrible decision to make, for it meant breaking the barrier of flowers, fighting my way into the realm of the fabulous.

I had, I think, my hands in my pockets, and I stood at the edge of the clump looking perfectly natural so that neither the guard nor the flowers would suspect what I was up to.

My mind was in a turmoil. It was going to carry me off, to kidnap me, and I stood there motionless in the presence of the flowers. The bugle sounded the end of recreation.

One of Bulkaen's splutterings ended as follows: "You remember the times we went all the way to Bel Air to get butts?" No doubt some kids did go beyond the sacred limits of the grounds, but they themselves transported those baleful properties and imparted them to the remotest thickets. Perhaps certain children escaped these spells, for I realized from what he said how different Bulkaen's life at Mettray had been from mine. Bel Air was a sanatorium two miles from the Colony, and only the boys who worked in the fields could go there, accompanied by the head of a shop. When they returned at noon and in the evening, they would talk about Bel Air, and their stories were unintelligible to those of us who worked in the sedentary shops, but this hardly mattered to us because almost all the field-workers were jerks, and if Pierrot spent most of his time in the fields, that means he must have been a jerk, unless he created and made possible the character of a big shot or of a chicken with chapped hands, dirty smock and muddy clogs. Perhaps he actually performed that miracle. He has performed others in prison, where I find that the windows let in too much light, that footsteps are not quiet enough, that the guards are too mean (or not mean enough. I should like them to be disgustingly gentle). In short, we're tied to your life by too many strings. I think that my love of prison is perhaps the subtle well-being of plunging into a life amongst men whom my imagination and desire wish to be of rare moral beauty. This well-being is only slightly attenuated by the fact that prisons lose their hard glitter as they come to be frequented by honest people and as pimps take on the qualities of solid citizens. In prison, when the sun that streamed through the window scattered the cell, each of us became more and more himself, lived his own life, and lived it so acutely that we ached, for we were isolated and were made conscious of our

imprisonment by the brilliance of the fête that dazzled the rest
of the world, but on rainy days it was otherwise and the cell
was merely a shapeless, pre-natal mass with a single soul in
which the individual consciousness was lost. What a sweet
feeling when the men of whom it was composed loved each
other.

At night, I often stay awake. I am the sentinel at the gate of
the sleep of others, whose master I am. I am the spirit that
hovers above the shapeless mass of dream. The time I spend
there pertains to the time that flows in the eyes of dogs or in
the movements of any insect. We have almost ceased to be in
the world. And if, to cap it all, rain is falling, then everything
sinks, engulfed in the horror where only my galley remains
afloat on those ponderous waves. On rainy nights, the
storm-tossed ship rolled gunwale under. The thick squalls
seriously disconcerted the males whom nothing frightened.
They did not commit any rash act, of the kind inspired by fear,
but their features and gestures were lightened by a sudden
sharpness. Their past crimes were purified by their being at
last so close to God. By lighter I mean that the gestures and
faces of the crew belonged less to the soil. The friendly danger
did away with all boredom, all trace of what did not pertain to
the immediate moment, it scraped them clean, leaving only the
essentials required by the manoeuvre. We went back and forth
in the dark warm rain. Our naked torsos were gleaming. At
times, without recognizing each other, men would embrace as
they passed in the darkness and would then rush to do their
job, with their muscles both excited and softened by that single
caress. The most light-footed of the pirates swayed in the
rigging, but I carried the lantern in the most tangled knot of
the manoeuvre, and it was at times a knot of rough love. The
sea was roaring. I was sure that nothing could happen since I
was with those who loved me. They were sure that nothing
could harm them since the captain was there. And in my
hammock I would fall asleep in his arms where I would continue making love despite the fatigue of the love in which I had

just indulged. My life on the galley threaded its way into my
daily life. One day I heard myself thinking: "Anger fills our
sails." And it was enough for rebellious colonists to be called
mutinous for the night's confusion to settle on my days.

Our loves at Mettray! The child couples, the males of
which were sixteen! I was sixteen, a girl's age. Fifteen is thin
and seventeen too hard. But sixteen has a ring of delicate
femininity. I loved Villeroy, who loved me. Because he was a
child himself (he was eighteen), he was closer to me than
anyone (with the exception of Pilorge) ever was. I was more
amused than anything else at his making love to me the first
night, for I thought it a game despite the fact that his narrow,
brutal face was drawn with passion. He was contented with
this make-believe, but later, when one deep dark night I dug
his tool into me, he almost passed out—and I too—with
gratitude and love. A blond curl, damp with sweat, mingled
with my hair in an image of us that was projected in heaven.
His face was discomposed by the active quest of happiness. He
was no longer smiling. With my arms around him, I looked at
that phosphorescent face bent over me. We were children
seeking our pleasure, he with his awkwardness and I with too
much skill. I broke him in. I deflowered my pimp. But he
discovered quite naturally the sweetest caresses. That brute
became timid when making love to me. He called me Sapodilla.
One evening he even called his penis "my brute," and mine
"your little basket." They kept the names. I now know that
without uttering them we exchanged the most beautiful words
of love in the enchanted style of Romeo and Juliet. Our love
sang in that heartbreaking dwelling. We were isolated by the
bedlothes that hung from both our hammocks down to the
floor where we were enlaced. The colonists knew about our
love, they knew that we weren't stringing pearls behind our
brown woollen curtains, but who would have dared say a
word? Old Guépin himself once realized what it cost to touch
the chicken, the kid, of one of the bruisers of Family B. He did
not yet know who I was when one Sunday, during physical

training, he dared punch me in the shoulder from behind because I had botched a movement. I swayed and fell forward. Villeroy went up to the old man. His teeth were clenched and his thighs already quivering with the shudder that precedes the blow. "You bitch!" he said, looking at Guépin. Perhaps the latter wanted it to look as if he thought the insult were aimed at me, for he replied. "Is he a pal of yours?"

"Yeah, so what?" growled Villeroy.

"Then you ought to teach him the movements. That's your job."

He said this in a gentler tone. But in falling I had scraped my hand on a flint pebble. I was bleeding. The blow and then Guépin's insult had wounded Villeroy, chiefly, I think, in his pride. But we know the mechanism of the emotions: when you are carried away by anger (anger carrying you), it is enough for anyone—a suffering child—to pass nearby for your whole being, which is already exasperated, to open to pity, which is love. Anger had brought tears to the edge of my goon's eyelids, tears which pity sent flowing to his mouth. He grabbed my hand and kissed it. I was dumbfounded at what he was doing. Did he himself realize that his gesture was exposing him to the danger of being ridiculed by the others? A trickle of pink drool hung from his chin, and suddenly it was a crimson scarf rolled around his neck. The child in this finery turned black with ferocity. His face was contorted. As for me, my anguish, in order not to choke me, could only explode in a kind of joyous sob through which I saw the crimson, unable to hold fast, fall with shame and emotion on that handsome athlete's arm. For the space of a second, Villeroy was shaken by a signal of alarm. Finally, there was a rift of light. With the back of his sleeve he wiped off the blood that was mixed with tears, snot and foam, and charged at old Guépin head first. "He sailed into him." He beat him up as if carried away by the spirited drive of this expression. That was how I beat up Charlot during the medical examination ten days after meeting Bulkaen.

I have said that I had to perform a striking feat, not so much to compel Bulkaen's recognition as to be raised to his tragic level. I had been on the alert for the pettiest circumstances: a mispronounced word, an angry gesture, a guy brushing against me, a wink, in order to make them continue in a fight leading to the other's prayer or my death. It was during the medical examination that I met the kid known as The Wasp. He didn't get out of the way fast enough as I hotfooted it down the stairs, and I jostled him. He simply made a mild comment, but I "worked myself up."

"Shut your mouth," I said.

"What's the matter with you, Jean . . . You were the one . . ."

"Shut your mouth, I tell you, or you'll get it in the puss."

I had stopped for a fraction of a second, being at the turn of the stairs. I pushed him violently against the wall and ran down to the corridor on the ground floor where the inmates were lined up, awaiting their turn to see the doctor. Under the impetus of my momentum and inner speed I found myself facing Charlot. Bulkaen was near him. A sunbeam fell through the glass of the roof and sent shadows scurrying down the corridor. Charlot's authority lay in the curtness of his gestures and the comfort of his voice. When I arrived, he moved to the right, behind Bulkaen, and I was astounded to see the spread fingers of Charlot's rough and gentle hand pressing on the kid's left hip. I was stabbed to the heart. Rage spiralled up within me. I stood there motionless, ten steps away. The hand moved. It grazed the cloth with a kind of light caress, then fell away. Finally my chest swelled. I breathed more freely. I felt a bit ashamed at having been wrong, and perhaps my eyes grew dim at the knowledge that Heaven was carrying its solicitude to the point of gratifying me with false prodigies—with an illusion of evil and the knowledge that this evil is an illusion —when I realized it was the shadow of another hand, with spread fingers, that was playing on my friend's hip. But hardly

had the shadow drifted away when I heard Charlot say to his
attentive cronies:

". . . and, boys, the number of women I can take on. Four
times a day don't scare me."

I snickered, for I had walked up to them, and I said:

"You're piling it on." He turned around.

"I'm telling you it's so, Jean. When it comes to that, I'm
supernatural."

I hated Charlot ever since I thought he had been sharp
enough to discover the subject of my reveries, but that day my
hatred was aggravated by my thinking he had been so cruel as
to have Bulkaen at the back of his mind throughout the conversation, and I smouldered with repressed hatred. In addition,
I was afraid of seeming dull to Bulkaen because I never joked,
and I had to refrain from joking because when I laughed I lost
my self-control and ran the risk of revealing the affected side
of my nature. I forced myself to adopt a bearing of great
severity which made people take me for a boor, whereas any
tough could kid around without endangering his prestige. I
answered:

"You're supernatural? Ah, I get it. You get the angels to
help you."

I kept my hands in my pockets. He saw that I was trying to
rattle him. He cut short my irony, which required an
immediate reply that would end the matter.

"You heard what I said! Call me a liar!"

"Right, you're a liar."

But as soon as he started the sentence "When it comes to
that, I'm supernatural," I repeated to myself, "I'm going to
sail into him! The little prick! I'm going to sail into him!" I
repeated the phrase mentally, twice. Excited and uplifted by it,
I didn't wait for him to hit first. I sprang at him. And we
fought furiously, in the presence of Bulkaen, who was perhaps
amused. Whenever I was about to give in, the memory and
soul of Villeroy guarded me. I had the better of it because
Charlot fought fairly and I was vicious, as at Mettray. In my

fury, I could have killed him. I had the muscles and youth of
Villeroy, and not of Divers. I borrowed, I stole the beauty of
his stances. A lock of blond hair, taken from God knows
where, fell over my eyes. I was quick as lightning. I had to lick
Charlot because Villeroy would have licked him. It was with
Villeroy's shiny weapons and his failings that I fought. The
guards grabbed me, Charlot was carried away.

The guards rushed over to pick up Guépin. No one dared
take Villeroy to the quarter by force. He was told to go there
himself. He went alone, after shaking my hand. I realized that
something was expected of me, and so, utilizing the teachings
of my big shot, I took a sock at Guépin from behind. He
reeled, but he had time enough to turn around, and we went at
each other: perhaps the shame of being thrashed by an old
man who was still quite agile. I was a sorry sight when I
entered the quarter, but I stood as upright as Villeroy, who
was two yards in front of me.

We spent a month there, he in a cell and I in the drill squad.
When he got out, his rank of elder brother of Family B was
intact. He was feared. Among the other kids, Villeroy had the
gift of carrying things off with great dash; his proclamations,
even the slightest of them, had the sparkle of the proclamations
to the Grand Army. Once when he was asked his opinion
about a fight between Deloffre and Rey and what he thought
about the way Deloffre had fought, he answered very coolly,
"I can't say. On the one hand, I have no right to say anything
against a guy who fights like a wildcat, and, on the other, I
can't stand the guy. I'd feel sick to my stomach if I said
anything good about him. I'd rather keep my mouth shut."

The four or five big shots of the family also had their
chickens, whom everyone respected, except, occasionally, a
solitary, irreverent, insensitive and upright youngster who
wasn't afraid to say to me, "If you strut around that way, it's
because of your guy."

In my book, it's Harcamone.

On the docks, a crown of rope which slants because it was

carelessly coiled covers a bitt with a heavy plait, with a tarpaulin or cap: in like manner, Harcamone, who was always unaffectionate and alien, was capped on Sundays with a flat beret.

My pimp forced my mouth open with his tongue. I licked his shaven head, which should have been hairy, and I felt my face being beaten by the nervous, curly blond locks he ought to have had. I fell asleep for a few minutes and was stabbed by dreams more heart-rending than those of the sleeping gunner stretched out on the rammed member of his field-piece. Later on, though without waiting too long, we loved each other more artfully. Before leaving for the shops—he worked in the sabot shop and I in the brush shop—we shook hands, each with a smile of what I then thought was complicity but which. as I now realize, was one of tenderness and confidence. During recreation, his duties as elder brother and his dignity as a big shot obliged him to hold court, and when I sometimes approached the circle of men, he would lay his hand on my shoulder. The big shots got used to my presence. In order not to be unworthy of such a man, I overdid my virile posturing. I was helped a number of times by my irritation, which I knew how to transform into the generous anger that generates courage. One day, in the yard of Family B, a little tramp started joking, quite amiably, about the colour of my smock. He said, as I remember, "It's like Villeroy's eyes." I laughed, but my laughter was a little too shrill, I realized it, so did the others, they were all watching me. I felt foolish. I grew more and more irritated. My heart was pounding away. I felt hot and cold at the same time. Finally I began to tremble and I was even afraid my trembling might be visible to the pimps. They saw it. My agitation increased. I was losing self-control. And Divers was present. Divers, with whom I was already secretly in love, was a witness of my agitation, the only cause of which was the poor quality of my nervous system. I suddenly realized that I had to use this agitation, to make it look as if it were due to anger. With a slight shift, the signs of my confusion could all become signs of a splendid anger. I had only to transpose. I clenched my teeth and moved my cheek-bones. My face must have taken on a fierce expression. I let myself go. My trembling became the trembling of the anger that benefited from my sickly agitation. I knew I could risk any gesture. It would have extraordinary breadth, but that breadth would no longer be ridiculous, for it would be caused and sustained by the anger itself. I pulled myself together and tore into the kid, who was still laughing at my smock, at me, and perhaps at my confusion.

Whenever a big shot who was on the war path started heading for me, the fear of blows, physical fear, made me back away and double up. It was so natural a movement that I could never avoid it, but my will made me change its meaning. Before long, I fell into the habit, when stepping back and bending over, of putting my hands on my thighs or bent knees, in the posture of a man about to dash forward, a posture whose virtue I felt as soon as I assumed it. I had the necessary vigour and my face became surly. My posture was no longer due to the jitters but was a tactical manoeuvre. I would use only my right hand when I pissed; the left one stayed in my pocket. When I stood motionless, I kept my legs spread. I whistled with my fingers at first, and afterward with my tongue and fingers. All these gestures soon became natural, and it was owing to them that I was peaceably admitted, upon the death of Villeroy (upon his departure for Toulon), to the society of the toughs. Bulkaen, on the other hand, was a little man of whom Mettray had made a girl for the big shots' use, and all his gestures were the sign of nostalgia for his plundered, destroyed virility. I cannot do better than compare myself to the child I dreamed of being, some abandoned youngster of remote origin, diabolical, a gitano, for whom complicated machinations involving the theft of documents and murders plotted with the help of a daring adventurer made it possible to enter a noble house that was protected by its tradition and arms. I became the centre, the keystone, of a

strict family system. On my sixteen-year-old shoulders would
rest all the glamour of the genealogies of which I would be the
issue and provisional end. I would be a big shot among big
shots, and it would no longer be known that I was only a
chicken. Come what may, I had to conceal my deep-seated
weakness, because all the same you sometimes have to "put up
a front" and "fight it out." Nor did I ever accept anything that
was given to me out of kindness. But in that I was helped by
my proud nature, which refused all gifts, though you can live
comfortably when you have freed yourself from pride and even
though there is pleasure in knowing that you reap an advantage from a jerk whom you favour with an ironic thanks. But
along with the sweet feeling of being free from grim pride, I
gradually became aware of the unambiguous and disturbing
thought that I had taken the first step which leads to begging,
to flabby attitudes—which a very strong, very virile thug can
allow himself because he knows he will quickly regain his
rigour—and as soon as I let myself put on the slightest act in
order to get or be given something, the soul of a beggar was
born to me, and it was bound to be fed and fattened by a host
of petty capitulations. I had opened the door to a new life. I
had to barricade myself.

The evening . . . We wanted to sleep together a whole night
long, coiled up and entangled in each other until morning, but
as that was impossible we invented one-hour nights, while
above us, in the dormitory that was woven with tackle to which
the hammocks were attached, the night-light which burned like
a lantern, the surge of sleeping, the steel of the cigarette-
lighter striking the flint (we would say: "Listen to the
alarm-bell"), the whisper of a youngster, the moan of a jerk
whom the big shots called "a poor martyr," and the exhalations of the night, made us castaways of a dream. Then we
would unglue our mouths: it was the awakening from the
short night of love. Each would stretch his limbs and climb
back into his hammock and we would go to sleep, lying head to
foot, for the hammocks were so arranged. When I was alone,

after Villeroy had left, I sometimes conjured him up beneath the covers, but the sadness of his leaving soon lost its original meaning and became a kind of chronic melancholy, like a misty autumn, and that autumn is the basic season of my life, for it often sets in even now. After the sunshine, in order that my heart, which is hurt by such brilliance, may rest, I curl up within myself so as to return to the wet forest, the dead leaves, the mists, and I enter a mansion where a log-fire is blazing in a high fireplace. The wind to which I listen is more lulling than the one which moans in the real firs of a real park. It rests me from the wind that vibrates the tackle of the galley. This autumn is more intense and insidious than real autumn, external autumn, for in order to enjoy it I must invent a detail or a sign every second and must linger over it. I create it every instant. I dwell for minutes on the idea of rain, on the idea of a rusty gate, or of damp moss, of mushrooms, of a cape puffed out by the wind. When such a season clouds me, every nascent feeling, instead of rising up furiously, subsides, and that is why there was no violence in my jealousy with regard to Bulkaen. When I wrote to him, I wanted my letters to be sprightly, trivial, indifferent. In spite of myself, I imbued them with my love. I would have liked to make it seem powerful, sure of itself and sure of me, but I infused it, despite myself, with all my anxiety. I could have rewritten my letter, but sloth prevented me. I call sloth a kind of feeling that says to me: don't start over, there's no point. It is something within me which knows very well that it would be useless for me to take pains to appear strong and display self-mastery, for my wild nature will always be visible through a thousand and one cracks. No, I have lost in advance. I shall therefore voice my love. I now trust only in the beauty of my song. Whom did Bulkaen love? He seemed to remember Rocky in too great detail. But Rocky was about to disappear from our universe, and I am not sure it displeased me to know that they loved each other. It was hard for me to tell whether Bulkaen was in any way intimate with other big shots, for a queer's gestures in

the presence of his man are never equivocal. The meeting of
two friends in public never occasions a shocking gesture: they
shake hands and their talk is free and easy. I therefore was
unable to tell whether there was an understanding between
Bulkaen and the men from which I was excluded. I think that
the hour of my love struck when he asked, in a group of big
shots:

"What's daybreak?"

I said:

"It's dawn."

Someone continued:

"It's the fatal hour."

"Oh, I'm not kidding myself," said Lou with a smile. "I
know I'll get it."

He had said it so simply that the grandeur of being
predestined went hand in hand with that simplicity. He
transcended me and, had he asked me to, I would have given
him the kid then and there. When I saw Bulkaen again, he
seemed not to remember that I had fought. He made no
allusion to it, and I myself made no attempt to draw any pride
from my victory, though I felt like doing so. It seemed to me,
however, that the mere demonstration of my force had been
enough, and I dared not run the risk of hitting my victim. I
had the advantage of being more vigorous, since I was better
fed, but I wasnt sure that, even if he had been beaten, he
would have been willing to give in. Actually, in order to
achieve my purpose I had to use force, power, and not violence, and hitting him would have been proof of my violence
and a confession of weakness. Besides, wouldn't Bulkaen, who
was used to the violence of the inmates of Fontevrault and
Mettray, love me all the more if I used mildness? He had, to
be sure, sent me a note in which he said amiably that I had
been violent, but perhaps he said it in order to please me,
knowing that the big shots like to be considered brutal. I
thought for a moment of reminding him of the fight, but as he
was two steps higher, he towered over me, and as I looked up

to him when I spoke, at the first word: "When . . ." my voice took on an intonation such as might be used in addressing a live statue, and I tried to go up three stairs, passing between him and the wall of the stairway. I thus made a quick movement, but perhaps he thought I wanted to kiss him and, nimbly dashing up a few steps himself, he ducked and laughingly cried out: "What are you doing about Hersir?" I caught up with him on the next landing, where we bumped into a guard who was on the way down:

"Together again, those two," he grumbled. "Get the hell back to your shops or I'll report you."

We held our tongues and disappeared, Bulkaen to the right and I to the left. I definitely felt that my love was endangered not by Rocky but by Hersir. I had met Pierrot Bulkaen eight days before and had been at Fontevrault for twenty-five, and Harcamone had been waiting thirty-five days to be executed.

Mettray. I don't know much about Evil, but we must indeed have been angels to remain poised above our own crimes. The gravest insult among toughs—it is very often punished by death—is the word "cocksucker," and Bulkaen had chosen to be precisely what that vilest of words designates. He had even decided that it would be what was most personal, most precious in his life, since in prison he was first of all, before being a crasher, a pal, a "regular guy"—and though he was all that—he was first of all "a guy who does a blow-job." When you saw him, with his usual scowl of disgust, spit the words "little fag" at a jerk, you would never have thought that he himself was a chicken. Thus, there do exist fellows who voluntarily, and out of choice, are, in their heart of hearts, what is expressed by the most scurrilous insult, which they use to humiliate their opponent. Bulkaen was an angel for managing to maintain his balance so elegantly above his own abjectness.

Children who have been given a taste of sex at an early age are serious-minded, their features are hard, their mouths are distended by a repressed sorrow that makes their lips quiver delicately, their eyes are icy. I noticed this among the minors at Fresnes Prison whom I used to meet when we took our walk and all of whom had been between our thighs, and among the kids who frequent the Montmartre bars and cafés where friendship in all its force and fragility was revealed to me by a thousand and one gestures. But in order to see these children more clearly, call up the dreams provoked by your reading of pulp fiction. Michel Zévaco, Xavier de Montépin, Ponson du Terrail and Pierre Decourcelle have furtively introduced into their works the light, flexible figures of the mysterious pages who strewed death and love. Those pages wielded daggers and poisons with a delightful smile, with the casualness of fatality. A curtain or hanging or door of a wall, of which you caught a glimpse for a few lines, hid them too soon. They will appear later. And you, in order to get to them more quickly, though without admitting it to yourself, you skipped the pages, regretting that the books were not composed solely of the following matter: the adventures of adolescents in doublets unlaced at the supple, sturdy neck, wearing trunk hose, the fork of which bulges with their balls, and with the penis compressed so that it does not jut out when they pass the servant-girl or princess whom they will not screw until evening. The pulp-novelists have no doubt secretly dreamed those adventures, and they have written their books in order to suggest them, to give them the presence of a watermark, and they would be greatly astonished if they were told that the Pardaillans and One-eye were pretexts for handling those swift demons who are as nimble as trout. I ask you to conjure up their bodies and faces, for it is they who reappear, with a rose in their fingers and a whistle on their lips, in the breeches and smocks of the colonists. They will be those of whom one says: "It wouldn't be much of a loss if . . ." They will be Bulkaen himself, and he more than the others. The slightest questions, in order to be dealt with, required a stern mouth and cold eyes, attentive hands deep in pockets, stiff postures suddenly broken up by a tigerlike suppleness. All the adornments which my language glorifies and sometimes creates: Divers' member, his eyes, his gestures, his hands, the veil of his voice, all these adornments cloud over. Divers grows dim while Bulkaen remains luminous. He does not seem to be staggered by Harcamone's staggering presence and death-struggle. His gestures are as light and his laughter as joyous as ever. On neither his face nor arms is there any of the sadness I thought I saw on those of the other prisoners.

The matter of the leggings had been going on for a long time. During his stay at Mettray, every colonist contrived to amass a treasure. It was made up of what had been obtained by confiscation, fraud, theft, inheritance and transaction. Although everyone received the same equipment when he arrived, it was quickly transformed, depending on whether he was clever or lacked boldness. Either the youngster's sabots remained just as heavy, his smock just as new, and his tie just as sharp-edged as when he received them, in which case, he was a jerk; or else he swapped it all for personal effects that were less hick. Within a few days, he had sharpened his sabots with glass, knocked his beret out of shape, and opened a second pocket, which the guards called a false pocket, on the left side of his pants. The other big shots helped him. He had his case, his tinder, which was made of a burnt handkerchief, his flint, and the steel swivel. For the distinguishing mark of the big shot was this small piece of steel with which he struck the flint to light cigarette butts on the sly. As they advanced in authority and seniority, the Toughs grew rich on gifts and thefts, on confiscations, exchanges. When the big shots left the Colony, they dispersed their treasure among their friends, and we could thus see old-timers with trousers white as snow, light and supple as a result of washings, amazingly delicate clogs and sabots which very often had been split in fights but which they preserved, like a precious Chinese porcelain vase, by piercing the cracked parts together with hooks or brass wire. Some pairs were ten years old. They had been worn only by big shots. They were famous, they had a name. When studding them with iron—for the clogs were studded—one took infinite precautions. There were also the smocks. When they were new, they were stiff and bright blue. Those of the big shots were distinguished by their suppleness and the paleness of the faded blue. As for the leggings, they were the subject of numerous quarrels, for they were taken back in the spring and re-issued every winter.

The big shots arranged with the elder brother to get first choice. It was among the big shots that fights broke out. The leggings were supposed to show the shape of solid, powerful calves, which looked even more imposing because the trousers were bunched up underneath.

"Riton, keep in step."

"I am in step."

"No, my boy, you're not."

"Come and make me keep in step!"

In order to fall into step Rilton would have had to take a little hop, a kind of dance step. He loathed the thought of hopping. So he added:

"It's not the dancing period!"

Divers went over. Riton removed his hands, which he kept like all the big shots, flat on his stomach, between his pants and shirt. Divers didn't let him complete the movement. He suddenly bent and slackened his body, he kicked Riton in the chest with his left foot and shot an uppercut at him with his right fist. No sooner did Riton drop to the ground than Divers went at him again with his feet and fists, in keeping with the inexorable method of Mettray.

The pace of the boys who were being punished had slackened. The line began to sway. Out of the corner of his eye, Divers saw what was happening. He spun around three times with a kind of waltz movement that carried him four yards away from his victim and, despite his panting, he said, in a tone of voice a little too high because he must have had to breathe harder in order to stop puffing:

"And the rest of you, put some life in it! One . . . two! . . .

One . . . two! . . . One . . . two! . . . Hun . . . two! . . . Hun
. . . two! . . ."

Without realizing it, he was uttering the Mettray war cry. I
smiled. He must have seen my smile and understood it, but he
did not respond. And he stood there motionless in the corner
of the room, in his Tabernacle, with only his voice and eyes
alive.

Let us be astonished that a young man is handsome from
head to foot, that the curve of his lashes is as graceful as that
of his toenails, that the weight of his hams is in proportion to
the weight of his jaw . . . The intention is perceptible: it was
evidently to make a beautiful thing with a given number of
beautiful things. Divers had that absolute beauty. His voice
was grave, but I mean this, primarily, in the sense of gravity.
In addition, it was firm, solid, so that a long speech could be
hacked out of it—unlike mine, which breaks at a trifle—and
his voice is not, as sometimes happens, tacked on to him, but is
composed of the same hard matter as his body and the pattern
of his gestures to which I felt it so assimilated that I am still
unable to dissociate them. His voice composed his very cells. It
had exactly the same severe tone as his flesh and his will. A
few days ago, Divers was singing. His voice has remained full
and throaty. When the song was over, I realized that another
more distant one was being sung during the first, which kept it
from being heard; then, the second one stopped, so that
another even more distant one could be heard. Each was
different from the other and appeared when the preceding and
closer one ceased, somewhat as, when a veil is drawn away,
you see another underneath which was invisible when the first
was taut, then a third, and so on ad infinitum, veils increasingly light. In like manner, when a song stopped you could
perceive that there was another beneath it and then another
beneath the latter and so on to the curved infinity of the
prison. It was not until three songs had already been drawn off
that Harcamone perhaps heard, far away, *Ramona* and
recognized the slightly tremolo voice. That mournful voice is

another flaw through which Divers' deep tenderness escapes from his toughness. He sings silly tunes. At first I suffered when I heard his voice carry ugly songs over the prison yard, but gradually the very beauty of the voice was imparted to the tunes, and these tunes excite me when I hum them. As for Harcamone, he never sings. In addition to all this was the fact that Divers had been drummer and band-leader at Mettray, that is, in the Sunday parade he marched in the first rank of the drummers, but to the right. Bear in mind that he was not the only one in front. He was to the right. He was in the rank and yet not in it. The only way of expressing the excitement that this aroused in me is to compare him to a singer in a cabaret who sings, not on the stage but, without getting up, at the table where she has been chatting. He and she are the one who is suddenly designated. The one who stands out. He handled the drumsticks with a masterful firmness that distilled a song from his marching and playing. At times, during the Sunday parade in the presence of the director, he was slightly off to the side, but that was intentional on his part, for he never broke the line. When the band marched by us to take its place in front, toward the chapel, I saw him press onward from the end of the world, impassive and solemn, carrying his drum, which thundered and sang. That joyous music accompanied his acts, approved the maddest, foulest of them. Music is the approval of action. It is joyous and drunk when it approves drama. His drum applauded him. On his shaved head sat his blue Sunday beret, wide and flat as a pancake, weighted with the yellow tuft of the musicians (one feels that the yellow will powder them with its pollen) and so soft and floppy that it almost fell over his eyes and right ear with ambiguous elegance. His thighs hit against the drum, and his legs, with their firm calves, perfectly outlined by the khaki leggings, which fave a scaly effect, carried him forward. It was clear that he loved that children's game which leads processions to some joyous or dire festival which he still seems to be directing. Even as a trusty he sometimes plays in the void, recapturing the grace of his adolescence. I cannot help but mention too those moments during the walk when, instead of going straight up to the room, he huddled in a dark corner of the stairway where, as we passed in front of him who stood there laughing, every colonist and I myself had the sudden, brief revelation of the mysterious lure of prisons, and Bulkaen stood against the wall in the same way. Ah, despite your loving me, you too-handsome child, whom does your beauty love in secret? I want to know what other beauty, perhaps inaccessible to yours, which I see slightly clouded with sadness, but perhaps moved by yours, though neither you nor anyone else—except me if I want to go to the trouble of finding out—can tell. It may well be that Lou or Divers or Harcamone, or others more dangerous for me because less potent, have been struck full in the face by the explosions of his laughter.

Divers loved his drum with its accessories, the adornments and leather fittings (I am always excited by the beating of a drum, and my body still vibrates with a muffled echo when I repeat to myself what Divers murmured to me one evening as his mouth rested on the folds of my ear:

"I'd like to tear off a piece with you! ")

All the wounds that those budding thugs inflicted on me have scarred over, but this word itself tells that there was blood.

In the disciplinary cell I can very often chat with Divers. His position as trusty makes it possible for him to come up to me. Facing the wall, I talk to him. When I saw him the day I was sent there, he was at first astounded to learn that I had risked death to see him. It was a few days later, when he was talking to me about it, that I said to him:

"After fifteen years, I still thought about you. It was in order to see you that I swallowed the phenobarbital."

This cry of love moved him, for he had remained as simple and gentle with me as in the past. I also took advantage of the presence of one of the more decent supervisors to remind him rapidly of my former love for him. He believed me:

"But now," I said, "it's pure friendship."

The number of convicts per cell has tripled, even quadrupled, because of the lack of room in the prisons. In the disciplinary quarter, every cell contained two men, for the night. The same evening that I spoke to him, Divers managed to take the place of the man who shared the cell with me at night. When we were locked in, we chatted like pals. I told him about my life and he told me about his, and that he had spent six months at Calvi with Villeroy:

"He was quite solid on you, you know. We often talked about you. He thought a lot of you."

"To be solid" was the expression used at Mettray to designate a big shot's friendship with a chicken. "He's solid on him" meant: he took him on. And now, after fifteen years, Divers repeats it to me when talking about Villeroy. He tells me about Calvi and what fun it would have been for me to make love freely to mutinous seamen. He spoke again at great length about Villeroy, but a surprising thing happened: as he went on talking, the image I had retained of my big shot grew dimmer instead of clearer. Divers adorned him with qualities of which I was unaware. He referred several times to his powerful arms. Now, Villeroy had very ordinary arms. Finally he dwelt on the way he dressed and then on his whang, which he said must have been something special since he had won and kept me. Gradually the old image of Villeroy gave way to another one, a stylized one. I thought at first that the colonist had changed, but I realized from something Divers said that he was talking mainly about the Villeroy of Mettray. He wasn't joking. I didn't dare think he was in love with him. Finally, tired from walking within bounds all day, I wanted to kiss his cheeks and go to bed alone, but he grabbed me in his arms and hugged me tight. I broke away:

"We're pals," I said.

"But that makes no difference."

"I think it does."

"Come on."

He hugged me tighter.

"You're crazy. We're not going to fuck around, especially here. If we're caught, they'll give us another month."

"Just tonight."

"No no, stay there. Let's be pals."

"But I said it makes no difference. On the contrary.'

He kept smiling as he spoke, with his mouth almost pressed against my face, and when he let go of me, he urged me to give in as eagerly as he had in the past, though he had known at the time that I was Villeroy's kid. And in that eagerness, in that ardour, I sensed, with a rather slight uneasiness, a kind of deep despair, which cropped out at the surface of him, a despair that made him very simple and unsure. The porcelain of which the boy was made had a crack in it, I don't know where. Despite his smile, I discerned an appeal in his voice and gestures. We made love all night. Our shaved heads rolled round each other, with our rough cheeks scraping, and I would have accorded him caresses that I had bestowed only upon Villeroy were it not that my love for Bulkaen, which was in its most intense period, kept me from unrestrained voluptuousness, but nevertheless that night made Divers think I was deeply in love with him, for I was trying to drown the grief that had been caused me that very evening by Bulkaen's voice when he spoke from his window to Botchako, who was locked up a little farther off. From the big room, where all was silent, we all heard the dove-call which he made with his mouth and which was answered by the same signal, and above our heads the conversation, which I could not make out, began in the early darkness without my being able to intervene or to join in it. You know what the pangs of jealousy are like. I was jealous, and it was my excruciating anxiety that made me accept Divers' proposal; and despair, with the fury it arouses, made him believe in the passion of his ardour. For the first time since I knew Bulkaen I managed to come, and perhaps I did because it seemed I was merely carrying out an act which should have been performed—and perhaps had been performed in desire—at Mettray. My love for him solaced me, which proves that my quest for pleasure was always a quest for love. It pained me to know that Bulkaen spoke to Botchako in the darkness, but I hoped that their talk was an illusion which a bit of reflection would destroy, for at Mettray a scene in which the play of voices created a certain confusion was rather quickly dispelled. Besides, what had I to fear from a possible friendship between Bulkaen and a few bums, and between him and Rocky? I had already suspected, before he asked me to write a poem about the love between two bums, that there was a connection between his friendship for me and the breaking up of an older liaison; I then realized that it involved a dramatic separation: his man was being taken away from him, but that liaison had long since been undermined by a host of sly little facts which I sensed when Bulkaen said to me "that he was fed up with bums, that he had always been fooled, that he hated their guts . . ." Rocky did not seem to me much of a danger.

I loved Villeroy with tranquillity. My love was all the stronger—that is, my confidence in Villeroy was strong—in that I was afraid of being consigned, abandoned, to faggotry. I loved a man to the point of getting into his skin, of adopting his ways, and I became quite adept at discovering in others the mannerisms one steals from the person one loves. Hell has degrees, so does love, and I reached its lowest circle and its heights when, in the quarter, where I was putting in a week of punishment for having insulted the supervisor of the brush shop, I heard, through a skylight, Villeroy's voice instructing another boy who was being punished and who was to be let out the following day to tell Rival, a bruiser in Family A, that he was still thinking about him. Jealousy again maddened my heart and dried my mouth. I loved my man! My very depths must have screamed it. On the spot I became what any fag is without his big shot: a temple of anguish. And then I quickly realized that Villeroy was not being punished and that the voice from the wall could not be his. That voice was gentle and, if I may say so, superficially gentle and moving, but swollen with manly serenity. It reminded me of the light floating silk of the trouser legs of certain Russian and negro musicians who make the cloth ripple by manipulating their pockets. Delicate though it be and stirred by gentle waves, the silk conceals the heaviest male gear, which dents it and can sometimes split it and appear in the pride of nakedness. I can also say of the voice that it was the beating of a drum behind a cloth. As Villeroy was not being punished, my lump of anguish melted. But it quickly filled my throat again. Its size became immense. The voice I had heard was Stokley's. He had been imitating Villeroy. With amazing speed I remembered having imitated the gestures and, despite myself, the voice of a hoodlum with whom I had been in love. Stokley was a big shot in Family A; there could be no question of even a hidden liaison between Villeroy and him, but I realized how secretly he must have loved Villeroy to have stolen his voice. And I imagined him submissive to my man. The betrayal was killing me. Finally I calmed down. Villeroy's voice could not be imitated, and if I thought that Stokley *had* imitated it, I was mistaken. His voice was actually very husky and raucous, for he was a teamster on the institution's farm and dealt with horses, but the echo of the cell softened it by swelling it, the thickness of the walls filtered it and made it tremble slightly. I slowly realized this and to some extent even invented it so as to comfort myself.

During drill, the men spat at random, sometimes on a fellow inmate who was marching by. They upbraided each other with oaths of astounding hardness and beauty, but I was sure that somewhere inside those golden-necked brutes, perhaps between the shoulder-blades, was hidden a rift of tenderness, for I had noticed the delicacy of the expressions relating to the life of the filthiest sailors. Those bruisers dare say, when the galley leaves port: "the galley's off," and also: "to dip sails," and: "standing rigging," and also this jewel: "to get under way," and they call the interior of the sheathing "the fur." And the

most violent of them hold these fragile poems between their
teeth as they sometimes hold in their fingers the twigs and
threads which will be the masts and gear of a schooner
imprisoned in the crystal of a flask. And the sadness of the sea,
shattering the peace we had regained, gave us all pathetic eyes.
The wind beat against the sails. The oaths clung to the gear,
from which men fell to the deck, and the most extraordinary
view of this which I recall is that of a sailor's curly head
trembling in the wind and mist and with the rocking of the
boat, and framed by a buoy which was itself entangled with a
rope, and it was that same head, in a similar buoy, which was
tattooed on Pierre Bulkaen's left shoulder. That was the
surprise he had promised me and which he had once shown me
on the stairs when he suddenly opened his jacket and shirt:

"Look, Jean, take a squint at your little guy."

I have not yet told you anything about the pirates' garb. It
was merely a kind of long pair of drawers, but pulled up above
the knees. The torso was bare. Though captures in the South
Seas were sometimes colourful, fate never allowed the men to
be rich enough to clothe themselves. Often, when they were all
huddled together in the hold, the sight was so beautiful that if
anyone had tried to photograph them, the plate would have
registered only a rose. By that flight across the sky I escape
from death. A trigger opens a trap-door through which I fall
into a vengeful, imaginary world.

At night, here, in Fontevrault regained, we let our hearts
and pricks sob, here where our pimps once grieved as we do.
But we did not suspect that the Prison had its bosses and
chickens. Could it possibly think about us? Moreover, in the
little village of Fontevrault, a slate-roofed village of a thousand
souls (if I may use the expression, knowing that the place is
inhabited by two hundred turnkeys and their wives, women
who dare say of us among themselves: "They're just lousy
riff-raff."), the Prison occupies the site and has inherited the
importance of the former abbey, and every convict, when, in
summertime, he sees looming above the patrol walls the green

treetops on the hills surrounding the local spring, recognizes, within himself, in his very humility, the proud soul of a monk of old. The men would tell each other stories about their life on earth, which was also a nocturnal life in which they went off on expeditions with throbbing hearts. They would say, "I took the feather and the blocks," that is, the jemmy and the wedges which were used in forcing doors. Concerning a woman who returned unexpectedly to an apartment he was visiting, a crasher says, because he beat her up until she fell: "I spread her out." And a pimp, to some contemptible rival: "Sit down on my cock and let's talk business." Another, a newcomer among them, who misused an expression which meant "to eat pussy," said one morning, meaning that he had jerked off, "I kept pulling back my eyelid."

All the delinquents first learned French. Later, they heard argot and repeated the words. They were young, and the words charmed them just as they did me. But whereas it took me a long time to be imbued with the charm and then to exploit it by talking argot, they, when very young. instinctively took over the charm and gave up French. They understood it and yielded to its grace completely. It took me a long time to find myself, a long time to enter into my nature, which I discovered, after much effort, only later, and I am living in my thirties what the hoodlums lived at twenty.

I even heard talk about "periods of love" in such a tone that I realized the expression was to be taken in at least two of the senses which it can have, and I still wonder, when I hear words which have three or four different and sometimes conflicting meanings, what worlds are confused with the usual world we think we have named, though we have no more named it than we have another, and sometimes a third. Who within us addresses that universe and mentions it? We sensed from here that similar and even finer words flowed from the mouth of the Golden Voice with the rush of smoke that rolls from the lungs of a smoker's broad chest, and I was shaken to my depths by the thrill that must stir young men with heavy voices when they feel that round, warm voice rolling from their throat through their open or parted lips. These deep voices (deep not in timbre, but owing to a muffled hum which makes them roll and vibrate softly, and even growl slightly) are often to be found in toughs. They betray buried riches which would be envied by that lady who wished to adorn her vocabulary with diamonds and pearls. These deep riches are the natural sign of pimps. I accept them, along with what they indicate, but though it may be true that a pimp can be recognized by his turtle-neck sweater, his hat, his shoes, his cap and, in the old days, his ear-rings, we wonder why this particular attire, which was the product of a general and frivolous fashion, was considered by them to be desirable and why they adopted and preserved it until each detail, even when isolated, became the symbol of the pimp, the most brutal of men, he whom the kids, and they themselves, admire above all: the man who has not been taken in by love. The knight stronger than love. But what pimp is this faultless knight? I recall Rey, a good-looking but plucky little tough. There was no reason to say he wasn't a man, for his gestures, voice and bearing were tough. It was only the words he uttered which tried, unsuccessfully, to be tender, and here again we see a sign of virility. He was a man. But who or what was responsible for the taste which made him choose that fancy, fawn-coloured corduroy shirt-jacket, which was not the kind of thing pimps wore but which he was wearing when he arrived at Fontevrault? Hence, it is rare in prison for a man not to reveal his inner delicacy in one way or another, but the question of delinquents' attire is not settled. I would like to know why bell-bottom trousers have been in fashion among us so long, though the lower part is as ample as an evening-gown, and in fact lots of fellows even widen it with an inlay so that the trousers cover the shoes. Why do we take in our waist so much? Perhaps it is not enough to trace the origin of this to the navy by explaining that sailors were once pimps in sea-ports, but this explanation is nevertheless disturbing, for though sailors who were discharged and became

pimps and hustlers might have been nostalgic for their garb
and have wanted to go back to it—and recapture at the same
time the poetry of sailors' movements—by altering their pants
and jackets, it should be pointed out that the garb of pimps
antedates that of gobs and goes back to that of the seamen of
old, of the crews of galleys, of the Knights of the Mooring.
Like us, the men of Fontevrault opened their skylights in the
evening, and they were surprised, were astonished, to see the
thousand skylights of the section opposite and to know the
happiness of seeing themselves behind its walls since they were
those who saw them and those who were behind them. They
would stand there for a second, amazed by the suddenly
withdrawn horizon, and they said good evening to each other
from window to window. They knew the diminutives of each
other's Christian name: "Jeannot, Jo, Ricou, Dédé, Polo" and
also those light, fragrant nicknames which were poised on the
pimps' shoulders, ready to resume their flight, and which I like
to think were words of love whose secret was still unknown to
us at Mettray where the boys called out—as from friend to
friend, cruelly and blunderingly by name—passionate declara-
tions which they make to each other, if they do not scream
them, at night. They knew only those names and the sound of
their voices. In the darkness, the half-open windows tossed
titles of novels to be exchanged. Thus there floated beneath the
stars, from Fontevrault to Mettray: *Princess Billion. The
Rope around the Neck, Under the Dagger, The Gypsy's
Tarots, The Blonde Sultana.* Carried by the wind from their
open mouths, the words flew like streamers from a shroud of
mourning on a funeral ship. They knew only their voices, and
perhaps that was how crushes began. For voices love other
voices. Our encaged gods, their heads looking out of the open
skylights, adored each other in like manner. At times, a
younger one, a boy of twenty, sings a hooligan song, as
Bulkaen most often did before he was killed. In *Nocturnes,*
this word itself rhymes with "funeral urns," which are, in the
song, the hearts of hoodlums. We listen to it, a song that might

shatter the walls. We listen to it fervently. If he bungles a high note, someone yells: "Bye-bye, bugger."[1] He doesn't mean that he assumes the singer has a wild rose tattooed on his thigh or that his shoulder is branded with a *fleur de lis*, but that he hopes the child will be entered. The voices that were locked up at night in every cell of Fontevrault must have been as heavy and hollow as that which is singing this evening "Leave and don't look back." This song disturbs me more than any other because when I was a young colonist I brought it with me from the outside, probably from Petite Roquette where some child had introduced it. Upon my arrival, the oldtimers felt me out and they saw immediately that I would "fall." They let me alone that evening, bundled up as I was in my stiff new clothes, on condition that I sing.

"What tonsil number do you know?"

Their argot was half-baked. Though a few of them were from the working-class quarters of Paris, others came from the provinces, by way of Paris. Yet I did hear at Mettray an expression which is not used in prisons, but only in the penal colony. To wit: "to defend one's pants." Is it the similarity of situation that created it both here and there? Perhaps an escaped or discharged convict went back to Mettray to meet his chicken behind the hedges and advise him to defend his pants, or perhaps a colonist-murderer exported it from Guiana in his bundle.

That same evening I sang *Leave* for them in the middle of the yard, *Leave,* which Yvonne Georges and Nini Buffet used to sing. The colonists listened. Every greenhorn had to name the new songs he knew, then he sang them. He thus paid a gracious entrance-tribute. For the oldtimers, it was a fragrance of light tobacco, a flavour of woman that he brought with him. We learned *My Paris, Two Loves Have I, Place Blanche, Strawberries and Raspberries, Hallelujah.* But the favourites

---

[1] Bugger: *effleuré,* meaning, in argot, "one who is buggered". The following sentence is explained by the fact that the root of the word is *fleur* (flower).—Translator's note.

were the soulful and violent ones that spoke of love, leave-taking and rapture. I sang for the whole crowd in the middle of the Family B yard, and the elder brother liked my voice so much that he picked me to be his chicken. Though my voice was clear and pure, it did not have the subtle trembling, the kind of quiver of Italian voices that makes the singer's neck tremble as one imagines the neck of a cooing dove trembles. Toscano's voice had this quality and he was later to steal a male from me. But Mettray did not produce any of those characteristic ballads in which the colonists sigh their sadness.

The last time I met Botchako, he was humming.

I stopped to listen with another group of big shots. He smiled.

"Didn't they sing where you were with Guy, at Mettray?"

"Sure they did. The usual songs. Why?"

"Why? At Eysse . . ."

"Were you at Eysse?"

"I just said so. We used to make up songs. There were guys who thought them up. And there were some that guys brought from other colonies, from Aniane, from Saint Maurice, from Belle Ile . . ." But never from Mettray. The following are refrains from Fontevrault:

> The colony has gone elsewhere
> Its name has disappeared
> And instead there's a big prison
> Whose name is Fontevrault
> Which means grave . . .

And:

> In a sad prison with blackened walls
> Two young prisoners walk slowly round and round
> Wearing their garb of shame they bow their heads
> A number on their arm like real convicts
> I wonder what they could have done
> Are they murderers, gangsters, tramps
> People who let nothing stand in the way
> Of killing and robbing honest workers . . .

The ballads of which Botchako spoke could not have been produced at the colony because it was not surrounded by walls. Our nostalgia was deep, but the melancholy that developed there was not intense enough, it did not accumulate, it did not beat against walls and rise up like carbonic-acid gas in a grotto. It escaped during our walks or when we went to work in the fields. The other reformatories, Aniane, Eysse, the jails, La Santé, the state prisons, are surrounded by walls. Suffering and sadness are unable to flee, they are thrown back by the barrier, and these were the plaints that Botchako sang and wanted to hear.

Thanks to my singing the first evening, I was at first spared the shame of prostitution. Instead of my going from hammock to hammock or seeing all the males come crawling at night into mine, my pal, my big shot, my friend saw to it that I was respected. Even before I laid my bundle—a blanket containing my equipment—on the bench, near the window of the mess-hall, they tested me. Rio tipped the bench, and my belongings fell to the floor. The others smiled all around me. I picked up my pack. Rio made it fall again. I looked him in the eyes.

"Are you doing it on purpose?"

"Can't you see, lunkhead?"

The kids all laughed at this reply. Whereupon there occurred within me a phenomenon the like of which I never experienced again. I had a feeling that the rest of my life depended on my attitude at that moment. I was suddenly endowed with a very profound political sense, for I realized that the children's insight was extraordinarily acute. They were testing me in accordance with a very sure method, and, depending on my reaction, I would be classified as a big shot, jerk or fag. A tremendous fear paralyzed me for three seconds, and then, straight off, clenching my teeth with the rage of feeling weaker than Rio, I said, exploding the "p":

"You lousy prick!"

He was already at me. I didn't back out. I was saved. But

what amazing skill the children display in choosing their friends, and spontaneously, without conniving. They eliminate the weak unhesitatingly. Generally their flair sufficed; if not, they knew how to test us, to elicit the reactions that affirmed the "man" or denied him. I defended myself, and Villeroy took me under his wing. Tenderness between us was rare. From this point of view, I can say we were Romans. No tenderness with him, but, far better, there were at times gestures which had an animal grace. He wore around his neck a small metal chain to which was attached a silver medallion of the Sacred Heart of Jesus. When we made love, when he was tired of kissing my eyes, my mouth would meander over his neck and chest and would glide down to his belly. When I reached his throat, he would turn slightly and let the medallion that hung from the chain fall into my open mouth. I would close my mouth over it for a moment, then he would pull it back. When my mouth ran over his throat, he would thrust the medallion into it again. His prestige required that I be the best dressed of the youngsters, of the minors. The day after my arrival, I already had, for Sundays, a broad beret, broken in accordance with the colonists' fashion, and, for weekdays, a dashing police cap, and also a pair of light clogs, the tips of which were sharpened with a piece of glass and which were filed down to such a point that the wood was as fragile as parchment. Unbeknown to his superiors, every colonist fabricated his own cigarette lighter, burned a handkerchief to make tinder and stole a piece of steel. At night, he retailored his trousers so that, when worn with leggings, they clung to the thighs. Each inmate, whether he was a big shot or the chicken of a big shot, contrived to work up his own equipment. Because the big shots said ironically, when speaking of fags who got reamed: "They're right, they relieve suffering humanity," I could not help associating the expression with that of the church: "the humanity of Good Suffering," and I regarded my need to make the big shots "come"—which has now been transformed into a desire to make the minors come—as the sign of a charity which was so potent that it even seeped into my vice, and it may well be that I am slowly discovering, with the help of luck, the Charity buried within me. Perhaps, by dint of my writing about it, it will emerge pure and streaming with light, as certain children emerge dazzlingly from my poems because I have obscurely sought them there, with long patience, amidst a riot of words, for I sometimes find the innumerable abandoned rough drafts in which, as a result of my saying "you" to no one in particular, this secret prayer gradually grows more beautiful and creates the boy to whom I address it. As the quest for saintliness is painful in all religions, each of them grants the seeker, as compensation, the glory of being face to face with God, in accordance with the idea of Him which it imposes. It had been granted me to see Harcamone, to witness from my cell, in spirit, with greater precision than if my body had been close to his, the wonderful unfolding of his highest life, the one he attained by leaping above himself: his life lasted from his death sentence to his death. And those scenes of ravishment are perhaps the pretext for my writing this book, which is as treacherous as the mirror systems that reflect the image of you which you did not compose.

I thought of calling my book *The Children of the Angels*. A verse in *Genesis* tells us that: "the sons of God saw the daughters of men that they were fair; and they took them wives of all which they chose." And *The Book of Enoch:* "The angels chose each of them a wife, and they went in unto them. And the wives conceived. And they brought forth giants whose size . . . They devoured all that men could produce. The angels taught the children magic, the art of making swords and knives, shields, breastplates and mirrors, the making of ornaments and bracelets, the use of paint, the art of painting the eyebrows, of using precious stones, and all kinds of dyes, so that the world was corrupted, impiety grew and fornication multiplied."

When I came across these texts, it seemed to me there was no better way of painting or depicting the secret realm of the colonists. With a rush of dizziness I seize upon the idea that we are the youthful descendants, learnèd by birth, of Angels and women, devoting ourselves with the surest of knowledge to the secret fabrication of fire, clothing, ornaments and practices which border on magic and unleash wars with their glory and their dead. With what high indifference do they act? It must not be thought, for example, that the Order of Tattoos met in formal session. It gave rise to none of the ceremonies invented by people who play, whether they play at war or at being apaches. The colonists indulged in no play-acting, loathed all affectation. The business of tattooing, decisions, restrictions were matters of course. No master held court in a strange costume. A little steely-eyed tough decided curtly: "Takes more than that for the guy to deserve a tattoo for big shots. If he ever tattoos with anything but a flower. I'll attend to him myself."

The Order thus remained pure, and the more pure in that, not being officially established, membership in it could not be sought as an honour. In principle, it did not exist. It resulted purely and simply from the kindred boldness of a few boys who eventually designated and revealed themselves by the sign of the Eagle, or the Frigate, or some other sign.

In my early days, Beauvais was still there. All he said to Villeroy was: "Oh, say!", but words have the meaning one gives them, and the fact is that our entire language was a code, for the simplest exclamations sometimes signified complicated insults. "Oh, say!" meant, in this case, "You're not the whole works. I've got something to say too." Villeroy went at him. They "gave it to each other" with a rising excitement that, if we are to believe novelists, was perhaps increased by the sight and smell of the blood flowing from their gums, nostrils and eyebrows. No one would have dared intervene, for it was a sacred combat. Villeroy had rejected Beauvais' application for the Eagle. The month before, he had granted him the Frigate. As for the Eagle, let him wait, but Beauvais tried to disregard him. He died as a result. You will understand my emotion when I thought I saw the Eagle on Bulkaen's chest.

I do not know whether the others (crashers or the various kinds of delinquents) had noticed and recognized his beauty on the stairway when we went down for our walk; they all became perturbed when he drew near. I mean that the men lost their bearings for a brief instant, but an instant of which I was aware. They would suddenly waver, for no reason. Near the corner of the wall where he usually waited for me, the men turned to him imperceptibly and hesitated a moment before going up. The stairway will bear the eternal mark of all that excitement. It still vibrates with the first kiss that Pierrot gave me there and with his flight, which was swift and slightly stiff, like that of a chamois. His fleeing so hastily left me pensive. I thought it was due to his wanting to hide his embarrassment at having dared give me, of his own accord, a kiss which I had stopped expecting, for perhaps his brusque manner concealed great delicacy. But could he have loved me? Life had left its mark on me, despite the care I took of my body and face. I mean the many heartaches and pain I suffered in my free life, for prison keeps one young. The faces of crashers who have aged in jail are calm and relaxed, fresh as a rose; their muscles are supple. Some of them are still serving their sentence, and despite the hunger that ravages us they are the masters of love here. Rocky had arrangements with his pals in the bookkeeping department, with the trusties, with the bakers, and I am still surprised that Bulkaen did not take more advantage of it. Once, however, on the stairs, he took a loaf of bread from under his jacket, broke it in two on his knee—I saw the thrilling ripple of his forearm muscle—and handed me half. I recalled that gesture several times, and judged him thereby. His telling me, quite spontaneously, that he had bread and his giving me part of it warranted my thinking that spontaneity was the basic element of his character, that he was thus acting in a way which was faithful to himself, that all his acts sprang from the same sudden spontaneity, which is easily confused with frankness, but frankness is the will to hide nothing, whereas spontaneity is the inability to hide anything, because the reaction immediately follows the stimulus.

I therefore thought his gestures were spontaneous. I was wrong. Having seen him spontaneous once, I thought him frank because he was spontaneous. I thus tended to believe him, and I believed him when he told me later, when he stated, in his blunt, spiteful tone, that he had broken with Rocky. Actually, he had offered me the bread because someone had just offered it to him; pleasure had expanded his soul and vanity led him to act rashly.

Rocky was big and strong, but not exactly handsome. I now know that he knew I loved Pierrot, but he never showed it. Perhaps he had broken off with him either because he no longer loved him or because he realized that their destinies would not allow them to love each other. I saw him only on rare occasions, and I would have liked friendship to unite us in our love for Pierrot. Such friendship, and even love between two rivals, was not impossible, since we both liked men.

I have seen boys tattooed with the Eagle, the Frigate, the Naval Anchor, the Serpent, the Wild Pansy, the Stars, the Moon and the Sun. Those who were most charged with blazons had them up to their neck and higher. These figures adorned the torsos of a new chivalry.

A chivalry, but also a kind of imperial nobility had been created, one that took no account of earlier tattoos which might have been engraved in prison or other reformatories. Nevertheless, the prestige of the older parchments made the big shots here respect the big shots who had been tattooed elsewhere. On our arms was a little wild pansy, but though the men at Fontevrault had dedicated it to their mothers, we had it tattooed around a little scroll which bore the inscription: "The Golden Voice," which was the initial sign of that purposeless order. We had our bodies tattooed with adornments so that the flower and scroll would be set in a framework worthy of them. Some were cruelly branded with brutal signs that ate away their flesh like lovers' initials graven on aloe leaves. I would gaze with anguish at the men who were devoured by drawings as the crews of galleys were by salt, for the tattoos were the mark—stylized, ornate and flowery, as all marks become, whether they grow more intricate or less—of the wounds they would suffer later on, sometimes in their heart, sometimes on their flesh, whereas in days of old, on the galley, pirates had those frightful ornaments all over their body, so that life in society became impossible for them. Having willed that impossibility themselves, they suffered less from the rigour of fate. They willed it, limited their universe in its space and comfort. Others were tattooed like the interiors of sentry-boxes, and it was in their shade that I buried myself.

When Divers was at Mettray, he was not yet tattooed. I remember the whiteness of his body, his skin, his teeth. He now has, on his left shoulder, the head which I have seen. When darkness set in, he slipped into my bed. I could not say anything, the other prisoners would have heard us, and I received him on my pallet with wild gratitude. His desperate fire and passion can be explained by his having been deprived of love. For an hour, we devoured each other with kisses.

Like the others, Divers joined the Navy when he left Mettray, and he did not go only to Toulon. All the colonists, who are let loose all over France, youngsters with many thighs, run away from Mettray like warriors who break ranks and flee; also like schoolboys. They have chosen to be sailors. Their seeds of crime will fertilize harbours, seas, ports of call. They will have women, but I dare not think that these kids who for so long were courtesans, or males who adored them, can ever get over the wound that Mettray left in their hearts, minds and muscles. When Rio is in a port and wants to be both gentle and cruel to a girl, instead of calling her Jacqueline he will say to her, stressing the word very tenderly, "My Jackie." And the word would calm him, as it calms me when I think of it.

I need calm, the great calm, that recalls the night when the galley sailed on a warm, smooth sea and the crew made me climb the main-yard. The sailors had stripped me by taking off my pants. I dared not even struggle to free myself from their laughter and insults. Any gesture would only have entangled me even more in their shouts. I remained as still as possible, but I was already sure I would reach the top of the mast. I was at the foot of it. I saw it looming pure and straight against the pale, twilit sky, clearer than the cross. With tears in my eyes, I put my thin arms around it and then my legs, folding one foot over the other. The frenzy of the men was at its height. Their cries were no longer insults but excruciatingly cruel growls. And up I went. No doubt it was this more fiery explosion from their chests that brought the captain from his cabin. When he reached the circle formed by the crew, I was already half-way up the mast, and the cries subsided as an emotion of another kind came over the convicts. While climbing, I saw the captain arrive. He remained outside the circle, watching it and me in turn. I kept climbing. I realized that he would not have dared interfere with the torture. He would not have remained master of the men, and I knew they would have turned their exacerbated temper against him. Perhaps the captain was gripped by the same emotion that was immobilizing the crew. The men were no longer even growling. They were panting, or perhaps their growling seemed to me, from the height I had reached, to be only a panting. I got to the top. I was about to touch the pinnacle. I fell and awoke the next morning in the firm arms of the captain, who lay in his hammock which was hooked to the part of the boat called the boom!

Every big shot at Mettray was the mystic betrothed of some tough, a betrothed with sinewy arms and brutal thighs. The wedding veil on his insolent head could be woven, with fervour, only by the fishermen, young or old, who sit on the piers weaving with their thick fingers the brown veil or the gown for the handsomest of their pirate captives.

I realized that Divers had been jealous of Villeroy and that in talking to me about him, in describing him as more glamorous than he really was, he was embellishing the rival so as to feel he had triumphed over a superman. But I recall a remark

of Divers' at Mettray that burst from his lips, that finally burst
from him, without his realizing it. We were inventing fanciful
ads to put in a newspaper, and I asked him what he would ask
for. He answered straight off: "A little guy," it's first a fiery
tie that crackles in the wind of a romping waltz, he was
expressing his deepest desire. Divers had brought off, better
than I, the wonderful trick of passing for a tough, whereas he
had the soul of a fag.

He got up to go to his own bed. As the night-light was on, I
could see in the semi-darkness a tattoo on his shoulder, and
the drawing seemed to be that of a young man's head. That
was the only tattoo he had. But that head which he had
brought back from there on his shoulder! That little head
which had been brought back from a special expedition, like
the mummified, shrunken head of a Jivaro from the Amazon.
This pimp was tattooed, and I was staggered at the thought
that he had asked me to go down on him. It's strange that I
loved him nonetheless, but that can be regarded as the result of
the slow working of depoetization. I remember that at Mettray
Gaveille was tattooed from toe to eyelid and that he let himself
be reamed. When I saw him go behind the laurels with his big
shot, my heart sank at the thought that it was the visible form
of a male—a male flower—that was going to be deflowered. It
was the profanation of a labarum covered with sacred writings.
Divers shifted on the bed, and as his shoulder caught the light
I saw that the tattoo was the very same one that Bulkaen had
flashed on me as a surprise: a sailor's head in a buoy.

The entire next day, during the torture of marching, Divers
made friendly signs to me. He had the same furtive alertness
he had had at Mettray. But I responded halfheartedly. My
jealousy must have been taking revenge for what I thought was
Bulkaen's betrayal, and all day long, during drill, I mingled his
life with mine. Neither at night nor the following day did I
quit my reverie. After an unbridled but imaginary life with him
for days on end, I came to his death at about two in the
morning. As I have said, I could conceive only a violent death

for that child who was violence itself, and I invented it in the secrecy of a march to the scaffold. When it was time to get up and my door was opened, I was mad with grief at having lost my friend, though thrilled with the grandeur of having been involved in the death of such a creature, but when I wanted to regain my footing in everyday life, I called to mind the particulars of the actual Bulkaen, and I realized that all my jealousy was dead, killed by his death. In trying to conjure up the head of the sailor, I no longer knew whether it was imaginary or real or on which shoulder it was.

When the big shots wanted to needle a jerk or an available chicken, or a bleater (a squealer), they would go looking for him. He would generally be leaning against the family wall. The big shots would stand around him in a semi-circle as follows: at the jerk's or chicken's or bleater's right, one of them would rest against the wall with his arm out; a second would lean against the shoulder of the first; the third against the second; and the last, at the left, would be in the same position as the first. The boy would be caged, a prisoner. And the big shots who had stepped forward with smiles on their faces, and who kept smiling even during the pleasure they took in the inflicted sacrifice, would spit oysters and frightful insults in his face. When the yeggs made friendly advances to me, and even smiled, when they were sure I was shacking up with Bulkaen, I was afraid they might change into wild beasts, that they might form the diabolical circle and close in on me, and instead of creeping into my shell, as I would have done at Mettray, I assumed a somewhat disdainful and distant attitude. I kept away from their group.

Bulkaen had been jerking off. For several days I noticed rings under his eyes. The ring of shadow marked his face, almost masked it, for he had a pale complexion and extremely fine skin, which was even finer above his cheekbones, under his eyes. In the morning, the rings indicated that he had indulged during the night in his true pleasures. Those private pleasures still disturb me, for I wonder whom he loved in the secrecy of his nights, in the secrecy of his heart and body. If I judge from myself, who love only beauty, he must have loved a handsome boy or beautiful girl, but his apparent femininity, and his stay at Mettray, led me to think that he no more loved a girl whom he conjured up at night than he did a delicate boy (the latter can be found here, and he could have had as many as he liked or have shown that he wanted one, but he ignored all of them.). The conclusion was that he had a crush on a big shot. I've seen too many couples in which the more handsome of the two puts up with the more homely not to think that this has to do with a law of nature, a law of compensation which consoles me in a low kind of way, and I didn't have the heart to think that Pierrot was in love with the handsomest of the big shots (to be sure, he did say to me one day that he *had loved* Rocky, and added: ". . . he wasn't a bad-looking guy . . . ," but I know Rocky, he's not the kind one conjures up at night for solitary pleasure), for if he loved the handsomest, who was also a bruiser (I refer to Lou Daybreak), why wasn't he his girl? Should I have thought that Lou was insensitive to Bulkaen's beauty? Or was it that Bulkaen was so feminine that at night he liked only to be loved by the strongest, who was also the ugliest, by Botchako the bandit? I do not remember ever having known a former Mettray boy who became a pimp. The profession of procurer is learned gradually, through contact with other successful, practising pimps who guide the beginner in his career and encourage him. One has to start at an early age, and we stayed in the reformatory until the age of eighteen or twenty. After that, we joined the Navy. At Mettray, we dreamed of a woman only to caress her. Our sadness yearned obscurely, hopelessly, for a woman whose tenderness would be a consolation for our unhappiness. The fact is that our dreams were mostly dreams of adventure. Our purity was such that, though we were not actually unaware of it, we did not know, in our heart of hearts, in our flesh which desired and longed for it, that there was an "underworld" in which men lived off women, just as we did not know that there were carpenters, wool-carders, salesmen. We *knew*—wanting to know—thieves, crashers and racketeers.

This book has required great effort and pain. I am writing without pleasure. With even less relish I plunge head first into the adventures of that exceptional childhood. No doubt I can still produce darkness within me and at the landmark of a memory be thrilled with stories of my past. I can still re-shape or complete them in the tragic mode which transforms each of them into a poem of which I am the hero, though I no longer do it with the same passion. This is the luxury I allow myself. In the cell, gestures can be made with extreme slowness. You can stop in the middle of one. You are master of time and of your thinking. You are strong by dint of slowness. Each gesture is inflected in a flowing curve. You hesitate. You choose. That is what the luxury of cell life is composed of. But this slowness of gesture is a slowness that goes fast. It rushes. Eternity flows into the curve of a gesture. You possess your entire cell because you fill its space with your engrossed mind. What a luxury to perform each gesture slowly, even if it be lacking in gravity. Nothing can completely dispel my hopelessness. It would start taking shape again because it is governed by a gland whose secretion is internal. It trickles, slowly at times, but with never a moment's stop. In speaking of Mettray, I tend to use symbols, to define facts and interpret them rather than show them. Mettray afforded me spectacles as great as that of Pierrot sprawled out, silent, frothing, knocked off his feet by a bruiser's fist, or as when I once said to him:

"Rocky, that goof of yours . . ."

He burst out laughing. He was so prompt that I thought all his gestures were the direct expression of his feelings. I was terribly sorry. He burst out laughing, but the hand that shot to his heart showed me he was hurt. I was also cruel enough to think that the wound would remain when the laugh had gone from his face. The laughter beautified him. I was therefore dismayed at the thought that the harm I dared do him was expressed on his face by a recurrence of light. He himself felt that his gesture might reveal his suffering, and as his hand had clenched when it sprang to his heart, he opened it, pressed it flat, and pretended to be supporting his chest because he was laughing so hard that he coughed. I also point out that this forced laugh was that of an actress—a great coquette—it was a stylized laugh, the kind emitted by elegant women who try to show off, the laugh that their sons have stolen because they were always graciously at their mothers' side, nestling in their satin trains and bare arms. Bulkaen could have caught such a laugh only from his mother. I still remember that he dashed up the stairs and, when he reached the top floor, leaned forward. I saw his face lit up by the glass of the prison roof. A kind of peace came over me, that is, I felt myself strong with his beauty, which entered me. I was probably in a state of adoration. I have used the word enter. I have done so deliberately: his beauty entered me by the feet, went up my legs, rose to my body, to my head, spread over my face, and I realized it was a mistake to attribute to Bulkaen the sweetness it instilled in me, that desertion of my forces which left me defenceless before the overwhelming beauty of the work, for that beauty was in me and not in him. It was outside him since it was on his face, in his features, on his body. He could not enjoy the spell it cast on me.

Each individual detail—the smile of the mouth, the gleam of the eyes, the smoothness, the paleness of the skin, the hardness of the teeth, the star at the intersection of certain features —pierced my heart with an arrow that each time dealt me a delicious death. But he was the archer who bent the bow. He bent it and shot. He shot not at himself but at me.

Official personages sometimes have the luck to see a patch of sky through a gap or flaw. It surprises them. They are not used to seeing it, and it, being reprehended, gains thereby. I have been wanting to see Mettray again in the autumn, and I conjure it up here, alone in my cell, with words that carry me away. I have been wanting to make a pilgrimage to it, in thought, with Pierrot and to make love to him in a hedge of laurels wet with mist, on the damp moss and leaves. We walk up the avenue of chestnut trees with the grave pace of the bishop when he came to visit us. We walk in the middle, as slowly and solemnly as he, and I am sure that the loving couple which we form is inspecting our little companions, who are invisible and present. They bless the consecration of a marriage which took place in the chapel one night, fifteen years ago.

When the Bishop of Tours visited Mettray, his car arrived by the highway, at the far end of the lane of chestnut trees where the chaplain, the director, Dudule, and the nuns, who kissed his finger, awaited him, and he, in his lace, escorted by a host of abbés and shaded by a red and yellow parasol, walked across the colony, from the road to the chapel, between two double rows of close-cropped colonists. A throne had been prepared for him near the altar. He settled himself on it. Then the evening service was held, and Dudule made a speech welcoming the bishop, who replied by addressing the colonists in particular, whom he called stray lambs. In the early days of the war, old ladies with pale blue hearts entered into conversation by talking about "our little soldiers . . . our little braves"! They, in the trenches, jerked off at night with their mudcaked hands. God's little lambs, sitting in the pews with their hands in their pockets, did likewise. Though the big shots were the first everywhere, in chapel they deliberately sat in the last pews, at the very back, so as to be in the shadow during services. They did not even deign to stand up or kneel. The jerks up front performed these movements for them, and no doubt also prayed for them. But when the bishop came, they wanted to be in the first row. On other Sundays their indifference was so like an absence that I can say they did not even go to church, and when they were all in the choir, they had, despite their importance, the awkwardness and subtle grace of village boys in church on Easter Sunday. I shall try to render the tone of Dudule's speech of welcome:

"Most Reverend Sir,

The Director has permitted me to speak on his behalf, and so I welcome Your Excellency to our midst. The entire institution of Baron de Courteille (the founder of the establishment) is aware of the signal honour of your visit. Ours is a troubled age. The Church and Society feel threatened by the sly attacks of the Demon. The diocese of Tours has the good fortune to be in the safekeeping of the most vigilant of pastors. Your Excellency has continued with utter rectitude the care showered upon us by Monseigneur de Montsanjoye which has been traditional for centuries in our God-beloved Touraine. We know that Your Excellency has more than once turned his thoughts—with most paternal kindness—to this institute of re-education and religious and moral regeneration to which we are dedicated. The bishopric of Tours has already provided the Mettray Farm Colony with considerable sums and has employed its kind solicitude in choosing chaplains worthy of itself, of the institution, and of us. For that, too, we must thank you, Your Excellency. The colonists, those repentant sinners, take pride in your visit and also desire to show they are worthy of it. The announcement of your arrival was welcomed with calm inner gladness. Indeed, they recognize the great honour of your presence amongst them, and there can be no doubt that from this moment forth they are resolved to lead a godly life. Your Excellency will allow me at this point to add my personal gratitude and tribute to the general tribute. Indeed, I had the honour of being presented at the episcopal palace, and though the delicate welcome accorded to the Colony's humble servant was due to the interest inspired by that great charitable institution, it must nevertheless be mentioned today as an additional honour."

The bishop replied:

"Mr. Director, Mr. Assistant Director, My Young Friends,

I am deeply moved by this welcome which is indeed an indication of fidelity to the principles of your holy religion. It is a very deep comfort to me, coming from cities where perverse unrest tries to make men forget God, to enter this oasis of religious calm. We are familiar with Baron de Courteille's splendid achievement, and we are aware of the sacrifice and devotion it entails. The Director and Assistant Director are collaborating, with single-hearted will, in a sphere which we know is different and yet similar, to the success of that sacred undertaking: the rehabilitation of wayward children.

Saintly women have also devoted their efforts to this work. We must, through our holy ministry, convey to them our full encouragement and assure them of the beauty of their lives. We have been struck by the care with which our arrival was prepared for. The decorations of the chapel are in exquisite taste, and this tribute to God must indeed be encouraged. Abbé Viale, your chaplain, of whose devotion we are aware, is convalescing from a long illness which he bore with religious resignation. To be sure, sickness is sometimes given to the just by God, Whose purposes are unfathomable (At this point the bishop smiled at the chaplain, to whom he said: But that God, Who is all goodness, knows His lambs, and if one of them is torn by thorns, He takes it in His arms and brings it back to the fold.)."

Then turning to the colonists and raising his voice so as to make it quite clear that the rest was addressed to them:

"My young friends, it was not the Lord's intention to let your souls stray eternally. A group of pious men have devoted themselves to setting you on the right path. They will spare you the pain of knowing that house of detention whose proximity should be a continual, a daily reminder of what is right and wrong. Although they are supported by the purity of their intentions, it is indeed true that their task is a hard one. They must struggle with the demon that dwells, alas, in the souls of many of you, and the struggle is a frightful one. And yet we are hopeful, and even certain, that they will triumph. Our Lord said: Suffer little children to come unto me. Who could be so hard-hearted as not to heed that appeal of the divine child and to prefer the black, burning bosom of the devil? Ah, to be sure, this colony is a nursery of men who are on the side of God. Persevere, therefore, on that path which we observe with close interest. The Holy Roman Church can only be happy that you do so. We are going to pray for our Holy Father the Pope, for the sick, for prisoners and for the departed."

The colonists listened, but particularly when the bishop referred to Fontevrault and told us that thanks to this house of God (Mettray) we would be spared prison. We were then hoisted to the utmost height of attention, hoping that a personage so well dressed, so escorted, so learnèd, so close to God, would reveal something startling about Jo with the Golden Voice and about the whole prison, but the bishop must not have known anything definite for he merely touched lightly upon the matter. We sat there breathless, and our profitless attention quietly expired, like a suppressed fart in a drawing-room.

The bishop then handed his crook to an attendant who laid it down near the throne, and, standing at the top of the twelve stairs on which the altar rested, he raised the monstrance and was about to bless us. It was at that moment that, like a solemn elevation, the fight broke out between Rigaux and Rey. The matter of the leggings had come up again. After remaining quiet for a long time, it finally exploded. I never knew what started the brawl—perhaps Rey winked at Rigaux's chicken, perhaps some gesture with the shoulder—but they fought magnificently over nothing, at the foot of the altar. They fought fiercely until blood flowed (at Mettray you kept hitting your opponent when he was down, when he was gasping for air), until death ensued, unto damnation. While the bishop stood at the top of the stairs with the raised monstrance, hesitating to bless us, the two dancers kicked each other in the head and chest with their iron-shod heels, punched and butted, clawed each other (clawing plays a very big role in children's fights), panted mysteriously. For once the idiotic heads of the

families rushed to separate the two heroes and take them dying
to the disciplinary quarter, which was quite simply called the
quarter or the hole. The bishop finally blessed us with only his
hand, with his hand of felt. He made a gesture of pardon. He
left with dignity as we stood bare-headed. He did not know
that the fight, that dance in honour of the Blessèd Sacrament,
was going to continue throughout the colony for almost two
weeks between the partisans of Rey and Rigaux. The partisans
fought with unusual ferocity. One shoulders a musket out of
necessity and one enlists out of duty, but in war one fights to
the death out of love. No family was on the honour roll for
weeks, and the flag, which was kept on Sunday by the family
that had not been punished during the week, stayed in its black
cover, in the darkest corner of the reception hall.

Although the toughs chose their favourites from among the
best-looking youngsters, the latter are not all destined to
remain women. They awaken to manhood, and the men make
room for them at their side. The following also happened,
which is not so very strange: their good looks got them into
the severe gangs. The attractive chickens were so well received,
almost on an equal footing, that the sight of them on such
familiar terms with the toughs made you forget that they could
be stuck, whereas the fact is that they were the most trans-
pierced. But, strong in their grace, they carried off their faggotry so grandly that it became an embellishment and source
of energy.

The author of a beautiful poem is always dead. The Mettray
colonists realized this, and we spoke of Harcamone, who had
killed a nine-year-old girl, only in the past tense. Harcamone
lived among us, but what circulated in the Colony was only his
splendid envelope which had entered eternity. When we spoke
to him, we never mentioned his crime, about which he must
have known even less than we. What remained behind and
moved about was a friend. He was a friend to every one of us,
and he was perhaps the only one. He never had a big shot or a
chicken. He was polite to both, even to the jerks. I suppose he

led a very chaste life, and I rather think that his hardness and lustre were due as much to his chastity as to his crime. When "ass" or "chicken" was discussed in his presence, his face remained impassive. When questioned about the matter —which happened very rarely, for no one would have dared, and the only ones who did dare were newcomers who did not yet respect him (I mention this so that you will believe in the children's delicacy)—he would shrug his shoulders, neither scornfully nor with disgust. I was once on the point of asking him for details about the person and habits of other young murderers, which shows to what extent I felt that they were all members of a family—for example, the Atrides—that they all knew each other, that they were familiar with each other's ways, even if they were separated by a period of fifty years, since they were united by relationships that led to their knowing, loving and hating each other from one end of Europe to the other, just as a prince of Baden can speak knowingly of the private life of a prince of Toledo.

I imagined deep rivalries among them, maledictions on young heads, at times the death sentence or exile. It should be noted that Harcamone's voice had certain foreign intonations, though I was never able to tell what language was involved. Nevertheless, he spoke argot, but there was something else that characterized him: though he was sturdy, he was much less tough physically than the other big shots, he was less muscular and his bone structure was less rugged. In fact, he seemed swollen (though not bloated) with a very heavy juice. The newspapers had mired him in the epithets "the killer," "the monster" . . . His raised head and curled upper lip must have been kissing or receiving the kiss of a transparent being that hung from the sky by its bare feet.

At the Colony, Harcamone was a plasterer and a mason. He was powdered with plaster from head to foot, and his hard, fine face took on a delicate softness. The Colony must have been doomed to damnation for a thousand other marvels, but the charm alone that was worked by his face would have been sufficient. Harcamone had a limp. The others would say laughingly in his presence that he was probably back from the penal colony where he had had to drag a ball and chain, but this pleasantry left him cold. When I slipped out of the brush shop for a minute to take a leak, I would sometimes see him crossing the Big Square with a ladder on his shoulder. And the ladder was the final touch that made of him a drama whose intensity was due to its brevity and whose brilliance was the effect of the power of its reduction in space to a single actor. On his shoulder it was the ladder of escape, of kidnappings, of serenades, of a circus, of a boat, it was scales and arpeggios and God knows what. The ladder carried him. The ladder was the murderer's wings. He would sometimes stop in his tracks and, with his chest arched and one leg stretched behind him, would turn his head sharply to the left, then to the right, cock one ear, then the other. He was a doe that stops to listen. Joan of Arc must have done likewise to hear her voices. When he murdered the girl, he came so close to death—perhaps to get to us by going through storms, by escaping from ship-wrecks—that at the age of eighteen he regarded the life he continued to live as if it were a postscript. His life had already been cut short, for he had known death. He was familiar with it. He belonged to it more than to life. This, too, gave him that funereal air. For he was funereal, despite his grace, funereal as are roses, which symbolize love and death. When he crossed the Big Square, he was elegance strolling arm in arm with the lie. I have since known youngsters who were destined to be locked up in state prisons. One of them who told me how he was given fifteen years, with hard labour, for committing murder did so with such haughty elegance that I would have blushed had I pitied him. I felt that the murder was enabling him to be what everything within him was tending toward: a tough among other toughs. And though he must have known, for fiteen years and afterward, those islets of regret for what you call a wasted youth, this in no way negates his act or his desire. On the contrary. His longing to be a big shot was great enough for him to sacrifice his youth and life to it—we are confronted here with one of those miracles of love that make the worshipper, at the risk of jeopardizing body and soul, desire to adorn himself with the attributes of his idol. You ought to see how the kids whom God does not grant these heroic opportunities approach the insolent pimps when they happen to meet on the stairs, at medical inspection, or in the showers. The little delinquents go to them by instinct. They surround them, they listen to them open-mouthed. The pimp impregnates them. And if you shrug your shoulders at what seems a ridiculous ideal, you are wrong, for they obey the amorous impulse which makes them resemble the person they love, a tough, until the time they finally become that person. They then lose, in hardening, the thrilling tenderness that was imparted by the movement of marching to their goal, the inconsistent flow—which is only a transition—of yearning youth to maturity. Everything within them then forgets that amorous march. They have become commonplace pimps who no longer remember the adventure they had to pursue in order to be these pimps. They, in turn, will be a pole of attraction to other minors, for this is the means, perhaps an impure one, that God uses to fabricate the impassive men of the prisons.

Another of Harcamone's embellishments: his hand swathed in white. Was it his skin or his too delicate flesh? Or his occupation? A trifle would injure him. Perhaps there was nothing wrong with him and he feigned injuries! Yards of white gauze were wound around his hand, and that was how he appeared at meals, as if emerging from extraordinary escapades, a survivor of scuffles, of brawls, of clashes. Those dressings made him cruel, him the gentlest of angels, but transformed our hearts, when we beheld him, into those of nurses.

Like lots of tough guys, he wore on his right wrist a broad leather band studded with steel and copper, and as its primary purpose was to relieve and support the wrist when it was under strain, it was called a "wrist-support," but it had become an ornament, a symbol of manliness. It was laced on by a leather cord, at the bend of the wrist.

The Colony, including Divers, rotated about that axis: Harcamone. But it, including Harcamone, also rotated about another axis: Divers. And about Villeroy and many others. Its *centre was everywhere.*

Shall I speak of the bums? They were the black, ugly rabble, scraggy and grovelling, without which the patrician does not exist. They too had their slave's life.

Larochedieu, that jerk with putrid feet eaten away by pus, Larochedieu, that stool-pigeon, the official squealer, with his bony body and coarse skin, once had to undress in the yard to show the head of the family the mark of a punch that he had complained of receiving on the Bel Air road. And on a level with his left breast, I read, penned in ink (a kind of superficial tattoo): "Pietro M.D.V." And I remembered the floorboard engraved with the words "Pietro, the master of the vampires[1], that's me!" He would not have dared to have that tattoo made. Nor did he have the courage to make it himself. Perhaps he was afraid of being incited by the violence of the sign tattooed on his skin and of thus being forced to live thereafter in peril of his life.

How my throat tightened whenever I chanced to see those little bodies which were almost entirely blue from head to foot. I would find myself confronted with the terrible expression of a destiny which pushed those children deathward, allowing them to see life only from far away and through an inviolable, undecipherable netting of blue lace.

But the name Bel Air, of which Bulkaen had reminded me earlier, makes me turn away for a moment from everything that has fascinated me in my memories and makes me see the true grief, the lamentable suffering of those children bent over in the beet-fields where they worked winter and summer. They would move through the fields slowly. Their vivacity was bogged down by their muddy sabots. Their youth and all its

[1] In French: "Maître des vampires," thus M.D.V.—Translator's note.

bright charms were caught in the clay like a nymph in a tree. They were chilled by the rain and the icy gaze of the head of the shop who stood in their midst, motionless and upright. It was through them that the Colony suffered. When I think back, remembering that Bulkaen was one of them, my heart melts with a kindness of which I thought I was devoid. May I be forgiven this cry of love and pity. Bulkaen no doubt suffered greatly, and he was too proud to show it. From his letters too I can tell that he shone to the very end. I excited him by my glowing replies. He spoke to me of escapades that continued all the way to Spain. His letters, which were written by himself, in his own words, seemed to report, in cryptic language, secret adventures in which we were bandit chiefs in a gloomy sierra. Bulkaen was a hazel wand that, with a single stroke, transformed the astounded world. But I felt that in the most intricate and reckless of his projects in which I was involved, he kept thinking of Rocky, for he once said to me, without my asking, that it was he, Rocky, who had asked him, before leaving, to write the poem about the penal colony. I realized that his delicacy had invented this explanation in order to console me. He gave it to me not when I was upset, but when he thought he was the cause of my being upset, that is, when—while talking to me about something else—he was thinking most intensely about Rocky. We were alone on the stairs. I laid my hand gently on his shoulder. He turned his head. His gaze sank into mine. He was carried away. Without thinking, he told me about their exploits, how they went from one floor to another, through luxurious, overheated apartments, about the doors that gave way, the trampled carpets, the dazzled chandeliers, the devastation, the agitation of the raped, gaping furniture, the silver complaining in their hands, the dough.

"Who the hell cares if they know it! I'm telling you. We'd go into the joint. We'd knock things around. We did all our jobs together. We couldn't work any other way. We'd break in, in broad daylight. The jimmy, the wedges, and bang . . . we'd

break in, we'd close the door behind us. We were both caught
... We ... We'd get down to work ... We were both caught
inside ... once ... Who the hell cares if they know it ...
Once ..."

It all came gushing out of his open mouth. I removed my
hand. I turned my head a little. He kept going all alone, far
behind and within himself. He was walking without my help.
He kept talking. His voice clouded over. From the fear and
happiness of the first stair to the actual danger. Huddled
together, incorporated into each other for greater security, they
broke the lock in two minutes, entered quickly, stole very little
and fled. The second job, when their excitement was so great
that they rolled on the huge bed of the gutted apartment and
indulged in the finest orgy of love that either of them had ever
known, leaving in their wake a pair of spotted sheets. I listened, drinking in the words he rattled off though in a low
voice. Then I put my hand back on his shoulder. Was it true
that he had loved so deeply? We were so far away that a
prisoner went by without seeing us. I held Bulkaen pressed
against me. He turned his head slightly. The depth of his eyes
was revealed to me. It conjured up, by its clearness, the Bay of
Along (though I am not calling it that), and to my happiness
was added the glory of uniting to my love the most thrilling
landscape in the world. I was holding in my teeth the stem of
the rose I had stolen from Harcamone's mysterious garden,
and his mouth crushed the flower on mine. All the stalwarts of
the jail must have shuddered, and all the criminals. A mysterious thread of kinship, a delicate affinity, unites the
criminals of the whole world, and they are all affected when
something happens to one of them. They are stirred periodi-
cally, like Japanese black bamboos which are said to flower
every fifty years wherever in the world they may be. The same
flowers bloom on their stems, in the same year, in the same
season, at the same hour. They make the same response.

In his lyrical cries, which were uttered in a muffled voice
that was muted even more by the hand he put to his mouth, I

recognized the same emotion that accumulated deep within me
when I did a job. It had not been able to express itself so
readily, it had not released itself in such beautiful acts, with
the collaboration of so warm a soul as mine. It had remained
solitary in the pit of my stomach, but Bulkaen was now giving
it the perfect form of which I had secretly dreamed.

I always carried out my burglaries alone, from the first day
to the one that brought me to Fontevrault, and in that course
of time I was constantly purifying myself. I did my jobs in
accordance with the rites I learned from conversations with the
men. I respected the superstitions. I evinced a wonderful sentimentality—the sentimentality of the hard-hearted—and I
would have been afraid, as they were, of drawing down
lightning from heaven by taking a child's piggy-bank from the
mantelpiece and emptying it into my pockets. But that aspiration to purity was constantly impeded by my intelligence,
which, unfortunately, was too crafty. Even during the most
brazen jobs—including the robbery at the Museum of
P.—while involving my physical person to the utmost, I could
not keep from supplementing standard courage with my own
particular ruses, and on that occasion I invented the business
of shutting myself up in a historical piece of furniture, a kind
of round-topped chest, spending the night there, and tossing
the unhooked tapestries through the window, after walking
around on my heels (one walks more silently on one's heels
than on tiptoe beneath gilded ceilings, amidst illustrious me-
mentoes) and finally realizing that any Saint Just can vote for
the death of the tyrant and bedeck himself, in the secrecy of
darkness or of solitude or of reveries, with the crown and lilied
cloak of a beheaded king. My mind still encumbered me, but
my body was supple and strong, like that of any crasher. That
life saved me. For I was afraid that methods which were too
subtle might, by dint of subtlety, have more to do with magic
than with intelligible intelligence and might put me, despite
myself—literally: against my will—in contact with the spells I
dreaded, with the invisible and wicked world of elves. That

was why I preferred the direct means of crashers to all the intricate concoctions of my mind, for the brutality of the former is frank, earthy, feasible and reassuring. The enviable brutality of Botchako the gangster, his fury, were like those of a lone creature at bay aware that it resembled a lone creature. When he was in a rage, the guards kept away from him, or else waited for him to cool off. Brulard was the only one who dared approach him. He would enter Botchako's cell and lock himself up with him, and he would leave when Botchako had calmed down. We supposed that the cell had been transformed into a fabled den where seduction and exorcism took place. What actually happened was this: Brulard would go in—it was Botchako who told us about it—and in order to calm him the turnkey would find fault with all his colleagues, his superiors, the warden. They would both work themselves into a state of violent indignation which would gradually die down, and the appeased brute would sit on the stool with his head in his hands.

At Mettray, we went to the toilet as follows: the shit-house was in the yard, behind each family dormitory. At noon and at 6 p.m., on our way back from the shops, we would march in line, led by the elder brother, and stop in front of the four urinals. We would leave the line in fours to take a leak or pretend to. At the left were the latrines, which were four or five steps high so that the crap can was on a level with the ground. Each boy stepped from the line and went to one or the other, depending on the need he felt. He would let his belt hang from the door to show that the place was occupied. There was never any paper. For three years I wiped myself with my forefinger, and the wall whitewashed my finger.

I love the Colony for having given me such moments. Idiotic vandals—Danan, Helsey, Londres and others—have written that penal homes for children should be destroyed. They fail to realize that if they were, the children would set them up again. Those inhuman kids would create courts of miracles (that's the word for it!) and perform their secret,

complicated rites in the very teeth of well-meaning journalists.
War was beautiful in the past because in shedding blood it
produced glory. It is even more beautiful now because it
creates pain, violence and despair. It breeds sobbing widows,
who take comfort or weep in the arms of the conquerors. I love
the war that devoured my handsomest friends. I love Mettray,
that paradise in the heart of royal Touraine, which is full of
little fourteen- and sixteen-year-old widows and of males
struck by lightning in the fairest places. The dead Bulkaen and
Harcamone are now within me, in crypts which are as strange
(to my eyes) as the dark, windowless capitular room of the
abbesses of Fontevrault. I could call it infernal if hell were
damp and sad. No light, the icy air, the height. They must
have engaged in indescribable ceremonies around the tombs of
the Plantagenets, of Richard the Lion-hearted. There the
monks and nuns celebrated a forgotten liturgy which I faith-
fully continue.

Despite Divers, who is nearby, despite Bulkaen, it is the
memory of Harcamone that visits me. That eighteen-year-old
murderer whom the Colony had changed into a mason, with a
plumb-line, water-gauge and trowel in his hand, decided to
climb, mysteriously, certain walls. He was indeed the demon of
the Colony, a demon that haunted it and that still visits me. I
shall never forget its last appearance when it went so far as to
become incarnate, to my great joy, and to make roses bloom.
Its impertinence baffled even the warden of Fontevrault, who
was a very elegant gentleman, with a ribbon in his buttonhole,
and who was shrewd, very shrewd, probably very intelligent.
He must have been interested in rehabilitating the prisoners,
but the murder committed by Harcamone baffled him. By
putting together bits and pieces of the silent conversation of
the guards, I was able to reconstruct the scene in the prison
courtroom which preceded the questioning by the Judicial
Police and the judge. Harcamone appeared before a warden
who was dismayed at being confronted with a mystery as
absurd as that of a rose in full bloom. He wanted to know the

whys and wherefores of the murder, of the guard's falling at
the murderer's white feet, but he was up against Harcamone's
ignorance, nor could he count on a false explanation, for the
murderer was stronger, thanks to his destiny, than any means
of punishment practised in French prisons, the most effective
of which is to put a man in irons, on dry bread. But condemned men are already in irons, and a practice which is more
respected than the regulations requires that their bowl be filled
at every meal. In order to punish Harcamone, the warden had
to wait for the death sentence to be commuted to hard labour
for life. He trembled with impotence. He realized that to beat
the murderer or to have him beaten would be a childish
pleasantry. Standing between two guards, with his feet in
chains, Harcamone looked at him somewhat quizzingly. The
guards were absolutely at a loss. Finally, Harcamone saw a
look of such anguish in the warden's eyes that he was on the
point of admitting that he had borne Rose-wood a hatred
that only death could resolve. He hesitated. Just as he was
about to break down, he heard the warden say, "Take him
away. You're a poor specimen." He was taken back to his
cell.

I suspect him of having had affinities with the members of
the crew who stirred up rebellion on the galley. Life on board
was not easy. It cannot be treated as an elegant adventure on a
charmingly poetic vessel. I knew hunger and lack of kindness
there when the captain accumulated within himself the electricity of the clouds so as to discharge his men of some of it.
There was one day which was worse than the others. Our
nerves were jarred by a storm that didn't break. In fact, the
tension was so great that we didn't want it to break at all, for
the result could only have been a kind of terrifying miracle, the
birth of a god or a star, of a plague or of war. I was squatting
at the foot of the top-gallant mast when the captain drew near.
I knew that he loved me. Nevertheless, he gave me an evil look
in which I could see all the boredom, all the anguish, of being
human. A trifle would have been sufficient pretext for him to

talk to me. He came a little closer, then stepped back and
without effort uttered his cry: "Ho! boys!" His voice re-
sounded in the oppressive calm. The pirates came running. We
were surrounded in a trice by a hundred and fifty huskies
whose sweating bodies gleamed in the sun. Oh, of course, I
was intimidated by all that hardiness, but even more by being
accorded the honour of witnessing such a spectacle. Those
males with rippling muscles leaned against each other's bare
shoulders familiarly. Some of them had their arms around the
others' necks or waists. They formed an unbroken circle of
hard, bulging flesh through which passed a current powerful
enough to blast anyone so imprudent as to dare let his finger-
tip touch one of the clamps of muscle. The captain did not see
them. But one could feel that he was allowing his soldiers to
live before his eyes in a state of the most nervous intimacy. He
was still standing in front of me. His thighs swelled in his
breeches, and grew so hard that a muscle split the cloth. The
rip revealed an amber flesh so fine that I expected to hear it
sing.

That kind of almost silent scene always enthralled me. I
spun them from myself, and yet the pirates were so real that I
suffered in my flesh, my pity and my love.

"Anger swelled our sails." I often repeated that expression.
It goes back perhaps to the time when, curled up in my
hammock, I was a galley packed with stampeding males.

The buccaneers, as I have said, never got rich, any more
than we did, and if I feel deep relief—despite the disappointment that, without masking it, accompanies it—when I bungle
a job that I expected to make me rich right away, the reason
may be that the job would have done away with all necessity
for acting, for crashing again (our acts should spring from
necessity), but also a sudden necessity would have enabled me
to carry on much bigger operations, and that's what I was glad
to avoid, for I feel that it is not my destiny to be a great
bandit. In becoming one, I would have departed from myself,
that is, from the comforting regions to which I flee. I live in a

small dark realm which I fill out. And to be a bandit of stature
is not the destiny of any of us, for it requires qualities which
were not developed by Mettray and which we do not cultivate
in prison. The poetry of the great birds of prey eludes me.
Gangsters of stature have none of those wounds which our
childhood suffers and which it itself causes. Thus, Harcamone
failed, despite his loftiness.

Bulkaen must really have been the better part of me for me
to deprive myself even of food for him. I would have given
both my eyes for him to love me. But can anyone fully realize
how I felt when one afternoon, after leading me to the fifth or
sixth step of the stairway, he put his arm around my neck and
said, straight to my face, "All right, pal . . . a kiss." I tried to
pull away, but he pressed his mouth against mine. Under his
sleeve I felt the muscle of his arm. As soon as he kissed me, he
backed against the wall and said, "I'm spotted, Jean." He had
seen or thought—or pretended—he had seen a guard go by.
He ran down the few steps and left for his shop without saying
a word, without shaking hands, without looking back. I was
still under the shock of that cry which recalled the voice of
Inspector Peyre: "All right, my boy!" And that other, with
which he broke away: "I'm spotted." In the face of danger he
had not thought of me. But the following day I received
another blow. Hidden behind a line of prisoners, I would not
have been able to see him were it not for the fact that he was
facing the glazed door. I thus saw his back, but also his
gestures in front of him. He had joined Rocky and he made the
gesture of handing him the loaf of bread I had given him
shortly before. Then he seemed to change his mind. He took a
quick look around and, with his head down almost under his
arm, in the shifty way he often had of doing very simple
things—though this wasn't simple—he bit into the bread and
smiled at Rocky, offering him the wet side with the marks of
his mouth and teeth. Rocky smiled at his friend's smile. He
grabbed the bread, made the same shifty movement, took a
bite from the part that had been bitten into and ditched the

bread under his jacket. All these events had taken place in the
panes of the door. If I had dashed forward to deal with
Bulkaen or provoke Rocky, I would have been sent to the hole
right away. It would have meant trouble for Bulkaen. I felt, on
my right side, a kind of big emptiness. Managing not to be
seen by either the guards or Pierrot, I stepped back into the
line of prisoners and sneaked off to the shop. I realized for the
first time in my life that novelists are right when they say that
their heroine, after a highly tense scene, can hardly drag herself around.

When I dreamed of a prick, it was always Harcamone's
—which was invisible at the Colony—in his white canvas
trousers. Now, that prick, as I learned later from one of those
indiscretions common among hoodlums, did not exist. The
prick merged with Harcamone; never smiling, he was himself
the stern organ of a supernaturally strong and handsome male.
It took me a long time to know of whom. The truth of the
matter is that Harcamone belonged to a pirate prince who had
heard about us. From his galley, among his coppery riff-raff,
that is, also covered with copper ornaments, sailing and
sizzling far from here, he had sent us his superb organ, which
was as ill-concealed in the guise of a young mason as the
murderer himself would have been in the guise of a rose. And
that's why I was all agog when he went by or when, during the
day, I thought of him or of it, and at night, in the dormitory,
when we sailed until dawn, until the bugle call that opened the
window of morning, announcing for all the world, except for
us, the loveliest summer day.

What I preserve, inscribed in my eyes, is the dance performed by three hundred children in thrilling postures. One of
them hitches up his belt with both hands horizontally flat, one
in front, the other behind. Another is standing, with his legs
spread, at the door of the mess-hall; with a hand in his trouser
pocket he pulls up one side of his little sky-blue smock, that
kind of stiff surplice which the big shots wear very short. For
there is a fashion. This fashion is similar in principle to that of

crashers and pimps, it answers to the same secret com-
mandments. The big shots created it.

It had not been the result of a capricious, arbitrary decision.
A stronger authority than that had created it, the authority of
the big shot who had to impose his torso and thighs, who
retailored the jacket and breeches and who accentuated the
severity of his face by rolling a stiff, broad blue neckerchief
very high around his neck. The Sunday head-gear was the
sailor's beret and the pimp's cap. Its tassel was a rose that
made the Colony go back another five centuries to the days
when pimps wore rose and hat, they to whom Villon said:

> *Lovely children, you are losing*
> *The loveliest rose of your hats . . .*

It was worn, as we know, in crasher style. The Colony was
a place of high fancy in the blossoming heart of France. I am
speaking of fancy and not of frivolity. When a child discovers
black lace for the first time, he receives a shock, a slight
wound; it staggers him to learn that lace, the *lightest* of *fa-
brics*, can be a frill of mourning. Thus, let us realize, with that
twinge of the heart, that there exists a grave fancy, an austere
fancy, precisely the one that governs the scenes which flow
from my eyes until I actually participate physically in those
marvels.

Every inmate of Fontevrault has to leave his anthropo-
metrical measurements in the prison archives. I was therefore
taken, at about two o'clock, from the big cell to the record-
office to be measured (feet, hands, fingers, forehead, nose)
and photographed. It was snowing a bit. I crossed the yards,
and when I returned it was also dark. On my way through the
cloister, in the doorway of the stairs leading to the second
yard, I almost bumped into Harcamone, who was being taken
to the record-office by a guard for some formality or other.
His head was bowed. He took a little hop to the left to avoid
walking in the snow, and he disappeared.

I returned to the big cell.

This apparition gave me a shock which was all the more violent for being brief.

I went back to the drill squad, the pace of which was both rhythmic and gliding, but though I was breathing in the upper world, colliding with the air exhaled by the chests of murderers, the very logical part of me remained present in the disciplinary cell, and as I passed Divers I said to him:

"I've seen him."

I had to talk very fast because of the guard and I wasn't able to see the look on Diver's face as I had already passed him.

The severity of prison life thrust us into ourselves, from where we sometimes came up with gestures that were laughable and strange to the turnkeys and main screws. We found there the solitude whose grandeur was revealed to me very early, thanks to an unjust charge.

Punishments bristled with painful angles: the "silo" of the African Battalion, the "grave" of the discipline squads, the "quarter" at Mettray, the "pit" at Belle Isle, the "big cell" here. We've all been belaboured by them.

I rack my brains trying to find some device, some artifice that would enable me to convey to you the peculiar feel of certain moments at Mettray. How can I make you taste and understand the—I must say flavour—the flavour of Sunday mornings, for example? I can tell you that we left the dormitory a little later than usual. That the morning had been prepared for by an active vigil in which we smoothed our neckties with the back of a brush; then, when we went to bed, more inclined to fatigue since we would get up at seven oclock, abandoning ourselves, so to speak, to that life, we were less tense. We would fall asleep with the hope of Sunday, of rest, a Sunday adorned, laden, with harassing, familiar, formal ceremonies, and we would reach the following day after going through—borne by stronger, surer arms—a confident sleep. In short, it was a slight freedom after the methodical week. We would leave the dormitory more or less as we pleased, depend-

ing on our mood or our love. I shall also tell you that on
Sunday mornings the head of the family would give Deloffre
the razor and, before mass, on a bench in the mess-hall,
Deloffre would shave the downier cheeks. The others, unoc-
cupied and amazed at being so, though it was the same every
week, would stroll about the yard.

Nevertheless, I am sure that I have not rendered the very
particular feeling I had Sunday mornings. The bells would
ring, announcing mass. A big shot would shave my cheeks and
caress them. I was sixteen years old. I was alone in the world.
The Colony was my universe. No, it was the Universe. Family
B was my family. I was descending into life. I was descending
my life with, beside me on the table, a piece of newspaper
crowned with shaving lather. Nothing I tell you will enlighten
you. I await the poetical expression of what I have to say. The
feeling was perhaps composed of my abandonment, my grief
and, at the same time, the happiness of my being there. It is on
Sunday mornings in particular that I feel all this simultaneously. At times some casual fact puts me on its traces, for
example, at night if I make an effort to relive Mettray, to
recall the precise details of the colonists' faces or their peculiarities, or the sight of shaving lather on a newspaper. But this
feeling—or its reflection—flares up within me. I cannot make
it last. If ever I do, *will you know* what Mettray was like? But
I think it is as hard to render as to convey *to you* what the
odour of my mouth is to me. However, I shall tell you that the
white banners, the cedars, the statue of the Holy Virgin in the
wall of Family E were not commonplace things, the kind you
can find anywhere. They were signs. In a poem, ordinary
words are shifted around in such a way that their usual
meaning is enriched by another: the poetic import. Each
of the things, each of the objects that recur to my mind composed a poem. At Mettray, each object was a sign that meant
grief.

We did not know that prison days were poor days, that the
jailed pimps had a sickly pallor, that they were bloated and

unhealthy and that the youngest and least husky of the guards
considered it fun to beat them till they cried for mercy with the
humility of a famished dog. Prisons are inhabited by shadows
that pace up and down the cells, between the door and the
window, silently, gliding rather than walking, on cloth slippers.
This stack of haunted rooms was comparable to collections of
crime magazines. However deeply I leaf beneath the pages, I
find, as if superimposed, another photo of a criminal. This
brings to mind the voices which fused one evening, and of
which I have already spoken. I descended, as the saying goes,
to the lowest levels of abjection. Here, from cell to cell, it's the
same. To be sure, there are the guards, the lawyers, the cops,
but they exist in order to make our shame (and its splendour)
more meaningful by contrasting it with their nice, worthy lives.
I have held those piles of paper in my hands, and my fingers
contracted over them. I am not writing a literary phrase: my
fingers made that movement. It was perhaps out of despair
that I crumpled them, in order to bring them together, to make
of them a mere shapeless heap that I could the more easily
have swallowed: so as to do away with it or to communicate
its virtues to myself. Bulkaen said to me one day, speaking
about Clairvaux Prison: "You realize, Jean, we kept our arms
folded all day long. Weren't allowed to say a word. If you just
moved your head, the guard sent you to the trusty. The trusty
beat the hell out of you. It was sure as fate. There are guys
who stay that way without moving, for years. There was no
danger of the guards giving them the hole. Even if you touched
them, they wouldn't answer. I think Rocky did the same as the
others. Poor guy, he thought. . . ." I realized that through the
memories of Rocky's gestures or deeds or words, Bulkaen had
gone, far from here, in search of Hersir. Rare is the big shot
who does not resign himself. Even the most stubborn break
down sooner or later. At Fontevrault, all that remains in
abeyance is a friendship, a mass of friendship, which unites us
all despite our particular hatreds that are suddenly signalized
by screams or impulsive acts. Like them, the mutest friendship

often manifests itself by those sudden cries that are as violent as a sob.

Shall I speak of the Mettray evenings so as to give you some idea of their monstrous sweetness? For want of anything else, against the curator's wall were a wisteria vine and a rose-bush which mingled their flowers and odours. Around five in the afternoon, in summertime, a vegetable incest would waft its fragrance toward a band of youngsters between the ages of fifteen and twenty who, with a hand in a torn pocket, were stroking themselves. After supper, in summertime, we would go out into the family yard for a few minutes. And the sweetness of which I speak was due perhaps to the brevity of the respite we were allowed. We had too little time to organize a game (but, in fact, have I ever said that we played?). We never played. All our activity had practical aims: concocting a brilliant polish for our sabots, hunting in the yard for a flint that would fit in a cigarette-lighter. We would dig up the pebble with a kick of the heel. If Monsieur Guépin saw anyone bend down and put something into his pocket, he would rush up and, without a word, search him. I could weep with emotion at the memory of those fifty grown-ups who guarded us, regarded us, never understanding us, for they played their role of torturer in all faith. And the three hundred kids who fooled them! We would exchange butts, would hold rapid confabulations about a getaway, and everything was done with gravity. This secret game went on throughout my existence, during all kinds of official occupations, during working hours in the shop, in the mess-hall, at mass, during our peaceful and avowable life, as if lining it with a satanic backing. It would continue during the break at noon, when the guards and bigwigs of the Board of Directors and distinguished visitors thought we were enjoying our rest period. But what shall I say about the shortsightedness of the guards? The shrewdest of them was Gabillé, the head of our family. The expression "to get a finger-job" meant to let a big shot first stroke your buttocks and then stick his finger (the index) up your behind.

The gesture was a gallant one. It was our equivalent of a light woman's kiss on the corner of the mouth. The expression was slightly transformed over the years. And when I say over the years, I do not know to what distant past I am referring, since the Colony is only a hundred years old. We knew from birth that a fellow who beams is one who shoots, who comes, and in that too I see a proof of the children's fabulous and common origin. I am surprised, however, that the web of our jargon was not tighter. Perhaps because we spun a little of it out of ourselves each day. But I now feel that the French language will never be able to render what we said and thought. The following is the expression as transformed by a big shot: "I took a finger-job." It was as if one said: "I stole a kiss." The finger-job was taken during meals, in the yard, while marching, in chapel, in short wherever it could be performed—very rapidly—without the guards suspecting. They heard the expression, it flew from mouth to mouth. And Monsieur Gabillé heard it before the other guards, because he was more alert. One day, in the mess-hall, merely wanting to josh Villeroy, who had rings under his eyes and whose cheeks were hollow, he said to him smilingly:

"You got a finger-job again last night."

He meant that Villeroy had jerked off. The boy took it in the usual sense. He sprang from the table, foaming at the mouth. He charged at the chair of the dumbfounded Gabillé and, knocking him over, hammered his ribs, back, teeth and forehead with the iron-shod heels of his clogs. Gabillé and Villeroy were lifted up, one dying and the other dead-drunk. That was how I lost my man, for he was taken to the quarter. When he got out, he was transferred to another family.

I was saying, before launching out on this digression, that during the noon break we continued our secret activity and, since we were, as a rule, idle, that this activity grew more stealthy and embroidered the yard with a very subdued, smooth pattern of mysterious figures, and this was the work of children brimming with stories.

Not every one of their stories (the one about Deloffre's hand, about Villeroy's heart) was known to us in detail, but either because its author had spoken about it in a nebulous way or had arrived at Mettray escorted and preceded by a reputation that had accumulated at Petite Roquette, the stories finally came to be known, though in a rather vague, loose form, for, as I have said, only the glory which he created for himself here was valid for the colonist, and the feats of arms, even the glorious, superhuman exploits that had brought him to the Colony, meant little. Except, of course, in the case of Harcamone. Thus, each story was known in a legendary form, with more or less vivid touches. One could feel that an atmosphere hung over a few children who were involved in an adventure in which ringed fingers were clutching a terror-stricken heart.

In the evening, we did not have time enough to undertake anything, and we would bask in its stillness. Boats are said to be caught in ice; we were caught in a sudden vacancy. The proximity of night, whose cousins we were, the scents, the depth of the air, perhaps acted upon us without our knowing it. Our gestures grew softer, and our voices too. We were already asleep with the sleep of men when the bugle blew. We would fall into line and march up the stairs to the dormitory where, after a few formalities still accorded to humans, our life as colonists would take shape. Colonists was one of those words which to us were base, but which we had made our own. Though it was not inscribed on marble in letters of gold, we had seen it engraved on our men's torsos or arms, but it nevertheless remained base, we knew it, and we steeped ourselves in that distinguished baseness. The word "offender" makes no more sense at the Colony than it does in prison. Had anyone uttered it there he would have made a fool of himself.

Fontevrault is full of gracious gestures. There is the gesture of Carletti who breaks cigarettes and slips them under the door of the hole for another pimp who is being punished. For the performing of these gestures, the prison is full of famished

bruisers whose pale white faces are idealized by their thinness
and by the white canvas hood which they have to pull down
over their faces when they take their walk and which they wear
on their shaven heads. One hears the following arrogant
answers:

The guard: "Take your cap off."

The broad-shouldered guy, motionless: "Can't, chief."

"Why can't you?"

"I got my mitts in my pockets."

Meanness, arrogance and toughness have sharpened his
voice. Just as severity and asceticism dry the body and mind
and make them more nervous, so ill-humour has given the
tough's voice a whip-like elegance. It lashes.

The prison contains other gestures.

Take this one, the gesture of a youngster and of dozens of
others which they make behind the guards' backs and the
transformation of which, like the evolution of certain slang
terms, I have observed over the years: the hand slaps the
thigh and slides up to the fly with the movement of grasping
the penis as if to piss, a gesture which becomes the following:
after slapping the thigh, the hand, still flat, goes up to the
mouth and makes the sign that means "fed up."

The nasty gesture of a guy who quickly slips a few lice and
bedbugs—found on himself the night before or the same morning—under the door of a hated but too hefty rival. He bends
down fast and blows them into the enemy cell.

It's all so real that I wonder whether it is real and whether
the prison isn't a house of illusion.

Bulkaen excels in these discreet games.

Attracted to men (those who say: "We men, you jerks"),
he takes pleasure in their ways. I expected him to display signs
of unmistakable femininity by virtue of which I would have
completely dominated him. I would sneak a look at his handkerchief, stupidly hoping to find it spotted with blood by a
nasal, and monthly, haemorrhage, to which some inverts are
said to be subject. These are their periods. But the more I

examined the boy, the more brutal and menacing he seemed, despite his smile. Generally, because of his boldness and firmness and his pretty face, the pimps were friendly toward him in an indulgent sort of way. Even though he carried no weight, they would let him take a drag. He mingled with them, and they didn't spurn him. One of the crashers might have taken him under his wing and used him as a helper, giving him a fair share of the profits, and then have rewarded him with his friendship, but I said to him:

"In any case, his friendship, even if he cares for you, won't outweigh his love for a woman. Sooner or later he'll drop you. And he'll never give you the kind of love you really want."

He realized this, but he realized it upon reflection, when he thought it over. He knew that what I said was right and that my love would be stauncher, but he was already abandoning me, forgetting my love which would not fulfill him. Enraptured by the men, he ran to them. I dared not reproach him. In addition, I was disturbed by his attitude toward the toughs and, even more, by his attitude toward Rocky. Though they were still friends, they never touched each other. No attitude could have been more dignified. It was not hypocrisy, for one could tell they were friends from such signs as the following: they used the same linen, the same knife, they drank from the same bottle, one of them would sometimes say to the other: "All you've got to do is write" and you could feel they had the same friend or the same woman. But never did they display their love otherwise than by displaying their friendship.

One morning I saw Bulkaen in a corner of the corridor. He was, as always, in a group of big shots who were standing and talking with two convicts who had been in a penal colony. I drew near. I was about to touch him discreetly on the shoulder and motion to him to come, when I was struck by the drift of the conversation and at the same time noticed that he let Botchako lean on his shoulder. One of the convicts had escaped from the colony and, having been caught, was waiting at Fontevrault to be taken to Saint Martin de Ré. The other was also passing through. The latter, who had got himself charged with a new offence in France so as to be brought back for trial, was giving the other one news of the colony. I heard him mention familiarly the names Mestorino, Barataud, Guy Davin . . . and others. I stood there agape. The two men were speaking casually—as of acquaintances, some of whom they liked and others of whom they hated—of all the princes of crime who had become big names, thanks to the newspapers. They were talking about them quite simply, and I was as astounded as bystanders must have been when they heard Murat speak familiarly to Napoleon. The two convicts were using, with horrifying naturalness, a language that seemed to us as strange as the vegetation of the jungle, which perhaps had given birth to it. We could feel that the words rose up from a remote region, like eructations from the stomach. They spoke an argot of argot, and they seemed unaffected by Harcamone's presence. The colony no doubt had a murderer a thousand times more potent. I stood there listening. I assumed an attitude of detachment, with my hands in my pockets, so that when Bulkaen turned around he wouldn't realize how excited I was. But when someone tipped us off that a turnkey was coming and the group broke up, Bulkaen was under such a spell that he didn't even seem to feel that Botchako was moving away from his shoulder, was liberating him, and I had to touch him. He suddenly came back to earth. His gaze trembled when he saw me, and he said:

"Oh, Jean, you've been standing around. I didn't see you."

"Well you can see now. I've had my eyes on you for an hour."

He went off, hardly burdened by my reproach, to the games and activities of the toughs.

I did not know quite what to think of the advances made to me by the big shots, Pierrot's friends. However, I feared a trap, which he himself perhaps hoped would bedevil me. I decided to respond to their smiles with a piece of impertinence. Which was the following. Botchako was at the top of the stairs with a few other big shots. I was on my way down from the dormitory when he came over to me with his hand open, hiding a lit butt in his bent palm.

"Here, pal, take a drag," he said.

And he handed me the butt with his usual smile. Obviously he was according me the privilege of preceding the other big shots who were awaiting their turn. Obviously too he was making a polite advance to me for which mere politeness required that I show some respect, but I assumed an air of indifference to the honour he was doing me. However, I put out my hand and said:

"If you like."

I saw that I was on the point of being obliged to take the butt and have a drag, but suddenly I recognized, a few feet away, a guy, a pimp, I had known at Fresnes. I drew back my hand, which I had extended toward Botchako, and moved it toward the pimp, at the same time noisily expressing my surprise and delight at seeing him again. As he was on his way down, I quite naturally went along with him, pretending to forget the homage of the drag. Then, thinking that my gesture might look like too-premeditated insolence and thus lose the element of contempt I wanted it to have, I suddenly stopped on the third stair and acted like a person who has just forgotten something. I turned around and started to go up again. The pimps were watching me. Seeing Botchako only in profile, I sensed that his face was clouded with shame. I felt that the brute's decency was being tortured and was muddled in a confused episode in which I appeared and disappeared as disdainfully as an actress. He was also hurt because I was a crasher, a guy who was hostile to pimps. I ought to have been up there with him, and here I was, going down the stairs and laughing with a young hustler. I scowled and flipped my hand the way one does when deciding not to bother about some trivial matter, and I went downstairs. In that way, my gesture did not seem calculated, and my contempt for his advances, which were sought by others, sometimes in a cheap way, disturbed Botchako deeply. I could hear him say, in a gentle, trembling tone, to the fellow nearest him:

"Drag, Milou."

It was a triumphal moment for me, and I went downstairs, carried away by a sudden friendship for the pimp who had been feared at Fresnes and whom a farsighted destiny had called forth to give my exit grace and brilliance.

At reveille, the bugler on duty opened the window and, still bleary-eyed, in his night-shirt, put one foot on the window-sill and with a tragic howl set the sun going. He raised up the fallen walls of an evil city. But everything is sweet to me, Colony, that comes from you, and that allows me a phrase which conjures up Bulkaen's chest opening out wide to expose to me, in the sunlight, the delicate gear of a deadly mechanism. Of the memories which I have, the saddest are joyous. Burials, festivals, and I know none more beautiful than the funerals we gave Rigaux and Rey. It befell the two greatest enemies to be given burial honours the same day, to be merged in a single ceremony. That double ceremony suggests to me that it is perhaps time to touch upon the mystery of the double.

There were two elder brothers in Family C. Here again I am confronted with the strangeness of the prodigious exception. Only Family C had elder brothers, and this fraternal double sovereignty disturbs me as much as the governing of the Russian empire by two child czars, as much as the double death of Rigaux and Rey and the ceremony, savouring more of a marriage than of a burial, which unites them for heaven.

I had a foreboding of palace tragedies, of struggles within the family between the two crowned children, rivalries that could have been carried, they too, to the point of death. Both boys were very handsome. The two faggots—for the elder brothers of Families C and D were always the chickens of big shots in Families A or B—governed the little race of minors, distributing whacks, slaps, kicks, insults, spit and, at times, unexpected treats and blessings. They did not rule in turn or over a given half of the domain. Their rules mingled, com-

plemented each other, one often destroying what the other
ordained, but despite their opposition it was impossible that,
involved with each other as they were by their very struggle,
they did not finally meet in an absurd region beyond
agreement and disagreement and there love each other. Those
two sleeping hearts reigned asleep and adored each other
behind the thick wall of their slumber. Thus do dead warriors
who have slain each other love.

It rained for the funeral. The mud of the little cemetery
soiled our black clogs. Our world often makes capital out of
brutal impoliteness. At Mettray it was common to hear a
child's mouth declare: "Go get browned by the Greeks," and
I have told how, at Fontevrault, the few minutes in the evening
when our windows are open often conclude. A word from
someone sets things going:

"And me, I ream you!"

"You ream the fanny of my cock, you bitch!"

"Your cock never had a fanny. It's your fanny that has a
cock."

And if the last to be challenged does not answer, a pal will
reply for him:

"Get someone to polish your chocolate machine."

And then:

"Get someone to stick his finger up your cornhole."

In citing these insults, I am not trying to make my book
picturesque, but the prisoners do shout them, along with
others, and in the darkness they seem to me the ardent but
violent call of unsatisfied prisoners who, in uttering them, sink
deeper and deeper into regions which are not infernal (for the
word has meaning only if it is far-fetched and not taken
literally) but still subject to the physical and moral laws of the
beginning of the world. Each individual has chosen (not
deliberately but in some obscure way) a phrase which recurs
to his lips more insistently, and this phrase, or formula, is his
substitute for an emblematic figure. It plays the role of the
tattoos on the skin of the big shots at Mettray and here.

It does not seem that the Roman, Hindu and Frankish nobilities of about the year 1000 or earlier enjoyed a religious prestige, a prestige more and other than religious, like that enjoyed by the crumbling nobility, and the reason for this, as I see it, lies in the creation of armorial bearings. It is not for me to study the origin of the emblems (animals, plants, objects), but I feel that the lords, who at first were military chiefs, disappeared beneath the escutcheon, which was a sign, a symbol. The elite that they formed was at once projected into a sublime region, against an abstract sky on which it was written. By virtue of being signified, written, it became the nobility. And the more mysterious the signs that wrote it, the more disturbing it was, compelling the churl—and the noble whom it transcended—to seek in it a remote significance. In like manner, the tattoos consecrated the big shots. When a sign, even a simple one, was engraved on their arms, they hoisted themselves on to a pedestal and at the same time plunged into a darkness remote and dangerous, as is every darkness. When the lord reappeared (a fragile human behind the escutcheon, which was weighted with a symbol), he was charged with the obscure meaning of the symbol and was dangerous, as are all the inhabitants of darkness, the inhabitants of dreams. Dreams are peopled with characters, animals, plants, objects, which are symbols. Each is potent, and when the one who occasioned it substitutes for the symbol, he benefits from this mysterious power. The potency of the sign is the potency of the dream, and it was likewise in the realm of dream that National Socialism went to search, thanks to an explorer of darkness, for the swastika.

Other facts, by singularizing us, isolated us even more.

We had our own little familiar, secret cemetery where our seniors slept. Before the coffins of the two children were taken to it, they were placed in a very simple, bare catafalque, and the bareness, which was that of the hearses of proud great men, conferred upon the young dead the nobility of sages.

Beneath the yews were the rows of graves of colonists who

had died in the infirmary, and against the wall, better sheltered, were those of nuns and chaplains who had shoved off with a natural death. And at the end of the cemetery, in two chapels, were the vaults of the founders, Monsieur Demetz and Baron de Courteille, who rested "among the children they loved so dearly," as is written on the black marble in the chapel. About ten of us had been picked to escort Rey and Rigaux. Deeply involved in our love, we were a united couple leading a dead couple to burial, just as, shortly afterward, I was to accompany the remains of Stoklay, and ten years later, in thought, those of Bulkaen united with those of Botchako, and, still later, those of Pilorge.

What was Stoklay to me? Apart from the many attentions he ventured to show me only when he knew that Villeroy wasn't around, our lives crossed twice. I once wanted to escape. Was it really because I was hopeless and unhappy? But the violence that quickens me when my hopelessness is too great would, at present, make me seek other means of flight. And I wonder whether a life sentence will not help me find them. I have already mentioned the taste—I emphasize the word taste, for I felt a sensation in my mouth, on the roof of the palate—the funereal taste of the words "preliminary hearing to confirm the mandatory sentence of life imprisonment," and it occurs to me, so that you may have a clearer understanding of my despair, to write that I was like the living leper who, with a taper in his hand, hears himself singing, behind his hood, the Office for the Dead, the *Libera me*. But hopelessness draws you out of yourself (I weigh my words). Mine was so deep that, in order for me to live (continuing to live being the important thing), my imagination first organized—and was first to do so—a refuge for me in my very fall and created a very beautiful life for me. The imagination being rapid, this was done quickly. My imagination surrounded me with a host of adventures which were aimed perhaps at cushioning my encounter with the bottom of the precipice—for I thought it had a bottom, but hopelessness hasn't—and the deeper I fell, the faster my mind worked, accelerated by the speed of the fall. My tireless imagination kept weaving. It wove other adventures thick and fast. Finally it ran wild, excited by the violence, and a number of times I had the impression it was no longer the imagination but another and higher faculty, a salvatory faculty. All those splendid, invented adventures took on more and more a kind of consistency in the physical world. They belonged to the world of matter, though not here, but I felt they did exist somewhere. It was not I who lived them. They lived elsewhere and without me. This new and, as it were, eager faculty which sprang from but was higher than the imagination showed them to me, prepared them for me, organized them so that they were all ready to receive me. It would not have taken much for me to withdraw from the disastrous adventure that my body was living, to withdraw from my body (I was thus right in saying that hopelessness draws you out of yourself) and to project myself into those other consoling adventures which were unfolding parallel to poor mine. Was I, thanks to tremendous fear, on the miraculous road to the secrets of India?

Child that I was, I ran away from Mettray. I no longer know what impelled me one Sunday afternoon to break the magic circle of flowers, kick off my sabots and fly through the countryside. Beyond the laurels, the ground sloped. I rushed down the meadows and groves as if I were rolling, instinctively choosing the edges of fields where my figure was more likely to blend with the landscape than elsewhere. I felt, I sensed, that I was being pursued. The river stopped me for a moment, long enough for me to realize I was winded. I heard footsteps. I wanted to continue along the shore, but I was out of breath. I think my clothes turned white with fear. I entered the water, and that was where Stoklay, without going in himself, caught me. He stretched out his arm. I don't know whether I was seized by the water or by the child child-stealer, but I remember how glad I was to be caught. The freedom I was winning—and which had already been won during my flight,

since my flight was my first free act—was too weighty a
matter for a kid accustomed to obedience. I was grateful to
Stoklay for stopping me (I am tempted to say here that I still
feel the same happiness when a policeman arrests me, and
perhaps I am happy only because of the unconscious recalling
of that childhood scene). His hand came down on my shoulder
in the classic manner. I almost collapsed in the water with fear
and love. With fear, for the monstrousness of the act I had
dared, my flight—a true deadly sin—from a clandestine
heaven, appeared to me in a white light. I finally came to my
senses. And then I was filled with hatred. Stoklay was very
decent. He said that old Guépin had made him run after me.
In short, he gave very noble reasons, whereas he forgot the
only right one, perhaps out of modesty, for he knew himself: it
was that, being strong and handsome and bearer of a name
which was so like that of Soclay, the murderer of the little
Marescot girl, he had a right to do the vilest things, or rather
he must have known that in his case vile acts turned into
heroic acts, and this was obscurely understood by the big shots
who, strong in their power, rather than repudiate one of the
handsomest among them, did not hold it against him for
having brought me back and who arrogated to themselves the
right to sell chickens and jerks to the guards.

Gripping my arm, Stoklay led me back to the Colony, and I
saw myself at his side as an escaped harem woman being
brought back by a warrior. Under cover of a grove, when we
were finally on the little road leading to the Colony, he looked
at me and with his right hand turned my head to his, but I felt
my face becoming overcast with such a haughty solitude that it
made Stoklay flee, that is, what was himself withdrew, left the
contour of that form, his body, left his mouth, eyes, fingertips
and through deep, slow, circuitous folds retreated faster than
electricity into, no doubt, the secret chamber of his heart. I
stood there in the presence of a dead figure that was watching
me. My revenge went further than I. To shake off his lethargy
he burst out laughing. Then, with a movement of his arm he

made me get in front of him. He grabbed me by the shoulders and, with a thrust of his hips, with a single powerful thrust, he pretended, laughing all the while, to ream me while walking. I was thrown ten feet forward by his steely movement. I continued on my way alone, in front of him, straight ahead, and that was how I returned to the Colony, sent back by the thrust of a prick. I went directly to the quarter. But as my trousers were wet, they left a big damp spot on his which, exposing an intimacy that he had only desired, was enough for him to be locked in a cell. He could very easily have defended himself by having me questioned, though one never knows how a questioning by the head of a reformatory will be conducted. The director of Mettray was no more a fool than the warden of Fontevrault who nevertheless lost his way in the simple complications of the adventures of inmates when they had the purity of Harcamone.

Stoklay, who perhaps was uncertain as to how I would answer if called upon for my poor testimony, refused to defend himself, perhaps too out of vanity, in order to be locked up for having screwed a young kid. He though that he in turn would take revenge on me by compromising me. He left the cell to join the squad a few days before I was released from the quarter (big shots who were punished were sent to a cell where they slept on the floor, and the other kids marched around the yard all day long: that was the squad). The cell regime, including masturbation, had fagged him. He was pale and skinny and could hardly stand on his feet. He begged the jerks for a crust of bread or left-over slops. Don't laugh at this. Every day I see hunger occasion other cowardly acts that are just as beautiful, humiliations compared to which his were nothing. One day he got into a fight with Bertrand, who was as weak and skinny as he. Before our eyes they dealt each other blows that were as soft as caresses. It was a struggle in slow-motion, with, on both sides, an occasional burst of violence that came to nothing. Only their eyes retained their force. It was still summer. The two children rolled delicately in the dust. They knew they were ridiculous in our eyes (for we were less free with our hands during the day and had only our nights for exhausting ourselves, but what nights on our hard boards!). They were hurt by this and kept fighting. They were ghosts who ripped each other from top to bottom and through whose laceration we could see the imprecise, yet very clear vision of the mysteries of death. I still do not dare speak too precisely of the tortures of hunger and the magic it generates. I have suffered so much from it and seen my friends suffer that my words, without my choosing them deliberately, will sigh my anguish, if not scream it.

In the quarter, the elder brother at the time was Piug, a magnificent husky who didn't let privations get him down. He separated the fighters with a kick and a smile. The two pieces fell apart, glad to be saved from themselves. To me the Stoklay piece was stamped forever with the very noble ridiculousness of physical exhaustion. A few days after I got out of the quarter, he entered the infirmary, where he died. The Almighty again wanted me to be chosen to go to the cemetery. I had to escort Stoklay all the way to death. The director went as far as the church. At Mettray, one no longer has parents. We sprinkled a few drops of holy water on the grave, and I left with the other colonists. It was on the way back that I heard Villeroy, Morvan and Mono talk about escaping. Métayer, who was near them, no doubt also heard them. They moved away from that king's son whose sad, freckled face made them uneasy. They ran away that same night.

There can be no doubt that within each cell the youngest inmates now dream of Harcamone's destiny. All their thoughts are dedicated to him, and it is also that part of Bulkaen which I lose. Harcamone was invested with the majesty of the victim and the rough beauty of the warrior. Thus, the phenomenon of the fecundating of young hopefuls by the bigtimers who are fraught with crimes as with glamorous insignia is repeated in the prison itself, but not quite in the same way, for this time the kids do not dream of being Harcamone—unless it be at the

hearings in criminal court—or of imitating him. They admire
his awesome destiny and they are ready for any act of humility
as relates to him. The condemned murderer's presence in their
midst, at the fortress, disturbs them, causes them a kind of
vague, drifting anxiety, whereas Mettray, which was also disturbed, though perhaps less deeply, dared the act of wanting to
become Fontevrault. I used to hope that the big shots of the
time thought about us who lived only for them and by their
code. I hoped that each of them was handsome and that he had
chosen a colonist to love secretly, inventing curious forms of
love and watching over him from afar. When talking about the
Colony I sometimes refer to it as "The Old Lady" or "The
Dreadnaught." These two expressions would probably not
have sufficed to make me identify Mettray with a woman, but,
in addition to the fact that they usually designate a mother,
they occurred to me, in connection with the Colony, at a time
when I was weary of my orphaned solitude and when my soul
yearned for a mother. And everything that one associates with
women: tenderness, slightly nauseating whiffs from the open
mouth, deep, heaving bosom, unexpected punishment, in short,
everything that makes a mother a mother (writing this
reminds me of the chaplain. In all his sentences he used the
"so" which is the voicing of a sigh and is common in feminine
conversation and literature: "We felt *so* happy. . . ." "I
suddenly felt *so* far away from it all. . . ." You can see the
ample bosom rising and falling. The priest's belly swelled out
in like manner. All his gestures started at his bosom, his hands
moved to and from it constantly, so that you wondered
whether the gestures sprang from a charity whose source was
in his heart or whether his bosom was the most important part
of his body). I endowed the Colony with all these ridiculous
and disturbing attributes of womankind, until there was
established in my mind not the physical image of a woman but
rather a soul-to-soul bond between us which exists only
between mother and son and which my undeceivable soul
recognized. I went so far as to address invocations to it. I

implored it to relive in my memory. That was my mystical period. The divinity was still wrapped in a solemn, faraway sleep, in limbo. Little by little the veils fell away from it. The mother materialized. In the cell, I really and truly returned to her throbbing breast and had real dialogues with her, and perhaps these transformations which made Mettray my mother added an incestuous feeling to my love for Divers, who had come from the same womb as I.

He appeared more and more fabulous to me. Everything about him still surprises and enchants me. Even the word "diversity" seems to me to derive from him as achillea, or the Achilles plant, derives from the warrior who nursed his heel with it. Divers often said, quite simply, "balls." He said it instead of "what crap." His face was hard. When I kissed him for the first time, on our wedding night (for though Villeroy had left the family, he looked after me and often, when we met behind the laurels, he brought me a piece of cheese from the kitchen), when I kissed him for the first time, I felt, along with the thrill of intimacy, the impossibility of communion with so handsome a face, a face that was continued by so handsome a body of so rigid a male. That head was as hard as a head of marble. It numbed your wrists. And cold. He did not throb. No flaw, no crack, gave exit to an idea or emotion. He was not porous. Some men are. A vapour emanates from them and enters you. Diver's face was less mean than strange. It was only when I kissed him that I recognized him a little, that he seemed to show himself in a new and disturbing light which revealed unknown perspectives. I felt the same emotion when I cut the photo of Pilorge out of a detective magazine. My scissors slowly followed the outline of the face, and the slowness focused my attention on details, the texture of the skin, the shadow of the nose on the cheek. I was seeing that beloved face from a new point of view. Then, as I had to turn it upside down to facilitate the cutting, it suddenly became a mountainous landscape with a lunar surface, more desolate and forsaken than a landscape of Tibet. I cut along the line of the forehead, I turned the page a little, and suddenly, with the speed of a racing locomotive, shadowy perspectives and chasms of grief rushed at me. The sighs that came from far away and blocked my throat were so thick that I had to stop several times before finishing the job. The view I had of a certain eyelid was so lovely that the two blades of the scissors remained open, not daring to cut farther into the paper. I didn't want to finish too quickly. I was abandoned in a gorge or on a peak, staggered by the discovery of a murderer's face. I thus caressed that insolent youngster a last time, as we caress a word when we think we possess it. That is how—by taking them unawares, by approaching them from unusual angles —one discovers the extraordinary composition of faces and postures, and certain virtues of Bulkaen were revealed to me just as accidentally. When he said to me (and it was nine days after I had met him) on the stairs, as he took my mouth:

"A smack, Jean, just one."

Bulkaen had opened for me the door to René Rocky's heart. I was in the habit of calling a kiss a peck. Bulkaen had said "a smack." As erotic language, such as we use in dalliance, is a kind of secretion, a concentrated juice that flows from the lips only in moments of the most intense emotion, of plaint, as this language is, in other words, the essential expression of passion, each pair of lovers has its own peculiar language, a language which has a perfume, an odour *sui generis* which belongs only to that couple. In saying a "smack" to me, Bulkaen continued to secrete the juice peculiar to the couple he formed with Rocky. A foreign, because new and unsuspected, body was entering my love for Bulkaen, but, at the same time, by means of that word I was brought into contact with the intimacy of the couple Bulkaen-Rocky. "A smack" were the words they murmured to each other in bed or in the windings of the corridors, and perhaps on that stairway. "A smack" is what survived of their ruined love, the odour that escaped from it after it had died. It was the very odour of the breath, and especially of Bulkaen's breath mingling with mine. Rocky had

intoxicated him with that word which was addressed to me,
and with those that accompanied it, and each of them had
certainly intoxicated the other with it until they were both
quite giddy. I suddenly learned that Bulkaen had had a
love-life as deep as mine, with a past equally charged, for the
word that rose to his throat and the gesture that perhaps
moved his hand were what are said and done when there are
two and the two love each other in keeping with the secret rites
of a deep love. In watching over Bulkaen's fidelity to myself, I
was entering Rocky's friendship, and it was over his fidelity to
Rocky that I also watched.

Chance, secretly wooed, soon showed its face. Eight days
after we had met, I was on my way up from the shop at noon
when I tore one of my slippers and bent down to mend it, thus
letting everyone leave the shop and go by me. A guard
remained behind with me, but when I finished and stood up I
was on the landing of Bulkaen's shop. Bulkaen was on his way
out. He was second in line, Lou was first. Both of them, like
all the others, had their hands in their belt, flat against the
stomach. Lou put his right hand in front of his eyes to shelter
them from the light. Bulkaen did the same, but whereas Lou
placed his hand flat on his forehead and left it there, Bulkaen
slowly slid his palm over his shaved head. He moved it back to
his forehead and left it there. Then, with perfect timing, Lou
continued on himself the movement begun on Bulkaen's
forehead. He brought his hand down over his eyes and slowly
put it back into his belt, and Bulkaen, with a slight delay, made
this same movement on himself, but a little more briskly, so
that his hand entered his belt at the same time as Lou's
reached his. They hitched up their trousers simultaneously.
Even without my jealousy I would have been greatly disturbed
by two inmates, one following the other, who seemed to agree
secretly to share a movement as simple as the one they had just
performed, but my excitement of the past few days made me
magnify the event to fabulous dimensions. Acting as if I hadn't
noticed them, I joined my shopmates in the refectory. I felt I

was at Bulkaen's gate since I had not had time or room enough
to insert into the connections of their movements even the
intention of one of mine. It was essential that I enter him at
any cost. Divers at least was more able than the dead Pilorge
to defend his face and the reflections of his heart. Perhaps it
was also this defence that made him tremble, made him move.
The continual fear in which Divers lived was very deeply
hidden beneath an external candour and boldness, it was
buried in the depths of his being. At times it cropped out on
the surface, which it took over. But that deep, muffled fear
always made Divers, to a slight degree, a kind of prisoner.
None of his gestures was quite pure. They were those of a
statue on which light and breezes play. Their outline was a bit
blurred. When I held his face in my hands, I held the face of a
dream character that had come to life. I was horrified by the
impossibility of making it love me. I realized, when he said to
me laughingly: "I'd like to give you a shot in the pants," that
he wanted to because I was the kid most sought after, but it
was enough for him to make that remark in his deep, gruff
voice, which was surprisingly weighty in such a finely chiseled
mouth (those sinuous little lips usually adorn chubby faces;
that's what his mouth was like, on a lean, colourless face). He
made a single statement which stripped him of his boyhood but
attired him in splendid frippery. He was a king. As rich and
powerful as the captain of the boat whose member loomed up
from the billows of lace and silk with the solemn authority of a
cannon in the shade of branches firing terrible shots at the
galley after each of which there was a recoil, the memory of
which moves me more than the shot itself, for it was the
skillful recoil of the loins that thrust again, without stopping,
that thrust beneath the lace like the grey monsters of German
gunnery which are veiled by the camouflage netting woven by
us in prison and strewn with leaves and flowers. But I have
had to wait seven years to learn that he loved me. Seven years
have hardened his features, but have also humanized them. His
face is less smooth, life has left its mark on it. I had just

left—when I went down to the hole, when I joined Divers—a Bulkaen both nasty and charming who was doing his best to love me.

Divers said to me:

"When you left, the head of the family made me sleep next to the elder brother in your hammock. God damn it, I jerked my head off thinking of you! In your hammock, you realize! I couldn't believe you were hot for me there. I always had a feeling you were making a monkey of me. Because you're a kidder! You remember when Villeroy locked us in the mess-hall? I must have looked like a prize jerk to you!"

"A jerk? Yes, pretty much."

One Saturday afternoon, Villeroy, Divers and I were standing a little apart from the others, near the open door of the mess-hall, and were joking about the crush I seemed to have on Divers but which no one dreamed of taking seriously. At Mettray, I had to distort the face of my love, because it was stifling me. It had to come out, I had to tell it, to scream it, but fearing lest the slightest word annoy Divers, lest he jeer at it and arrest the tense gestures, the caresses, the contacts that freed me a little of my amorous burden, I exaggerated the expression of my love to the point of caricature. I ridiculed Divers, my love and myself. With the result that I loved on a very pure plane, with sentiments that were very beautiful but that were seen only as reflected by one of those loathsome mirrors you find in amusement parks. Divers feared my irony. But the caricaturing of the words and gestures of love had destroyed within me the glamour of love, or rather: I got used to loving within the framework of the ridiculous, or in spite of it. I mean that whenever I discovered something ridiculous about a boy, some blemish, a stain on his beauty, it did not prevent me from being in love with him. I even went so far as to be in love because of it. Over-weary of loving, I even followed and spied on youngsters who quivered with grace, until the spell was broken. In order to be rid of an amorous burden, I would wait for the moment, for the glance that revealed the speck of ugliness, I would wait for the angle that brought the ugliness into view, the line or volume that destroyed the beauty, but, on the other hand, it often happened that when I had seen all aspects of the boy, he would sparkle with a thousand other lights and would trap me in the mingled charms entangled in his multiplied facets. And the blemish I discovered would no longer be enough to free me. On the contrary. While seeking it, I would discover each time a new aspect of the masterpiece. Am I to regard this as the origin of my sexual perversities? I have adored lovers one of whom had flat ears, another a slight stammer, a third who had lost three fingers. They would make a long list. I had done such a good job of belittling Divers, I had saddled him—and his relations with me—with so many grotesque ornaments, that the whiteness of his skin, which at first had been loathsome on someone else, was acceptable on him, then it became a charm. And that may very well lead me ultimately to scatophagy—the mention of which used to make me nauseous—and afterwards even further, perhaps to madness, owing to my love of convicts in the cells where, no longer able to recognize my farts in the tangle of mingled odours, I came to accept and then to relish indiscriminately those which came from the pimps and thereby to accustom myself to excrement. And perhaps I allowed myself to drift into this so readily because in that way I estrange myself from the world. I am carried along in that fall which, cutting by its very speed and verticality all threads that hold me to the world, plunges me into prison, into foulness, into dreaming and hell, and finally lands me in a garden of saintliness where roses bloom, roses whose beauty—as I shall know them—is composed of the rims of the petals, their folds, gashes, tips, spots, insect-holes, blushes and even their stems which are mossy with thorns.

Villeroy joked about my love for Divers, of which he saw only the contortions, but he did not forget I was a chicken. He was mindful of my future and my dignity. Thanks to him, my gesture had more fullness. A stronger wind swelled out my

gesture, which conjured up a youngster bent over his handle-
bar and racing down a hill, with the wind of the ride puffing
out his shirt in which a hard, straight, little chest was erect. He
wanted me to have a manly upbringing. Thus it seems that
even when I was young I refused, in my dreams, to be a fair
captive on the galley but was rather a cabin boy in order to
reserve the possibility of *growing up* at the captain's side and
taking his place. One would almost think these were precepts
of honour (a kind of warrior's honour) that were handed
down from big shots to chickens. He would not have put
up—as no big shot did—with having a chicken who was a
queer. He made me fight, but that was not enough. In order
that the blows I dealt have more meaning, in order that my
authority and power be greater, I had to protect someone. He
therefore decided that I would have a chicken. He himself
chose a kid from Family E, a smart youngster who laughed in
my face when, one summer afternoon, behind the laurels,
Villeroy introduced him to me and, pointing to me, said to
him: "He's going to be your man. I'm telling you so."

Villeroy wanted me to "lay" the little guy before his eyes.
One evening, he arranged an appointment behind Family B. I
don't know how the kid managed to leave Family E and cross
the big yard without being seen, but no sooner did he arrive
than Villeroy made him lie down in the grass and nettles.

"Pull down your pants," he ordered.

The kid lowered his trousers. It was evening. Though
Villeroy couldn't see me blushing, he could tell from my
constricted gestures that I felt ashamed. He said to me:

"Go on, Jean, let him have it."

I looked at him. I felt like flinging myself at his knees. What
worried me was the thought that he would love me less, would
find me less graceful if I assumed the male's position in his
presence.

He spoke again:

"Well? What's the matter. Make it snappy, you don't have
time. What's the matter? Got stage-fright?"

Lying on the grass, with his behind bared to the wind, the kid waited, patient to the point of indifference. Villeroy seized my arm.

"Wait, I'll help you. I'll take him first."

He stretched out on the kid, but with his head raised like that of a snake. He said to me:

"Get down there, in front of me."

I squatted, facing the kid. Villeroy must have stuck it right in, as he usually did.

"Go on, quick."

Here there should follow the description of a children's game which I invite you to complete.

As Villeroy could not kiss the kid, he darted at my face a look that united it with his in a long kiss. Though he came quickly, I finished before him. The three of us stood up without any embarrassment. The kid was the least embarrassed of all. Villeroy pushed him toward me.

"Got to kiss each other."

I kissed him. Villeroy added:

"Now he's your man."

Then, turning to me:

"And you, you've got to stick up for your kid."

And, after these furtive movements, reassuming his bossy tone as an elder brother, he said to him:

"All right, now get going. We've seen enough of you."

When the boy had left, Villeroy took me amicably by the neck and said:

"Well, my little man, was it good?"

We joined the guys who were about to go up to the dormitory.

I was strong. I was breaking away from Villeroy, but, as I was attracted by Divers, there was the possibility of his wrecking my effort to be virile by loving me. However, he was amused at my love for him. Villeroy found it piquant to arouse his own jealousy. He suddenly pushed Divers and me into the empty mess-hall and shut the door behind us. Enclosed in the same darkness, we stood there startled for ten seconds. Pulling himself together, Divers cried out:

"Oh! the dumb jerk!"

In the dusk, despite the dusk, I sensed his embarrassment. I drew near and tried to kiss him, but he stopped me with a laugh. I laughed too and said: "You're the one who's backing out." He laughed again in the darkness and said: "That's right, I'm backing out." My heart swelled with tremendous shame, for I realized he had been making a play for me until then only in order to string me along. He had been pulling my leg when he said to me: "Cutie, I could go to town on you." He hadn't meant it, it had been only big-shot talk. I then realized my ugliness—my close-cropped hair, the fuzz on my cheeks—for I still thought that most of the big shots were looking for the woman in me. I didn't manifest my confusion and started banging on the door, begging Villeroy to let us out. He opened the door and laughed at us. I don't know what he was trying to accomplish by locking us in. Perhaps he wanted to humiliate me, for one evening—and I, his cherished chicken, whom he showered with love, couldn't possibly have doubts about his friendship too—one evening, after mess, he ordered me to go to the sink and dry the dishes. I stood up, quite surprised, and in front of everyone he threw the repulsively greasy dish-mop in my face. Then, amused at his prank, he gave a huge horse-laugh, which insulted me.

I betrayed my big shot without guile. Children all betray with this same guilelessness, and I wonder whether, despite the betrayals which I suspect, Bulkaen did not love me. Perhaps he loved me all the more, or would have loved me had I possessed him. I had to make up my mind to take him.

When I got back from the shop where they made camouflage nets, I looked around for him. He wasn't there. I was afraid he might have sneaked over to Shop 6 to try to get news of Rocky. I turned to Rasseneur, who was walking at my side, and asked him whether he had seen Pierrot. But Lou Daybreak, from the depths of his cadaverous countenance,

answered instead, in a simpering voice which he tried to make
sound casual. He also pretended not to know about my fondness for Bulkaen. He said:

"The turnkeys let him slip out to see his pimps. He went up
ahead."

I didn't bat an eyelid. I kept walking in line, outwardly
calm. Rasseneur corrected him: "That's just talk." Again I
heard Lou Daybreak behind me:

"Botchako's trying to shack up with him."

When I reached the foot of the stairway, the light went on
as if by concerted chance, and at 5 p.m. the prison suddenly
had the look of a bakery busying itself silently in a city which
is still asleep. I shoved aside the first few men who were
already on the stairs, and dashed up the three flights. He was
standing at the top, upright and motionless, as he usually
stood, with his hands in his belt, against his stomach. Seeing
me rush up that way made him smile, and because he was four
steps above me he looked as if he were smiling at me from on
high.

"You slut, you bitch," I said in a low, breathless voice, for I
knew I no longer had the constraint of the discomfort caused
by physical effort.

"But Jean, what's eating you?"

Counting on his spontaneity, I was expecting a prompt
reaction. I was expecting a punch. I thought he would have a
violent reflex that would prove his spontaneity. It didn't come.
I screamed in a whisper:

"And as for your guy, I'll ride his deck."

Suddenly I realized that I had no claim on him. I did not
have enough natural authority to assert myself and require that
he belong to me by virtue of a single look of mine or by a
laying on of hands. I knew, in addition, that in prison the word
friendship means nothing when it does not imply love.
Therefore nothing obliged him to be faithful to me, except one
thing: physical possession. But I had never possessed him, not
even in my dreams. He repeated:

"Jean, what's eating you?"

The flock of inmates who were behind me were coming up. We heard them.

"Go away, Jean, I beg you. If they see us together again, they'll start bullshitting about me."

But I went up to him, with my jaws clenched and trapped his waist in my arms. I held him firmly. I was amazed. He didn't even try to break away. With an imploring look, he said:

"Jean, let go of me!"

And, in a whisper: "I'm your kid, I swear to you."

I let go of him and he fled to his cell. It was time. The silent penitents were there. I joined them, but I felt that only if I had him would I be his friend and possess the rights that go with friendship. And it is friendship that I conjure up every night, a friendship ever deeper, ever closer. I want to possess Bulkaen. Is possession the right word? Our revels so merge our bodies. . . . I report that a few nights ago I imagined a most beautiful love-scene with him, and I felt the sadness of it only upon awakening, when I realized that he was dead, that his body was rotting in the prison cemetery, next to Botchako's.

The more I write about Bulkaen, the less attractive I find him. I have given life on paper to a paragon which I have adorned with all the beauties of my friend. I have stripped the flesh-and-blood Bulkaen whom I see emerging little by little from banality. I wonder whether he ever did possess all the charm that I discovered in him and that thrilled me so. Perhaps it was Bulkaen's role to be loved, and the ecstasy aroused by this love made it all the more possible for me to discover —thanks to language—the qualities of the ideal creature who is now fixed once and for all. The reader may ask whether I did not love Bulkaen precisely because I found these qualities in him *too*. I cannot answer.

I loved him less and less, and I would have stopped writing him those love letters which I wanted to be the most beautiful letters ever written. He no longer inspired me. I had got all I could from him—either for lack of means or because he himself had been emptied. By the play and tricks of language, he has helped me to portray a human being, to give him life and force. But what exactly was his role?

It is with words of love that I have recorded in this book his acts and gestures, all the attributes of his personality, which stands forth spiked with sharp angles. But as I no longer need, for the work of art, to seek within me—or to find there without seeking—the expressions that sublimated him, when I think of Bulkaen living with our life, I content myself with *seeing* him carry on without the help of magic words. I no longer name him. I have said all I have to say about him. The work flames and its model dies. And when I rejoiced in having already given all the loveliest names I could think of to other youngsters who are entombed alive in my books, it was perhaps with the vague idea of preserving Bulkaen, outside my writings, as a physical being whom I had loved with my gratified flesh. And now I feel only infinite pity for the poor birdie that can no longer fly because I have plucked all its feathers.

Although Bulkaen was not the fiery archangel, the archangel Harcamone, whose adventure transpired in Heaven, that is, in the highest region of myself, the reader is not to use these words as a pretext for thinking that Harcamone never existed. I knew the murderer. He strode the earth, at my side, but he continued so far that I was the only one who witnessed the full extent of his ranging. The expression "in the highest region of myself" also means that I had to strain every fibre in order to see very high or very far within me, because I could barely make out the patterns, the diagrams inscribed there by the vibrations produced by Harcamone's human gestures, by his deeds on earth.

Although Bulkaen was not that Archangel, neither did he have the sad destiny of Divers. I never spoke to him about Harcamone in so many words. Though he worshipped him, he did so secretly. His modesty would have been shocked. But he worshipped in the depths of his heart. Had I brought that cult to light, he would have recoiled from it, and from me too. Divers liked prison the way one likes everyday life. He took its everyday pattern as a matter of course, without embellishing it, without wanting to embellish it. He knew he was a prisoner for life. Bulkaen waltzed through prison because his natural rhythm was the waltz, but he hoped that his whirling would bring down the walls and whisk him off to the sun. His body sang a hymn to action, to freedom. I have said that he was joyful, that he taught me joy, and I have written what precedes in order to make you realize how bewildered I was when I received his message asking for a poem about the penal colony. Mettray had dealt him a telling blow. He was mortally wounded, despite his laughter and health. Nothing would prevent his being dragged down like the rest of us by that lethal weight. No doubt he had risked death—he will find it—in order to free Rocky. After his own bars, he would have cut those of the convict. He wanted to save his lover. I see Bulkaen as belonging to the mob of youngsters who hang around the prison in which their younger or older friend or accomplice is locked up and who smuggle in (thanks to an obliging guard) linen, cigarettes, and a word of hope tinted with love. These lithe, silent figures, ravaged despite their smiles, prowl around all the prisons of the globe. They are called lost souls.

Each of the lapses of my love for Bulkaen enhances the splendour of Harcamone, but then, in order to devote myself entirely to the affection which I forsake and then return to repentantly, I would like Bulkaen to give him up, to be unaware of him. Words have no power over Harcamone's image. They will not exhaust it, for its matter is inexhaustible.

Novels are not humanitarian reports. Indeed, let us be thankful that there remains sufficient cruelty, without which beauty would not be. Prison regulations concerning criminals are strict and precise, and rightly so—with respect to the code of special justice in the service of beauty—for they are one of the tools that will shape and fashion the hardest and, at the same time, most delicate substance: the hearts and bodies of murderers. Let us not feel pity if, that very evening, after being informed by the Court in *words*, Harcamone was informed of his condemnation in *fact* by a whole body of details which made him mount, as it were, a flight of tiers by which he passed from the state of man to the state of death, and of which he could perhaps have taken advantage in order to escape, for we ought to be able to make practical use of certain extraordinary states which are granted us. I think that the term "supra-terrestrial" would be appropriate to this new mode of being. They therefore began by refusing to let Harcamone go up to his old cell. When he was taken to the clerk's office, he was granted the following frightful consideration: they did not go through his pockets. They did not beat him, which surprised him. The guards had been very rough with him. The day he stabbed Rose-wood, he was handcuffed and all the guards beat him, one after the other. He screamed. They kept beating him, and when he was removed from the cell where the torture had taken place, he was covered with blood. He had to be transported by attendants to the cell that had been reserved for him until the court passed judgment. All along the way, he lost blood. He was the dead man and the murderer. They maltreated him even more when they sensed his power, but what would they have said had they learned of his miracles, that the rose means love, friendship, death . . . and silence! In their minds, Harcamone would have taken his place in a mysterious society whose language was taught by learnèd and subtle Chinese! Two guards and an officer took him in hand and escorted him to the condemned cell. The guard who opened the door did so with solemnity, with a kind of tenderness, a feeling which was not perceptible in his gesture, but I know that this turnkey was suddenly moved to pity, ready to burst into tears. The slightest suspicious-looking fact, a fact out of the ordinary, can give him a shock and engender that wondrous virtue: charity. A trifle, and his heart would open. The door made the usual, terrifying sound of a door.

This chapter of my book will be only a song of despair, and I am afraid that this last word flows from my pen frequently. Harcamone entered first. He entered despair itself, for from then on the ceremonies ceased and there ensued the removal from the world in which the body had nothing to fear. Indeed, the pomp of the Criminal Court may set us dreaming of an elaborate funeral with the collaboration of a very special clergy in which the accused, who as a rule is already condemned, plays the monumental role of a man living at the climax, at the pitch of paroxysm, since all that display is in his honour, since he is the heart which sends out its blood so that a gigantic body may live, that body being: the pomp and circumstance of the Court, the soldiers, the spectators and, outside, the mob that mingles his name with the name of death, and farther off, the newspapers, the radio, an entire attentive people that is nerved, as it were, with a more secret, hidden element, which he also quickens with his supernatural sperm, the adolescents, their throats taut with anxiety, who will bear forever the scared stigmata of the decapitation. He made the acquaintance of the too-precise details of death, those which deal with the body and with which the body is preoccupied. Here ended the sublime, and never was word more apt. The cell was similar to the one on the second floor in which he had lived during the three months he had been awaiting trial. Similar, though with certain fearful particulars. Infernal horror does not lie in an unwontedly, spectrally, inhumanly, deliberately fantastic setting. It accepts the setting and ways of everyday life. A mere detail or two transforms them (an object that is not in its right place, or that is upside down, or that can be seen from inside), takes on the very meaning of that universe, symbolizes it, revealing that this setting and these ways pertain to hell. The cell was like the others, as was the life that Harcamone would lead there, but the window was half bricked up, and the open grill in the door could be closed only by a small grate, like the Judas-holes in convents. Outside, near the door, was a high wooden stool where the guards would take up their post, in turn, so as not to lose sight of the murderer for a second, and would thus be able to keep an eye on him while remaining seated. This cell was really special. Hardly had Harcamone entered than a guard arrived, followed by a trusty carrying sheets, blankets, a coarse shirt, a towel, a pair of slippers, and a homespun jacket and pair of trousers. Harcamone sat down on the bed, and a guard began to divest him of the civilian clothes he had been allowed to wear for the hearing. He first removed the tie, then the shoes, then the jacket, and when Harcamone was completely naked he helped him on with the shirt and then the homespun jacket and trousers. Harcamone did not touch his clothes. He was at the very centre of one of those states which may be called magical. Harcamone was a sprite, and sprites do not touch their earthly rags. He did not utter a word during the operation. The chief guard said:

"I think you can count on mercy."

But neither Harcamone nor anyone answered. When he was dressed, he sat down on the bed again and sank into a kind of sea which made his body so light that he no longer felt it. The body is familiar with the kind of over-fatigue one feels after a long hike, when you suddenly drop down anywhere. Something else too plunged him into that sea which lulls galleys and their crews. It was a very particular noise and an operation so unusual that it seemed to be going on elsewhere. A shock was needed, the kind that comes like a bolt from the blue and awakens you. It was then that he saw, kneeling at his feet, on the bare floor, four guards who were riveting a chain to each of his ankles. He touched the edge of his sleeves first, then his trousers, which were tightly drawn over his thigh. He was scared.

A deafening roar again arose outside. Bulkaen told me later that he could make out the words "Kill him! kill him!" That's false, for the dormitory windows face the yards and the shops, but nevertheless I believe him, for crowds have always sent up this cry of acclaim to the murderer returning in his chariot from the Law Court to his prison.

It is impossible for the Black Maria that brings the condemned man back from Court to return otherwise than slowly, for it is laden with the weight of all the funeral ornaments, with the weight of the sky. Today the engine runs low, but when the carriage was drawn by horses—and that is how I still see it—the horses walked and panted breast-high in black mud. The axles creaked.

There are two kinds of procession, one in which the murderer is alone with his guard—this is the less tragic—and one which contains, in the other tiny cells, his accomplices whose lives are spared. They are in a transport of horrible joy. They are only a song of life, a waltz in which violins are entangled, and this waltz is silent and grows funereal so as to accompany the fellow-inmate who is already dead and jokes about death, tortured to the heart of his heart at having skirted life so narrowly, since they who mean most to him, the cronies he adored this morning, whom he hates this evening, are preserving it. Harcamone had come back alone.

If criminals were judged by a Court that was outright fantastic, that is, a Court dressed like devils in an opera, in a scary carnival, or were composed of inhuman, superhuman beings, like priests for example, the sessions would be less terrifying. But composed as they are of men involved in commonplace everyday existence who suddenly—without losing their humanity, since we have all been able to see how they retain the idiosyncrasies that show they are men—become judges who decide about death, we are bound to conclude that one aspect of men, an aspect of ourselves, remains in close touch with hell, since this part of us suddenly refers to it. The horror would indeed be less great if one were at grips with a ferocity that shows hell to be far from man than if one discovers hell within him. We can then no longer hope for the miracle. Harcamone's chains were riveted on, not by order of a mysterious, fabulous will, but by that of a human will, the popular will that had here delegated four guards who were doing a blacksmith's job as well as blacksmiths themselves would have done it.

Harcamone wanted to speak, to say something, he didn't know what, but the words dried in his throat. He then realized that he had to keep silent so as to remain engulfed in that sea of torpor. The guards could speak, could bustle about. They belonged to the world which is concerned with chains, which rivets bolts, which shuts doors. He himself soared above that world.

"Are you hungry?" asked the chief guard.

Harcamone shook his head.

"Wouldn't you like some soup?"

He said "No no" in a very low voice. Harcamone had eaten nothing since morning, but the guard realized that he had better not insist. He motioned to the others to leave, then closed the door behind him and locked it. A guard had already been assigned to duty at the grate. He sat down on the stool and began his vigil. Harcamone thought of going to sleep, which meant having to stretch out on the bed, but his feet were so heavy—the chain—that he had to take hold of them with both hands in order to lay them on the edge of the bed. There was a rattle of iron, which made the guard look more closely. Harcamone seemed to be sleeping. He had dropped his head on the bolster. There is little need to tell that he relived the hearing, transforming it to his taste, for his own good, into an acquittal. But whenever he came to a painful detail—an error on the part of the lawyer, a wrong answer, a violent reaction of the judge—he winced with shame and rage. How had Napoleon been able to sleep and awaken at will? Night was falling. The cell was almost dark, when suddenly there was a brutal brightness that struck the white walls. The guard had put on the light. This shock destroyed the torpor that had been creeping over Harcamone. He realized that the light would be on all night long, and for forty-five nights.

I learned from Bulkaen how the news reached the dormitories. The trusty of the hole who had helped in the dismal operation returned to the cell he shared with Bulkaen, who was being punished at the time. It was next to Dormitory 8. With his spoon he tapped out on the left wall the seven beats of the signal for attention: "My shoes . . . are shipping water!" Bulkaen scratched with a nail on a piece of paper the words "death penalty" and, above each letter, its number in the alphabet. The first cell in Dormitory 8 answered with the same signal, and Bulkaen (the more agile-fingered) who had the paper in front of him transmitted the message. D—one, two, three, four; E, one, two, three, etc. The news made the rounds in the same way from Dormitory 8 to Dormitory 6, from 6 to 9, but the whole prison was already being riddled with a muffled hammering, with a multitude of beats coming from all sides and going in all directions. The mournful message was penetrating the walls. It was running, it flew faster than treacherous news carried by the wind, above the jungle, among savages. It eluded the guards' pursuit. The walls, the echoes, the ceiling, the vents were deeply moved. In the darkness the prison lived with an intense, universal life a night of July 14th[1]. The trusty and Bulkaen were drunk with the excitement of having unleashed an activity as violent and amorous as the emotion aroused by the announcement that the Homeland is in danger. A tapping on the right wall made them jump. They thought that an action was going to dim the present one, though they regretted not being able to sink entirely into its nausea. Bulkaen again took the spoon and replied to the signal. Then they listened: "One . . . two . . . three . . . four . . —D" A silence Then: "One, two, three . " The cell on the right was informing them of the death penalty.

The night was thick.

Behind the prison walls, the crowd was leaving, withdrawing its cries, its insults, its clamour. Silence reigned.

The prison was silent. No one dared sing. The guard ate a

---

[1] July 14th, the French national holiday, commemorates the storming of the Bastille.—Translator's note.

cold meal while waiting to be relieved by a colleague. And outside, around the prison, a few youngsters, leaning against the mossy tree trunks with their foreheads bent and their eyes often closed with fatigue and grief, kept watch, while others slept on the grass where a moonbeam fell. This sign of supernatural fidelity fills me with tremendous despair, for it heightens the pain of being abandoned by Bulkaen when I was waiting for him, or a word from him, in the hole. But I imagine how tough I can seem to others, for Bulkaen's toughness was likewise composed of the deep grief of finding himself abandoned. That tremendous sadness surged up in him, but stopped at his eyes, which pride kept from weeping. And it was that repressed sadness which constituted his toughness. The fear that I might abandon him when I was upstairs made him write to me every day, which obliged me to reply. This fear softened him a little. He saw that I thought about him constantly. He felt I was close to him. He kept weaving the bond that joined us, and his hand kept tightening it. But I felt a kind of peace rather than bitterness. As soon as the kid no longer needs me, my function disappears and along with it everything that was necessary, therefore pure, therefore dazzling, in my relations with him. But I could no longer do anything for him from the hole. And I couldn't count on my authority, despite our last scene together. I was at the top of the stairs. I waited for him to leave his shop so that I could give him a note. He rushed up to me with a smile. Perhaps he thought I was going to go to him, but I didn't move. He ran into me, and I stood still. My immobility surprised him, he smiled. I remained impassive. He gave me a slight push, trying to shake me, but I still didn't move. He pushed me harder. I seemed made of stone. He persisted and was seized with a violent rage that lit up his eyes. He hit me in the face. Anger welled up from deep within me, as did a huge, silent laugh that was invisible on my face and that further excited my anger, that kindled it. I realized that the moment for subduing Bulkaen had come. I let him hit me again. He had lost his

smile. And suddenly I was a kind god who can no longer put
up with men's insults or arrogance, and I smacked him. He
was at first amazed by the riposte that had been so slow in
coming. With my whole body bent toward him, I dominated
him, I wanted to crush him. He pulled himself together and
tried to parry, but his slightest gesture excited me. I went at
him with my feet and fists until he lay crouching on the steps,
about to topple into a pathetic position which did not even
arouse pity in me. "Stand up," I said, with my mouth foaming.
He jumped to his feet. I started whacking again, but he made
no further effort to parry or attack, so that I was very close to
him, and he was not defended by any obstacle. I touched him.
My body touched his. I kept whacking away, but his heat
mingled with mine. My cheeks were flaming and so were his.
In order to avoid a smack in the face, he made a quarter turn
with his chest. I missed him, but I lost my balance and leaned
against him. My thighs were touching his. My blows lost their
violence. I pressed his body to mine, standing up, with his
back on my chest. My right hand took hold of his face, tried to
turn it around, but he resisted. I imprisoned him more tightly
in my legs. I wanted to kiss him on the mouth, he turned
away; he put his two fists on his eyes. I tried to pull them
away and I felt myself repeating the execrable gesture that had
led me to Mettray: my cruelty, when I was sixteen, made me
gouge the left eye of a child who, frightened by my pitiless
stare and realizing that his eye attracted me, tried to save it by
putting his fist to it. But my grip was stronger, I pulled his fist
away and put out his eye with my knife. Bulkaen made the
same gesture of protection. I clung to him. He didn't try to
break away. I squeezed him a bit harder . . . then I suddenly
made the hoodlum gesture of bending him by violently putting
one hand on his stomach and the other on the back of his neck.
I held him that way for ten seconds, without daring to do
anything else. I felt he was conquered. I heard his choked
breathing, I myself was puffing a little. When I let him go, we
both felt ashamed.

Still hostile-looking, with my teeth clenched, I said to him:
"All the same, I've had you."

"In spite of me. You didn't get anything at all. I had my pants on."

"It's the same thing. I came. And besides, I'll have you whenever I like."

"Jean."

We looked at each other.

There was no astonishment in his eyes. We seemed not to realize that there had been no apparent reason for the fight, but we both felt, deep down, that it had had to take place.

"Get going. We've had enough."

He went off, adjusting his rumpled clothes. I was the master.

For me he was now no more than the kid he had been at Mettray, the one he had never stopped carrying within him, as I could well see. I returned to my shop, and, because I had replied contemptuously when my name had been uttered in a tone of appeasement, I was, thanks to that scene, carried back, in particular, to our Sunday walks outside the Colony.

On Sunday afternoons, after hearing vespers in the chapel, we would go for a walk, with the band and flag heading the procession. We strolled along the country roads, sometimes as far as La Membrolle, and once even came within sight of Fontevrault. We saw the prison windows to which the inmates were perhaps clinging, watching us approach, listening to our music that floated toward them. We played only high-stepping airs and military marches, led by the sixteen-year old buglers and drummers. It was to these that we marched. In that region, where the most ordinary house has the elegance of a prince's dwelling, there are many castles. We would pass them along the road. As we went by, our troop would grow silent. Seeing them at such close range, each of us who, during winter nights, toward morning, had dreamed he was the lord of a manor so as to escape the horror of a shameful awakening, in the cold, to the accompaniment of abuse, thought he was seeing his dream suddenly draw near. He thought he was going to enter and find himself lord and master. He both thought so and didn't think so. We would continue walking. As we left the castle behind, the conversations were resumed. Our private story was over. But we would turn around from time to time so as to be quite sure that the castle was moving off. That was how I always saw them, so far away from me, and at night, in my hammock, in order to escape from our vile life, I often dreamt of their mirrors, their rugs, their marbles. They were dream-objects for so long a time and with such intensity and I am so poor that I cannot believe real ones actually exist.

Bulkaen himself once said to me:

"I've always been broke," an admission which, after his death, I blushed at having heard, for it belied what he said in his pressing letters which reeked of sincerity: that he had always got a swag. My thefts have never succeeded in putting me into immediate contact with wealth, but they have done better. Books with heraldic bindings, the Japanese vellum of de luxe editions, the long-grained moroccan copies, the flat ones with coats of arms, the old gold of the tooling, were inter-spersed with Chinese statuettes, onyx and vermilion signets, silks and laces, and transformed my room into the deck of a pirate ship after the sacking of a gabion.

I was emerging from a now forgotten dream, and as I leaned over the edge of my hammock one night, I saw a trap-door fall back noiselessly under Villeroy's berth. Villeroy was no longer sleeping in his place. I stayed awake until he returned, trying to figure out how he had managed to unnail the boards, with what knotted ropes or sheets he had gone down from the dormitory to the mess-hall, and with whom. To go where and do what? Perhaps the whole band of big shots had just leaped into the darkness a few feet away from me without my suspec-ting it. I dared not go and look into the hammocks where the others were lying. I waited two hours, or more, or less. I remember hearing someone at the end of the dormitory hum: "Lovingly rock and sway . . ." It sounded to me like: "Loving

a cock..." Finally, there was a faint sound in the mess-hall
below, and, raising the boards, Villeroy's head appeared, then
a bust that was severed for a moment, and then the most
thrilling part of his body and a knee on the edge of the
opening, while the other, which was bent in the taut trousers
because the foot had been placed on the floor, was the head
of a nurse beneath the stiff veil. Villeroy was wearing his shirt
and trousers. He pulled up a rope that I hadn't seen which
must have been tied to the hammock rod. Finally he stood up
and, seeing me awake, came over and told me that he had just
met his pal Robert, a crasher who had recently got out of the
jug.

"From where?" I asked.

"Oh, from Fontevrault. I saw him yesterday. He slipped me
a note."

He said this with a certain constraint, which was due perhaps to the fact that a touch of anxiety had stopped his breath
and that he had to speak in a low voice. Then he exhaled a
little more air, and as he inhaled he rapped out, somewhat
hoarsely:

"My pal's got quite a build."

The bulk of the confession was made. He could now develop
it in a simpler tone. He added:

"He couldn't take me with him tonight because he still
hasn't found a getup for me. But keep it to yourself, get me?"

He whispered this with his mouth at my ear. The sentences
entered me and made me fall to the bottom of a dark world
where, in order to be fully admitted, I had only to put my arm
around Villeroy's neck. He would not have dared reject me,
but I dared not make the gesture. Moving his cropped head
close to mine, he added, for now anything was possible:

"Do you smell how good I smell?"

I sighed with a sigh that welled up from the depth of my
gloom: "I do," very feebly, for I would have screamed. Then,
and the most fraternal excitement enveloped us, he added in a
somewhat casual tone:

"I smell good. He kissed me."

And he made the gesture peculiar to a person smoking on the sly: when he has taken a drag and the smoke has emerged, the hand waves in front of the mouth, warding off and scattering the smoke. (This is one of the many gestures that consecrate the big shot, that make him a member of the Clan.) Thus, Villeroy made the gesture without even having to scatter his smoke: he feared that his friend's fragrance might remain in his mouth and betray him. That caused the final dizziness. My man, my tough, my guy, he who kissed me and gave me his fragrance, let himself be kissed, caressed, by a more potent big shot. A crasher had kissed him! So thieves kissed! As I write down this memory, my heart contracts, for I realize it is not impossible that Lou Daybreak, very secretly in the eyes of all, loved Bulkaen. In order for me to realize it, a trap-door had had to open in the darkness. Thieves kissed, and so thieves were simply fragrant young men who kissed. Am I to regard this as the origin of my taste for theft? Though we did not plan jobs with the precision that later governed our schemes in prison, we devised wild fantasies that carried us beyond seas and mountains, that made us skip long periods and prepared us to admit robbery into our lives. Above all, they enabled us to merge the life which we projected into the future with the bold, tortured existence of the thugs of Fontevrault. Those pimps carried us in their pants.

I love the act of stealing because I find it elegant in itself, but above all I love twenty-year-old thieves whose round mouths open on small, fine teeth. I loved them so much that I was bound to resemble them sooner or later, my heavy, choppy gestures were bound to grow lighter and ultimately acquire those youngsters' superior elegance, and in the course of my thefts I must have made, not the gestures they would have made in similar circumstances, but the graceful gestures for which I love them. I loved furtive, slippery thieves: I became furtive, slippery, with the result that the police and their informers tracked me down fast. I realized later that it was wiser to curb within me the charming person whose role I was playing. I held him in check. I assumed his quick-wittedness, his mind which was alive to opportunity, but I rejected his gestures. Little by little, he disappeared within me. He melted away. I stopped making the gestures I would have liked to see made, and performed those which were specifically required by the particular circumstance. But he kept watch within me. He was actually my guardian angel. And that was how I came to employ gestures that were strictly my own, dictated solely by necessity, and I finally got rid of the elegant scamps who haunted me. I had to overcome only the shame of the cunning required of us, if only for a second, by the act of robbing. The need to hide, even for a fraction of a second, made me blush, but I also realized that the thief must transform this necessary cunning into a factor of delight. The thief loves darkness (to lie low and watch, with his gaze sliding or seemingly elsewhere, is to be in the darkness; to wear a mask or make-up is to be in the darkness). You have to love robbery. Young thief, always be borne by the reverie that makes you the resplendent creature you would like to resemble! Only children who want to be bandits so as to resemble the bandit they love—or to be that bandit—dare have the audacity to play their character to the very end. It is essential that your gesture be beautiful. Any gesture performed in suffering, wrought of suffering, born of suffering and danger, deserves respect, despite the contortions it brings to the face, despite the grotesque postures of the body. Couple these gestures for their beauty, just as the youngsters of whom I'm speaking do what they do for the beauty of being a big shot. Theft is beautiful. Perhaps you will be disturbed because it is a brief, very brief, above all an invisible gesture (but that's the marrow of the act) which makes the thief despicable: just time enough for him to look around and steal. That, unhappily, is exactly the time it takes to be a thief, but transcend that shame, after exposing it, showing it, making it visible. Your pride must be able to undergo shame in order to attain glory.

We were savage children who went far more deeply into cruelty than our idols, the bold gangsters. But though I have lost the ability to steal the bruisers' adornments, do not be surprised that, at the beginning of my stay in the hole, I unwittingly gave myself a bruiser's build when I drew a pencil sketch of myself on a paper bag for Bulkaen. I drew myself with the muscles I knew I had and I knew I was strong. It will take Bulkaen's death and the knowledge of his treachery to deflate me.

Thus, the Colony acted on the man I would be. That is what is meant by "the bad influence" of which pedagogues speak, a slow poison, a deed that bides its time and puts forth unexpected blossoms. The kissing of Villeroy and that crasher's kiss did everything, for I was still astounded at the thought that each male had his own glorious male, that the world of force and manly beauty loved in that way within itself, from link to link, forming a garland of muscular and twisted or stiff and thorny flowers. Those pimps were always being women for someone stronger and handsomer than they. They were women less and less the further away they were from me, all the way to the very pure pimp who dominated them all, the one who lorded it over the galley, whose lovely penis, grave and distant, moved about the Colony in the form of a mason. Harcamone! I was at the other end of that garland, and it was the weight of the world's virility that I bore on my strained back when Villeroy went down on me. And I was dazed with an almost similar dizziness when I learned that Hersir had been in the reformatory at Aniane.

Aniane was a closed colony, girded with impassable walls, as was Eysses too. We were familiar with all the particularities of the kid pens, for at Mettray our only conversations were about prisons and pens. We would say to each other: "So-and-so got nabbed, he's at Belle Ile." "So-and-so is at Aniane." And we uttered those names, which would have frightened or amazed a child still living with his family, as casually as an inhabitant of Singapore says: "I'll be passing through

Sourabaya." The climate of Aniane must have been more oppressive than ours because of the walls, and the children who grew up behind them were to us very different from our colonists; they were crowned with another vegetation, other branches continued their hands, other flowers; but yet they were colonists, like us, like me, and I, who come from a kid pen, love a boy who comes from a pen, who loves a boy who goes back to the pen, who loves a boy who comes from a pen.

Villeroy kissed me on the mouth, but I did not yet dare put my arm around his neck, and I remained alone at the brink of dizziness, unable to fall into it.

One day, and I still feel the tremendous pain of it, we learned that Toscano had finally let himself be reamed. He was on duty in the mess-hall, and while we were in the yard after the mid-day meal, he had gone to get a jug of water at the drinking fountain. Immediately all the village girls surrounded and joshed him, for a gust of wind had to pick just that moment to make his shirt cling to him, transforming it into one of those housecoats which I have seen on Marguerite in engravings that adorn the text of *Faust*, and this happened just as the child was completing the transformation by wiping away a tear or brushing aside, like hair or a veil, what was merely drops of water that the wind had blown from the fountain. Thus it often happens that an accidental gesture makes you the chief character of a famous historical scene or that an object is so placed that it reconstructs the setting in which the scene took place, and we suddenly feel we are continuing an adventure interrupted by a long sleep or else it seems there exists only a limited repertoire of gestures, or else that you belong to a kind of heroic family, each member of which repeats the same signs, or else that you are the reflection in time of a past act, like the reflection in space seen in a mirror: in the subway, supporting myself at times with both hands on the thin vertical column between the doors, have I not been the reflection of Joan of Arc at the coronation in Rheims holding the staff of her standard? When I looked through the grating

of Bulkaen's cell, I saw him lying on his stomach on his white
bed, with his arms folded on what was supporting his chin, in
the very posture of the Sphinx and ready for sex, and I was in
front of him, an Undecipherable, with a pilgrim's staff, the
questioning Oedipus. And what else wasn't he whenever I went
to his shop to see him on the sly and his fellow-workers would
say to me:

"He'll probably end by shipping you off to the chain gang."

I could laugh and joke, and Bulkaen could join in with me,
we were veiled by a kind of crape, for the joking had the
natural smell of all prophecies and the shadow of grief on his
face was the shadow of the big straw hat on the shaved face of
a convict. We are a book of familiar and living history in which
the poet can decipher the signs of Eternal Recurrence. The
fault that Toscano bore on his face was already known, for
Larochedieu had seen Deloffre leaving the chicken's hammock
the night before. Thus, that lofty virtue had given in. It's not
hard for me to imagine all his struggles and wiles and combats
protected by the horror of being a classified, definitive chicken,
protected by contemptuous public opinion, but combating
these too and combating pleasure when Deloffre's bare arms
rested on him. He had yielded. And we who, like him, were
characters in an old-time song surrounded him at the fountain.
The others jeered at him. As for me, I was a sad gallant. When
the radiant Deloffre came along, he put a foot on the fountain
and laid his fist on Toscano's crimson shoulder. The big shot's
arrival silenced the girls.

There was naturally a bitch who had Toscano sent to the
quarter. I heard a group of kids discussing it. I asked:

"Him in the hole? What's he done?"

"He did a blow-job on his guy and was nabbed."

Toscano became a little princess and we played at vying for
the big shots, and one evening, in the shower room, the last
evening I ever saw him, Bulkaen had time to make a similar
confession to me. He had managed to enter my little booth on
the pretence of asking me for soap. I was already dripping.

The hot water enveloped us in a white vapour. He thus managed not to be seen by the guard, who was himself invisible. I was soaping myself, I wanted to push him out. I said:

"Go hide your mug, that little mug of yours."

He chuckled.

"It's not my fault if I've got a mug like a whore. That's how I am. At Mettray, I gave lots of guys a run for their money ... There were fights about the least little thing ... When I was there, it was over me and also another little guy named Régis that the big shots had the most fights ... at times ..."

He muttered this while soaping himself. The water fell on his bent back, on his neck. Our soap was lathering.

As he went on talking and telling me the story of my own life, I relived the Colony, under the flowering chestnut trees in the dust of the brush shop. I could see Dudule's ridiculous, sniffing moustache.

Bulkaen kept muttering away:

"... at times we saw each other during recreation. I'd say to him, 'Well, Régis, how many fights did you cause today?' Or else I'd say: 'I bet you I make Millaud—Millaud was his big shot—get into a fight with my guy, that I get him to beat the shit out of him.' He'd say, 'It's a bet. But you won't.' We were kids. We were fourteen or fifteen. So I wrote a note and then went to see my big shot. I said to him: 'Say, look at what Millaud sent me.' They met during recreation. My guy socked the other one: 'Go after my kid. We'll fight it out, if that's what you want.' The other guy didn't back out. And biff! bang! They went at it till blood flowed."

He rattled on faster and faster. The memory was irritating him. His teeth were almost clenched when he finished. His bare, tense, outstretched arm was busy between his feet. He was trampling and kneading the lather and the dawn.

He laughed and tossed his head.

"I gave lots of guys a run for it ..."

I took his hand, but hardly had I grazed it than it disap-

peared streaming into the opaque fog. And streaming was the
very word the turnkey used when he told me about his death:
"He was streaming at the foot of the wall . . ." one rainy night.
It seems he died that very day, conjured away by the steam.

Since seeing Divers again, I have noticed signs on him that
would perhaps not have been found on Harcamone or Pierrot:
traces of women. Harcamone's toughness and destiny had kept
him away from love of any kind.

As for Bulkaen, he had spent so little time in freedom, had
been so little involved in civilian life that the Colony's influence had not had time to wear off. He had always lived in its
halo and his gestures remained caught in that stifling
shade—the shade of the rose-laurels—despite his efforts to
thrust it aside. But Divers had known woman. I gathered this
first from his language, for he spoke quite naturally about
menstruation, about having the rag on. He also used the word
"lay" instead of "screw." Anyhow, in his boldest gestures
there is a modesty which we do not have.

I would have liked to make an apologia in this book for theft
too. It would have pleased me if my little friends had been
elegant thieves, as keen as Mercury. Were we really thieves? I
think not, and this surprises me, and hurts me. The crimes of
which we boasted would recall, by their strangeness and splendour, the barbaric embellishments with which actors no longer
know how to adorn themselves: espionage, rosewood coffins,
princely loves, drownings, hangings by sashes, wooden legs,
pederasty, births in caravans and so on, which once made them
extravagant idols. Thus, the children in this memoir knew how
to adorn themselves. They would arrive here with a past that
was generally tragic and noble. It flowed from their cruel,
sukly little mouths as they kept inventing it. They must
therefore be that too since I show them as being that. I am not
inventing. If I have viewed them from a certain angle, it is
because, seen from there, that is how they looked—which may
be due to a prismatic distortion, but which is therefore what
they also are, though unaware of being it. Now, the most

audacious of the youngsters, the one who dared the most extravagant finery, was Métayer.

I was thinking chiefly of him when I said that all children are sons of kings. Métayer was eighteen years old. I loathe having to describe young men who are homely, but that one set me dreaming so much that I am willing to recall his red pimples, triangular, freckled face and sharp, dangerous gestures. He told those who were most attentive, and particularly me, that he was a direct descendant of the kings of France. He would rattle off genealogies between his very thin lips. He pretended to the throne. No one has ever studied the idea of royalty in children. I dare say, however, that there is not a single kid who has ever looked into Lavisse's or Bayet's or any other *History of France* who has not thought he was a dauphin or some prince of the blood. The legend of Louis XVII's escape from prison was particularly responsible for these reveries. Métayer must have come across it. He had elected to be heir of the kings of France. Métayer's megalomania must not be confused with my passion for imposture which made me dream of introducing myself into a powerful family. The point is that Métayer thought he was a king's son or grandson. He elected to be king in order to re-establish a destroyed order. He was king. I desired only to commit a sacrilege, to soil the purity of a family, just as I would have soiled the caste of big shots by introducing among them the chicken that I was.

My memory of that child grows clearer as I write about him. He was royal because of his sovereign conception of his person. His skinny naked feet in their sabots were poor princely feet on the icy tiles of a Louvre, or on ashes. What elegance and what superior sobriety in comparison with the celestial and ostentatious eloquence that Divers displayed in every one of his gestures. One was the prince and the other the conquistador.

The big shots of Family B were unaware, or pretended to be unaware, of Métayer, who continued to harbour within him, secretly guarded, the idea of his royalty. But the haughtiness of that living tabernacle, with its lofty gestures (such as Stephen the deacon must have made when he swallowed the host to save it from profanation), secretly irritated us. Secretly, that is, we did not allow our hostility to be apparent, and did not even realize we were affected by it. Then, one evening, our hatred exploded. Métayer was sitting on the bottom step of the stairway to the dormitory. Did he think he was the sainted King Louis beneath the Oak of Justice? He was talking. Someone dared to jeer. Whereupon there was laughter, to which he responded with scorn. Then all our accumulated rancour suddenly broke the dams and flooded him: blows, slaps, insults, filth, spit. The family remembered that he had probably blabbed about the escape of Derelle, Leroy and Morvan. Whether true or false, an accusation of that kind was a terrible thing. Not a single child thought of verifying it. They punished cruelly on the basis of suspicion. They executed. The royal price was executed. Thirty howling kids bore down on him more savagely than did the Knitting Women on his ancestor. In one of those pockets of silence such as often form in tornadoes we heard him murmur:

"They did that to Christ too."

He did not cry, but he was clad on that throne with so sudden a majesty that perhaps he heard God Himself say: "You will be king, but the crown on your head will be of red-hot iron." *I saw him.* I loved him. My feeling was comparable in a way to the kind of fear I felt at school when I had to draw a face. Faces are defended by respect. They resemble each other in that they are images. Drawing the main lines aroused no emotion in me, but when it came to achieving resemblance, I was paralyzed by a difficulty that was not only material, physical, but one that was of a metaphysical order. The face remained therefore before me. And the resemblance escaped. Finally, my skull suddenly burst. I had just seen that its chin was individual, its brow was individual . . . I was advancing in knowledge. Métayer was Métayer when, amidst the brawl, he shattered the sky by placing his two hands wide open in front of his chest in such a way that the thumb-nails touched, like the hands carved on Jewish tombstones. One must sometimes give in to attitudes. The necessity that governs me relates to an inner theatre of violent games.

Divers would sometimes say to me laughingly:

"Come into my hammock, I'll make you ask for more, you'll see if I'm well hung."

One day, Harcamone got drunk. Wine could not pickle an angel on a mission, but it did turn him blue. Coloured by the blue wine, he meandered all over the Colony, stumbling, tottering, hiccupping, belching, without anyone's seeing him. The memory of that powdered murderer lurching among the laurels still sets me dreaming. Ah! I madly love all that strange masquerade of crime. Those princes and princesses of high, shameless audacity, those "Marie Antoinettes," those stunning "Lamballes" emit charms that stagger me. The smell of their armpits after a race is the smell of orchards! Harcamone, drunk, with his dick beribboned, was singing in the yard! No one saw him, but did he himself see anyone? Even though his eyes were open, they were shut.

It was I who replaced Harcamone as reader that evening. For in each family, while the others ate, a colonist read aloud from a book in the Bibliothèque Rose[1]. It was the murderer who usually read in the Family B mess-hall, but he was drunk; I therefore took from his hands the children's book in which all the inoffensive words bore the appearance of being allusions, which were strange to the head of the family and were understood only by us. It was then that I read the following sentence by the Countess de Ségur: "The rider was on a goodly steed (*Ce cavalier était bien monté*)[2]." Although it meant that he had a fine mount, Divers, when saying "*bien monté*," conjured up his splendid genital apparatus, and I, in uttering the sentence, transformed Divers, to my amazement

[1] A nineteenth-century series of stories for children.—Translator's note.
[2] In argot, the phrase means "the rider was well hung".—Translator's note.

and for myself alone, into an impetuous centaur.

Medical care in the Mettray infirmary was no better than it is here. Divers, who has ral (or syph) goes for a weekly injection (piqûre), which he calls, like the other patients, a *piquouze*, a word fabricated by the secret tenderness the pimp feels for both the remedy and the ailment from which he suffers but of which he will never be cured. However devoted the nuns may be, they will never be able to dress the damaged flesh. Nevertheless, the infirmary was a paradise to us. It loomed out of our daily fatigue like a cool resting-place because of its whiteness: glaze of the coifs, of the aprons, the smocks, the sheets, the bread, the mashed vegetables, the porcelains. We sometimes felt like burying ourselves in that glaze, in that snow. On that high summit, Sister Zoé had planted the iron staff of the black and red standard of despotism. She bullied the little fellows who, from bed to bed, shot glances at each other in words of love. I once saw her rap Daniel's fingers (he was the new bugler) with a big convent key. Was it by contact with a thousand children who were more like girls than boys that the sister had taken on that manly bearing? The kid growled between his clenched teeth:

"I'll get even with you, you bitch."

She heard him and made him leave the infirmary before he was cured of his boils. We left together, but he managed to join his chicken Renaudeau, of the Arc family, who was waiting for him behind a hedge of laurels.

But fate had still other ways of opening my eyes, or of opening the darkness in two so that I could see into it. Have I told you that Divers once called me "My drum"? He beat me gently with his fine, elegant drumsticks. One day at noon, when he was returning from the drum-and-bugle school with his instrument, we found ourselves alone for a moment, behind the others. He was carrying the drum on his back. With a brusque movement, he turned it around so that it was in front of him. He stroked its top-skin two or three times with his palm. Then, what sudden rage seized him? Darker and fiercer

than a knight, he turned it over, and with his fist he burst the
bottom-skin, into which his wrist sank, vibrating with emotion.
Finally, he pulled himself together, laughed with his lovely wet
mouth, and, still panting a little, said to me, close to my
mouth:

"I've had you after all, you little tramp. You can't deny it.
Take a look at your pants!"

He had just lifted up my skirts with jaunty promptness. I
was crushed on a couch or a bed of cool moss by that weight
of wonders. It is only when the sperm has cooled that the
princess who has been raped by a palace guard thinks of her
dignity! A swift scene exploded within me: "Get out of here,"
I screamed inwardly. "Get out of here! All right, now get out
of here! I can't control myself in your presence!" The con-
quering guard lowered his head and looked at me shiftily, as if
he had said: "I'll get you, you slut!" I cried out again: "I
must be livid with rage." Divers had displaced the drum, and
on the dwindling bump I saw the same stain whose warmth I
felt on mine. I made a few awkward, foolish, absurd gestures,
which were gestures of exorcism intended to cast out the joy
that the guard's vigorous body had accorded the princess.
Then I was filled with the gloom that suddenly comes forth at
the approach of death. Our heart clouds over. We are in
darkness. A similar darkness warned me of Bulkaen's death.

At first I knew nothing definite, but it seems to me that
Bulkaen's name was hoisted above the prison and floated
lightly and that the waves it displaced caused me the indefinable uneasiness that I felt even in the centre of the Big Cell.
The idea of escaping must have charmed him.

Working a little every day for more than a year, squatting
and hidden behind a pile of rags in the tailor shop, Botchako
had managed to cut out a kind of trap-door in the floor. The
work—I saw it five or six days after his escape when I went to
get an armful of patched pants—was of Chinese precision and
delicacy. He had used a paring-knife or scissors. I don't know
which. Then, with the same tool, he had hollowed out a cavity

in the main beam big enough to lodge his bent chest; his legs
were to hang on either side of the beam, in the void, above the
capitulary chamber. He worked on this for a year. The night
he decided to leave, he wormed his way into the slot with a
provision of cigarettes—found God knows where—and bread.
Then a friend scattered rags over the closed trap-door.

When, at six o'clock, the turnkey came to get the prisoners,
he counted them, as he did every evening. The staff hunted for
the missing man all over the jug, they didn't find him. They
thought he had escaped. It wasn't until the third night that he
got away.

I also learned that he had earlier stolen a hack-saw from the
foundry. He waited a few days until the excitement that the
theft created throughout the prison died down. He was not
suspected. The guards increased their vigilance, the rounds
were tripled and were made more carefully, but two weeks
later the matter was forgotten and supervision resumed its
normal rhythm. According to what we gathered from
Botchako's explanation, it was he who had first unsealed the
window of the tailor shop and sawed through a bar. Then he
had gone down to the yard. Bulkaen hung a string from his
window and pulled up the tool with it. He sawed through a bar
and went down the same way as Botchako. By helping each
other they managed to climb over the first wall, and when they
reached the patrol lane Botchako tossed the gadget that he had
constructed with iron strips from the spring of his mattress: it
was a kind of harpoon at the end of a rope, which was rolled
around his waist. The harpoon was supposed to catch on to the
top of the wall. Bulkaen was the first to start climbing, but the
alarm was given by the police dogs. There was the sound of
barking, then a frenzy of howls. We were all eagerly listening
in our beds. Suddenly a cry rang out in the darkness: "Stop
or I'll shoot." And the following is what I was told. Bulkaen
had to climb faster. The guards arrived. Botchako grabbed the
hanging rope and also started climbing. The claw held fast, the
rope was strong, but the stone at the top of the wall was not

bedded. It was raining. Under the weight of the two bodies, the stone fell in a single block, without swaying. Botchako broke his legs. Bulkaen tried to get away. He dashed at the three guards who were arriving with their revolvers raised. One of them fired. Bulkaen stepped back. The dogs rushed at him. He stepped farther back, against the wall. The guards approached in order to seize him, but though wounded, I think in the thigh, he struggled. He fought the dogs and the guards. He didn't admit he was captured. He struck out at the guards with his feet and fists. One of the blows hit a revolver, which fell, and Bulkaen saw it gleaming at his feet. He quickly picked it up and fired at the guards, but six other guards had come running up with the chief supervisor. My friend was nailed to the wall by a machine-gun. He collapsed. I cannot help seeing him—with his hands around his mouth like a megaphone, mutely crying: "Help!" and dripping with rain—disappear slowly into the smoke, water and explosion of twenty or thirty deadly flowers of fire.

Botchako was groaning. His legs were still under the block of granite. He was carried to the infirmary. He died a few days later, without regaining consciousness. Lou Daybreak's comment was:

"Pierrot'll find his boy-friend among the angels."

I'm sure that the band of pimps was kept informed by Lou of all the rivalries and secret rumours in our group. Did they despise us or, on the contrary, were they excited by that incessant movement, that perpetual emotional exchange?

The two men were buried in the little prison cemetery. One day, shortly thereafter, there were five of us on pallet duty (filling old mattress ticking with straw). The turnkeys were becoming more familiar with a few inmates. They spoke of one thing and another. We joked with them a little. One of the fellows said:

"Were you there, Monsieur Brulard, when Bulkaen and Botchako tried to make a getaway?"

And while we stuffed the pallets, and despite the rule that

forbade him to talk to us about such things, and in such a tone, the guard, who knew of my friendship with Bulkaen, as did all the guards, related, for he had been present, what had happened that night. He laid stress on the rain, which had bothered him, so that I would realize how it had treated Pierrot. The dust stung my eyes and irritated my throat, but his account did not make me cry. He dared say: "He was your pal," but I made no reply. The others continued doing their job without looking at me. He did not forget a single detail, neither the bullets that entered Pierrot nor those that ricochetted against the wall, nor his twisted mouth, nor his silence. Later, I got other, more brutal information, but I had neither the moral freedom to admire, nor the time, nor was I surprised. I followed Bulkaen's scarlet adventure as a passionate expert, as a witness who remembers an earlier one that was a kind of dress rehearsal for this one. I felt nothing: I observed, and it was the crowd of inmates who informed me of the beauty of the adventure. From the staring eyes, the suddenly gaping mouths, the silences, the sighs of the mob surrounding me, I realized dimly that I was hearing a more beautiful passage, and that it was to be admired . . . Someone said to me:

"He put his foot on a piece of cement that was sticking out. It gave way . . . It seems that's how he broke his leg . . ."

The muffled "oh" that rattled in their throats told me that the narration was thrilling. I had just heard an account, in a joyous tone, of my friend's death, but I was so exhausted that the crowd had to lend me its soul in order for me to feel. Three days later, I learned that it was from the hole that Bulkaen had escaped. In the case of Pierrot, there was no question of the family's asking for the body, no one knew whether he had a family, and as for Botchako, if it is true that every prisoner must put in the time to which he was sentenced and as he still had three years to go, his family will not be able to claim his body until three years have elapsed . . . I learned from the gravediggers that both bodies were thrown into the common grave. Pierrot was buried in the blue lace of the tattoos that covered his whole body: the buoy and the gob, the girl's head of hair, the stars on his nipples, the boat, the pig on his prick, the naked woman, the flowers, the five dots on his palm and even the slight stroke that lengthened his eyes.

When a sucker has been robbed of a valuable object and files a complaint with the police, we say: "The sucker sang a fart" and also: "He sang a dirge." To God I sing a dirge!

Your death, Bulkaen, hesitates and is surprised to see you arrive dead. You have preceded me. Being dead, you have transcended me, you have traversed me. Your light has gone out . . . Like poets, precocious heroes die young! Despite myself, it is in a solemn mode that I shall speak of you, of your life, of your death. Bulkaen! Among so many other loves, what were *you*? A brief love, since I saw you only twelve days. Chance might have summoned me to sing another.

I do not claim to be giving you full knowledge of all the mysteries (and to be unveiling them) that were dormant in the Colony. There were lots of other things as well. I'm searching. They sometimes occur to me, but they flit through my mind without leaving traces. Without a trace on paper. You have to wait, they will appear at the end of the book.

Shall I also speak of the colonists' smile? And particularly the extraordinary smiles, bantering and saucy, roguish and amiable, more whorish than those of girls, with which, when they walked by, the kids led on the big fellows and Bulkaen excited the guys with tattoos? I'm sure that, as he once said to me, he made "hearts beat and hearty guys beat each other up."

They performed only acts that were useful. This may seem extraordinary after my saying that their lives were modelled on those of prisoners, but this miracle did occur and I shall try to demonstrate it: though each of the activities was a reproduction of the same—or what they thought the same—activity in prison, it was always warranted by an immediate necessity. They did not play. Primitives and children are grave. If you

observe any joyous revels among them, it is because the joy is
so great that it exhales from these games (which are always
religious) and bursts into laughter. The revels are not
improvised. They are themselves useful acts, being, rather,
ritual gestures of the cult of a divinity whom they must win
over. The execution of Métayer was a revel, it began with
immolation and continued with orgiastic frenzy. In short, I
think that those children's joy was of a bacchic order, a kind of
drunkenness caused by certain cruelties so intense that the joy
could be expressed only by a hoarse but also musical laugh,
and if they sometimes smiled, it was because they were unable
to resist—and did not dream of doing so—that whirling,
musical joy which envelops all high tragedy. But their laughter
was sombre. Flowers are gaiety and some are sadness become
flowers. And the laughter of the colonists, the laughter of
Harcamone in particular, produced only a slight eddy on the
surface of his face, whereas one could see that he himself
continued to live in a thick bed of slime, of mud, from which
an air-bubble sometimes rose up: a tear. And the whole
Colony composed one enormous Harcamone.

But the adolescents are behind the walls. They no longer
yearn for us and, at the far end of the Touraine countryside,
Mettray is forsaken, in short inoffensive. Is it possible that
time, in weathering the rigid prison, has so smoothed the
angles as to make of it a romantic tomb pleasant to the eye and
sweet to the heart? When I saw the Colony again, grass had
grown between the stones, thorns were piercing the leaves
from the windows that so many colonists had straddled with
their thighs at right angles. The panes were broken, swallows
nested in the building, and the dark, shadowy stairway, which
allowed us to exchange so many kisses and caresses, had collapsed.

After glancing at these ruins, the sadness of my soul will
never be cured. I advanced slowly and all I heard was the cry
of a few birds. I found only a corpse. I know that my youth is
dead. Nothing remains of the presence of so many hoodlums

on the walls and floors of the cells in the "quarter." I took a
walk around the Colony, then a longer walk, then another, and
as I strolled farther and farther away, describing wider and
wider circles, I felt my youth dying within me. Can it be that
that monstrous thicket of vipers which had enticed so many
boys withered in its prime? I still hoped that a colonist would
appear before me, and I hoped to see a fatigue squad, commanded by the head of a shop, appear at the bend of the road.
I placed my faith only in the latter miracle which would
suddenly revive the abandoned Colony after a five-year torpor.

My having seen it again in that state of desolation stops the
play of invention. My imagination dries up, but, in compensation. I turn to my youth; I fall asleep in it. I try to revive it by
every possible means. The stern band that gave all its rigidness
to that place which was naturally so gentle has gone away,
scattered in the other reformatories of France, and so I must
seek the memory of it within myself. I realize that I loved my
Colony with my flesh just as, when it was reported that the
Germans were preparing to leave, France realized, in losing
the rigidity they had imposed on her, that she had loved them.
She squeezed her buttocks. She begged the supplanter to
remain inside her. "Stay a while," she cried. Thus, Touraine
was no longer fecundated.

In my sadness, I feel such a need to go rampant that I could
tear out my heart and throw it in your face.

Where do the angels' progeny now meet? My beloved Mettray! If the simple precept of Jesus, "Love," was to give birth
to the most extraordinary pack of monsters: metamorphoses
into flowers, escapes by angels, tortures on the rack, resurrec-
tion. I turn to my youth; I fall asleep in it. I try to revive it by
kissed lepers, canonized guts, flowers condemned mirthlessly
by notorious councils, in short an entire legend which is called
Golden, the even more overwhelming miracles with which our
families teemed were bound in the end to unite, merge, mingle,
cook, boil in cauldrons so as to make visible in the depths of
my heart the most scintillating of crystals: Love. Pure and

simple love that I vow to the memory of those warped and sinuous families.

Again love, which fills me with insuperable bitterness because I thought I had discovered it between Pierrot and Botchako, who was called here—a title equal to that of Khan—Botchako the Bandit. He was ready to bugger any queer, and there was nothing of the bashful lover about him. To come along with his swaying walk, his hands in his belt, and take on the first little guy he took a shine to, that was more or less like him. But to dare come and free Bulkaen from the hole and go off with him! For it was from the hole that Bulkaen escaped. He stayed there only one day, the day of my arrival. I was therefore unable to see him in the disciplinary room.

You can easily imagine my joy and despair when I learned of it. He had finally been sent to the hole. He had managed to be punished in order to see me, as I both hoped and feared he would. He had given me proof of his love, and that proof was not annulled by his flight, for it would have been easy for him to escape from his dormitory cell, and Botchako had not been sent to the hole.

When one of the guys in the Big Cell said to me one morning, after his death:

"I saw him go by too when I was sweeping the cells. He was on the carpet . . ."

"You saw him? Where was he coming from?"

"I told you, from the council room."

Deep gratitude rose from my whole being to all of Creation which allowed such a moment, and I wondered by the same token at the wretchedness of our destiny which, just as I was about to take hold of my happiness, caused death to intervene.

"Why the council room?"

"He smoked in the dormitory."

But another inmate from Bulkaen's own dormitory corrected:

"It wasn't him who was smoking. It was Daybreak."

"So?"

"So? Pierrot said he was the one."

"Him, Pierrot. Pierrot said to the turnkey: 'It's me, chief'."

And I realized that it's awful to understand the workings of our friends' loves because we ourselves have been involved in the same system. At Mettray, in the dormitory, I had taken Divers' fault upon myself. Bulkaen accused himself of Lou Daybreak's crime.

And did Botchako know about it when he dared free the kid? He had displayed consideration, incredible delicacy, in his relations with Bulkaen, with Pierrot, and had wanted to cap them by escaping with him, that is, by joining him in the greatest peril either by saving Pierrot or making him a party to his bold jobs in a life of adventure. Both of these reasons oblige me to inquire into what there was about Pierrot that was so special, what made him different from the chickens in the jug, and what it was that had made him be elected by a master. There is still another question: if he chose Bulkaen as accomplice in order to escape, it was because he recognized in him the chief qualities required of a comrade-in-escape, namely coolness and courage, which are manly qualities and which Bulkaen possessed to such a degree that I can say of him that he was insensitive, icy, blind. I was able to hope that our mingled memories of Mettray would entangle Bulkaen and me in a kind of confusion in which he would lose his way and which, with its lakes and windings, he would perhaps take for love. Perhaps he would get lost in the meanders of an earlier life and would love me as one twin loves the other who was once half of himself. But this explanation was the product of words, and the facts are different. Bulkaen did not necessarily have to love me because I reminded him of Mettray; I myself loved Bulkaen because of Mettray, though I love Mettray as much as I do only because Bulkaen was the prettiest kid there. The love I bore Bulkaen was mingled with his contempt for me. This proposition may seem incoherent. I would like the reader to reflect on it. This contempt, emanating from

Bulkaen, unleashed by him, entered me without violence and tainted my love. It slowly disintegrated me, it destroyed my life.

Everything collapsed. All that remained for me was to kill Bulkaen or myself, for there was no further reason for existing since my role, whose function was to give me that happiness and pain, and death, had been performed.

But Bulkaen was higher than I. I was sure I would never reach him. And even though I saw him in his wretched reality, as a sad hoodlum with an unwashed face and a mind glutted with the sentimentality of poignant songs, songs true to life, he was higher than I because he was prouder. He looked down at me from on high. He did not love me, I loved him. He was the demon that incited me to greater toughness, greater boldness, greater love: Bulkaen was my virility, as Harcamone was that of someone else.

In order to love the man who had these qualities, Botchako himself had to manifest the few gaps in his coolness and courage through which the courage and coolness of the other entered him. Botchako was thus gentle and weak, and perhaps he sincerely desired my friendship when he offered me a drag. I am still ashamed of having rejected friendship and, even more, what symbolizes it here: the cigarette butt.

At Mettray, it was enough to hear a big shot say to Stoklay: "It was Rigaux who gave me a drag" for me to suspect the big shots of being linked by a bond of friendship, by a complicity that kept away the jerks and chickens, and yet no pledge of unity had been expressed. They recognized each other rather by snap judgment, by instinct. The same tastes brought them together, the same distastes. The *touche*[1] was the "touchstone." The rare butts, wet, sucked, black, dirty, exquisite, were signs of wretched tenderness as they passed from mouth to mouth, each of which was swollen with the mean, sulky expression one sees in children whose souls are

[1] *La touche,* the sharing of a cigarette by several prisoners, each of whom takes only one puff.—Translator's note.

heavy with sobs, in delicate children whom despair quickens. Since nothing melted them, the big shots never cried, nor did anyone else. The upright, rigid little men in their blue surplices, with their hands in their pockets, jaunty, curt, spiky, inhuman by dint of toughness, walked up and down the lanes, went through the hedges, beneath a summer sun worthy of their fragile ruggedness. They were unaware of the charm, the pleasantness, the abandonments of an indissoluble group because they were unaware of friendship and its treasures. Thereby too they were Romans. But knowing love, they wanted the little tramps. The big shots loved without violence, and in order to defend their love for each other—or rather for the distinguishing marks of the caste—they needed an opponent. The opponent is necessary, for he keeps love within bounds, he gives it form. These lines are dikes which he batters, which he assaults in thus becoming aware of himself.

Daniel had gone back to his job of bugler. One morning when he was at his post on the deserted square (near the pond, so that he would always be ready to blow any call ordered by Guépin), Sister Zoé, who was on her way from the infirmary to the chapel to hear low mass, went by not far from him. The child's heart must have frozen with rage. He no doubt thought of his kid who had cut his finger because of the sister in order to stay with him. He said good morning to the sister, crying out: "Good morning, Sister Zoé." When off duty, the nuns were quite agreeable. She therefore answered good morning. The bugler went up to her. When they were face to face, they were also very near the pond. The vigorous youngster shoved the old woman with his shoulder. Utterly astounded, she toppled into the water. Her skirts kept her afloat for a moment so that she looked like a huge, ridiculous water-lily, but they very quickly absorbed water and pulled her down. She was mute with fear and shame. The contact of the water with her legs, thighs and stomach, the novelty of the element she was no longer used to, paralyzed the virgin. She dared not make a movement or utter a cry. She sank. There was still a slight

eddying at the surface, and then the pure calmness of all April
mornings. Beneath the chestnut flowers, the virgin drowned to
death. The child, with another jerk of his shoulder, readjusted
the red and white sling of his bugle, put his hands back into his
pockets and calmly and slowly walked away from the pond. It
was not until the next day that the corpse was discovered in
the water. The obvious conclusion was that there had been an
accident, that she had lost her footing. The following Sunday,
before mass, the director assembled the colonists in the reception hall and told them about the accidental death of Sister
Zoé, and he urged them to pray for her.

Villeroy's transfer to Family H had freed me a little from
my fidelity. That was the period of my shame. The shame was
never glaring. It was never spoken of aloud in my presence,
probably because of the proximity of Villeroy who was
assumed capable of suddenly appearing to defend his little guy,
but the shame enveloped me as do certain odours that emanate
from you and that people pretend not to smell. Yet from a
certain kind of silence, from a puckering of the brow, you feel
that they know. Every night the pimps took turns coming into
my hammock. Our love-making was rapid, but Larochedieu
learned about it. I was taken to the Council Room, which was
near the quarter. It was a small, whitewashed room with a
green-covered table and two chairs. The director was sitting at
the table. Dudule was at his side and behind him, on the wall,
hung a huge crucifix. All the kids who were being punished
that day were waiting at the door for their turn to be sentenced
to: eight dry breads, ten dry breads, eight *piquets* (two hours
a day of tiring movements performed in the yard of the
quarter, instead of recreation) or a month in the quarter or
one or two months in the cell, but most often it was cell or
quarter until further notice. I too waited at the door. The
sound of the culprits' iron-shod sabots as they marched in step
entered my soul and stripped it of all hope: "One! Two! One
. . . Two . . . (a word here: The elegant thing to do was to
distort the "one, two" as much as possible, for example:

"Fuck . . . you" or "cunt . . . pooh," in short to make a kind of
grunt. The more savage and odd the grunt of the elder
brother, the more he was feared and respected. I think back to
the power of that cry which was due to the resemblance with
that of an animal, of a beast. If anyone had said simply: "One,
two," he would have been ridiculous. The cry was a male's cry.
It disturbed the chickens. When, after a pause, the cry was
taken up again, it was the empire of man that, after a brief
respite, subdued us. In order to indicate its power, one must
speak of a war cry, of tattoos, of strange seals, of ornamented
sceptres, of the laying on of phalli. Each male had his own
command, which corresponded to the shape and size of his
penis). I waited at the door of the Council Room. I was
already hiding in my mouth the piece of steel of my lighter so
as to smuggle it in when, after judgment had been passed and I
had left the council room, the chief guard, M. Bienveau,
stripped me and searched me and then threw me into the cell. I
went in. Dudule took a sheet of paper and said:

"You were seen leaving a hammock that wasn't yours. It's
disgraceful! "

And the director, the entire skin of whose cheeks was
trembling:

"It's disgraceful! At your age! "

I was given a month in the big cell.

When a young fag was in the big cell, the guards thought we
slept at night, but the big shots would organize their cruel
games. Just as the toughs talk nastily to the women they
subdue, calling them yapheads and ass pedlars, so they spoke
to the children about the smell of their bruised feet, of their
unwashed asses. They would say of a youngster whose toenails
were too long: "His nails are curling." They would also say:
"Your crap basket." "I'm going to shake your crap basket." I
can rightly say that the pale, submissive kids were led by the
rod and whip of fierce expressions. Nevertheless, the youngsters were dainty delights whose loathsome rind had to be
removed, they were like very young soldiers who are enveloped

in barbed wire from which they may fly away with the wings
of bees but in which, for the time being, they are roses caught
on their stems. The toughs enveloped the kids in those
frightful networks. One day, in the quarter, they curtly ordered
Angelo, Lemercier and Gevillé to wash their feet. I was present. I did not tell them to take off my shoes and socks, out of
humility in relation to the toughs: Deloffre and Rival of
Family B, Germain and Danier of Family A, and Gerlet of C,
but out of consideration for Villeroy they did not require me to
perform the chore. It was Deloffre who invented the ceremonial. Each of the three children had his function; Angelo
carried a pan full of water; Lemercier soaked his handkerchief
in it and washed the feet of the barefooted big shots; Gevillé
pulled out his shirt and dried them. Then, all three together,
on their knees, kissed the washed feet. Was it horror that
seized us when we entered the big cell? The naked torsos of
the motionless big shots gleamed in the darkness. The smell
was that of urine, sweat, cresyl, shit. And from their flowery
mouths the big shots spat smacking gobs of spit and envelop-
ing insults. Lorenque, who was present, must have been
secretly in love with Angelo, for he tried to defend him, though
in a rather casual way, against Deloffre's harshness, but the
kid felt that Lorenque wasn't a real big shot. Lorenque said:
"Let him alone, go on, don't be a pain in the ass."
Deloffre dropped the matter, but shortly thereafter he made
the angel, who was shuddering with disgust, clean his nostrils
with his tongue. Lorenque spoke up again:
"Hey, Deloffre, stop picking on him! "
But this time Deloffre's face took on its dirty look. He said:
"Listen, half-pint, you'd better butt out of this."
He was in a temper, not to be trifled with. Meanness, which
also made him look as if he were scared of a smack in the puss,
aroused in him such violent rages that they upset his whole
organism. He had the intelligent and evil appearance of certain
phials of poison, of reptiles and daggers (the kind called
"misericords"), but a meanness as hard, sharp and serene as a

jewel, as a ring, for the theft of which I am now in prison. A
fit of meanness could go as far as murder, and it is in this
sense that I have used, with regard to him, the word meanness,
that weapon which kills. In the eyes of Harcamone, he had the
dead face of the little girl which sparkled with the deliberate
meanness of all the objects that have got you into trouble.
Harcamone must have been unable to look at him without
hatred.

Angelo sidled gently up to Deloffre. He laughed at
Lorenque and said to him:

"Why are you butting in?"

He wanted to seize the opportunity to curry favour with the
big shot by siding with him against his knight. Lorenque said
nothing. That clinched the disgusting agreement that had been
established against the one who was punished. Angelo cleaned
the hoodlum's nose with his tongue.

I have described this scene because it took place in a disciplinary cell similar in every respect to the one in which we
have been grouped here, at Fontevrault, where I have just been
given an account of the epilogue of a love story. There were
about ten inmates in the cell, none of whom must have known
about my friendship with Bulkaen. I noticed among them a
former trusty of the sixth division. The sixth remained, for me,
the mysterious division, to which I had never yet been, but to
which Bulkaen had often gone without telling me: it was
Rocky's division. I asked the trusty whether he had ever known
the latter. He answered that he had. He specified: "He was
tall and thin. A decent guy. Yes, I knew him, but he left for
the Isle of Ré. Before that, he'd been married here. Not very
long ago." Married "legitimately." At that moment there
flashed in my eyes the heartbreaking vision of a wedding in
which the bride was Bulkaen himself, wearing a white satin,
bare-shouldered dress with a train, carrying orange blossoms
in his arms, and with lilies on his shaved head. The emotion
that shook me was due to the recollection of that wedding
beneath the stars at Mettray. My slightly faltering image of

Rocky merged with that of a bride and groom in full dress, of convicts in love, in a setting of red carpets and green plants. But a consolation, a very sweet peace, entered my heart, for I felt sure that Rocky had married in prison because he no longer loved Bulkaen. I was sure that Bulkaen knew about the marriage and resented it, and I was avenged for his contempt for me. But at the same time I regretted that we were not bound—Rocky, Lou Daybreak, Botchako, Divers and I—by a savage friendship like that of Cleopatra's five warriors, to whom we would have turned over our united fortunes to buy for one of us (designated by dice or cards) a night of love with Bulkaen.

As a result of having been at Mettray, I am kind, that is, my kindness toward the humble is composed of my fidelity to those I have loved. Had I risen up into the hyperboreal solitude of wealth, my soul would have been unable to blossom, for I do not love the oppressed. I love those whom I love, who are always handsome and sometimes oppressed but who stand up and rebel.

One does not live forty years of one's life or one's entire life among children and angels without an error in one's reckonings. And the torturers of children are scented with the children's scent.

M. Bienveau was the grand master of the quarter. His mouth was shut over his clenched teeth, and his dark gaze could not be seen behind his pince-nez. He wore, in summer and winter alike, an extraordinary yellow straw hat encircled with a broad sky-blue faille ribbon. Bienveau was posted in a small room, the window of which looked out on the yard of the quarter where we marched round and round in the rhythm given by the elder brother. Protected by a screen, he would strike from a list the one bowl of soup of the kid who stumbled or chattered in silence. For the summer he had devised a system of being brought pans of cool water and he would watch us die in the sun while he took foot-baths that lasted three hours. He died of something else. The whole Colony accompanied him to the village cemetery, but when we left the chapel and the band leader lowered his arm to direct the funeral march, the Colony's great joyous soul exhaled in the whirlwind of a silent *Marseillaise*.

Just as here, in Fontevrault, it is the disciplinary cell that concentrates, that elaborates, the very essence of the prison, so, at Mettray, the Colony drew its power of love from the quarter and, even more deeply, from the big cell where a few big shots, labouring the darkness, emitted waves that will not stop for a long time to come.

The death of Bulkaen and that of Botchako ought to have edified them, sanctified them, but in all canonizations there is a devil's advocate, and in this case it was again Lou Daybreak. He said:

"So what? Botchako was a jerk, like lots of . . ."

"That's what *you* say."

"Ask the Weasel. They worked together. Botchako the Bandit, the yegg, he couldn't snag the letters in the apartments. Didn't dare read them! Question of delicacy. And a guy like that threw his weight around!"

But though Bulkaen's death magnified him only in *my* eyes, it also placed him in a region of myself where I can reach him. However, let me add the following: as soon as I learned that it would be impossible to see him again, since we were separated by the rules of the hole, I realized, to my despair, that I loved him so deeply that I was unable to utilize his image at night for my solitary pleasures. Shortly thereafter, his death heroized him for a few days and he was sacroscant, but now that his flame is dying out, I feel that I am going to love him tenderly. Our joint adventure is taking on a more human aspect in my memory. When his toughness falls away from him, a gentleness clads him; each of his acts, even the fiercest, becomes mild.

My memory preserves only those which soothed me, those which expressed the hidden and intermittent love he felt for me, though at the same time he despised me. And as for the fierce acts, I am able to retain only the cracks in their marble through which there escaped, like vapour from a sulphonator, his more than human sweetness. In short. I am aware that I loved only a kid, who requited my love, a kid who was voluptuous since he was so very tender, and now, after his death, there is nothing to prevent me from coming because of and with him, and it is as a result of his death, which does not make him inviolable, that I violate him. And in fact it was last night that I forced his spectre to confess to me: "Baby, I wish I had a fist up my ass to take what you ram into it." And in order for my gesture to be easier, I accumulate in Bulkaen all the signs by which I can see him quite otherwise than as a hero. I recall with pleasure the bright look of astonishment in his eyes when he told me, on the ninth day of our friendship, that his big shot in the Joan of Arc family loved him for the first time. He suddenly remembered the cherry pit he had swallowed. Parents threaten their children by telling them that if they swallow a cherry pit a flowery shrub can sprout from their stomach. The sperm could have sprouted within him and produced a child there. I even remember that at Mettray he was a field worker and thus one of the jerks. That subtracts nothing from his charm, but rather adds to it. What jerk didn't have the heart of a big shot?

For Winter, beauty was a hard blow. The toughs took a fancy to him. and he had to suffer being reamed by twelve cocks and the shame of its happening almost publicly. Long afterward, when he told me about his life as a young pimp in Paris, a delicate emotion that arose from his past shame made his voice and face waver a little, and in fact his whole being. The trace of the humiliations in the cell was transparent behind his rough gestures. Certain scars appear when we rub the injured limb.

His pretty mug and his nonchalance excited the big shots, and they gave themselves a treat.

"I've just treated myself to a little guy." Thus spoke Divers, who added for my benefit:

"You'll have a little punk's dick, you too."

Unfortunately, Winter did not suffer the miseries of prostitution for long. I would have liked to see that urchin archduke in the supernatural realm of our reflections, I mean of that higher world into which we plunge and where we are damaged to the point of shame by the peckers, chests, thighs and claws of the big shots who leaped from a sublime sky into his cavern. Winter cut off his eyelashes in order to be less handsome. He was transferred to another family and became a jerk. But I had seen him wipe away his tears after being scoured by the jissom of a dozen big shots. He was assigned to Family C, which was composed almost entirely of chickens, including the elder brothers. One was the kid of a yegg in Family B and the other of a pimp in Family A who stuck up for them and saw to it that they were respected. And in the mess-hall the little chickens ordered a jerk who was making noise with his sabots to stand against the wall and eat dry bread, and they added, very loudly:

"He lets himself get reamed and a jerk like that makes a rumpus."

This magnificent bumptiousness prevented smiles and protests.

I don't know whether I would have invented perverse postures all by myself, but it's impossible for the poet not to be influenced by words and turns of phrases, and even more by the persons who reveal them to him by uttering them in his presence for the first time. When Divers was wooing me in the grotesque way I have already described, he once said to me, laughingly:

"Come on, pussy, I'm going to tongue you up the nose."

And he accompanied the words with a spiral movement of his tongue.

Divers made gestures which could only be those of a male. When I sat down at the table, I didn't take hold of my chair by both sides and slide it under me as I usually did. I put one hand between my thighs and pulled it forward. That's a man's gesture, a horseman's gesture, and it seemed so impossible for me to make that it slightly unseated me. And then I kept doing it, and now I'm used to it.

For three years Divers was the handsomest boy in the Colony, where there were a hundred splendid adolescents. He dared—and was the only one who did—to have his pants retailored so that they would be skin-tight. That part of him was a focal point of the Colony. Even when he wasn't present, I felt that my eyes were fixed on it. And, what was strange, the slightest of his gestures (whether he raised an arm, made a fist, ran, jumped astride my handsome pimp, lunged) or the mere sight of one of the seemingly inoffensive parts of his body: his bare or clothed arm, his strong wrist, the back of his neck, his narrow, motionless shoulders and particularly the proud calves outlined by the canvas trousers (actually, the calves of the strongest and handsomest kids were modelled by the cloth) made us realize instinctively (reminder of Harcamone's swelling muscles) that beauty lay in that vigour, that those features could give us prestige, since—on the sly our hands would tighten the floating cloth of the trousers so that the bulge left by the calf stood out; we would tighten the thighs and buttocks so that they bulged (that was another way of deliberately getting a hard-on)—it was enough to see any one of those details on Divers to feel that it was only a modest representative of his precious packet of genitals.

The five blue points, tattooed on his palm in the form of the five of a dice cube—but at the base of the thumb of the others where it meant "Fuck the police"—had, on Divers' fist, an extremely grave meaning, to be sought in the Bible and in my mythologies, for those points were ornaments on a priest who served a cult (I never knew which). For the first time I understood musicians who express passion with song. I wish I could write out the melody I heard in Divers' gestures.

During marches, or when we went from the mess-hall to the stairs or from the reception hall to the family cottage, Divers would sometimes get behind me and try to keep in step with me. He would stick to me with precision; his right leg would shoot forth and stick to mine, then his left leg would do the same. His chest was almost on my shoulders, and his nose and breath on the back of my neck. I felt as if I were being carried by him. It was as if he were already on top of me and had screwed me, laying me out with all his weight and also drawing me to him as the eagle drew Ganymede, as he was to do that fourth night when, better prepared, I let him enter me deeply and he swooped down on me with his huge bulk (a whole sky falling on my back), his claws digging into my shoulders and his teeth biting the back of my neck. He was planted inside me, pushing into my soil and, above me, unfurling a bough and a leaden foliage.

(Through the open collar of his white shirt I saw the edge of a blue-and-white striped jersey. What kind of fidelity makes him keep that sailor's skin on his own? But I understand men's pleasure when they see a woman's chemise showing. Beneath his civilized air, on his polite, reasonable words, I see Mettray showing, and what I see is as exciting as the blue and white triangle in the opening of the shirt.)

I have already said that the head of the family slept in a small room at the far end of the dormitory. We always found a way of escaping the supervision of the guard who spied on us through a movable little pane set in the wall. He was prompt and alert and his whole bearing was furtive and guilty, because his glances and gestures were quick and brief, and yet it was frank because they were direct. This mixture is not infrequent. I found it in Bulkaen too. Youngsters can shift quickly from pliancy to the vigour that makes you believe in their purity. One night, Daniel crept under the hammocks in order to steal. The colonists do not rob each other. They are strong, and a thief would be beaten to a pulp, or they are weak, and what need would there be for the big shots to get up at night to steal? If they want a thing, they make the owner hand it over politely during the day.

So, I saw Daniel.

The next morning, after prayer in the mess-hall, before breakfast—soup and black bread—we learned that the supervisor's watch and tobacco had been stolen. That same evening, Daniel was missing at roll-call. He had been seen for the last time, at about three in the afternoon, going from the brush shop to the latrines. It was assumed that he had run away. But three days later his little corpse, which already smelled, was discovered in a laurel hedge. He lay there abandoned, with his teeth exposed. An eye had been plucked out and his body had been stabbed fourteen times with a paring-knife. I thought I was the only one who had seen Daniel prowling under the hammocks, and I didn't know how to link his death with his nocturnal expedition. As I lay in the sleeping dormitory with my eyes peeping above that sea of motionless waves, I no longer dared look night in the face. Each little shaver, though barely swelling out his hammock, was charged with the mystery of death.

Since Toscano and I were close friends, I would occasionally join him at night, unknown to his man, Deloffre, who loved him. Beneath his hammock we would crouch on a blanket and roll up in another, and we would chat. The nature of the friendship I must have felt for Toscano was so pure that when we pledged our troth I felt so purified that I was willing, the same evening, to make love with Villeroy, as I did every evening, but a kind of overpowering chastity prevented me from feeling any pleasure. I pretended that I felt sick and quickly dug into my hammock to find my way back, not to Toscano, but to my freindship for him. Several times in succession he had refused to climb out of his hammock, where he remained curled up in the sleeping-bag. Once, before I left him, he whispered to me:

"Do you happen to know if cabin boys have their hair cut?"

I realized immediately that he was referring to the Royal Navy, but I didn't know what to answer, for though I had read lots of adventure novels about eighteenth-century pirates, stories about boarding, shipwrecks, storms, mutinies, hangings

from the maintop, and though I knew about the extraordinary
forecastle, I was lost in schemes (involving rum and negro
slaves, gold and smoked meat) that were described in closely
printed lines on dirty paper, but I don't know whether cabin
boys of the period had their hair cut. I suppose they were
vermin-ridden. Finally, one evening the kid was willing to fold
back his covers, climb out of his hammock and resume our
chats. No doubt the reason was that he had finished the story
which had embarked him on a brig that carried the pirate flag,
the Jolly Roger with a death-head, or on the galley that took
him from a penal colony to plough the Caribbean Sea. And the
very evening of this return from the finest of voyages, he
secretly called me and showed me the silver watch that Daniel
had stolen from the head of the family. I asked him how he
had got it, but he refused to tell. The police had turned things
topsy-turvy in their effort to find the killer, but they came
from Paris with methods that are right for the usual kind of
murder and utterly wrong for the world of children. It was at
Brest Prison that I learned how the story ended. I found
Deloffre there and he spoke to me with great emotion about
Toscano, who had drowned before our eyes. In his excitement,
he didn't even realize that he was also telling me about the
murder of Daniel. He had seen him—just as I had—enter the
room of the head of the family. The morning of the theft he
said nothing, but around noon he met Daniel by a laurel hedge
and demanded part of the booty. The thief refused to share it.
A fight followed and went on until Daniel, who had been
stabbed fourteen times with a paring-knife (our knives were
sharper, fiercer, more dangerous in our hands than actual
daggers), fell dead and bleeding in the dark laurels. He had
not screamed. The fight had taken place in silence, among the
silent branches. For me, the Touraine countryside is strewn
with little frail or muscular bare-armed corpses, without any
comforting curl of hair to weep for them. Tight-lipped and
with their teeth clenched, they died an Italian death. The
murder took place behind a clump at a crossing of corridors, of

passages, of ebony hallways, of ranks of men-at-arms meeting
successions of columns in three directions. It was, by virtue of
the heroic presence of a sixteen-year-old child, the peristyle of
a Racinian palace. Deloffre took the tobacco for himself and
the watch for his faggot, and I can't help admiring the heroism
of the chicken who didn't love his big shot and never opened
his mouth to squeal on him and who only once was so
imprudent as to show me the watch.

A week before he left for Toulon, Villeroy, of Family H,
officially sold me. He sold me to Van Roy, a big shot who had
once been discharged but whose bad conduct brought him back
to the Colony. I finally realized where he had got the pieces of
cheese with which he had been stuffing me. They were my
price. For three months Van Roy had deprived himself of his
portion in order to buy me, and it was I myself who had
devoured my dowry as it was being paid. The matter was not
treated as an act of sale, but one afternoon in the yard, in the
presence of Deloffre, Divers and five other big shots, Villeroy
said that he was turning me over to Van Roy and if anyone
present didn't like it, let him say so then and there himself
before picking on Van Roy. I feared and hoped for a moment
that Divers would speak up. He said nothing. And all the other
kids, who were already aware of Van Roy's views, said that
everything was in order. Then, seizing me from behind, Van
Roy brutally locked me in his arms and legs. A month later, he
took a fancy to another chicken, whom he sold. He then turned
me over to Divers, whom I married in a wedding of which I
have spoken.

Deloffre must have been a Parisian and must have often
taken the subway and noticed the outlandish poster telling how
to treat a person who has been asphyxiated. One afternoon of
one of the three Julys I spent at Mettray (the second, I
think), we all went down, led by the band, to the river that
flowed to the bottom of the hill. Bathing trunks had been
distributed and we were supposed to dry ourselves partly with
our towels and for the most part in the sun. We stripped in the

presence of the guard, who wore a celluloid collar and black tie, and the sight of those four hundred children in the meadow, on the bank of the river, offering their skinny bodies to the water and sun, was charming. The river was shallow. Toscano swam out a way with Deloffre. He must have fallen into a hole. He disappeared in the water, and Deloffre brought him back in his arms, drowned. He put him down on the grass of the meadow. The entire Family B was there, and we were some distance away from the head of the family. We were thunderstruck. Deloffre stretched Toscano on his stomach and sat astride him. He began his rhythmic pressures as advised by the subway poster. This poster is illustrated by a curious drawing: a young man straddling the back of another who is lying on his stomach. Did the memory of that picture (evoked by the necessity of the moment) arouse obscene thoughts in Deloffre (he told me later that it did), or was his posture itself sufficient? Or the proximity of death? The rhythmic pressure was at first desperate but big with hope, with mad hope. The despair subsided at the slightest hope. His movements grew slower, but though less rapid, they were extraordinarily vigorous, they seemed charged with a spiritual life. Naked in the green meadow, with the sun drying our bodies, we formed a circle of worried, anxious souls. Most of us stood upright, a few were leaning forward. We were afraid of witnessing the kind of miracle in which Joan of Arc brought dead children back to life. Deloffre seemed to be taking in an excess of life (which he drew from his intimate relations with the powerful nature of noon) in order to revive Toscano. His friend mustn't die! And on the day of the funeral, during the procession, I'm not sure that he didn't reproduce instinctively on himself, with his arms, Toscano's usual gestures and, on his face, his friend's tics and smiles, performing behind the coffin the exalting function of the funereal Archimime. Deloffre's penis grazed his dead chicken's buttocks, which were outlined by the wet trunks. We all saw it, but none of us would have dared say a word. Deloffre might have whistled to call his dead friend back to life, whistled or sung, as Bulkaen's big shot whistled in the past.

(I have written "in the past" with regard to Bulkaen. At the present time, Bulkaen presides at all my memories of the Colony. He is their father. He is thus prior to all.) When his big shot was preparing for love, he made Bulkaen whistle a tango softly.

"Boy, what I've been through. The funniest things, I'm telling you, Jean," Bulkaen said laughingly.

I wasn't laughing. That gesture reminded me of a rite of the earth, for the Vendée peasants are said to play the violin and accordeon so that the donkey gets a hard-on and fucks the she-ass.

Deloffre's gesture in that green grass was sacred. Nobody laughed.

Finally, there was a moment when he was completely shaken with little shudders: it was neither the wind drying the water on his shoulders, nor fear, nor shame, but pleasure. At the same time, he collapsed on the dead body. His grief was frightful and we realized that it would have taken a woman to calm him.

Since then, I have been to the big cell, and I have seen the noblest, most vigorous pimps, broken by drill, fall to their knees. Because they muttered words in too low a voice, I have seen turnkeys with dark torsos and pectorals of solid gold stiffly assume the postures of animal trainers and cudgel their bulging muscles. The pimps scream when they are beaten. They scream like their whores. And their cries rise up to me through girders, walls and cellars. This is a school in which men are transformed. Just as one sees Romans in the movies beat their slaves, so, in the cellars of the prison, I have seen jailers whip splendid, almost naked suns until blood flowed. The victims writhed beneath the thongs, they dragged along the floor. They were more dangerous than tigers, as supple but more cunning, they could disembowel the hard-eyed guard. And he, more insensitive to tortured beauty than his indifferent arm, kept whipping relentlessly. He carried out his metamorphosis. From between his hands the pimps emerged pale with shame and with lowered eyes. They were girls ready for the wedding.

Just as Fontevrault had its revolt, we had ours.

Not a single piece of paper circulated in the Colony, but all the big shots knew what was going on. We were sustained by something other than a hope of freedom, which would not have been sufficient to uproot us from our habits. Love was needed. It was Richard who took the movement in hand, and the impetus he gave it had the dash and drive by which he himself was animated. Deep down, we didn't want to escape, for we had a feeling that if there did exist a brilliant, worldly life in which crooks and racketeers and pimps and gigolos could strut about in patent-leather shoes, we would never find, except in jail, a dark, cavernous house with winding corridors where we could prowl about as in the Colony. But apart from the fact that the revolt seemed to us to come from a loving authority, we wanted it for its own sake. By revolt I mean a mass escape, for since the Colony was not confined by a wall—and since an explosive charge requires the worthiest possible setting—no explosion was possible. I am not quite sure that I have thus far succeeded in showing that usually our life was not frantic, was not nervous. No storm gathered in our families as in a valley, for the electricity of our brows and hearts always found a thousand ways of escaping through the flowers, the trees, the air, the countryside. Though our lives were tense, it was only because of the tragic attitude of children who measured and challenged each other. We wanted to whip up the waves of a one-day wrath so as to feel its full leaden weight fall and crush us. No one seemed busy. The chickens who were let in on things by their males kept their mouths shut. No one spoke with treasonable intent or out of weakness. The order was: to unnail three or four floorboards in each dormitory—as Villeroy had done—and to drop to the mess-hall, get out into the countryside and then scatter, one by one. The order was clear—one by one, but we knew that the darkness would quickly bring the kids together again in couples, and then in bands. We did not envisage this very clearly, for despite an idiotic hope that made the project seem a sure success we felt the unlikelihood of its success.

The idea of escape smouldered cautiously among us for four days. At least, that was as long as I knew about it. We would get together in little groups and, leaning against a wall, would discuss ways and means. One of us would shoo off the jerks, the way one shoos flies, to prevent them from approaching. I don't think that any one of us let the secret out. The departure was set for a Sunday-to-Monday night.

I don't recall exactly what I felt when the rumour spread in the afternoon that Van Roy and Divers had ratted on seven of the ringleaders. Divers already held the position that made everyone respect him, that of a high and mighty big shot. He had the additional advantage of knowing how to avoid fights and thus of never being in the situation of a loser. I despised him for his betrayal, though without withdrawing my love. In fact, I even forced myself to make it more violent so as to leave no room for contempt, but I felt I was shying away from him and almost instinctively I turned my back at the sight of him, whereas formerly my face would turn toward his sun. The whole Colony knew about his baseness, but no one seemed to hold it against him. The Colony had just lived through four wonderful days of hope. It was still breathing the smoke of the hot ashes. That was enough for it. But that same evening there was a bolt from the blue: Van Roy, one of the seven who had been arrested, was discharged, though he had not even put in three months of good conduct. In general, you had to put in a year. We understood. A horrible injustice had made us accuse Divers. But the harm that had been done within me had a lasting effect, and the contempt I felt for him a whole day long was to leave its mark on my heart. Nevertheless, my instinct had not been wrong. It had recognized that Divers was not a genuine male, that he was a usurper, for as soon as I learned

of Van Roy's betrayal, this big shot's prestige was heightened
in my eyes. He had dared make a terrible gesture, one which
sent six of his handsomest friends to the reformatory at
Eysses. Thus, the dangerous revelation that the strongest big
shots were squealers was repeated. I say "repeated," for I had
gathered as much when Stoklay prevented me from escaping,
and I had sensed it long before when I once heard a big shot
tell a silly lie: in the quarter, the elder brother, who had cuffed
a youngster for not keeping in step, said to him:

"I purposely smacked you so the guard wouldn't put you on
dry bread."

And I took pleasure in imagining their granite-like mass
undermined by a deep, winding network of mole-hills. I was
learning that traitors were born among knights, among the
noblest, the haughtiest, and that Divers had been unable to
betray for the very reason that he was gentle by nature and
was trying hard to be tough by observing all the appearances
of toughness. And when he left the Colony for I don't know
what destiny, bound for some port, I felt a deeper thrill
at night when I relived the minutes of love I had been
given by that worm-eaten pimp: Van Roy. I would fall
asleep in his arms. I was more *his* "little woman" than that of
Divers.

The real revolt took place a year later. I was told about it
by Guy, who had arrived at Mettray the year I left it.

"It was like this. We were lined up in the morning to go to
the shops. Guépin was calling the roll. He sees a guy, I forget
who, slipping a pal a piece of steel for his lighter. So he comes
up and starts yelling. He wanted to see the steel. The other
guy told him to go take a shit. They were going to fight, but
the pimp was a big shot, and the other big shots got sore. So,
you get it, all the other guys, instead of staying in line, wanted
to watch. They broke ranks despite (the word "despite" seemed
to him too literary, he repeated and pronounced it in a very
tough, vulgar tone) despite the bosses of the shops and the
heads of the families. It was a regular riot. And they began

yelling. Suddenly some guy shouted: 'Let's set the joint on fire and clear out!' "

Then there was real confusion. The guards were bewildered by the children's strategic skill. Several buildings were slightly burned, the colonists fled, a few guards were killed, screaming as they died: "I have children, remember that I have children." The most guilty (63) were sent to Eysses for ten years.

Toward the end of my stay, my nights at Mettray became anxious. One of them left me the memory of the greatest fear I have ever known. I awoke in the darkness; my eyes groped about before I recognized I was at Mettray, and I was happy to know I was there. Fear clung to my shirt, dampened my sheets. I had just lived through one of the most frightful nightmares of my life. With accomplices whom I no longer remember I must have seen an old woman killed on an embankment. The only thing I recall clearly is the scene of the jewels. I stepped on those which had fallen, and dug them into the slime with my heel. Then, when my accomplices had turned around, I picked them up. I was sure I had not been seen, except by the young man at the bottom of the slope who had witnessed the murder of the old woman with complete indifference and thus knew I had not taken part in it. I therefore did not mistrust him, and I bent down and picked up the jewels before his very eyes. There were three rings—two bands for any of the fingers, and one which had a particular form: a kind of small hood cut from an emerald—or topaz, I no longer remember—and meant to cap the thumb. I put them into my pocket. They were worth a great deal, but a sum in small coins, small as spangles . . . The young man minded his own business. Then, when I had picked up the jewels, he laid his hand on my shoulder and said:

"What have you got there?"

And he duly arrested me, for he was a detective disguised as a young man. I didn't dream at first that I would be guillotined, but little by little the thought rose within me. Certainty invaded me in little waves. I was awakened by anguish, and I was relieved to find myself in the cell. But the dream had such a ring of truth that when I was awake I was afraid I had not quite dreamed it, had not merely dreamed it. The fact is that it recounted, while deforming and actually continuing, something that had happened the day before. I had taken advantage of a colonist's release to swipe all of Van Roy's tobacco and hide it in my pallet. As the boy who had been released left the dormitory before waking-time, Van Roy did not fail to accuse him of the theft when he learned of it. He flew into a terrible rage and had no scruples about searching all the pallets. He looked into mine too. He would have killed me if he had discovered his tobacco there. He searched carelessly and found nothing.

And whenever I recall that dream, the same anguish that clutched me when I awoke swoops down on me, because the dream seems to be the highly retributive epilogue of the entire adventure that I am transcribing, the adventure occasioned by a seemingly trivial fact: Divers' betrayal of Harcamone, in which I became an accomplice by helping and absolving him.

And, as at Mettray, I had had the feeling that the dream had not sprung from nothing—as dreams often seem to do—I have just had the feeling that that entire part of my life had deep roots in this dream and was its flowering in the air (I was about to write "free, pure air," alas!).

I had done nothing to gain Deloffre's confidence, but perhaps he remembered that I had been Toscano's friend during my chicken period. One evening he spoke to me again about the latter's death and told me how horrible it was to be haunted by the kid. I asked whether he believed in ghosts. It wasn't a question of that but of the semblance of love he had made on the corpse. That outlandish ceremony on a catafalque of flesh appeared to him to be what it must have been to everyone: a profanation. He lived in the shame, in the horror, of having screwed a corpse and above all of having taken pleasure in the act. After the drama, he had to live in the tragedy. He once said to me:

"I have the feeling I was present at my birth, that I came out of him right after his death. My skull is his, my hair, my teeth, my eyes are his! I feel I'm living in the dead body of my little sweetypuss!"

It was there, no doubt, beyond the slightest doubt, that I could find the deep, tangled, clawed roots of my dream, and this sudden revelation gave rise to another. If the dream seemed to be the prolongation of another, in the way that I myself was the prolongation of Divers, wasn't the crime of which we became guilty by letting Harcamone be punished the prolongation (rather than the repetition) of an earlier crime? I mean the following: I was not much aware of the resemblance there was said to be between Divers and me because the only mirrors in the Colony were the tiny hand-mirrors—one per family—that the chief loaned on Sunday mornings to the colonists whose job was to shave us. I therefore didn't know what I looked like, for what I could see of my face from the outside, in the lower window-panes, was too imprecise. Besides, the colonists who had once spoken about Divers' face apropos of mine seemed to give no further thought to the resemblance. However, it intrigued me, not that I very seriously believed in any actual kinship, though I did invent one, an even closer one, if possible, than a family kinship, so as to be able to entangle our love with violent incest. Without his being aware, I would gaze at his face, which I also thought was mine. I tried, unsuccessfully, to engrave all his features in my memory. I would close my eyes so as to try to reconstruct it there. I came to know my face through his. His height—he was taller than I—and his age—he was eighteen and I sixteen—instead of troubling me made me regard myself as a replica of him with a two-year lag. It seemed to me, if you like, that I was destined to repeat for the balance-sheet of 1926 and 1927 the eminent gestures with which he had adorned the years 1924 and 1925. I was continuing him. I was being projected by the same ray, but I had to focus myself on the screen, had to make myself visible, two years after him. He himself never spoke to me about our mysterious resemblance. Perhaps he was unaware of it.

I now know that he is much better-looking than I. But my solitude impelled me toward that resemblance until I wanted it to be perfect, until I merged with him. In like manner, the two elder brothers of Family C regarded each other as do identical twins, those whose twinship is due to the division of a single biological cell, those who are sure of having been one and the same and who were sundered by a sword-stroke. Having also heard that as a result of mutual love and of living together a certain husband and wife had come to resemble each other in a disturbing, almost comic way, I was thrilled by the hope that Divers and I had, in a previous existence, grown old together and been a very united and loving couple.

I therefore buried myself, as I have said, in the depths of the atmosphere created here by the secretly united presences of Harcamone and Divers. Harcamone lived in the twists and turns of a slow, complicated death that wound in and out of itself. Without saying anything expressly, Divers and I communed—by virtue of our haunted looks and gestures—in Harcamone's death. The extraordinary purity with which I endow Bulkaen, the living light, the moral rectitude with which I adorned him, had given my aspiration toward Harcamone, and the form of his destiny, the semblance of an ascension. I felt I was rising toward him, and this necessarily made me place him very high, radiant, in the very stance of Bulkaen waiting for me at the top of the stairs. But this interpretation was erroneous.

If customary saintliness consists in rising heavenward toward one's idol, it was quite natural, since the saintliness leading me to Harcamone was its exact opposite, that the exercises which were orienting me were of an order other than those which lead to heaven. I had to go to him by a path other than that of virtue. I did not seek access to brilliant crime. The abjection in which Divers remained—and the more intense abjection of our two united wills—drove us head downward in the direction away from heaven, into the darkness, and the thicker the darkness, the more sparkling—hence, the blacker—Harcamone would therefore be. I was happy about his agony, about Divers' treachery, and we were more and more capable of so ghastly an act as the murder of a little girl. The joy I feel when I am told of certain acts which the multitude call infamy should not be confused with sadism. Thus, my pleasure when I learned of the murder of that fifteen-year old child by a German soldier was caused by the simple rightness of the audacity which dared, by massacring the delicate flesh of adolescents, to destroy a visible, established beauty in order to achieve a beauty—or poetry—resulting from that shattered beauty's encounter with that barbaric gesture. A Barbarian smiling at the top of his statue was knocking down Greek masterpieces all around him!

Harcamone's influence acted truly in accordance with his perfect destination: through him our minds were opened to extreme abjection. I cannot avoid using the figurative terminology that is commonly employed. Do not be surprised if the images that indicate my movement are the opposite of those that indicate the movement of the saints in heaven. You may say that they rose, and that I lowered myself.

It was then that I made my way along those winding roads which are, in truth, the very paths of my heart and of saintliness. The ways of saintliness are narrow, that is, it is impossible to avoid them, and when, as ill luck would have it, one has ventured upon them, it is impossible to turn around and go back. One is a saint by the force of circumstances which is the force of God! Bulkaen was a jerk at Mettray. It is important to bear this in mind, and I must love him, since I do love him, because of that, so that neither scorn nor disgust will find the slightest opening. He himself would have hated me had he known that that was why I loved him. He would have thought my heart was full of tenderness for the little tramp he had once

been, and that was why I treated him with severity, as one
treats marble. I loved Bulkaen for his ignominy.

In order to reach Harcamone I had to go by way of the
opposite of virtue. Other signs too led me gradually to the
stupendous vision which I am going to describe. But I am
already the belated young man who presses onward in the
twilight and says to himself, "It's behind those hills, it's in the
mist, behind those glens." He is wrung by the same emotion as
the soldier who was fighting in the African darkness, who
crawled along, rifle in hand, and said to himself. "Behind those
rocks is the holy city." But perhaps I must sink even deeper
into shame, and one of the most painful memories of Bulkaen's
childhood recurs to me. Bulkaen was a tragic character because
of his passionate, excessive temperament, and also because of
the circumstances of his life. When he assured me that he
loved prison (he told me so one morning during recreation,
displaying his unlined face), I realized that there were people
for whom prison was an accepted way of life. The fact that I
myself took pleasure in it would not have been enough for me
to believe it, but suddenly the handsomest of the prisoners
assured me that he loved prison. In like manner, when the
convicts march round and round the big cell with their arms
folded on their chests and their heads bent in the posture of
worshippers approaching the Holy Table, they display, if the
guard or trusty calls them, a closed, stubborn forehead,
frowning eyebrows, a terrible look, because they have just been
torn from one of those deep plunges into reverie where they
move about nimbly. He loved the prison toward which he was
falling, for it uprooted him from the earth, and I feel I would
have been powerless to fight against it because it was itself the
form that fatality had taken to achieve its chosen end.

As others took upon themselves the sin of men, I shall take
upon myself this added horror with which Bulkaen was burdened. When Divers learned that I loved him, he made a point
of telling me himself what I am going to relate, for he stayed
on at Mettray two years after my departure. There he met

Bulkaen, who knew Van Roy; the latter had been discharged but returned a year later because he had committed new offences.

In telling me this, Divers did not realize that he was thus presenting a Bulkaen who was qualified to join our group of outcasts.

I TAKE THE SUFFERING UPON MYSELF AND I SPEAK.

"I put on my most form-fitting pants, and I wonder by what miracle he managed, during the hour that noon recreation lasted, to elude the guard, who was constantly on the look-out. Van Roy assembled the seven most important big shots of the family (including Deloffre and Divers) in the yard behind the cottage. Then he went to get me. As soon as I saw him approaching, I realized that my time had come. They were going to proceed to my execution.

"The Colony then became one of the most agonizing dens of hell. It remained sunny for the flowers, foliage and bees, but it contained evil. Every tree, flower and bee, the blue sky, the lawn, became props of an infernal place and site. The scents remained scents and the pure air just as pure, but evil was in them. They became dangerous. I was in the centre of a moral hell whose purpose was my torment. Van Roy came up to me with a rather casual air and a faint smile on his lips. Pointing to the far end of the yard, he said:

"All right, get going! "

"My lips were dry. Without answering, I walked ahead and, without being told, stood against the back wall, the one facing the latrines. From there we could not be seen by those who were playing in front of the cottage under the supervision of the head of the family, and they must have been given orders to keep away during the entire recreation period. When I arrived, the seven big shots, who were standing with their hands in their pockets, engaged in discussion, stopped talking. Van Roy cried out in a joyous tone:

" 'Here we go, boys! Fifty feet away! '

"He placed himself in front of me, at the said distance, and yelled:

" 'Open your mug, you bitch!'

"I didn't move. The big shots laughed. I dared not look at Divers, but I felt he was as excited as the others. Van Roy yelled again:

" 'You going to open that dirty mug of yours?'

"I opened my mouth.

" 'Wider!'

"He came up to me and spread my jaws with his steel grip. I stayed that way. He took his distance again, leaned over a bit to the right, aimed, and spat into my mouth. An almost unconscious movement of deglutition made me swallow the gob. The seven of them howled with joy. He had spat straight, but he made them pipe down so as not to attract the attention of the head of the family.

' 'Your turn,' he cried to the others.

"Then he grabbed Deloffre by the shoulders—Deloffre was laughing—and, pulling him over to the place he had just left, made him take the same stance. Still shaking with laughter, Deloffre spat in my eyes. The seven of them took their turn, in fact several times, including Divers. I received the spit in my distended mouth, which fatigue failed to close. Yet a trifle would have sufficed for the ghastly game to be transformed into a courtly one and for me to be covered not with spit but with roses that had been tossed at me. For as the gestures were the same, it would not have been hard for destiny to change everything: the game is organized . . . youngsters make the gesture of hurling . . . it would cost no more for them to hurl happiness. We were in the middle of the most flowery park in France. I waited for roses. I prayed God to alter his intention just a little, to make a false movement so that the children, ceasing to hate me, would love me. They would have gone on with the game . . . but with their hands full of flowers, for it would have taken so little for love to enter Van Roy's heart instead of hate. Van Roy had invented this punishment. But as the big shots grew more and more excited, their gusto and high spirits began to gain on me. They moved closer and closer until they were very near me, and their aim got worse and worse. I saw them spread their legs and draw back, like an archer stringing a bow, and make a slight forward movement as the gob spirted. I was hit in the face and was soon slimier than a prickhead under the discharge. I was then invested with a deep gravity. I was no longer the adulterous woman being stoned. I was the object of an amorous rite. I wanted them to spit more and thicker slime. Deloffre was the first to realize what was happening. He pointed to a particular part of my tight-fitting pants and cried out:

" 'Hey! Look at his pussy! It's making him come, the bitch!'

"At that point, I closed my mouth and started wiping my face with my sleeve. Van Roy rushed at me. He butted me in the belly and knocked me against the wall. The others stopped him."

Bulkaen was the very picture of shame. The memory of him was a powerful aid to me when I undertook the bold adventure of assisting Harcamone, not immediately with my physical presence, but with my mind, which I shot toward his cell with the violence of an arrow.

I am going to try to tell about that experience—in which I was supported by Bulkaen's soul—with the utmost precision. I ask the reader to pay close attention.

Thus, my whole body—almost my whole mind—struggled in Harcamone's presence, and my difficulty was all the greater in that Divers was plaguing me.

Finally, on the forty-seventh day after Harcamone was sentenced to death, after assisting him in all his nights and sustaining him during all his endeavours, weary, exhausted and discouraged by my efforts to enter into relations with the occult powers, I was ready to receive Divers.

It may be that my eyes were ringed with fatigue and my face flushed with fever, for that very evening, after marching round

and round the big cell all day long and when I was still deeply
involved in the harrowing experience, I saw him go up to Dédé
Carletti and heard him say, "I've got to talk to Jean tonight.
Change cells. Go into mine."

Carletti made a sign with his eyes and muttered, "All right,
sure thing!"

The stroke of a gong. Drill is over. Stock-still in the
position in which the gong caught us, we waited for the guard's
order: "To the cells. Forward, march."

We went up to the cells. As the guards' assignments were
changed every day, they did not know exactly in which coop of
the dormitory each of us slept. The one on duty that evening
noticed nothing wrong when he saw Divers at my side. I was
so tired after the past four nights, which I shall describe, that
as soon as I got to the cell I threw myself on the pallet without
undressing. Divers fell on me and covered my face with
kisses.

"Jean!"

I opened my eyes. He was smiling. He hadn't the slightest
inkling of the reason for my fatigue. He probably thought I
was being coy. I had not even strength enough to answer. He
arranged his legs between mine, then he put his arm under my
head. After a few seconds, he thought of arranging the
blankets. He must have felt cold. I was still in a state of utter
exhaustion. My effort and failure had caused me great
suffering. I had spent the past four nights working.

That was the period when I lay on the wall-cot all night
long and stared into the darkness. Bulkaen had been dead for
two weeks. Every morning I left for the hole, and my cell
remained bare and empty. I kept only the paper bags (which I
hid in the hole of the latrine pail) on which I jotted down what
is to follow. I would crouch on the wood of the cot, trying hard
to occupy as little volume as possible by folding my legs under
me, and I covered myself as much as possible so as to remain
in darkness. Can the name reverie be given to the workings of
my mind or of whatever faculty it was that enabled me to live

in Harcamone, to live in Harcamone as we say to live in Spain?

Despite my admiration for his destiny which had been so grimly brought to its fatal conclusion, I could not prevent a tremendous despair from wringing my heart, for Harcamone was still a creature of flesh, and I pitied that battered flesh. I would have liked to save him, but being myself a prisoner to the nth degree whose body was bound, weakened by hunger, the only aid I could venture was that offered by the mind. Perhaps this is more helpful than physical boldness. And still another time I went back to the thought that a simple escape was possible by methodical use of the marvellous. I questioned my mind, and the exercise in which I engaged was not a reverie. With my eyes wide open under my jacket, I lay and thought. A way had to be found. Harcamone was harrying me. The appeal period was going to expire. I haunted Harcamone more than he haunted me. I wanted to help him. He had to succeed . . . He had to keep his wits about him, to gather his power as one gathers a mob. He had to nourish himself so that his body would not be feeble. I watched over him, I tensed my mind. I stiffened it. I forgot whatever wasn't Harcamone and his flight from the physical world. I ceased to recognize the sounds that announce the trusty's arrival with the bread and soup. Finally, on the fortieth night, I had a revelation: Harcamone's cell appeared within me. He got up. Wearing only his shirt, he went to the window. It still seems to me that as he walked his whole being screamed. He climbed to the window-sill, and, when the sky was on his face, he calmed down. Having escaped from his darkness, he pissed with a new and naïve gesture. A clap of thunder boomed within me when I saw this god who was scarcely unaware of what he was shake the drops from his penis without hearing, as I did, the cry of a voice that called out to him. Did he know that the flowers, forests, stars, seas and mountains that had been trod by his musical step were drunk with him? The moon was full. The window was open on a countryside livid with terror. I trembled lest he escape through the open wall, lest he call for help to his other in the stars and lest the sky crowd into the room and snatch him before my very eyes, to his other in the sea and lest the sea come rushing in. From my cell I saw the helpless god's terrible and prodigious signal to the others of the night, to the doubles, to his lords, to himself away from here. The fear and hope of witnessing the transformation made my mind so clear, so sharp, that never have I understood anything with such astonishing precision. He already had one foot in the winter of heaven. He was going to be whisked up. He was growing thinner so as to slip between the bars. He was about to flee upon the night, but something snapped. He no longer seemed to know his empire and, without haste, stepped down from the window-sill. I still feared for a moment that he might come to my bed to question me about the angels or God. That would be asking me something he knew better than I, and so I would have had to give a false explanation for him to understand me.

He went back to bed without knowing anything of the danger or the prodigy. As for me, I closed my eyes, and it was a well-earned rest. As a result of having dared watch this preparation I was strong with the strength of that king of a destroyed country who, when confronted with a miracle, had the nerve to oppose it and thwart God. I was strong in the knowledge that I was operating in accordance with the poetic powers. That entire exercise had been governed by what I am obliged to call the soul of Bulkaen. He himself was the centre of a group of children and girls at a table in a café from where he saw, beyond the habitual, an illuminated golden altar where the scenes in Harcamone's cell were concealed. Though he seemed little interested in them, he did take an occasional look, but his mere presence was proof that he approved the drama. He was helping me. I fell asleep. When I awoke, I didn't say a word to anyone, neither when I went to the big cell nor in the corridors nor in the washroom nor at meal time. I avoided Divers, but perhaps he was avoiding me. When I arrived in the hole the morning after the second night of this crisis, I was still holding between my teeth the stem of the rose which I had stolen from Harcamone and which my fervour preciously guarded. I do not know whether I was transfigured, but the lines of my face were probably altered, for Divers, recognizing me by what had not changed, my clothes, came up to me, and I admired his courage, for he whispered to me, "You're not the same!"

I am tempted to write: "I was about to swoon." That would be untrue, physically speaking, for I never faint, but I was tremendously excited at the thought of being the mystic betrothed of the murderer who had let me have the rose that had come directly from a supernatural garden.

Perhaps Divers supposed that my nights were occupied with less dangerous dreams, with his image or that of some other lover. He was jealous of me. It therefore took great courage or great cowardice—in any case, he was deeply troubled—for him to wait until that evening and impose himself a whole night long. He did not suspect how I had been working. He therefore managed to get into my cell in the way I have described. He stretched out near me, on the cot. He kept pecking my face with quick, dry little smacks. I opened my eyes.

The warmth of his body had aroused me. I hugged him a little, despite myself. His presence and this love delivered me from the miracle I had almost caused. He responded to my embrace, light though it was, with an impetuous gesture that opened my trousers (which, as I have said, were belted by a piece of string). The string snapped. I was leaving Harcamone. I was betraying Harcamone. And the exhaustion of those four nights vanished and was replaced by a delicious well-being. My having risen to the surface after a long engulfment protracted the feeling. After the night when Harcamone was snatched by the window and almost fled, and after the day of drill that followed, I went back to my cot, and, with my head still hidden, like that of a chicken under its wing, I started working again. My forehead smashed the walls, scattered the darkness, I called to faithful poetry for help. I

was in a sweat. It was then that there began for Harcamone
the chapter I would have liked to entitle: "Message to the
Children of France." In the evening, when all the free voices
of the night were still and the guard could not hear from the
corridor (where he had fallen into the habit of reading his
screen-story), Harcamone stood up, silently, for he had
learned how to wear his chains noiselessly, and flattened himself against the wall of the cell, beside the door, facing the
window. In that position he could not be seen by the jailer, but
he himself could glimpse a patch of sky, an indifferent sky,
without definite constellations, but in any case a sky of France
covering a silent, beloved countryside where, to grieve our
hearts even more, all that could be heard in the stillness of the
night was the sound of an invisible bicycle coasting down a
hill. His body was flat against the wall. In addition to grief, he
was filled with tremendous hope, a hope legible on his eager
face. This hope induced total rigidity. A sudden start arched
his back against the wall. He said: "It's time," then, a
moment later: "You've never had a break like this." His right
hand moved away from the wall, grazed his fly, the cloth of
which heaved like the surface of a sea shaken by a terrible
inner storm, and then opened it. A bevy of more than a
hundred doves pressed together in a rustle of wings. emerged,
flew to the window and entered the night, and it was not until
morning that the youngsters who keep watch around the
prison, lying in the moss behind the tree-trunks, awoke in the
dew with the dove of their dream nestling in the hollow of their
hands.

But that was not the awaited miracle, and time was pressing.
Harcamone was getting restive, and his restiveness was
exhausting me. Finally, the following night, hence the third of
the experiment, he thought he was ready to try his luck. He
felt my help coming to him from behind the walls. In the late
afternoon, he lay down and waited for night. When it had quite
settled around the prison, he made a movement: the chains
did not rattle, or was the guard asleep? He heard nothing.

Nevertheless, Harcamone stood up very cautiously. He did not know whether the night was dark, for his entire existence was being lived at the incandescent centre of a raw white light. He approached the door, holding up his irons, but hardly had he taken three or four steps when the irons opened and fell to the floor noiselessly. Harcamone did not fluster. He must have been used to the courtesy of objects. He pressed his ear to the door and listened: the guard was asleep. He filled his lungs with air. The thing was going to be difficult. He therefore uttered a silent invocation: he summoned all his energy. Magical operations are exhausting. They drain you. A person cannot perform them twice in one day. You must therefore succeed at the first try. He went through. He went through the door first, accompanied by such music that the fibres of the wood were torn painlessly, and then he went right through the sleeping guard. As he went through the door, he left his clothes behind it, and his tattooed arm impressed upon the guard's arm the arrow that pierced a heart on his own. Finally, he found himself in a corridor where the light was softer than that of the cell. He was naked, and his muscles were so bulgy that they looked padded, like the legs of football players in their socks. All his muscles were erect. To get to the stairway at the end of the corridor he crossed a zone of shadow. As he walked on his heels, his rump bounced up and down like that of a bather walking on pebbles. Not a sound. On his back, thighs, shoulders and stomach, the Star drew close to the Serpent, the Eagle to the Frigate. He went up the stairs. When he reached the landing, he spent a long time looking for a certain door, and when he found it, he tried to go through it, but the fatigue of the first operation made him falter. He waited a while for a guard to come and open it for him (just as we used to wait at our cell-doors in Santé Prison for a passing guard to be so kind as to open the door of our jail and lock us up). He waited, but it was a foolish hope. He sank down in front of the closed door, behind which slept the men sentenced to the colonies. Had Rose-wood found him there, he might have said of him, as he once did:

"He's a Sunday boy-friend."

Toward morning, he awoke, passed through the sleeping guard again and went back to bed, shivering.

My desires needed a support, a pretext. Harcamone was this pretext, this support, but he was too inaccessible to be it for long, and Bulkaen, by appearing on the scene, bedecked himself with all the adornments secreted by my madness. He ordained himself priest. To the particular splendour that was all his own, destiny added even more by making him an elect creature charged with discovering the noblest truths. I learned, likewise from Lou Daybreak, that before leaving Santé for Fontevrault, Rocky had arranged for Bulkaen to spend a last day, a whole one, in his cell. Rocky had kept a little wine. They quickly said everything they had on their minds and, I don't know how, they came up with the following idea: they and the four other inmates piled all the mattresses in a corner, folded the bed against the wall and danced for hours. Since they were allowed to say good-bye before separating for what they thought would be a long time—they did not expect to see each other again at Fontevrault—after exchanging a few awkward words of friendship, they made the only gesture of love permitted in public: they danced. Barefoot in their laceless shoes, for hours, with the four others, a medley of singing and dancing. And the most ordinary dances, waltzes, javas, which they whistled as they whirled about. As I write, I see Bulkaen going round and round and peering into Rocky's dark eyes, still seeking Hersir there, and he must have been thinking of that day when he said to me (nine days after we had met): "The reflection of his eyes in Rocky's gave me a hard-on." They were desperate. But love and waltzing carried them off with a joyous, mad and tragic lightness. They had just spontaneously invented the highest form of theatre, they had invented the opera.

It is not to be wondered at that the most wretched of human lives is related in words that are too beautiful. The mag-

nificence of my tale springs naturally (as a result of my
modesty too and of my shame at having been so unhappy)
from the pitiable moments of my entire life. Just as the Golden
Legend flowered from a banal sentence to torture pronounced
two thousand years ago, just as Botchako's singsong voice
blossomed into the velvet corollae of his rich rippling voice, so
my tale, which issues from my shame, becomes glorious and
dazzles me.

I no longer seek in reveries the satisfaction of my amorous
desires, as on the galley. I witness Harcamone's life as an
onlooker who is disturbed only by the effect of the echo of
what the master's beauty and adventure would have produced
on himself in the past. And perhaps hunger, active though
cultivated, forced me into the very core of Harcamone's personality. He took on fat so that I would suffer less. He was
bursting with health. Never had he been more robust and I
more puny. Each day the trusty took better care of him than
the day before. His face grew a little fuller. He was acquiring
the majesty of glutted dictators.

As the fatal moment approached, I felt Harcamone getting
more and more tense, carrying on an inner struggle, seeking to
escape from himself so as to escape from here. To break loose,
to leave, to flee through the fissures, like a golden vapour! But
he had to transform himself into a golden powder. Harcamone
clung to me. He urged me to find the secret. And I raked up
all my memories of miracles, known or unknown, those of the
Bible, of mythologies, and I sought the likely explanation, the
kind of simple trick that enabled heroes to perform them. I
was wearing myself out. I took no rest. I stopped eating. On
the fourth day, a guard dared say to me, "What's the trouble,
Genet, something bothering you?" Hardly had he uttered
those words of pity than he shut up again. He freed himself
from our contact by a shrug of the shoulders and went back to
his reverie, which was as far away as ours. Divers glanced at
me and assumed, as did the guard, that Bulkaen's death was
preying on my mind.

Anyway, Bulkaen devised that last trick, which had been invented amidst the clearest signs of grief. He ran away, up the same path.

Whenever I touch my eyes, into which I used to dig my fingers, images still flow from them, images that used to follow each other so swiftly that it was almost impossible for me to name them all. I didn't have time enough. Pairs of sailors went by, cyclists, dancers, peasants, and finally Harcamone accompanying a little girl. As these characters were speechless, I was unable to learn her name. Harcamone was talking. They were walking together through a countryside which was familiar to me, perhaps because it was indeterminate. The girl was smiling. Harcamone must have been saying nice things to her. She might have been ten or eleven. Though I no longer recall her features, I could see very clearly at the time that her face was gentle and beautiful. Harcamone was sixteen, but his body was already on its way to that somewhat massive perfection in which he fulfilled himself a few days before his death. He was the emanation of a power stronger than himself. He was speaking into the child's neck, which was warmed by his breath. They walked deeper and deeper into the countryside. Bulkaen remained at his post. He continued to preside over the operation. At times, when I was confused and needed help, he would glance in Harcamone's direction (in other words, my spiritual activity would be shunted; my mind's eye would look away from Harcamone and I would see Bulkaen). He had hardly moved, save that he was on a bench, among the Daughters of Mary, or else his face had taken on the moving lines that go from the bear to the bird, but Bulkaen was present.

After the murder of the girl, Harcamone was sentenced to the Colony until the age of twenty-one, and he was called a monster. Nobody realized that one of the motives of the murder was the murderer's charming shyness. At the age of sixteen, he was frightened by women, and yet he could not keep his flower any longer. He was not afraid of the girl. When they were near an eglantine bush, he stroked her hair. The shuddering little bitch let him do it. He probably whispered something trivial, but when he put his hand under her skirt, she defended herself and blushed, out of coquettry—or perhaps fear. Her blushing made Harcamone blush, and he got excited. He fell on top of her. They rolled into a ditch, without a word. But what a look in the girl's eyes! Harcamone was frightened. He realized that the incarnation which had transformed him into a farm-hand was coming to an end. He had to fulfill his mission. He was afraid of the expression on the child's face, but the proximity of the little body that wanted to run away and, despite its fear, cuddled between the boy's arms, roused him to the first gesture of love.

Everyone has noticed that the flies of country boys are always short of buttons: negligence on the part of parents or teachers, defects in the garments, too frequent buttoning and unbuttoning, wear and tear of the trousers, etc. Harcamone's fly was open, and, almost by itself, his penis sprang out. The girl was still inclined to squeeze her thighs together, but she spread them. As he was taller than she, Harcamone's face was lost in the grass. He was crushing the kid. He hurt her. She tried to scream. He strangled her. This murder of a child by a child of sixteen was to lead me to the night when I was granted the vision of an ascension to the paradise that is offered me.

I was trembling (it wasn't my body, but something within me was really trembling) lest Harcamone faint. He walked through the corridors again after going through the door and the guard. I followed his course from door to door. I would have liked to guide him, but all I could do to support him in his quest was to impart to him my strength of mind. Finally, he stopped. The prison seemed deserted. Not even the sweeping of the wind outside could be heard (never does it burst into my too fast-closed corridors). Harcamone found himself in front of a door on which was hooked a card: "Germain, age 40, hard labour." He made a violent attempt to enter, but, exhausted by all his earlier efforts, he could

expect nothing more from our powers. We knew that behind
the door were Guiana and its sun, the sea that had been
crossed, the death that had been vanquished. Behind the door
were three murderers waiting to leave for the penal colony.
Harcamone was going to them, we know why. To them, as I
go to him. They offered him the peace of a Guiana bathed in
sun and shade, with palm trees, escapes, in the coolness of the
straw hat.

But he was drained. He dropped.

No one could hear me howling my anguish. I cried out
angrily, impatiently: "A religious silence!" I think that what I
meant was that there should be even more silence, but that the
failure was so beautiful that everyone should observe a religious silence. In any case, I expressed what was religious in my
feeling and even in my instinct. I felt myself blushing at having
uttered that journalistic phrase. My lips quivered. I fell asleep.
The next morning, when the guard opened the door of the
dormitory to wake us, I was in such a state of agitation, so
involved in inhuman adventures, that even my body suffered. I
was exhausted. Was I going to have to give up a dream that
was supported by so many caryatids? In order to calm it, I
would have had to be kissed by a child, a woman would have
had to let me rest my head on her bosom. The turnkey opened
the cell and went in to inspect it, as he usually did. I felt an
imperious need to go up to him. I even made a movement. He
had his back to me. I saw his shoulder and suddenly felt like
crying: I had made the gesture of touching that shoulder, the
same gesture that Bulkaen had once made. I was on my way
downstairs when he came running after me, and in the
momentum of his running his hand came down on my
shoulder. I turned my head around, he turned his to me, and
we stood there face to face. He was laughing.

"I feel good!" he said.

"Joy makes you pretty rough."

He became almost indulgent.

"Did I hurt you, Jean? Go on, I didn't hurt you, did I?"

His eyes were gleaming with inordinate happiness. His cheeks, which were usually pale, were flushed. I said:

"What's going on? What's the matter with you?"

"Listen, Jean, I feel so good that I almost did a dumb thing just before . . . It's plain joy . . . I don't know what's got into me . . . I was about to slap one of the screws on the shoulder . . . I raised my arm . . . I felt like touching someone's shoulder. Good thing I stopped in time! You can imagine! Then I saw you go by and I came running . . . Jean! I didn't hurt you, did I? I'm putting my hand on your shoulder the way you once put yours on mine!"

I snickered.

"It looks bad, my boy . . ."

I was upset by all that joy of his. I felt it was being directed against my happiness and I gave it a cold welcome. I added very curtly:

"There's no need for you to put on a show. It doesn't mean a thing to me. Beat it. The screws'll be coming along."

He left light-heartedly, still smiling. We had known each other ten days.

I now feel ashamed of having put out my hand to touch the guard's shoulder the way Bulkaen had touched mine.

The day was painful, the drill harassing. Yet it brought me peace, thanks to the magical power of the circular march. For, in addition to the peace of being within ourselves at last (by virtue of our stooping posture, our folded arms and the regularity of our pace), we knew the happiness of being merged in a solemn dance by the unconsciousness in which our heads dangled, and the comforting sense of unity that one feels in all round dances and other group dances when people hold each other's hand, as in the farandole or the kolo . . . We drew this force from the knowledge that we were bound to each other as we marched round and round. We also felt a sense of power, because we were conquered. And our bodies were strong because each profited from the strength of forty sets of muscles. It was only at the end of the very deep, dark tunnel that I saw Harcamone, but I was sure that when night came I would again be at the door of the locked coop, involved in his life.

But I could not continue the experiment much longer. I would have needed the training of Yogis.

In the evening, I almost dropped with fatigue, as I have said, into Divers' arms. When we were united, my fatigue fled. I stroked his head, which had been shaved that morning. That ball between my hands and on my thighs seemed huge. I removed it violently and brought it, despite its weight, to my mouth, which he bit with his.

I sighed: "Riton!" The mention of his name moved Harcamone further away.

He flattened his body against mine. Neither of us had taken off his homespun suit. It was I who thought we should undress. The cell was cold. Divers hesitated.

But I was in a hurry to be even closer to him. I did not want the oncoming darkness to find me isolated, delivered up by weakness to a danger which I felt approaching.

When we were in our shirts, we embraced again. The mattress was warm. We pulled the brown woollen blankets over our heads, and for a moment we lay still, as in the cradles where Byzantine painters often confine the Virgin and Child. And after we had taken our pleasure twice, Divers kissed me and fell asleep in my arms. What I had feared occurred: I was left alone.

I had obtained some tobacco and I smoked almost all night long. The cigarette ash fell on my blanket and on the cot. This sign too upset me, for I felt as if I were lying on a bed of ashes. And Divers' presence did not prevent me from resuming, for the last time, my activity as clairvoyant and ascetic, which was as keen as it had been the other nights. I was suddenly moved by the smell of roses, and my eyes were filled with the sight of the wisteria at Mettray. As you know, it was at the end of the Big Square, toward the lane, against the wall of the custodian's office, and was entangled in the thorns

of a bush of tea-roses. The trunk of the wisteria was enormous, twisted with suffering. It was fastened to the wall by a
wire network. Some of the overgrown branches were supported
by a forked post. The rose-bush was attached to the wall by
rusty nails. Its leaves were gleaming and the flowers had all
the tints of flesh. When we left the brush-shop, we sometimes
had to wait a while for the other shops to get ready so that we
could all march back in step together to the accompaniment of
the bugle, and it was in front of the mingled wisteria and
rose-bush that M. Perdoux, the head of the shop, used to make
us halt. The roses shot whiff after whiff at our faces. No
sooner was I visited by the memory of the flowers than there
rushed to my mind's eye the scenes I am about to relate.

Someone opened Harcamone's door. He was sleeping on his
back. First, four men entered his dream. Then he awoke.
Without getting up, without even raising his torso, he turned
his head to the door. He saw the black men and understood
immediately, but he also realized very quickly that, in order to
die in his sleep, he must not disrupt or destroy the state of
dreaming in which he was still entangled. He decided to maintain the dream. He therefore did not run his hand through his
matted hair. He said "yes" to himself, and he felt a need to
smile—but the smile was barely perceptible to the others—to
smile inwardly so that the virtue of the smile would be transmitted to his inner being and he would be stronger than the
moment, for the smile would ward off, despite his sadness, the
tremendous gloom of his abandonment which threatened to
drive him to despair, with all the pain it entails. He therefore
smiled, with the faint smile he was to retain until his death.
Above all, let it not be thought that he was intent on anything
but the guillotine. His eyes were focussed on it, but he decided
to live ten heroic, that is, joyous, minutes. He did not joke, as
the newspapers dared report, for sarcasm is bitter and conceals
ferments of despair. He stood up. And when he was on his
feet, upright in the middle of the cell, his head, neck and entire
body emerged from the lace and silk which are worn, in the

most trying moments, only by the diabolical masters of the
world, and with which he was suddenly adorned. Without
growing an inch, he became huge, overtopping and splitting
the cell, filling the universe, and the four black men shrank
until they were no bigger than four bedbugs. The reader has
realized that Harcamone was invested with such majesty that
his clothes themselves were ennobled and turned to silk and
brocade. He was clad in patent-leather boots, breeches of soft
blue silk and a shirt of old blond-lace, the collar of which was
open on his splendid neck that supported the collar of the
Order of the Golden Fleece. Truly, he came in a straight line,
and by way of the sky, from between the legs of the captain of
the galley. Perhaps because of the miracle of which he was the
place and object, or for some other reason—to give thanks to
God his Father—he put his right knee on the floor. The four
men quickly took advantage and climbed up his leg and sloping
thigh. They had great difficulty, for the silk was slippery.
Halfway up the thigh, forgoing his inaccessible and tumultuous
fly, they encountered his hand, which was lying in repose.
They climbed on to it, and from there to the arm, and then to
the lace sleeve. And finally to the right shoulder, the bowed
neck, the left shoulder and, as lightly as possible, the face.
Harcamone had not moved, except that he was breathing
through his parted lips. The judge and the lawyer wormed
their way into the ear and the chaplain and executioner dared
enter his mouth. They moved forward a little along the edge of
the lower lip and fell into the gulf. And then, almost as soon as
they passed the gullet, they came to a lane of trees that
descended in a gentle, almost voluptuous slope. All the foliage
was very high and formed the sky of the landscape. They were
unable to recognize the scents, for in states like theirs one can
no longer distinguish particular features: one passes through
forests, tramples down flowers, climbs over stones. What
surprised them most was the silence. They nearly took each
other by the hand, for in the interior of such a marvel the
chaplain and the executioner became two lost schoolboys. They

pressed onward, inspecting left and right, prospecting the silence, stumbling over moss, in order to get their bearings, but they found nothing. After a few hundred yards, it drew dark, though nothing had changed in that skyless landscape. They kicked around rather gaily the remains of a country fair: a spangled jersey, the ashes of a camp-fire, a circus-whip. Then, upon turning their heads, they realized that they had unwittingly been following a succession of winding paths more complicated than those of a mine. There was no end to Harcamone's interior. It was more decked with black than a capital whose king has just been assassinated. A voice from the heart declared: "The interior is grieving," and they swelled with fear, which rose within them like a light wind above the sea. They moved ahead, more lightly, between rocks and dizzying cliffs, some of them very close together, where no eagle flew. These walls kept converging. The men were approaching the inhuman regions of Harcamone.

The judge and the lawyer, who had entered by the ear, wandered at first through an extraordinary maze of narrow alleys where they suspected the houses (windows and doors were shut) of sheltering dangerous lovemaking punishable by law. The alleys were unpaved, for the sound of the men's shoes was inaudible; they seemed to be walking on elastic ground, where they lightly rebounded. They were skipping. The meandering alleys suggested a kind of Toulon, as if meant to contain the lurching walk of sailors. The men turned left, thinking that was the right way, then left, left. The streets were all alike. Behind them, a young sailor came out of a sinister-looking house. He looked about. In his mouth, between his teeth, was a blade of grass which he was chewing. The judge turned his head and saw him but was unable to make out his face, for the sailor was advancing in profile and turned away when he was looked at. The lawyer realized that the judge could not see. He turned around but was likewise unable to see the hiding face. I am still amazed at the privilege which allowed me to witness Harcamone's inner life and to be the

invisible observer of the secret adventures of the four black
men. The alleys were as complicated as the steep gorges and
the mossy lanes. They had the same downward slope. Finally,
all four met at a kind of crossroads which I cannot describe
accurately. It led down, again to the left, into a luminous
corridor lined with huge mirrors. They went in that direction.
All four questioned each other at the same time in an anxious
tone, almost ceasing to breathe:

"The heart—have you found the heart?"

And realizing at once that none of them had found it, they
continued their way along the corridor, tapping and listening
to the mirrors. They advanced slowly, cupping their ears and
often flattening them against the wall. It was the executioner
who first heard the beats. They quickened their pace. They
were now so frightened that they sped along the elastic ground
in leaps and bounds of several yards. They were breathing
hard and talking to themselves without a stop, as one does in
dreams, that is, so softly and indistinctly that the words merely
ruffle the silence. The beats were nearer and louder. Finally,
the four dark men came to a mirror on which was drawn
(obviously carved with the diamond of a ring) a heart pierced
by an arrow. No doubt it was the portal of the heart. I don't
know what gesture the executioner made, but it made the heart
open and we entered the first chamber. It was bare, white and
cold, without an aperture. Alone, in the midst of that
emptiness, upright on a wooden block, stood a young drummer
of sixteen. His icy, impassive gaze looked at nothing in the
world. His supple hands were beating the drum. The drumsticks rose and fell sharply and neatly. They were beating out
Harcamone's highest life. Did he see us? Did he see the open,
profaned heart? How could we not be seized with panic! And
that chamber was only the first. The mystery of the hidden
chamber remained to be discovered. But no sooner did one of
the four realize that they were not in the heart of the heart
than a door opened by itself and we saw before us a red rose of
monstrous size and beauty.

"The Mystic Rose," murmured the chaplain.

The four men were staggered by the splendour. The rays of
the rose dazzled them at first, but they quickly pulled
themselves together, for such people never permit themselves
to show signs of respect . . . Recovering from their agitation,
they rushed in, pushing back the petals and crumpling them
with their drunken hands, as a lecher who has been deprived of
sex pushes back a whore's skirt. They were in the throes of
drunken profanation. With their temples throbbing and their
brows beaded with sweat, they reached the heart of the rose. It
was a kind of dark well. At the very edge of this pit, which was
as murky and deep as an eye, they leaned forward and were
seized with a kind of dizziness. All four made the gestures of
people losing their balance, and they toppled into that deep
gaze.

I heard the clopping of the horses that were bringing the
wagon in which the victim was to be taken to the little
cemetery. He had been executed eleven days after Bulkaen had
been shot. Divers was still sleeping. He merely grunted a few
times. He farted. An odd fact: I had an erection all night long,
despite my mental activity which kept me remote from sexual
desire. I did not for a moment disengage myself from Divers'
arms, despite the cramp I had in an arm and leg.

Dawn was beginning to break. In my mind's eye I saw
Harcamone walking silently and solemnly on carpets that had
been unrolled so as to deaden the sound of his tread from the
cell to the gate of the prison. He was probably surrounded by
assistants. The executioner walked in front. The lawyer, the
judge, the warden and the guards followed . . . His curly hair
was cut. It was cropped close and fell on his shoulders. A
guard—Brulard—saw him die. He spoke to me about his white
shoulders. I was dumbfounded for a moment that a guard
dared speak that way about a man's adornments, but I quickly
realized that as Harcamone had been wearing only the white
shirt of the condemned, his massive, athletic shoulders were
particularly imposing as he mounted the scaffold in the mor-

ning light. The guard might have said: "His snowy shoulders."

In order not to suffer too much myself, I relaxed as much as possible. For a moment, I was so flabby that it occurred to me that perhaps Harcamone had a mother—everyone knows that all men who are beheaded have a mother who comes to weep at the edge of the police cordon that guards the guillotine. I wanted to let my thoughts run on her and Harcamone, who was already divided in two. I said softly, in my state of fatigue: "I'm going to pray for your mamma."

When Divers was awakened by the morning bell, he stretched and then kissed me. I said nothing. When, that same morning, a guard opened the door to take us to the disciplinary cell, I joined him in the corridor. His eyes were wild with panic. He had just read the tragedy of the night on the faces of the guards and of the inmates who were lined up in the corridor to go to the wash-room. As we were not locked in embrace we did not disembrace, but when we passed each other as we moved to and fro between the window and the door, we stopped for a moment and, without our realizing it, our heads bent forward by themselves, as when you kiss someone so that the mouths touch without the noses getting in the way. As for our hands, they remained in our belts. It was only when we heard the key make a thunderous din in the lock (the turnkey opening the door of the big cell), a noise which was reflected by the deep echo of the cell, that we realized we had gone out and that we finally felt the gravity of our situation. I do not mean the disciplinary or penal gravity. We felt that the moment was solemn since our heads had fallen into the habit of veritable grief, joint grief. Any other gesture that might have been interrupted by the key would, moreover, have been transformed into an augural signal. Jangled nerves and irritability made us see a meaning in all things.

Divers said to me:

"Jean, did you hear this morning?"

I said nothing, but I nodded. Lou Daybreak had joined us. He said to Divers jocularly:

"Well, rascal, how goes?"

Here again I heard the charming expression applied not to a youngster or a lover, but to a comrade, a friend, who is being honoured. It was no longer, yet it still was, a lover's word, a word belonging to the vocabulary of night. Then he added:

"Boys, it's over. They've made two out of Prettyboy! Who's next?"

He was standing erect, with his hands on his stomach. To us, to Divers and me, he was the personification of the fateful moment. He was dawn, daybreak. Never before had his name been so meaningful.

"Don't joke about it," said Divers.

"What's the matter? Getting weepy? Does it rub you the wrong way if I kid about it? It's not your fault if he got the axe."

Did Divers take this as a sly accusation? He answered:

"Shut your trap!"

Perhaps he remembered an expression for saying that a guy had smeared an accomplice: "He buried him." Lou answered gently:

"Ah, if I feel like it!"

Divers wanted to sock him. His fist shot out. Lou didn't budge. His name created around him a zone as impenetrable as that created by beauty around a face—for when I hit Bulkaen, it was never straight in the face—and when Divers wanted to punch him, Lou invoked, in a whisper, the charm of his name: Divers' left fist failed to get past the invisible obstacle, the enchanted zone. Flabbergasted, he wanted to try with his right, but the same paralysis made it so light that he held it back with his left hand. Confronted with the revelation of Lou's power, he gave up the struggle against the panting but smiling Daybreak.

Divers' gaze shone in Bulkaen's eyes during the scene on the stairs, when I wanted to kiss him. I saw that same terrible gleam, the gleam of the male who is ready to defend—don't laugh—his manly honour. Moreover, those were the only times I ever saw a look of such implacable decision in human eyes. Bulkaen was vicious. This evening, because the night is milder, I am led by reverie to imagine what Bulkaen would have been when he got out of jail if . . . I can see him saying to me coldly, with his steely eyes looking into mine, and refusing my outstretched hand: "Get the hell out of here," and then, seeing my bewilderment: "All right, so what, I took you for a sucker. Now that I don't need you, you can go chase yourself!"

This reverie was brought on because I had, long before, registered that cold gaze, which had been irrevocably closed to my fellow-feeling and which I encountered again this morning in the eyes of Divers. Yet I cannot believe that Bulkaen lied to me when he spoke of his friendship, and even his love, for knowing how devoted I was to him, no boy, whether queer or not, would have resisted the appeal of the kiss when I put out my arms to draw him to me. But if Bulkaen did lie, I admire his bumptiousness, and what tenderness is he not killing in me? God is good, that is, he strews so many traps along our path that you can't help going where he leads you.

He hated me. Did he hate me? I'm still struggling, far away, against his friendship with Rocky. I'm struggling like a magician who tries to prevent a charm, who wants to destroy a rival's spells. I'm struggling like a chosen victim who has been sighted and is already caught. I'm struggling without moving, with all my attention taut and vibrant. I'm waiting. I'll explode later on. I'm hardening. I'm struggling. Bulkean is bound to Rocky by a certain complicity. He must therefore be united to me by a closer complicity. Complicity in murder? I would like to take upon myself Harcamone's act of murder and share the horror of it with Bulkaen. But I can't help thinking that literature has dealt more than once with the subject of the supplanting of the important man by the lesser one, and even if, as a result of our closer, more dangerous collaboration, it's I

who am chosen, Destiny, by a haughty irony, will still be able
to make Bulkaen prefer Rocky. All things considered, I know I
won't ever win Rocky over, because he's bound to Bulkaen,
because, before I entered the picture, he braved with him, to
the very end, the dangers of a liaison that had to be defended
against the winks and whispers of the gang.

Though the day was dismal, it was shot through with the
joy caused me by the discovery, that very morning, of a tracing
paper showing a sailor's head in a buoy. It was a pattern that
was all the rage in the prison. More that fifty inmates, among
whom there was no particular alliance, had had themselves
tattooed with it.

The silence seemed light to me. But that evening Divers
arranged to be locked up in my cell. He must have felt, as I
did, the need for us to be united in mourning for Harcamone.
When he lay down, his muscles relaxed, and what I covered
with kisses was only a tired old lady. And I had never realized
that the kiss is the form of the primitive desire to bite, and
even to devour, as much as I did that night when I discovered
Divers' cowardly attitude toward his crime which, bleaching
his face, made him withdraw into his fragile shell. I felt like
slapping him or spitting in his snoot. But I loved him. I kissed
him, hugging him as if to choke him, giving him another kiss,
the most ferocious—into which a flood of rage welled up from
my very depths—that I have ever given any boy. I felt the
voluptuousness of dominating him at last! I was the stronger
mentally, and physically too, for his muscles were softened by
fear and shame. And as I embraced him I lay on him so as to
hide his shame. I even remember being careful to cover him
with my entire body, and then with the folds of my clothes,
which thereby took on the dignity of a shroud or an ancient
peplos, burying his head beneath my wing so that the world
would not see the woeful gaze of the humiliated male. We were
enacting a kind of golden wedding of a sorrowful couple who
no longer loved each other in joy but in sorrow. We had waited
fifteen years, seeking each other perhaps in other guys, ever

since the day I left Mettray, at which time he was in the quarter for some boyish offence.

At one end of the main corridor of the quarter was a frosted glass wall which was protected by bars and which was never open, except for a transom at the top. It was behind this wall that I saw Divers at Mettray for the last time. He had managed in some way to climb up to the transom, from which he was hanging by his hands. Only his head was visible: his body was wriggling heavily behind the panes, powerful and mysterious in the depths of those waters, even more disturbing with the mystery of morning. His delicate hands were clinging at each side of his face. He said good-bye to me in that position.

My memory stops at his face, as we stop at things which comfort us. I re-read his face as the lifer re-reads paragraph 3: "Persons sentenced to life imprisonment may, after a period of three years starting from the first day of such imprisonment, be liberated conditionally . . ."

Harcamone is dead, Bulkaen is dead. If I get out, I shall rummage in old newspapers, as after the death of Pilorge. As with Pilorge, nothing will remain in my hands but a brief article on cheap paper, a kind of grey ash, which will inform me that he was executed at dawn. These papers are their graves. But I shall transmit their names far down the ages. These names alone will remain in the future, divested of their objects. Who, it will be asked, were Bulkaen, Harcamone, Divers, who was Pilorge, who was Guy? And their names will inspire awe, as we are awed by the light from a star that has been dead a thousand years. Have I told all there was to tell of this adventure? If I take leave of this book, I take leave of what can be related. The rest is ineffable. I say no more and walk barefoot.

La Santé. Prison des Tourelles, 1943